ON THE OTHER SIDE

WAYWARD SONS
BOOK 5

HARPER JACKSON

PROLOGUE

Five months after high school graduation

RIOS

By late September, the island had gone quiet again.

Tourist season was over, and what was left of Hatterwick felt stripped bare. The boardwalk planks creaked in the heat, and the humid air hung thick with the scents of salt, sunscreen, and gossip. Without strangers to feed it, the talk turned inward, circling the same names like sharks lured by the scent of blood.

Mine most of all.

I'd just finished work at the docks, unloading the latest catch for the fishing company that signed my paycheck. Not a glorious job by any means, but it was who'd been willing to hire me fresh out of high school a few months ago despite the shadow hanging over me from the police investigation that had stalled without enough evidence for an arrest or a conviction. Not that the court of public opinion needed actual evidence to convict me.

My truck was still down—some clutch issue I couldn't fix

without parts that said paycheck still wouldn't cover—so I started the walk home. It wasn't far. At thirteen miles long and only three miles wide at its broadest point, nothing much on Hatterwick Island was far. The tide had gone out, leaving the mudflats slick and shining under the lowering sun.

Two old-timers outside the tackle shop fell silent as I passed.

They didn't spit anymore, which I guess counted as improvement.

"Evenin'." The greeting came automatically because my mama had raised me polite before she left us high and dry years ago.

Neither man answered.

I tried to focus on the glare off the water of the sound instead of the whispers.

Should've been him.

You'd think he'd be gone by now.

Same words, new mouths.

Four months on, and they still hadn't found fifteen-year-old Gwen Busby.

She'd have been a sophomore by now, along with my baby sister, Gabi. Instead, she'd vanished from the end-of-school-year beach bonfire like smoke into the night. They'd dragged every inch of the inlet and the deeper waters around the island, their hooks scraping bottom until mud clouded everything. Search choppers had beaten the air overhead for weeks, their rotors drowning out the gulls, while dogs from the mainland worked the dunes and maritime forest with their noses pressed to sand that held nothing but the ghosts of footprints washed away by tide and time.

Nothing.

Not a scrap of clothing, not a shoe, not even a hair tie to prove she'd ever existed at all.

By the end of June, the search parties that had repeatedly combed every salt-beaten inch of our scrap of land had turned into prayer circles. Old women with sun-spotted hands clutched their rosaries outside the Catholic church, their voices rising and falling like the rhythm of waves. By the end of July, those prayers had curdled into whispers that slipped through screen doors and across backyard fences like poison. And by mid-August, when the tourists had gone home and left us alone with our ghosts, everyone had settled into the comfortable certainty that she was dead.

Since they needed a villain more than they needed proof, they'd picked me. I'd been the last to see her alive—or thought I had—just a flash of her walking toward the cars when the storm rolled in. When news had spread that she'd never made it home that night, I'd gone straight to Chief Carson and told him every detail I could remember. How she'd stumbled a little in the sand, maybe from the beer, maybe from the wind that had already been howling off the water from the incoming storm. How I'd watched her disappear between the parked cars and figured she was heading home like all the other kids when the lightning started forking down.

That honesty had been my first mistake. My last had been thinking it would matter.

I crossed Front Street, dust rising in small clouds from my work boots, and heard the low rumble of an engine behind me. The sound was too clean, too smooth for the usual island traffic of rusted pickups and salt-eaten sedans. A black SUV crept along the curb like a predator stalking prey. Clean and new and expensive—the kind of vehicle that told you exactly who could afford to leave the island whenever they wanted, and who chose to stay just long enough to remind the rest of us of our place.

The Reilly family. Kin to the Busbys on the mother's side,

which made Gwen their blood, their loss, their grief to weaponize however they saw fit.

Mr. Reilly sat behind the wheel like a judge reading out a sentence he'd already decided, mirrored sunglasses shielding whatever passed for conscience in his eyes. I didn't need to see through the lenses to recognize his disdain. It radiated from him like heat off summer asphalt. Mrs. Reilly occupied the passenger seat with the rigid posture of someone who'd never learned to bend, her lips pursed like she'd caught a whiff of something rotten and couldn't escape the stench. Her gaze fixed on me with the kind of hatred that had been polished smooth by months of practice.

And in the back, Madden—dark hair pulled back in a ponytail so tight it might have been drawn with a ruler, posture as perfect as her grades, looking everywhere but directly at me, while somehow managing to watch my every move.

She was a year behind me in school—a senior now, with her sights set on some Ivy League future that would carry her far from this postage stamp of sand and spite. Someone I noticed, not because everyone knew she'd be valedictorian of her class, destined for bigger things than the rest of us even dreamed, but because something about those hazel eyes had always pulled at me. Not that I'd ever done anything about it. Someone like her would never have looked at the likes of me, even before the scandal.

She hadn't even been at the bonfire that night with the rest of the student body, too buried in test prep or college applications or whatever other serious business occupied the minds of people who planned to escape this place through merit instead of luck. That whole prim, proper, overachieving, stick-up-her-ass vibe should have been everything I wasn't interested in. But even I'd been able to see the way grief had carved hollows under her eyes in the weeks after Gwen disappeared, how she now moved around the island like someone walking underwater.

They slowed at the intersection, waiting for a cluster of men to cross—guys I'd worked beside last summer before all this started, before my name became a curse word that mothers whispered to keep their daughters close. One of them, Jimmy Kowalski, caught sight of the SUV and then let his gaze drift to me with deliberate slowness. "There he is." He pitched his voice just loud enough to carry over the engine noise. "The one who couldn't keep his hands to himself."

Sharp, ugly laughter erupted from the group—reminding me of the scavenger birds wheeling overhead, waiting for something to die so they could pick the bones clean. The sound echoed off the storefronts and bounced back at me from all sides.

Mrs. Reilly leaned forward and cranked down her window. When she pinned me with her stare, the weight of it struck like a physical blow, all that carefully cultivated blame and hatred focused into a laser that could have burned holes through steel. "You ought to be ashamed." Her voice carried the crisp authority of someone who'd never questioned her right to judge. "Walking around like you belong here, like you have any right to breathe the same air as decent people."

The words landed like a slap across the face, and the men nearby chuckled with the satisfied sound of people who believe justice was served, however crude. Mr. Reilly said nothing from behind his sunglasses, but his silence spoke louder than words. It was permission. Encouragement. A green light for anyone who wanted to take their frustrations out on the convenient target the police and his family had painted on my back.

I stood there with heat crawling up my neck like a rash, my heartbeat hammering so loud in my ears it nearly drowned out the jeers. Every muscle in my body coiled tight, ready for fight or flight, though neither option would solve a damn thing. Madden sat frozen in the backseat, her eyes darting between her parents and me like she was watching a tennis match where someone was about to get their head taken off. I saw her mouth fall open and caught the moment she seemed to realize words were coming out.

"They wouldn't still be looking at him if there wasn't a reason." Her voice rang clear and certain as a church bell tolling the hour.

The words weren't overtly cruel—not compared to what I'd heard from others—just delivered with the unshakeable conviction of someone who'd never had reason to doubt what the adults in her life had taught her. A smart girl repeating smart-sounding logic that seemed as solid as the ground under her feet. No doubt she'd absorbed those words and worse from her parents' dinner table conversations, their careful explanations of why the world worked the way it did and who deserved what. There was zero reason I should've expected her to contradict the people who'd raised her, fed her, shaped every thought in her head since birth.

And yet the remark hit me like a gut punch, stealing what little air I'd managed to hold on to.

The window hummed closed with mechanical finality, sealing the Reilly family back into their climate-controlled bubble. The SUV rolled forward with the stately pace of people who'd made their point and could afford to take their time savoring it, leaving behind nothing but exhaust fumes and the kind of silence that weighed heavier than noise.

The laughter that followed was low and satisfied, the sound of people who'd just seen their entertainment for the evening and found it exactly to their liking.

"Guess the Reillys said it plain enough," someone muttered, and the group began to disperse, their work done.

I turned my face toward the sound of the sea and started walking. The air tasted like rain and salt, though clouds hadn't yet rolled in. Every muscle in my body wanted to bolt—to catch the first boat out and never look back—but I couldn't. Not with Gabi still in high school, too softhearted for her own good, and Caroline running herself ragged trying to keep the lights on. Dad might not raise a hand the way he used to—not since I'd grown big enough to hit back—but the threat was always there, sitting in the next room, waiting.

So I stayed. Worked. Endured.

Home wasn't far—a weathered house near the marsh where the grass hissed with crickets. Caroline would already be there, working through the evening cleaning schedule before heading to her second job at the tavern. Gabi would be at the table with her homework, pretending not to watch the clock. Dad would be in his chair, silent and simmering, same as ever. I'd get home, wash up, make sure my sisters were safe, and keep my mouth shut.

Leaving would've been easy.

Staying was what hurt.

But if I left, who'd protect them?

The sun slipped lower, turning the sky toward the mainland the color of a burn. I stopped at the edge of the road where the marsh opened wide. My throat felt raw. I looked toward the water and said it again, the way I did most nights, quiet enough that the wind carried it away.

"I didn't hurt her."

The tide didn't answer.

It never did.

ONE

Thirteen Years Later

RIOS

The air was thick with humidity that clung to my skin and made every breath taste faintly like the sea. The OBX Brewhouse glowed against the deepening dusk, strings of Edison bulbs casting a warm glow along the edges of the cedar siding. I heard the crowd before I saw them. Music rolled through the open doors, and laughter spilled out over the crushed shell parking lot.

I hadn't planned on being here tonight. Hell, I hadn't planned to be on Hatterwick at all. I should've been hip-deep in my investigation, closing in on evidence that would nail the perpetrators to the wall. But the Navy had put the kibosh on that, calling me on the carpet in D.C. to answer for daring to upset the status quo.

The fuckers.

So when the Wayward Sons text thread had lit up this morning with Sawyer giving Ford shit about the ring and Ford confirming that tonight was the night and wishing Jace and I could be there, I'd found my way back to the island.

Unannounced. Uninvited. Pretending I wasn't already a knot of nerves.

I spotted Ford leaning against Sawyer's big contractor's truck in the parking lot, both hands braced on his thighs as if he couldn't quite catch his breath. Sawyer was right there, hand on his shoulder, probably giving him a pep talk.

"Do I need to find you a paper bag?" I drawled.

At the sound of my voice, Ford's head snapped up, and his face broke into a grin that made something in my chest ease for the first time in weeks.

"No way." He was already in motion, meeting me halfway across the lot and pulling me in for a back-thumping hug. "You actually came."

"You think I was gonna miss this? After Sawyer went and married Willa without so much as a warning to the rest of us?"

"Extenuating circumstances," Sawyer protested, following suit with another bro hug. "You didn't tell anybody you were home."

"Wasn't sure I was."

Ford's grin softened into something quieter, steadier. "Well, you're here now. That's what matters." He clapped me on the shoulder, a wordless welcome that hit harder than I'd admit. "Come on, before Bree figures out what I have planned."

Having seen the outline of his plan this morning, I laughed. "She's gonna kill you."

"Worth it."

The door swung open as we reached it, the rush of sound and warmth hitting like a wave—glasses clinking, chairs scraping, the low buzz of cheerful conversation rolling under Monty's voice as he did mic checks for karaoke. The scent of beer, a hint of fryer oil, and something citrusy from Bree's new summer shandy wrapped around me like a memory that didn't quite fit anymore.

The crowd was a mix of locals, tourists, and summer workers. Many faces I knew. Many I didn't. The Wayward Sons' old table by the stage was occupied by strangers now, but the Gray Beards still had their corner, and Willa was near the jukebox, waving a drink as she argued with Duck about the banned song list.

Then I saw them.

Caroline's dark hair caught the light as she leaned across a table, laughing at something her husband, Hoyt, said. Beside her, Gabi gestured mid-story, animated and bright.

My throat tightened. After everything we'd gone through growing up, I'd never tire of seeing my sisters like this—loud, safe, and happy. I moved in their direction, but I hadn't made it three steps before Gabi's eyes landed on me.

"Rios!" Her voice cracked through the noise like a firework. Heads turned as she launched herself across the room, and I found myself bracing as I always did when attention turned to me on Hatterwick.

"Hey, *pequeña*," I managed before she collided with me, hugging hard enough to knock the wind out of my lungs.

Caroline wasn't far behind, eyes wide, already demanding, "When did you get here?"

"On the most recent ferry."

"You could've called!"

"Would've ruined the surprise."

She smacked my arm but hugged me again anyway. I let the squeeze settle something frayed inside me, then eased toward the bar with Sawyer at my shoulder, tracking exits out of habit, trying to look like a man who wasn't constantly scanning for looks of derision and judgment. Mostly I saw folks who'd decided my visiting my sisters wasn't interesting enough to pay attention to—a position I was more than fine with.

Bree came around from behind the taps and wrapped me up in a quick, solid hug underscored by the scents of citrus and clean malt. "Good to see you, Rios."

"Great to see you, too." I pulled back, letting my gaze flick between her and Ford, taking in the way they stood close enough to brush shoulders, the easy intimacy that had been absent for so many years. "Glad you two finally got your heads out of your asses."

Ford shot me a cheerful middle finger over his pint, which made my mouth twitch despite everything I wasn't saying—all the things I'd learned to keep locked down tight when I was around decent people living decent lives.

Bree shook her head, amused and exasperated in equal measure, the sound of the room swelling and softening around us like the tide against the docks outside. "We've heard that often enough we're considering putting it on a t-shirt and selling it at the bar."

"It would be a bestseller." The words felt easy rolling off my tongue; the relief behind them did not.

She tipped her chin toward the impressive row of tap handles, pride edging her smile in a way that made her whole face light up. "You want to try the new beer? Dark Moon Rising just won a gold medal at Brewgaloo."

I took in the neat rows of sample glasses lined up on the polished counter, the way her hands stayed steady and sure even with the bar hopping around us and voices rising over the music. A normal moment between old friends. A good one, the kind I'd learned not to take for granted.

"Sure, I'll have a sample."

"Don't be silly." She waved off my offer before I could even reach for my wallet. "As a proper welcome home, you get an entire pint on me."

I let the warmth of that sit in my chest while she poured. The pint landed under my hand with a soft slide of glass on wood.

From somewhere just behind my shoulder, a name cut clean through the ambient noise like a blade, and every one of my muscles went taut. "Did you hear about Madden Reilly?"

I didn't turn around, but everything in me tuned in to the conversation.

"Miles and Gwen Busby's cousin? The one who moved out to Washington?"

"California. She was some big deal prosecutor out there. Emphasis on was."

"What happened?"

"Lost her job."

"Over what?"

"Helped convict an innocent man. New evidence came to light, and the conviction was overturned. Guess the guy had connections, 'cause next thing she knew, she was out."

"Ouch."

The pint was cold and solid in my hand, condensation already beading on the glass. I kept my face carefully neutral and let the anger that wanted to rise burn itself down to manageable embers instead.

Bree's blue eyes flicked up to catch mine, voice deliberately even when she asked, "Karma?"

I took a measured sip of the dark beer—rich and complex, with notes of chocolate and coffee her brewmaster, Monty, had perfected—and set the glass down carefully so it didn't thump against the bar. My tone stayed completely flat. "Maybe now she'll learn to think before she speaks."

I lifted the pint in a brief salute to Bree and stepped away from the bar, angling toward a spot against the far wall where I could see the whole room breathe—my sisters safe and laughing, the exits clearly mapped, Ford's nervous energy slowly coalescing into something that looked like purpose. I let the noise and warmth of the place fill my ears, replacing the echoes of the past.

Up on the small stage that had been set up in the corner, Monty tapped the microphone with one manicured finger. Feedback squealed through the speakers; the crowd responded with good-natured laughter and a few catcalls.

"Welcome, welcome to karaoke night at the OBX Brewhouse! Now, we've got some ground rules. Two-song limit per person. And if you're on the banned list—" he paused dramatically, scanning the crowd with mock severity, "you know who you are. Don't even think about it."

The laughter rolled through the room like a wave, easy and familiar.

"To kick things off, we've got a special treat. Please welcome Ford Donoghue and Bree Cartwright!"

Bree's head snapped up so fast I was surprised she didn't get whiplash, that carefully maintained bartender composure cracking at the edges like ice in spring. "Excuse me, what? I *don't* karaoke."

Ford's grin was pure mischief mixed with affection, the expression of a man who knew exactly what he was doing and was enjoying every second. He offered his hand with the confidence of someone extending a formal invitation to a dance. "Come on."

The chanting started somewhere near the Gray Beards' usual table—no doubt instigated by Bree's grandfather, Ed— and spread like wildfire. Her name bounced around the room in a rhythm that caught and built on itself. Ford's fourteen-year-old daughter, Peyton, was on her feet clapping, and both his mom and her wife's cheers rang clear as bells over the rest of the noise. I leaned back against the wall and let the sound work on me like a pressure release valve, watching my friend get thoroughly peer-pressured by people who loved her.

Bree shot Ford a look that should have been lethal, the kind that would have sent a smart man running for cover, then surrendered with an exasperated huff that anyone who knew her could read as pure affection underneath all that manufactured irritation. "Fine. But I'm blaming you when this goes horribly wrong."

She came out from behind the safety of her bar to a wall of cheers and applause. Ford tugged her up onto the little stage, both of them already swallowing laughter like teenagers getting away with something.

"What are we even singing?" she demanded, accepting the microphone like it might bite her.

Ford's eyes danced with barely contained amusement as he picked up the second mic. "A classic."

The opening notes of "I Got You Babe" filled the air, and Bree sliced him a look that should have peeled paint off the walls. "Really? This is your idea of a timeless classic?"

But Ford just leaned into it with complete commitment, and after a moment of what looked like internal struggle, so did she. They were off-key and fearless, ham-handed with the choreography and completely tone-deaf. Neither of them could carry a tune in a bucket if their lives depended on it. But the room clapped along and hooted encouragement. I spotted at least half a dozen cell phones recording the spectacle for posterity.

I felt the knot that had been sitting in my chest since I'd stepped off the ferry finally start to loosen. This was good—this warmth, this acceptance, this sense of belonging somewhere that didn't require explanations or apologies.

They finished with a flourish that was all theatrical nonsense, playing to the crowd like seasoned performers. Bree started to step away from the microphone stand, already laughing at herself, then stopped short when Ford didn't follow.

"What are you..." Her words strangled out completely as Ford dropped to one knee right there on the small stage. The entire bar seemed to breathe in and hold it, the silence sudden and complete.

"What?" she squeaked, shock and laughter braided so tight in her voice I couldn't tell where one ended and the other began.

Ford's voice carried steady as a ship's keel through the sudden quiet, and even though I'd seen the ring in our group text earlier, had watched him agonize over the timing and the words for weeks, hearing him actually say them still hit me like a wave I wanted to let carry me along.

"Bree Cartwright," he began, a slight tremor underneath all that determination, "I have loved you for most of my life. First as my best friend, then as the woman who stole my heart, and now as this amazing bonus mom to my kid. You're the missing piece I didn't even know I was looking for until I lost you. I was an idiot to ever let you go, and I don't want to waste another minute." He pulled out the ring box, and several people in the crowd actually gasped. "Will you marry me?"

For one heartbeat that felt like it lasted an hour, I heard only my own pulse hammering in my ears. Then the room seemed to tip toward pure joy, and Bree's laugh broke on a breath that sounded like yes before she actually managed to say the word out loud.

"I will marry you on one condition."

Ford didn't even blink. He probably would have agreed to anything in that moment. "What's that?"

"You never, ever get me up here again."

The place absolutely detonated—cheers and applause and whistles that probably reached all the way down to the docks. I didn't try to shout over the celebration; I just lifted my glass in a quiet toast, while Ford slid the ring onto her finger with shaking hands and pulled her up into a kiss that turned the whole bar molten with shared happiness.

It was nice to have something to celebrate.

Even if everything else in my life was falling apart.

TWO

MADDEN

The ferry deck was a parking lot with railings. We sat in two tight lanes, engines off, windows cracked. Heat shimmered up from the metal around us. Somewhere behind me, a toddler announced for the fourth time that his popsicle had "died," which earned sympathetic laughter from a row of sunburned adults in matching neon shirts that said FAMILY VACAY.

I stayed in my car with the seat pushed back, elbow on the sill, watching tourists take pictures of each other against the sliver of water you could see through the gaps. Phones up. Peace signs. Duck lips. A girl in a floppy hat recorded a slow pan of the horizon like she was panning across the Grand Canyon instead of a sound dotted with crab pots and a handful of sails.

Los Angeles had taught me how to disappear. You could walk three blocks there and shed one life for another. Hatterwick was the opposite. Here, you collected lives you couldn't set down—daughter, cousin, the girl who left, the woman who came back. You didn't vanish on Hatterwick; you got recognized, cataloged, recounted, misremembered. You became a story whether or not you wanted one.

A deckhand in a reflective vest appeared at the head of the lane, hand up, then rotated it in a lazy circle that meant "get ready." Doors thunked as people climbed back into their cars. Keys turned. Engines rumbled awake. The ferry shifted under us as the crew brought the ramp down. A cheer went up somewhere on the upper deck, because apparently ramps lowering were content now.

I checked my phone while we waited for the front row to move.

ASTRID:

You close?

MADDEN:

On the deck. Should be off in a few.

The dots popped up immediately.

ASTRID:

I'll meet you at the marina. Text me when you park.

MADDEN:

Will do.

I set the phone face down and put both hands on the wheel. My palms were damp.

We rolled in a slow, patient crawl. The sight line widened to the dock and the squat building with the snack bar and the rack of brochures advertising fishing charters and ghost walks. A kid in a life jacket bounced on his toes on the pedestrian side, waving like we were a parade. When it was my turn, I eased down the ramp and felt the ferry let us go.

The road off the dock was the same and not. New paint, wider shoulder, fresh striping that would have to be redone in a couple of summers. Banners announced a summer concert series in cheerful fonts over names of bands I didn't recognize. The gift shops had multiplied, colorful as candy; the old ice cream parlor still sat in its pretty pink shell like a time capsule someone had dusted. For a block, I let myself scan the street for Gwen the way I always did—out of habit more than hope. It was a reflex. It hurt anyway.

My cousin wasn't here.

She never would be again.

I followed the familiar route around the curve of the harbor, past the line of charter boats rocking lazily in their slips, until the old marina came into view. It had been upgraded by the new owners sometime since my uncle had sold the business. I spotted upgraded slips, fresh wood, new signage. Rows of masts swayed against the sky, and beyond them, anchored in its usual spot, sat my uncle's houseboat—a broad-hulled relic with white sides and chipped blue trim. The paint was dull from years of sea air and neglect, but the name was still clear on the stern: *Second Wind.*

I just hoped it could be that for me.

I parked in the open marina lot, cutting the engine. The silence that followed felt enormous. For a long moment I just sat there, watching the shimmer of light on the water. I hadn't set foot on this dock since before everything fell apart—before my cousin Miles's arrest, before California had burned through what was left of my faith in the world.

Now I was back with too many ghosts and nowhere else to go.

I texted Astrid that I'd arrived and opened the door. The air hit me like wet velvet when I climbed out. Damn, but I'd forgotten the oppressive humidity of the island in July. Sweat prickled instantly between my shoulder blades as I popped the trunk and pulled out my laptop bag. The rest of my luggage could wait until I got the keys turned, and the boat opened up.

The dock boards flexed underfoot as I walked, the wood sun-bleached and hot enough to feel through the soles of my sneakers. Every sound was amplified—the clank of rigging, the cry of a gull, the low murmur of water slapping against hulls. Most of the slips were full. Summer season was in full swing. A charter captain cussed amiably at a knot in a tone that told me business was good. A girl in a cover-up practiced a toe-touch jump off the end of a finger pier while her mom warned her not to break her neck in a voice that had "first day of vacation" optimism baked in.

By the time I reached the *Second Wind,* my nerves buzzed. The boat looked smaller than I remembered. No cheerful deck chairs now, no potted basil on the rail. Just a closed-up cabin and windows dulled by dust and time.

I stepped aboard, and the hull shifted under my weight, a slow, sleepy protest. The lock was stiff and the door sticky, but they both gave, and air that had been shut in too long slid past me—hot, stale, edged with old varnish and something like cardboard. I propped the door open with my hip and reached for the little breaker panel. I flipped the breaker switch and was relieved when the lights flickered to life. Stale, but not dead. A good sign. Another switch had the little fan above the stove sputtering to life. I set the bag down on the bench and moved around the cabin, propping open windows to get some cross ventilation going.

"Could use a welcome committee," I muttered.

As if summoned, quick footsteps sounded on the dock outside.

"Madden? You here?" Astrid's voice carried that same confident energy I remembered from high school—sharp, bright, always three steps ahead.

"In here!"

I heard the thump of sure feet climbing aboard. A moment later, she appeared in the doorway, and the boat seemed less empty by half. Her strawberry-blonde hair was pulled into a functional ponytail; her sunglasses were propped on her head; she wore a tank and shorts and the kind of sandals you could hose off without guilt. Her grin spread wide. "You made it!"

"I did."

Without warning, she darted in for a quick, tight hug, and for a second I forgot how to hold myself up. It had been so long since I'd had anything so uncomplicated as a hug from a friend. I relaxed a fraction, letting myself return the embrace.

"It's good to see you." She stepped back to study me in that quiet, assessing way she had. "You look... tired, but mostly okay."

"Mostly okay is generous." I gestured toward the door. "Bags are in the car."

We fell into motion the way you do with people you used to see every day: easily, without having to narrate it. The walk back along the dock was shorter with someone beside me. The parking lot buzzed—a woman wrestling a beach umbrella into the back of a rental, a couple arguing about check-in times, a guy trying to convince his dog that the unfamiliar grate wasn't a trap. Astrid took the heavier suitcase without waiting for a debate.

She hoisted it up. "What's in this, lead?"

I shrugged. "I wasn't sure how long I'd be gone, so I packed for all contingencies."

That earned me a lifted eyebrow, but Astrid said nothing as we trudged with the last of my stuff back to the dock. By the time we reached the boat and set the bags inside, the little fan had started to make an actual difference. I opened another window in the aft, and the air shifted enough to carry out a layer of stillness.

Astrid stood in the doorway, one hand on the frame, eyes sweeping the cabin and taking stock. "Not gonna lie—I can't believe your uncle's still got her."

I followed her gaze around the narrow galley, taking in the scuffed countertop and the curtain with a faded compass print. "I guess he couldn't quite let go."

"Yeah." She leaned her shoulder against the doorjamb. "After your folks left the island, and the Busbys sold their place, I figured this old girl would've gone next. Too many memories tied up in her."

"That's exactly why he didn't," I said quietly. "It's one of the last pieces left of Gwen."

Astrid nodded, her expression softening. "Makes sense."

The silence between us wasn't uncomfortable, just full of the things we both remembered but didn't say out loud. The search parties. The vigils. The way people used to glance at me back then out of the corners of their eyes, like proximity was contamination.

Astrid blew out a breath, shaking it off. "Well, she's still afloat. And she'll do you fine until you figure out what's next."

"That's the plan," I said. "Such as it is."

"Good." She hesitated, her thumb making slow circles against the worn leather of her watchband—a nervous habit I remembered from high school. When she finally looked back at me, there was something careful in her expression. "So, what actually happened out there? In California, I mean. I heard you got fired, but we both know gossip's like a game of telephone on this island. By the time it reaches the third person, you're either a disgraced criminal or a whistleblowing hero."

I grimaced as that familiar knot tightened in my chest. "Yeah, that's... not exactly wrong. Technically, I resigned." The word tasted hollow in my mouth, like I was still trying to convince myself it had been my choice.

Her brows rose, and I caught the skeptical tilt to her head. "Technically?"

"I was told the optics for me were better if I did it myself." I tried to make it sound like old news, but the words still sat like grit on my tongue. "So I did." Because I'd cared more about salvaging what was left of my reputation than I did about unemployment benefits or severance packages.

Of course, that had been before I realized exactly how wrecked my reputation was anyway. Before I understood that resigning wouldn't stop the whispers in courthouse hallways or the way colleagues would suddenly find urgent reasons to end phone calls when I walked into a room.

Astrid's eyes softened, and I saw something that looked dangerously close to pity cross her features. "Jesus, Mads. That sucks."

"Yeah." I swallowed hard, focusing on the way the boat rocked gently beneath us rather than the sympathy in her voice. "Not my best year."

She tilted her head, studying me with the same intensity she'd probably use to examine an injured sea turtle. "You here to lick your wounds, or start over?"

"Bit of both, maybe." I shrugged, trying for casual and probably missing by a mile. "I'm still working out what that looks like. Hell, I'm still working out what I want it to look like."

"That's fair." She gave me a crooked smile that reminded me of summer afternoons when we were kids, before everything got complicated. "You always did hate sitting still. Even in elementary school, you'd finish your worksheets and then reorganize your desk just to have something to do. Maybe that restlessness is what you need right now."

I let out a quiet laugh. "Don't curse me like that."

"Might be good for you." Astrid pushed off the doorframe as her phone buzzed in her pocket. She glanced at the screen and sighed. "I've gotta head back to the research station before the summer interns accidentally feed a pelican a glow stick or try to tag a jellyfish. But I'm glad you're here. Really. It's been too long."

"Thanks. It really has." I found that I actually meant it. "It's good to see you, too. Good to see someone who doesn't look at me like I might spontaneously combust."

"Lunch or dinner later this week? There's this new place that opened up where the old bait shop used to be. Surprisingly good fish tacos."

"Sure. That sounds perfect."

She reached out and gave my arm a gentle squeeze, her hand warm against my skin. "Text me when you come up for air, okay? Don't go full hermit on me."

Then she was gone, her footsteps echoing down the weathered dock planks before fading into the general hum of the marina. I watched through the small porthole as she walked back toward shore, her ponytail swinging with each step, until she disappeared behind a cluster of masts and rigging.

I sank onto the narrow bench beside my laptop bag, suddenly exhausted in the way that comes after holding yourself together for company. Looking around the small cabin, I took in the way afternoon light filtered through the open hatch above, casting shifting patterns on the worn vinyl cushions. The boat swayed gently beneath me, a rhythm I'd forgotten I missed.

For the first time in a long time, there was nothing I had to prove. No case to build, no reputation to salvage, no next move to calculate three steps ahead.

Just me, the quiet lap of water against the hull, and whatever came next.

For right now, that was giving this whole place a good clean. It might not help me take control of my life, but taking control of my space would be a start.

That was as much as I had in me right now.

THREE

RIOS

The ocean was louder on this side of the island. Not the lazy slap of the sound, but a steady hush and thrum that lived under everything, like a heartbeat you only noticed when the house was quiet.

Caroline's place almost never got quiet.

"Logan, shoes off before you run upstairs!" my sister called from the kitchen. "I am not mopping again tonight."

"I forgot!" came the six-year-old's earnest bellow, followed by the unmistakable clatter of sneakers being toed off at speed and launched toward the hall tree. One missed and pinballed off the baseboard. Logan whooped like he'd scored a goal.

Aubrey padded past me with the composure of a much older kid, a baby bottle balanced expertly in one hand, burp cloth over her shoulder. "*Tío* Rios, can you test the temperature? He likes it warmer than I do."

"*Sí, jefa.*" I took the bottle, tipped it to my wrist. "Perfect."

She nodded, satisfied, and took it back with grave efficiency. At eight, she had the soft voice and serious eyes of someone who'd decided she was an assistant adult. Mother's helper in a ponytail and mermaid pajamas. She bent over the bouncer where Eli vibrated with righteous fury at having to exist here on the floor when there were clearly greater heights in the world (arms, shoulders, ceiling fan).

"Here you go, squish." She coaxed the nipple into his mouth, and the fury dissolved into hungry snuffles. "Teamwork," she told him. "You and me."

"Bless you, baby girl." Caroline passed through with a stack of plates. She brushed a kiss over Aubrey's crown and aimed a look at me that said she'd slept maybe four hours total in the last two nights and would do it all again without complaint. "How many tacos did you eat? Be honest."

"An even dozen."

She snorted. "Liar."

"Okay, eleven and a half. Logan stole one and ate just the tortilla."

"Carbs are life," Logan announced from the stairs, hopping down each step like it was a personal trampoline. He stopped beside me and peered up with chocolate ice cream ringed around his mouth like a villain mustache. "Daddy says I can help him fix the deck light tomorrow."

"That so?"

"Yeah. Because I know how to hold the flashlight still. He said that's the most important job."

"It is." I nodded solemnly. "No ship was ever saved by a wobbly flashlight."

My nephew considered this, nodded, and sprinted for the bathroom. A beat later, the sink squealed to life, water blasting tile, followed by Hoyt's patient baritone: "Buddy, hands under the water. Under. That's right."

I leaned my hip against the long kitchen island and let it all wash over me—the clink of plates, the hiss of the dishwasher, the sweet-milk scent of Eli's formula, the lemon cleaner Caroline favored, the faint sunscreen tang that seemed baked into every surface from a summer lived outdoors. The house was a riot of color, reflecting all the warmth and chaos we hadn't had growing up. Caroline and Hoyt had built it together until it felt like something durable and loved. It was a good house. A home meant for comfort and relaxing.

My shoulders didn't get the memo.

They ached, coiled and ready, even here. Even safe. Night was the worst, and nights here had stacked up like cups in a game, all the sounds of a family layered one on top of another. Eli's midnight snaps into wakefulness. The soft pad of Caroline's feet. Hoyt's murmur. The click and whine of the monitor. The house settling. The ocean. The ocean again. My body cataloged each one, searched for threat in domestic noise, and never quite believed me when I said there wasn't any.

I hadn't told my family the truth. Not all of it. I was home because the Navy and I had agreed to part ways "quietly," and quiet had never been so loud in my head.

"Earth to Rios." Caroline slid a glass of water in front of me. "You drifting?"

"A little."

"Drink." She bumped my elbow with the glass until I took it. "And go sit down. You did dishes last night. You are officially off duty."

"You cooked."

"I assembled tacos. That doesn't count." Her mouth curved. "Besides, you've been kid-wrangling for three days. Hoyt owes you hazard pay."

"Add it to my tab." Hoyt appeared with Eli scooped easily into the crook of one arm. He pressed a kiss to Caroline's temple as he passed and transferred the baby with the kind of gentle muscle memory that made you trust him with anything.

"Your presence has been requested for bath time. You wanna swap bedtime?"

"I'm always on bedtime. 'Tis my lot in life." She angled her head into his shoulder for one second more with an expression of bliss that said she wouldn't have it any other way, before peeling away, already gathering Logan's abandoned art project and sweeping glitter-escaped sprinkles into her palm. "Aubrey, grab the story basket?"

"On it." Aubrey eased the now-dozy Eli from their mother's arms, jostled him with practiced rhythm, and marched upstairs like a tiny general escorting a prisoner of war to a very soft cell.

Hoyt watched her go, pride bright and unhidden. "She's a good kid."

"They all are," I said. "Even the sugar-possessed one."

"Logan! Five-minute warning!" Caroline sang toward the upstairs hall. She glanced at me. "You look like someone hit your pause button."

"Thinking."

"Dangerous." Hoyt jerked his head toward the door. "Come on. Porch."

We stepped through the wide sliders onto a wrap-around porch that ran the length of the house. The Atlantic stretched black-blue beyond the dunes, the horizon a thin smear of silver under a sky littered with stars. Ceiling fans whirred lazily overhead, and somewhere out of sight a neighbor laughed.

I kept one hand on the railing as we settled into Adirondack chairs. Old habit: touch the boundary, know where you are. The railing was solid and slightly warm from a day of sun. My back found the angle of the chair and protested. I breathed through it.

Inside, bath chaos started in earnest—Logan's dramatic odes to the injustice of shampoo, Aubrey's patient narration for

Eli's benefit, Caroline's, "You will not flood the hallway, I mean it." A family symphony.

"Day three crash," Hoyt said, not unkindly.

"What?"

"You." He propped his feet on the railing. "You come in on adrenaline, you ride on reunion and momentum for forty-eight hours, and then the noise catches up. It's a good noise," he added quickly, like he was afraid of offending me on his own porch. "But it's noise."

"It is a good noise." I scrubbed a hand over my face, scruff rasping my palm. "I love being here."

"But?"

I huffed a breath that wasn't quite a laugh. "But I don't remember how to sleep in a house."

He didn't fill the silence, instead letting the ocean fill it for a minute.

"Is that new?" he asked at last.

"Newish." I tipped my head back and stared up at the night. "It's been worse stateside since I discovered how loud 'quiet' is."

"You talk to anybody about it?"

I made a face. Talking wasn't high on my list of things to do.

Wind lifted the edge of the outdoor rug and let it drop. Somewhere below us, sand shifted in the dark. I traced the line of the dune fence with my eyes until the urge to pace eased.

"I will," I said finally. "I just... needed to get out first."

"Of the Navy?" Surprise tinged my brother-in-law's tone. Of course it did. I still hadn't told them the truth of why I was here.

"Of the box I was in." I flexed my hands on my knees. "I'm not ready to give you the long version."

"You don't owe me an explanation." He said it with the ease of truth. "You know that, right?"

"Caroline is gonna want one."

"She's gonna want to know you're all right." He tipped his chin toward the sliding door. "She knows where you've been doesn't come with easy stories."

"It's not a story," I said, sharper than I meant to. I sucked in a breath, dropped my voice. "Sorry."

Hoyt's mouth did that small not-smile he used when he was deciding to absorb rather than deflect. "What do you need tonight?"

I thought about saying nothing. I thought about lying and saying I was fine, because we all had our roles and mine had historically been the unflappable one, the one who could make a joke and shift the topic with a grin and a shoulder, the one who was made of angles and calm.

Honesty tasted like copper. "A place to be awake that doesn't keep your whole house awake with me."

"Yeah," he said softly. "Figured."

Aubrey's voice floated out through the screen, high and earnest as she continued the bedtime story: "—and then Max said, 'No gators in the bathtub,' and Logan said, 'But what if they're baby—' and Mama said, 'Nope.'"

Hoyt chuckled, thumb running along the arm of his chair. "You could take the guest room, but the baby monitor might make you crazy."

"It's not the monitor," I said. "It's... everything. And none of it is wrong."

"I know."

He let that sit. I let it sit with him. We'd both learned the usefulness of not rushing a fix. I appreciated his steadiness. Caroline deserved that in her life after where we'd started.

"You're still welcome here as long as you want," he said after a bit. "This is your home as much as ours. But I do have a thought."

"Hit me."

"The boat," he said.

I looked at him, and he looked back like he'd placed his piece on the board, and now we'd see if I moved mine.

"Are you gonna say you haven't used it much this summer, and you don't have time for sails because Eli eats hours like Pac-Man?"

"All true." His mouth twitched. "But that's not why I'm offering it."

"Why are you offering it?"

"Because you sleep better when you can hear water hit hull," he said simply. "Because you like walls you can touch without getting up. Because you're a man who checks the perimeter, and a 40-foot ketch is easier to check than a 3,500-square-foot house."

I stared at him. "That was disturbingly accurate."

"It's almost like I know you." He lifted one shoulder. "Take her for a while. I've got a slip down by C dock. It's quiet there. There's shore power. I replaced the bilge pump and the head last spring. She's ready to go. No pressure," he added quickly, palms out like he was approaching a skittish horse. "If you want to stay here, stay here. But if you want a door that closes on your own noise, I can give you that."

I looked past him at the dark line of the horizon and the way the stars doubled in the sliding glass reflection. I could already feel it—the way the world narrowed on a boat. The way problems did too. Deck, lines, mast, hatch, stove, berth, the soft thump of a halyard in a night breeze. A map I knew in my bones.

"You sure?" I asked.

"Rios," he said, amused now, "I am not only sure, I'm selfish. If you sleep, you will be human again, and then I can rope you into fixing my gate and hanging the cabinet doors I've been avoiding."

Because I knew he expected it, I smirked. "Ah. There it is. The trap."

"Always," he said cheerfully. "What do you say?"

Inside, the bedtime story rolled toward its end. Caroline's voice joined Aubrey's, steady and warm. A page turned with a whisper. Someone giggled. Eli hiccuped and sighed.

I swallowed. "I say thank you."

"Good." He clapped his palms lightly on his thighs and stood. "We'll walk down there after bedtime and make sure everything's fired up. Lights, water, shore power. You can move in tomorrow if you want."

"Tonight," I heard myself say.

Hoyt's brows lifted, but he only nodded, unperturbed. "Tonight, then."

We sat a minute more, both of us listening to the end of the house's evening song. My shoulders crept down a notch I hadn't realized they'd climbed. Space. A place to put my vigilance without resenting the people I loved for being noisy and alive.

Caroline slid the door open with her hip and stepped onto the porch, tucking a piece of hair behind her ear. Her pajama pants were sprinkled with cartoon lobsters. There was a smear of something unidentifiable on her shoulder. She was radiant with the kind of tired happiness that could only be earned.

"They're down." The gaze she turned on me was pointed. "You look a fraction less haunted. What did he say to you?"

"I offered him the boat," Hoyt said.

Caroline's face opened like the sunrise. "Oh, thank God. I was trying to figure out how to make that not sound like I was kicking you out."

"You are not kicking me out," I said quickly.

"Obviously." She came to me and put her hands on either side of my face, thumbs sweeping the sweat at my temples, the way she'd done when we were kids after Dad slammed a door too hard and the house rattled. "You are loved here, *siempre*. But you also look like a man trying to sleep in a beehive."

"That is an apt metaphor," I said dryly.

"Then take the boat and get some quiet," she said. "And come eat breakfast here in the mornings so I can see your face."

"Deal."

Her eyes searched mine. The part of me that had perfected the mask shifted, tried to slide it up. The other part—the one that had crossed an ocean for this porch—held still.

"You'll tell me when you're ready?" she asked softly.

"Yes," I said. The word caught for a second. "When I'm ready."

"Good." She kissed my forehead the way Mom used to, like it was a blessing. "Go with your brother-in-law. I will not wait up because I will be unconscious in eleven minutes."

She disappeared back inside with a little wave. Hoyt pushed up to his feet and offered me a hand I didn't need but took anyway.

"Come on, sailor," he said. "Let's go turn on your lights."

I followed Hoyt in my own truck. The drive took less than ten minutes, but it seemed like miles. Distance enough that I could breathe. C dock sat farther from the streetlights, tucked behind a line of taller pilings where the bigger boats moored up in storm season. Hoyt's boat rode easy, the masts clean lines against the sky. He stepped aboard first. I leapt up after, my legs automatically accommodating the familiar rock of hull underfoot. The deck smelled of sun-warmed rope and fiberglass. A different kind of home.

Hoyt moved through the cockpit by habit, flipping switches, checking gauges. Shore power hummed alive. Cabin lights clicked on one by one, throwing warm pools across the teak.

I stood in the companionway and let my eyes adjust. Everything was tidy—of course it was—but not precious. A blue blanket folded on the settee. Two mugs in the galley rack. A paperback face-down by the little berth and a pencil trapped in its pages.

Hoyt ducked his head out of the forward hatch. "She's all yours."

"Thank you." The words seemed inadequate, but they were all I had.

He took them as if they were more than enough. "I'll help you haul in your stuff."

"I'll get it," I said. "You go relieve Caroline from pretending not to wait up."

He laughed. "She lasted two minutes past her prediction. She is definitely out."

We stood there a little awkwardly, two men on a lit boat in a dark marina, and then he reached out and pulled me in for a hug I didn't know I needed until the second it started. Solid. Brothers, if not by blood. He thumped my back once and stepped away.

"Good night, *hermano*," he said.

"Night."

He headed up the dock, whistling under his breath, a tune I couldn't place. I watched him go until he hit the shadow line and disappeared.

I retrieved the bag with my essentials and went below. I didn't unpack. Didn't do anything to settle in. Instead, I turned off all but the little reading light near the aft berth, and sat on the edge of it with my feet braced on the floor. The boat rocked, close and sure. The sounds I could hear here were mine to inventory: water, wind, a fender creak, the occasional distant laugh. No monitor. No baby startle. No house bones. Only a perimeter I could monitor without moving. Doors I could see from where I sat.

I set my phone face down. I didn't need it to tell me anything right now. I stretched out and closed my eyes. For a long time, I breathed with the water. When my body startled, it had a place to land.

For the first time in too many months, the dark felt like a room instead of a field.

I slept.

FOUR

MADDEN

The taco place had taken over the spot where the old bait shop used to sit. Someone had painted the cinder block walls a saturated turquoise and strung a tarp for shade. Box fans hummed under the eaves, rattling the paper lanterns and the hand-lettered menu boards. The line spilled past a cooler of bottled sodas. The smell of grilled fish and warm corn tortillas wrapped the whole corner like an invitation.

Astrid waved me in from a picnic table half under the awning. "You found it!"

She'd staked out a spot with a view of the ordering window and the walkway, sunglasses in her hair, elbows planted like a general guarding a strategic position. Three students clustered around her—early to mid twenties—sunburned noses, university T-shirts, waterproof watches. The exuberance of people who didn't yet know where their limits were.

"I smelled it from two blocks away." I slid onto the bench and tried to ignore the itch between my shoulder blades that said half the patio had glanced up when I walked by. Maybe they hadn't. Maybe that was just the voice in my head that had learned to listen for whispers.

Astrid gestured between us. "My ducklings. Maya, Tyler, Priya. This is my friend, Madden Reilly. She's local stock, even if she ran off to the big city."

"Local stock," I echoed, wry. "I'll put that on my resume."

Maya—pale and freckled, with a sunhat big enough to shade a small village—pushed a paper cup toward me. "Horchata. It fixes everything."

"I'll take that under advisement." I glanced around again as the first cold sip hit me with twin blasts of sweet and cinnamon.

A kid two tables over tried to balance a lime wedge on his nose while his sister documented him for posterity. Gull cries braided with laughter and the crackle of the flat-top grill. Normal life. Loud and bright.

"I'm gonna put in my order."

I left them there and stepped to the window, trying not to appear as uncomfortable as I felt among all these people. I didn't want to meet anyone's eyes. Didn't want to risk finding someone I knew who might ask questions I didn't want to answer. When it was my turn, I ordered a couple of the day's special fish tacos and rejoined Astrid and her students with my tray.

"...N-17 and N-19 both started caving last night," one of the grad students was saying as I sat. "We logged sand temps at eighty-eight, so I'm betting on a boil in the next forty-eight hours."

"Make sure the interns know that means watch, not poke," Astrid said dryly, peeling the wrapper off her fish taco. "Last week I had to confiscate a selfie stick."

That got a round of laughter.

Priya flashed a smile as she shoved dark hair out of her face and resumed fiddling with the hair tie on her wrist. "At least they didn't try to 'help' a ghost crab out of a burrow again."

"Small mercies." Astrid shook her head and took a sip of her drink. Her phone buzzed on the table, the screen smeared with sunscreen fingerprints. She thumbed a quick reply, then set it face-down. "Anyway, tonight's team will rotate between N-17 and N-19 until midnight. Keep the red filters on your lights, and remember to flag the predation tracks before you fill in."

"Yes, ma'am," they chorused in teasing unison.

I smiled into my sweet tea, half-listening, half-watching the way this little crew orbited her—comfortable, competent, full of the kind of unguarded energy that came from doing work you believed in. Their hands moved constantly while they talked: one checking notes on a phone in a waterproof sleeve, another scrolling through photos of tracks in the sand, someone else jotting with a pencil on a crumpled Rite-in-the-Rain notebook.

They looked happy. Certain of their path in life. I couldn't remember the last time I'd felt like that about anything.

Astrid nudged me with her elbow. "You okay?"

"Just admiring how much smoother your job sounds than mine ever was."

She rolled her eyes affectionately. "Only because you never had to herd grad students. They eat more than sea turtles."

When the students finally cleared out, taking their trays, half-finished horchatas, and a cloud of laughter with them, the table felt bigger and quieter.

Astrid leaned back, ankle over knee, and sighed like a woman who'd been running at full speed since sunrise. "God, I love them, but I swear they make me feel ancient."

I pursed my lips. "You're thirty."

"Exactly." She pointed a chip at me. "Ancient."

I huffed a laugh and let my shoulders ease a little. "They seem good, though. Happy."

"They are. It's a nice change of pace. Most summers I get at least one who thinks data collection is optional and sunscreen is for cowards."

The breeze caught the edge of the tarp overhead, flapping it like a lazy sail. I watched it for a moment, letting the motion steady me. "You sound happy, too."

"Can't complain. Field season keeps me outside, my team's competent, and I get to come home to air-conditioning and actual showers." She tilted her head, eyes narrowing playfully. "You, on the other hand, look like someone still bracing for impact."

I winced. "That obvious?"

"To me? Always." She speared a piece of fish with her fork. "How's the houseboat?"

"Old, creaky, and exactly what I needed." Scrubbing the whole thing from fore to aft had been cathartic. She still needed the kind of TLC she'd only get off season and out of the water, but that sense of staleness and abandonment had been banished. I'd even picked up a plant while I was in town this morning.

"Good." She studied me for a moment, then grinned. "You know, I half expected you to chicken out. You've got that L.A. polish now. I thought you might wither in the humidity."

"I'm acclimating." I plucked at my sticky blouse. "Slowly."

Her laughter drew a couple of curious looks from nearby tables, and I fought not to shrink beneath their gazes.

"So, tell me what's been going on around the island lately." Better to steer the conversation toward other people.

"Well, you definitely missed a few things while you were gone. Sawyer and Willa eloped last fall."

"Wait, Willa Hollingsworth?" She'd been a couple of years behind me in school and one of Gwen's best friends.

"Yep. Total stealth operation. Whole town found out when they came back wearing rings."

"Wow. Didn't her parents disapprove of him?" Sawyer Malone hadn't remotely been of a social class the Hollingsworths would've approved of. I knew because my parents were cut from the same cloth.

"Well, probably, but Willa basically told them to fuck off and entirely cut them out of her life when she came back to the island at eighteen."

I tried to imagine the quiet girl I remembered doing such a thing and couldn't quite see it. For a moment, envy flared that she'd gotten out from under her controlling parents. "Good for her."

"I thought so. They're disgustingly happy."

"Double good for her." She'd always been an incredibly sweet girl. She deserved whatever happiness she'd managed to carve out of life. "What else is good news?" I wasn't sure I wanted to hear any other kind.

"Ford's back on-island, and he just proposed to Bree last week."

"I thought she hated him." They'd been besties from elementary school, but a few years after high school, there'd been some falling out. I didn't ever hear the details.

"So did we all. But whatever happened, apparently they worked it out. Oh, and he's got a teenage daughter. Not Bree's."

I blinked. "Wow. That's... unexpected."

"Took the whole island by surprise. Ford, too, from what we all know. She's a smart kid." Astrid took a sip of her drink. "Let me think. Oh, Lindsay has a new beau. None other than Corbin O'Connell."

My brain spun, sifting through names and faces and bits of

old knowledge about people I hadn't thought of in ages. "Didn't he go into the Coast Guard?"

"He did. Came back to help out when his daddy's knee surgery had complications. Lindsay's been working as office manager for their fishing company for years, and she ended up getting attacked at the office one night."

My hand shot out to close over Astrid's wrist. "Attacked?"

"She's okay. Promise. She was just concussed. Anyway, Corbin found her and went all bodyguard on her until they caught the guy, so she's been living her best romance novel life."

That dragged a chuckle out of me. "I love that for her. She's had a crush on him since, like, freshman year." I nibbled at my taco. "Sounds like it's been an eventful few years."

"It has." Her expression sobered, and I knew what she wasn't saying.

As if the universe was determined to bring it up anyway, a woman at another table murmured, "I still can't believe the mayor killed that man. Crazy world."

The words hit like a glass dropped on tile. The clatter of the patio kept going, but all the air seemed to thin.

The mayor. My cousin. Gwen's older brother, Miles, who'd been convicted of voluntary manslaughter for killing his blackmailer.

Astrid shot me a quick look. "Ignore them."

"I do." But it wasn't true. I'd been ignoring ghosts for years, and they were better at waiting me out.

Her hand brushed mine briefly, grounding. "How's your uncle?"

"He's... holding together." I managed to keep my voice steady. "Still working boats out of Beaufort. I think keeping busy is the only thing keeping him upright."

In the wake of his daughter's disappearance, he and my

aunt had eventually gotten divorced. With this latest scandal involving his son, I'd been really worried about him.

Astrid nodded. "Grief's funny that way. The motion's sometimes the only thing that keeps you from sinking."

"Yeah."

For a while, we just ate, the rhythm of it easy again, until she pushed her tray aside. "Listen, we've got a couple nests likely to boil Friday night. You should come out. Bring coffee and watch the hatchlings run. It's magic every time."

I hesitated. The invitation was so casual, so normal, it caught me off guard. "Are you sure I wouldn't be in the way?"

"Please. You'd be doing me a favor. Half of my interns are scared of the dark."

It probably wasn't true, but it coaxed a real smile out of me. "Then I'm in."

"Good." She gathered her trash and stood, slipping her sunglasses back into place. "I've gotta head back before someone tries to GPS-track a loggerhead. Text me later. We'll plan the night watch."

"Will do."

She leaned down to hug me, quick and fierce. "It's good having you back, Mads. Don't vanish again."

"I'll try not to."

I watched her cross the street toward her battered SUV. For a minute, I let the noise of the place wash over me.

I lingered after she'd gone, finishing the horchata in slow, deliberate sips. The fans ticked overhead. Somebody's radio flickered to a new song. A breeze lifted the edge of the tarp and let it drop, and for a blessed minute no one looked at me at all.

The walk back to the marina seemed shorter this time, sun sharp on the water, dock boards radiating heat. The *Second Wind* came into view, scuffed and stubborn and exactly where I needed her to be.

Movement to my right tugged my focus. The neighboring slip held a sailboat—sleek where my uncle's boat was boxy, clean lines and masts that made precise marks against the sky. A man stood on deck with a coil of line over one shoulder, back to me. He had black hair, cut close to his head, and shoulders that said strength without trying to.

For just a moment, I felt a stirring of heat as I admired the flex and stretch of those muscles beneath the tight black t-shirt. I wasn't here looking for anything with anybody. My life was the very definition of hot mess. But I was woman enough to appreciate the view of a very fine-looking neighbor. And if it reminded me of things I hadn't had the time or energy for in longer than I cared to remember, well, it was nice to know I wasn't dead.

He turned at the sound of my steps, and recognition slammed into me, along with an equally powerful punch of *hell no*. Because my next-boat neighbor was Rios Carrera.

The world tipped, then righted.

He looked different, and he didn't. The boy I remembered had been all restless edges and careless charm layered over anger he couldn't afford to show. This man wore silence like armor. His gaze locked on mine and held. No greeting. No surprise offered up for me to make sense of. Just watchfulness and something closed.

I had not prepared for this. I hadn't even known to. Every drop of moisture evaporated from my mouth as a hundred memories shot through me with the speed and sting of fish under a dock: my voice repeating other people's sentences because it kept the table calm; the way I'd stared straight ahead in the grocery store while two women spoke loudly about "boys who hurt girls," knowing he was two aisles over; the night my father said, "They wouldn't look at him if there wasn't a reason," and I'd said exactly that the next time I'd seen him. As if the system could not be wrong. As if being good meant agreeing.

Shame rose like a tide. I could either let it drown me or wash me clean.

"Hey." The word came out steadier than I felt. "Looks like we're neighbors."

He didn't move. The coil of line rested neat and controlled against his shoulder. Up close, the years showed in the finer lines at the corners of his eyes and a hardness in the set of his mouth I didn't remember. Whatever scars he had, they were his, and I wouldn't name them for him.

I could have turned. I could have pretended I hadn't seen him. Every muscle in my body wanted distance.

That part of me had gotten too much of what it wanted.

I stopped mentally editing to try to make this palatable. The truth needed to be spoken, even if it hurt me. "I know this is too little, too late, but I owe you a major apology. I was horrible to you after Gwen disappeared, and you had nothing to do with it. I'm sorry I added to the dogpile when everyone else on this island was already tearing you apart. I'm sorry I didn't stop to question anything. I was wrong. Period."

A gull piped somewhere above us. A fender groaned against pilings. The sailboat shifted a few inches and settled again.

He kept looking at me. Not past me. At me. Heat gathered at my hairline and slid, slow and humiliating, down my neck. He didn't owe me words. He didn't owe me absolution. I wasn't asking for either.

When the silence stretched, I nodded awkwardly. "Right. Well. I just wanted you to know that."

I turned, stepped onto the *Second Wind*, and set my hand on the familiar latch. The metal was warm. My fingers shook, a little tremor that made the clip rattle louder than it needed to.

The door gave. I kept my shoulders square and didn't glance back.

Inside, the cabin light made a soft pool on the counter. The fan ticked. I shut the door, leaned my forehead against it for a heartbeat, then pushed away and crossed to the small sink.

My heart was still running. It would stop eventually. I had done the thing that needed doing. No perfect words or rehearsed pauses. Only a necessary truth.

And the world hadn't spun off its axis.

Perhaps that was the lesson to take from this. I could speak truth and survive the consequences.

I wished I'd learned that years ago.

FIVE

RIOS

Noise spilled out of the open windows of the Brewhouse onto the outer porch. Fans whirred overhead, stirring the heavy air. The smell of fried fish and malted hops drifted in lazy waves. This time of day, it was mostly locals, who'd emerged now that the lunch wave of tourists had gone off for a nap or back to the beach to bake themselves all afternoon.

Sawyer spotted me first and waved from the back deck. "'Bout time, man. We were starting to wonder if you'd decided to steal Hoyt's boat and make a run for Aruba."

I slid into the empty chair. "I considered it."

Ford snorted, one corner of his mouth quirking. "You always did like to make an entrance." The tattoos on his forearms shifted as he leaned back, sunlight catching on the edge of his tea glass. "You eat yet?"

"Not since breakfast."

I'd put in my obligatory appearance at Caroline's first thing. She was still giving me The Eye—something she'd perfected since her offspring had been born—and I was gonna have to actually tell her the truth about my presence here, since, by everyone's expectations, I should still be deployed. But I wanted to talk it over with my brothers first, so here I was.

Ford flagged the waitress with two fingers. I put in an order for the blackened fish of the day and a Coke. Once she'd left, the three of us fell into the kind of silence that only happens when you've spent years earning it. No pressure to fill the gaps, no need to pretend. Just the hum of conversation around us and the creak of the boards under our boots.

Ford was the first to break it. "So, you gonna tell us what's really going on, or do we get to guess?"

I huffed a quiet laugh. "That obvious?"

Sawyer leaned back in his chair. "You've been back for near to a week. Not like you to hang around this long between deployments. We figured something was up."

"Yeah." I let my fingers drum once against the table before flattening them. "Something's up."

Ford's gaze sharpened. "You taking a new posting?"

"No, nothing like that." I took a breath and let it out slow. "I'm out."

That earned a synchronized blink from both of them.

"Out as in—?" Sawyer prompted.

"As in done. Separated. Or will be once the paperwork is done processing."

Ford sat forward, forearms braced on the table. "What the hell happened?"

The waitress came with our food, and I waited until she'd walked off before answering. "There was a case. Someone who's been preying on female sailors. One of them was a friend of mine." My mouth flattened as I remembered how I'd found Bridget brutalized because she'd fought back. "I started an investigation. Gathered enough statements and evidence to show a pattern going back a decade or more. A senior commander who believed his position entitled him to do any damned thing he pleased to whomever he wanted. But when I tried to run the case up the chain of command, I hit a wall of brass and old favors. They shut it down."

Ford's jaw tightened. "You pushed anyway."

"Yeah. And they pushed back. Made me an offer—early separation with full honors, clean record, and a quiet exit. The alternative was a long, ugly fight that wouldn't end with me in uniform or the son of a bitch behind bars where he belongs."

Sawyer's eyes darkened. "So you took the honorable route."

"If you can call it that." I picked up my fork, stabbed a piece of fish, didn't eat it. "I took the route that didn't end with me losing everything I'd built since I was twenty."

"The route that forced you to walk away while a predator is allowed to go free," Sawyer observed.

My teeth ground together at the reminder. "Yeah. They strongly encouraged the officer to retire, and so far as I'm aware, he took it. But it's cold comfort."

"That's bullshit," Ford said.

"Welcome to the military justice system."

For a long moment, none of us spoke. Somewhere inside, a blender started up. Somebody laughed too loudly at a bar joke. The ordinary sounds of life moved around us like nothing had shifted, even though everything had.

Ford finally said, "You did the right thing."

I kept my eyes on the distant sparkle of Pamlico Sound. "Doesn't feel like it. I had six women who trusted me to protect them, and they got to watch the bastard walk away with a handshake and a pension. And I got to pack my life into two duffels and pretend like it was mutual."

"Hell of a thank you," Sawyer muttered.

"Yeah." I jerked my shoulders, wishing I could banish the

images that still haunted my nights. "So now I'm here. Trying to figure out what the hell comes next."

Ford leaned back again, processing. "You thinking about staying?"

Once the answer would've been an unequivocal no. But despite the pain this place had caused me, my family was here. My friends were here. A part of me would always feel like Hatterwick was home. "Haven't decided yet." I chased a drop of condensation down my glass with my thumb. "Feels different this time. The island, I mean."

"I mean, it *is* different now," Sawyer said. "Now everybody knows Miles is the reason Gwen disappeared."

"Folks are still clutching their pearls over him killing David Galef last year," Ford added.

Yeah, I knew all of that. And yet. "People knowing our illustrious former mayor was more of a shit than they were aware doesn't automatically make them ready to rewrite the story. It's one thing to know the villain wasn't me. It's another to look me in the eye and admit it."

Ford's expression softened. "Most people know better now."

"Most people," I repeated. "Not all." Some would always look at me and see a brown man from the wrong side of the island. Someone less.

The waitress came back with refills. Sawyer thanked her; Ford tossed a few fries onto my plate like I needed moral support in the form of carbs.

"Hey, you could do worse than staying here awhile," Sawyer said. "Plenty of work. I can always use another set of hands on construction sites. And the marina is perpetually short staffed this time of year. Plus, you're half local legend. Some people actually like you."

I smirked. "You and Ford don't count as a majority."

"That's debatable," Ford said. "We're the two loudest."

The easy laughter helped bleed off the edge. For the first time in weeks, my chest didn't feel like it was caught in a vise.

Then I said the thing I hadn't planned to. "Madden Reilly's back."

Sawyer froze mid-bite. Ford's brows shot up.

"You're serious?" Ford said.

"Yeah. She's on the boat next to mine."

Ford sat back hard enough to make his chair creak. "You're kidding."

"I wish I was. She came over yesterday."

Sawyer's tone went skeptical. "Why?"

"To apologize." I took a sip of Coke. "Said she was sorry for what she said. For believing the rumors. For piling on."

Ford let out a low whistle. "That's... rich."

"It's something." I hadn't known what to think or say about it, so I'd said nothing, watching her walk away to the slip next door. "She looks like she's been through hell." Whatever her story was, it was written all over her.

I'd taken one look at her and seen the fragility that sat on her shoulders like a mantle of glass, and I'd wanted to step in and do... what? Protect her? Comfort her? Some asinine heroic bullshit that was an absolute no go even before I realized exactly who she was.

"Something about getting fired from her prosecutor job, according to the gossip mill," Ford said. "Maybe she got what she deserved."

"I'm not sure about that. No matter what she said to me back when, I can't take satisfaction in the fact that she looks like she's emotionally had the shit kicked out of her."

And damned if those earnest hazel eyes didn't still pull at me.

Sawyer leaned back in his chair. "Means you're still a better man than a lot of this town."

"She was right about one thing—it doesn't change anything," I said. "But it's more than most people have ever said."

Ford shook his head. "I'd have paid money to see that conversation."

"Wouldn't have been worth much. She spoke for thirty seconds. We stared each other down for a few more. Then it was done."

But apparently she was going to be next door, and I had to figure out what to do with that.

The sun had shifted enough that the awning's shade crawled across the table. My fish was cold, but I picked at it anyway.

Needing a subject change, I glanced up. "Anybody heard from Jace beyond what he said in the group text about Ford's proposal?"

"Not for a few weeks," Sawyer admitted. "Last I heard, he's still somewhere classified. Willa's hoping he'll make it home sometime this fall for a visit."

"Think he's a lifer?" Ford asked.

Sawyer leaned back and considered, now Jace's brother-in-law as well as brother-in-bond, as we all were. "Maybe. The guy doesn't exactly know how to do normal."

Ford snorted. "None of us do. You forget how to when half your adult life's been lived by orders."

Sawyer tipped his chair back, squinting toward the parking lot through the slats of the deck rail. "That or we just get used to the noise in our heads."

He wasn't wrong. The silence after structure had a way of turning on itself, filling up with the ghosts of should-haves and what-ifs. That static had followed me since the day I packed out of base housing.

I caught movement at the edge of the parking lot. A woman moving too fast for the heat, head down, stride clipped like she was chasing something she couldn't quite catch. Astrid Thompson. She blew past the line of parked bikes and tourists, eyes on her phone as she furiously tapped at the screen.

Ford followed my line of sight. "She's on a mission."

"She's worried." Even from here, I could see the tight set of her shoulders.

Astrid didn't even glance our way as she cut through the entry toward the main bar. A moment later the door swung shut behind her, muffling the burst of sound from inside.

"What do you suppose that's about?" Sawyer asked.

I shook my head. "Nothing good." Over the course of my career, I'd seen the faces of too many people who were close to their wit's end to dismiss it as something benign.

When Astrid emerged a few minutes later, her mouth was set in a hard line. She moved to the nearest table, speaking to the occupants and flashing her phone as if showing a photograph. Looking for someone or something.

I was already out of my seat headed for her before I'd consciously made up my mind. "Astrid? Something wrong?"

She exhaled a breath. "Hey, Rios. I hadn't heard you were back on-island."

"Haven't been for long. What's going on?"

Her gaze shifted as Ford and Sawyer joined us. "One of my grad students is missing."

She angled her phone so we could see the screen. An early twenty-something girl with wind-blown dark hair and a shy smile.

"She didn't show up for work this morning, and nobody's seen or heard from her. I feel like I've looked everywhere."

Another missing girl.

For just a moment, I flashed back to that long ago summer, when we'd combed every inch of this island looking for Gwen. We knew now why we hadn't found her. If we'd started sooner, right after the party, would it have made a difference? I had no idea. But I wouldn't make the same mistake again.

"When did you last see her?"

"Last night on the beach during hatching observation."

"And what time was that?"

Astrid scrubbed a hand down her face. "Um... it would've been around eleven-thirty, I think. I don't know for sure since I don't have her paperwork documenting. I didn't think anything at first. Kids oversleep. But when she didn't show by ten, I got worried and called. No answer. Then I went by her apartment. No answer there either."

My brain was already running scenarios as I continued asking questions. "Does she have a roommate? A boyfriend? Somewhere else she might've spent the night?"

"No roommate. It's just a teeny studio rental. And no boyfriend that I'm aware of."

"Could she have picked somebody up at a bar?" Sawyer asked. "Some of them are open 'til the wee hours this time of year."

"I suppose anything is possible, but she's never struck me as the type."

"And she's never done something like this before?" I pressed.

"No. Never. She's the one who keeps all my other students in line."

"Have you spoken to the police?"

"I tried to file a report before I came here, but they said since she's an adult and it hasn't been twenty-four hours yet, and there's no obvious sign of foul play, they can't do anything."

There were dozens of entirely valid reasons for the girl not to show. But after my years as a military cop, I had even more horrific scenarios in my head. The twenty-four-hour rule existed procedurally for a reason, but I well knew that a fuckton could go wrong in that span of time. If it had, time would be of the essence.

I exchanged a look with Ford and Sawyer and got nods from them both. One corner of Ford's mouth hooked into a wry smile. "You can take the cop out of the Navy..."

Astrid brightened faintly. "You're police?"

"I was naval police, yes."

She set a hand on my arm. "Will you help?"

"I've got no jurisdiction here, but I can absolutely help you ask around. I'm gonna need some more information."

SIX

MADDEN

The Sutter's Ferry Police Station looked even smaller at night. The squat clapboard building couldn't have been more different from the sprawling precincts I'd grown used to in Los Angeles. Just a single story, with one halogen bulb buzzing over the door drawing moths into its cone of light. But inside, it still held the ubiquitous scents I associated with police stations—the faintly musty odor of overworked air conditioning and the sharp bite of burnt coffee.

The wall just inside the door was covered in outdated flyers, including a MISSING poster with a familiar face. My step faltered as I took in this latest computerized rendering of what they thought my cousin looked like after all these years. Cheeks still round, hazel eyes still bright. Dark hair loose around her shoulders. She didn't look like me here. Would she have grown out of the resemblance that had made people believe we were sisters when we were young? Would I even know her if we passed on the street? Given what everyone now surmised had happened to her, the assumption was that she was dead. That was horrible enough, but after my years as a prosecutor, seeing the worst humanity had to offer, I knew that there were other options that were incalculably worse.

Tearing my gaze away from the poster, I hurried to catch up with Astrid as she marched toward the front desk, phone clenched in her hand like she'd bludgeon the officer who sat there if he didn't listen to her this time.

"—been exactly twenty-four hours. I want to file a missing person's report for my grad student."

"Of course. I'll just take down the…" He trailed off as he spotted me. "Madden?"

It took me a second to place him. He was taller and broader than he'd been in high school, his shoulders filling out the crisp uniform shirt in a way that spoke of years in the gym. The blond hair he'd once let grow shaggy was now shorn short enough to hide the natural curl I remembered threading my fingers through during stolen moments behind the bleachers. His jaw had squared out too, losing the boyish softness that had made him seem younger than his eighteen years when we'd graduated.

"Grant Willoughby." The name felt strange on my tongue after all these years. "I had no idea you'd become a cop."

My high school boyfriend grinned at me, and for a split second, I caught a glimpse of the boy who'd taken me to junior prom in his father's borrowed pickup truck. "Protect and serve." He tapped the badge pinned to his chest with obvious pride.

Knowing this was likely to veer toward the kind of small-town catch-up conversation that could eat away precious minutes while Priya remained missing, I tempered my own smile and kept my voice brisk. "Well, we could certainly use some of that protection and service just now. As Astrid said, she's here to file a police report for her missing grad student."

Grant sobered immediately, the easy grin sliding off his face as he straightened in his chair. "Of course. I've got the form right here." He swiveled toward the computer terminal, waking the screen with a sharp tap of the keyboard. The monitor flickered to life, casting a pale glow across his features. "Let's get the basics down first—full name, age, last time you saw her, that sort of thing."

Astrid rattled off the answers in a voice stretched tight with barely contained anxiety. The heel of her free hand pressed against the counter's edge like she needed the physical support to keep herself upright. I watched the concern settle over Grant's face as he entered each new piece of information.

A door down the short hallway creaked open, and Chief Bill Carson stepped out. I blinked in surprise, not expecting to see him here this late. As head of the department, there was no question he'd normally be home by now, likely asleep. But maybe it meant something significant that he'd stuck around. Surely he would have known Astrid would be back right at the twenty-four-hour mark, determined to make this official. The smallest whisper of that old faith in the system surfaced as he strode toward us.

"Madden Reilly." His weathered face, lined and leathery from decades of island sun, registered what looked like mild surprise. The years had carved deeper grooves around his eyes, like driftwood that had been blasted by sand and sea and time. "Didn't realize you were back on-island."

"Just for a while." I kept my tone deliberately neutral. The last thing I wanted was to get into the specifics of why I'd returned.

He nodded, seemingly satisfied with my non-answer, and

shifted his attention to Astrid. His posture remained relaxed, hands clasped behind his back in a pose that suggested he had all the time in the world. "Dr. Thompson. Back about your missing student, I assume?"

"Yes, Priya Shah." Astrid's voice carried the sharp edge of someone who'd been dismissed once already and refused to let it happen again. "As I told you earlier, she didn't show up for work this morning, and no one's seen her since last night's hatching observation. She's not answering calls or texts, and she wasn't home when I dropped by to check. You said you couldn't do anything for twenty-four hours. Well, it's been twenty-four hours and fifteen minutes."

A faint smile ghosted across his lips—the kind of patronizing expression that suggested he found her precision both amusing and slightly irritating. "All right, then. I suppose we can make it official."

He moved to peer over Grant's shoulder at the partially completed report, scanning the details that had been entered so far. "We'll start by asking around the usual places. The beach accesses, the marina, the bars. With all the crowds in town for the summer season, it's easy for someone to lose track of time, get caught up in the festivities." Carson's tone was measured and conciliatory, delivered in the practiced cadence of a man who'd spent decades explaining away concerns with the kind of confidence that was supposed to substitute for actual reassurance. "My guess is she's perfectly fine—overslept after a late night, lost her phone somewhere, maybe staying with a friend she met. Young people do impulsive things."

Astrid's eyes flashed with barely contained fury. "She's not that kind of person. Priya is responsible, organized to a fault. She has a detailed schedule for everything, and she wouldn't just vanish without telling someone. She's here on a research grant. Her entire future depends on this work."

"I understand your concern," Carson said, though his tone suggested he understood nothing of the sort.

My God, had he always been this level of condescending prick, and I'd simply been too young to notice? Or had the years in power crystallized something that had always been lurking beneath the surface?

My prosecutorial instincts kicked in, despite my current circumstances. "What exactly are you going to do other than casually ask around and hope someone volunteers information?"

Carson's gaze shifted toward me, still outwardly calm but with something sharper edging his voice now. A hint of the authority he was used to wielding without question. "We'll follow proper procedure, Ms. Reilly. Standard protocol for missing person cases."

The formal address wasn't lost on me—a deliberate choice to establish distance, to remind me that whatever standing I might have once had in legal circles, here I was just another concerned citizen.

Or possibly I was projecting.

"Surely we've learned something in the wake of my cousin's disappearance about the importance of fast, decisive action?"

Something flickered across his face—frustration, or perhaps the uncomfortable echo of an old failure that still haunted quiet moments. "That was a completely different situation. Gwen was a minor, only fifteen years old. Miss Shah is a grown adult with every legal right to go anywhere she pleases without checking in with anyone."

"That doesn't change the fact that something genuinely awful could have happened to her," I shot back.

God knew, after all the years I'd spent prosecuting predators and reading between the lines of case reports, after seeing the worst of humanity in stark detail across crime scene photos and victim statements, I could imagine far too many ways this story might end. The statistics on missing women, particularly young women traveling alone, weren't exactly comforting.

The police chief exhaled slowly through his nose, a sound that managed to convey both patience and irritation. "We'll give this matter due consideration, I assure you. I'll have the whole department looking into it first thing in the morning, but with the sheer number of tourists currently on-island for the season, I can't risk starting some kind of panic over what will probably turn out to be nothing more than a miscommunication. If anything about her disappearance starts to seem genuinely suspicious, we'll escalate our response accordingly."

So it was about optics, as always. The careful balance between appearing concerned and avoiding anything that might disrupt the delicate tourism economy that kept this place afloat. I should have expected as much.

Astrid's fingers tightened around her phone until her knuckles turned white. "She's not nothing, Chief Carson."

"I didn't say she was." He said it with the kind of calm that was no doubt meant to settle irate business owners and concerned citizens. "Now, I suggest you go home and get some rest. We'll be in touch if anything significant turns up."

Outside the station, the night air pressed against us like a damp blanket, heavy and wet with the kind of humidity that made clothes stick to skin within minutes. The cicadas were loud enough to drown out the rhythmic crash of the surf on the nearby beach. Overhead, the streetlights created small pools of yellow illumination that did little to push back the darkness stretching beyond.

Astrid stopped halfway across the small parking lot and raked both hands through her hair, the gesture one of pure frustration and helplessness. "He's not going to do a damn thing, is he?"

"No," I agreed, my voice flat with certainty born from years of watching the system fail people who needed it most. "He's going to make it look like he's busy while convincing himself that minimal effort is somehow enough."

She let out a shaky breath that might have been the precursor to tears if she'd allowed herself the luxury. "Rios said he'd help look for her. Maybe he'll actually find something concrete before the police bother to get serious about this."

I blinked, taken completely off guard. "Rios? Rios Carrera?" As if there was any other Rios on this island?

"Yeah, he's back on-island right now."

My brain offered a flash of that bare, muscled torso again. As if I needed *that* image burned into my brain just now.

Astrid shifted her weight, glancing toward the dark stretch of street beyond the station, where the shops had long since closed for the evening. "He used to be military police during his time in the Navy. He, Ford, and Sawyer started asking around earlier today when I first mentioned Priya was missing."

Military police. That wasn't anywhere close to what I'd imagined he'd end up doing. Then again, I realized with an uncomfortable twinge of self-awareness, I'd never really taken the time to know him back then, had I? I'd been too caught up in the community narrative, too willing to believe what everyone else insisted was obvious truth.

Astrid looked toward the car, her expression lost and uncertain in the dim light. "I can't just go home and sit there waiting for them to get around to taking this seriously. I'll lose my mind completely."

"Then don't wait. If Priya didn't go back to her place, where else might she have gone after finishing her work?"

Astrid considered this for a moment, chewing on her lower lip. "The grad students often stop in at Home Port after their night shifts. It's the closest bar to the beach research sites, and they stay open late enough to catch the crew when they're done with observations."

"Then let's go see if anyone there remembers seeing her last night."

SEVEN

RIOS

The docks were more than half asleep by the time I got down to Home Port. Not surprising, considering it was past midnight. A couple of trawlers still had their work lights on, halos glowing faint in the mist that clung to the water. Somewhere out on the sound, an engine droned low and steady, the hum carrying across the black expanse.

Home Port sat back from the marina, its faded sign lit by a single buzzing bulb. The wood underfoot was damp and soft in places, the air thick with brine, diesel, and the faint metallic tang of fish scales that never quite washed away. This was the working man's bar on the island, where tourists seldom wandered.

Out of habit, I made a slow circuit around the building, looking for anything out of place. There were only two exits. The main front door and one at the rear by the kitchen that led out to the dumpster. Unless they'd changed the layout since I'd haunted this place in my younger years, that rear door connected to the short hall beside the restrooms. Nobody but staff had reason to use it, but that didn't mean someone couldn't. So I took my time, scanning the area for any telltale signs of a struggle or anything else out of place. But there was no discarded phone. No dropped bag. No drag marks. If Priya Shah had made it here last night, as the grad students I'd spoken to earlier had claimed she intended, the docks had already swallowed the evidence.

Inside, the place was running on the low hum of late-night regulars. The air conditioner rattled but did its job, cutting through the humidity. Classic rock played on the jukebox, half drowned by the clink of bottles and quiet conversation. The pervasive scent of grease had saliva pooling in my mouth, reminding me that dinner had been hours ago. If the kitchen was still open, I'd grab a burger.

I'd been away from Sutter's Ferry long enough that the faces had changed, but the atmosphere hadn't. Dockhands, boat mechanics, a few locals finishing the night's beers. The kind of people who generally kept to themselves. There were some fishermen gathered around the pool table, blowing off steam after what was probably a multi-day trip out on the water. Nothing unusual.

And then I saw her.

Madden Reilly.

She stood near the far end of the bar, dark brown hair pulled back into a braid that even Outer Banks humidity hadn't teased into a mess. Something about all that neatness made me want to muss her up, just to see what she'd look like with wild curls and kiss-swollen lips.

I blinked.

Where the *hell* had that thought come from? Shoving it far into the depths of what the fuck, I focused on the rest of the scene. While Madden wasn't wearing a suit, her posture was straight and formal, shoulders squared, as if she were arguing a case in front of a jury. The three men she spoke to seemed amused more than offended. Their eyes scanned the length of her and saw only a pretty girl on her own. I watched their body language shift from amused to predatory. The big guy in front of Madden leaned closer, smiling in that way that was all teeth and no warmth. One of his buddies said something I couldn't catch, and the third laughed the kind of laugh that made every muscle in my body wake up and pay attention, even before the first guy reached a hand out to touch her.

I was moving before I'd even consciously decided. I caught the meaty guy's wrist in my grip before he could reach her, my hand wrapping around the thick bones with enough pressure to make my point clear without breaking anything.

"I don't believe the lady issued an invitation."

The big one's frown deepened as he turned to face me, his alcohol-glazed eyes taking a moment to focus. I released his wrist with deliberate slowness, letting my hand fall to my side but keeping my stance loose and ready.

"We was just talking." The words were slightly slurred around the edges.

"Looked like she wasn't enjoying the conversation." I kept my voice level. Better to diffuse the situation than turn this into a brawl.

"She didn't say that." His buddies had moved closer now, flanking him in that instinctive way men did when they sensed trouble brewing.

"She's saying it now."

I didn't raise my voice. Didn't need to. Years in the Navy had taught me that calm was what people feared most—the kind of steady control that suggested violence was always an option, just not the first one. I shifted my weight just enough that he had to either back up a step or bump chest-first into me, and I could see the calculation running behind his eyes as he weighed his options. The standoff lasted only two seconds before he broke eye contact, his gaze sliding away to focus on something over my shoulder.

His bravado deflated like a punctured balloon. "No harm meant." His friends echoed the same sentiment in mumbled agreement, already peeling off toward the other end of the bar where the pool table promised safer entertainment.

Madden's exhale was slow and controlled, the kind you use to tamp down adrenaline. Or temper. Her gaze flicked up to mine, all sharp edges and barely contained irritation. "What the hell do you think you're doing?"

"Stopping that from turning ugly."

"I had it handled."

"Uh-huh. That's why that asshole was about to lay hands on you."

"I can take care of myself." Her chin lifted slightly, no doubt intended to punctuate her point. Instead, it drew my attention to her lips, unpainted but still rosy. Would they be soft as a counterpoint to that sharp tongue?

Focus, Carrera.

"I'm sure you can. But that's not what was about to happen, and we both know it." I gestured toward the retreating figures. "Three drunk fishermen who've been at sea for God knows how long, and you standing here looking like some pretty little citified thing without a lick of sense to know where you actually are and the kind of men who frequent this place. The math doesn't work in your favor."

Her expression hardened. "Are you always this patronizing, or is that a new skill you picked up?"

"I'm not patronizing. I'm observant. And I'm not about to watch a woman get cornered and pretend it's none of my business. Not even you."

Something flickered in her expression—hurt, maybe, or just

surprise at the venom I'd managed to pack into those last three words. "Not even me," she repeated quietly, and I heard the way her voice caught just slightly on the words.

Fuck, I was a dick. I hadn't needed to say that. The words had just slipped out, carrying more baggage than this moment deserved.

Before either of us could unpack that, Astrid appeared. "Jimmy said Priya was here last night. He said she came in after midnight, sat over there by the wall with her laptop. Never saw anyone with her."

I followed the direction of her gesture to a small table by the window. Clean now, wiped down, nothing left but a faint ring where a coffee cup had sat. My brain started rearranging the timeline, narrowing down the window when the girl could have disappeared.

"We've been asking everyone else if they were here last night and if they saw her." Madden's words clipped with barely contained frustration.

"Obviously, you need to work on learning how to ask questions of people in a way that doesn't put them on the stand." Damn it, there went my mouth again.

She flushed, pink creeping up her throat in a way that should *not* be appealing. Her jaw worked like she wanted to fire back, but she didn't argue the point. Because she knew I was right, or because she was too tired to fight anymore?

If Astrid noticed the tension crackling between us, she decided not to comment on it. She shifted her weight from one foot to the other, exhaustion written in every line of her body. "Did you find anything else?"

Astrid deserved better than watching me and Madden tear strips off each other. I turned my attention back to her. "Not much. I spoke to her landlord earlier. She wouldn't let me inside without a warrant, but said everything looked normal when I pressed her to go check herself. The bed was rumpled, and her stuff was still there. No way to know if she's a bedmaker or not. Plenty of people aren't."

"Hopefully Carson's people will handle that now." Astrid's tone suggested she wasn't holding her breath.

"He took the report?" I asked.

She nodded.

I grunted, the sound carrying more disgust than I'd meant to let slip. "Then we're probably on our own."

Astrid's head jerked up, her eyes widening. "What's that supposed to mean?"

"Just that he's predictable." I chose my words carefully. No point in destroying her faith in the system tonight. "He'll make a show of looking, fill out the paperwork, maybe even put a patrol car around her building once or twice. But unless there's a clear sign of trouble—blood, signs of struggle, something that screams foul play—he won't rattle cages. Not with the summer crowd on-island and the tourism season in full swing."

Madden folded her arms across her chest, her expression grim. "That's pretty much my read on it, too. Politics over people. It's why we're here doing his job for him."

"It's unacceptable. I'm responsible for these kids!" Astrid scrubbed both hands over her face. "I'm going to have to contact her parents tomorrow if she doesn't show up. What the hell am I going to say? That I lost one of my research assistants, and the police think it's not worth their time?"

Face softening in an instant, Madden wrapped an arm around Astrid's shoulders and pulled her close. "That you're doing everything you can. That you care enough to be out here at midnight asking questions when everyone else has given up. She could turn up tomorrow morning with some perfectly reasonable explanation, and this will all be some huge misunderstanding."

She didn't believe that. The words lacked conviction. I didn't believe it either. Not after Carson's failure with Gwen. But neither of us was going to destroy whatever lingering hope Astrid had left. Sometimes, hope was all that kept you moving forward.

"Look, there's nothing else to be done tonight. You should both go home. Get some rest."

Madden's hazel eyes flashed gray in the low light of the bar, anger sparking there like flint against steel. "You think we're supposed to just stop? Go home and pretend a girl isn't missing?"

"I think fatigue makes mistakes." I kept my voice level despite the challenge in hers. "You'll help her more if you come at this fresh in the morning, with clear heads and steady hands."

She huffed a humorless little laugh, the sound bitter. "Some of us don't have the luxury of switching off. Some of us can't just compartmentalize everything into neat little boxes and file it away."

The words hit closer to home than she probably realized. "Trust me," I met her gaze, "you don't want to learn how."

That earned me another look I couldn't quite read—half anger, half curiosity, like she was trying to figure out what exactly I meant by that. Astrid tugged at her sleeve, breaking the moment. "Come on, Mads. He's right. For tonight, anyway. We're not going to find her stumbling around in the dark."

I followed them out into the parking lot, crushed shells crunching under our feet. The night air was cooler now, carrying the scent of low tide and rain building offshore. I watched them cross the dock, shadows moving through the pool of yellow light cast by the bulb over the entrance. Madden glanced back once, her expression unreadable in the darkness, then disappeared into a car with her friend.

They hadn't been wrong to ask the questions, but I didn't think either of them was the type to actually get the answers we needed. Could be I'd pick up a lot more by being a fly on the wall. So when their taillights faded, I went back inside.

The bartender looked up from drying a glass. "Carrera. Heard you were back."

"Jimmy." I nodded in greeting. "That girl Dr. Thompson was asking about—did you see her last night?"

"Yeah. Quiet girl. Sat over there." He jerked his chin toward the corner table by the window, beneath a neon beer sign. "Coffee, laptop. Left after one, I think."

"Alone?"

"Far as I saw. I was in and out of the back. Didn't actually see her leave."

"Anybody pay her undue attention?"

He shook his head. "Didn't notice."

"Thanks. Kitchen still open?"

"For a bit."

I ordered that burger and took a seat at the far end of the bar, facing the window where Priya had last sat. The faint reflection of neon shimmered on the glass, the docks beyond swallowed by dark.

Somewhere out there, she'd vanished.

And I knew, deep down, that if the system was already dragging its feet, someone had to move faster.

EIGHT

MADDEN

Astrid's office looked like someone had tried to cram an entire ocean into a twelve-by-twelve room and given up halfway.

Maps layered the walls—shoreline charts, satellite images with nest markers in red pen, printouts color-coded in ways that meant something to the people who worked here and nothing at all to me. A whiteboard behind her desk was crowded with dates and codes—N-17, N-19, S-03—each with a cluster of tiny notes. A battered metal file cabinet did double duty as a coffee station, the ancient drip machine burbling resentfully beside a jumble of mismatched mugs. Somewhere down the hall, pumps thrummed, keeping water moving through specimen tanks I hadn't bothered to count on the way in.

Maya and Tyler stood in front of Astrid's desk like they were waiting for a verdict as she scanned something on a tablet. The pair of them looked like they'd been dragged down the beach backward.

"Go home," Astrid ordered. "Eat something that isn't out of a cooler. Sleep. And do not come back on site until check-in tonight."

Tyler's throat worked. "If you hear anything—"

"You'll be the first to know," she promised. "Text me when you're home, so I know you made it."

They nodded in unison, relief and helplessness wrapped up together, and shuffled out past me. The door clicked shut behind them, and the room seemed to exhale.

Astrid slumped back in her chair as if someone had cut her strings. She tipped her head back, eyes closing briefly as the worn mesh creaked in protest.

I noticed the tremor in her hands. "Did you sleep at all?"

"Fits and starts." She rubbed the heel of her hand over her sternum like she could physically dislodge the worry lodged there. "Every time I closed my eyes, I started thinking about everything that could have happened to her. Every scenario was worse than the last."

Yeah. I knew that particular spiral far too well, both from Gwen and from the cases that had crossed my desk.

To keep myself from pacing, I dropped into one of the chairs opposite her. "Did you hear from her parents? Or whoever's listed as her emergency contact?"

"I called both numbers on her forms." Astrid's voice was flat. "No answer. Left messages. I didn't spell it out in those, just asked them to call me and told them it was urgent. I couldn't just say, 'Oh, hey, your daughter is missing,' in a voicemail. Especially not as her family is in India this summer visiting relatives."

"Good call."

"But I don't know what I'm going to say when they call back."

The computer on her desk chimed. A single bright ding that cut through the low mechanical hum of the building.

Astrid glanced at the screen and jiggled the mouse, presumably opening her inbox. Then her jaw dropped open. "It's from Priya."

I hurried around the desk and read over her shoulder as she opened the message.

From: Priya Shah

Subject: Departure

Dear Dr. Thompson,

I'm sorry for the short notice, but I've had a family emergency come up, and I need to leave the island immediately. I won't be able to return for the rest of the season. I appreciate the opportunity you gave me to work on the project, and I'm grateful for everything I've learned.

Sincerely,

Priya

We read it twice in silence.

"That's it?" I said finally. "No details. No 'I'm okay, don't worry'? Just... 'family emergency, I'm gone, thanks for everything'?"

Astrid's eyes raced over the lines again, as if more information might materialize if she looked hard enough. "This... this doesn't make sense."

"It's conveniently vague." My prosecutor's brain ticked through the phrasing on autopilot. "And stiff as hell. Does she normally write to you like she's drafting a form letter?"

"No." Astrid's voice sharpened. "She calls me Astrid in emails. We joke about sea turtles and coffee. If something had happened back home, she would've called. Or at least texted. She knows I'd move heaven and earth to accommodate her if she needed to leave."

"Yesterday, when you were blowing up her phone, there was nothing." I tapped the monitor frame lightly. "Now, suddenly, she has time and bandwidth to send this one paragraph of corporate goodbye?"

Astrid's fingers hovered over the keyboard, then dropped to the desk with a soft thunk. "I hate this. I hate that part of me is relieved to see her name at all, and the rest of me is screaming that this is wrong."

"It feels manufactured," I said. "Like whoever wrote it pulled 'polite exit email' from a template."

"Whoever?" Her gaze snapped to mine. "You think somebody else wrote this?"

"I think it doesn't sound like someone reaching out to the advisor they've spent months working under," I said carefully. "But I also don't know her. You do. What's your gut say?"

"My gut says I'm going to call her again." Astrid snatched up her phone and stabbed at the screen. She put it to her ear, pacing the small office in tight, agitated loops as it rang, then went to voicemail. Again.

"Priya, it's Astrid." Her voice wobbled. "I got your email. I'm... I'm sorry about whatever's going on with your family, but please call me back. I want to make sure you're okay. Just call. Or text. Anything."

She dropped the phone onto the desk hard enough that a

pen skittered off the desk, rolling toward the edge before I snagged it and set it upright in the mug with the others.

Astrid blew out a shaky breath. "I'm calling Carson."

"Good." I hadn't liked the way he'd talked to us last night, but I'd still let that old reflexive trust in authority smooth some of the edges. "Make him earn his paycheck."

The chief himself showed up ten minutes later.

Astrid startled when his shadow crossed the frosted glass, but I just sat back, unexpectedly hit by a ripple of déjà vu. That same steady gait. That same measured pause before entering a room, like he needed to school his features into professional calm. It tugged at something deep in my memory. Being seventeen, brittle with terror, watching this man set down his coffee and promise my aunt he would leave no stone unturned.

That calm certainty and insistence they were doing everything humanly possible had been the one thing keeping us upright in those early hours. Despite how he'd treated us last night, that's who I expected this morning.

But the man who stepped into Astrid's cramped office now... felt different. Or maybe I was. Maybe the years had made me harder, less willing to assume the best.

"Dr. Thompson." Carson gave her a courteous nod before his gaze moved to me. "Ms. Reilly."

Not Madden. And certainly not the softer, paternal "kiddo" he'd used when Gwen vanished. Apparently, adulthood had earned me a formal demotion.

Astrid gestured toward the computer. "We just received an email from Priya. It came through just before I called."

"So I understand." Carson stepped closer. "May I?"

She pulled up the message again and angled the screen toward him. I watched his eyes as he read it—once, without expression, then again, a tiny furrow appearing between his brows. Not confusion, exactly. Something closer to reassessment.

But he didn't ask the questions I expected.

No: *Have you spoken with her emergency contact yet?*

No: *Is this in character for her?*

No: *Do you suspect someone else might've typed this?*

Instead, he straightened, folding his hands behind his back in that same composed, reassuring posture he'd used in every press conference about Gwen.

Only this time, the tone didn't land the same way.

"You said last night she hadn't made contact at all," he said.

"She still hasn't." Astrid's voice broke over the words. "I called her twice after this came in. Straight to voicemail. She didn't text. She didn't call before she supposedly left. This isn't like her."

Carson nodded like he'd heard the same from countless worried parents, a small wrinkle of genuine sympathy appearing. "I can understand why this feels abrupt. But it does give us something to work with."

I waited for the next part. *Now we dig deeper. Now we widen the search. Now we take this seriously.*

But instead, he said, "This may actually fit with what my officers found this morning."

A faint chill slid down my spine.

Fit with. Like he'd already built a framework and now the pieces were clicking neatly into place.

"How do you mean?" Astrid asked.

"They conducted a welfare check at her apartment earlier," he said. "From what they observed, it appears many of her personal belongings have been removed. Clothing, toiletries, electronics."

Astrid's eyebrows pulled together, unsure. "This morning? Before she emailed?"

He didn't blink. "Correct."

I tried to process that.

It wasn't damning on its face—people did pack in the middle of the night. But something about the timing scratched against instinct.

Carson continued. "There was no sign of disturbance of any kind."

I waited again for the next logical step.

But we'll confirm that timeline.

We'll double-check with the landlord.

We'll pull camera footage from nearby structures.

Nothing.

He seemed almost... relieved. Like the existence of the email had smoothed over all the rough edges for him.

And that's where something inside me wavered. Not anger. Not yet. Not even mistrust. Just a creeping dissonance. This wasn't how I remembered him responding to uncertainty.

Astrid hugged her elbows, shoulders collapsing inward. "I don't understand. This still doesn't sound like her."

Carson's tone softened infinitesimally. "I know it's unsettling, Dr. Thompson. But it's not uncommon for young adults to make impulsive decisions in moments of stress."

Something in me twitched at that—old muscle memory from a very different case. He'd used a different vocabulary then. More urgency. More gravity. But maybe that was because Gwen was only fifteen. He'd said that himself the night before.

Still.

The ease with which he placed this email into the "voluntary departure" column... it didn't match the man I'd built my childhood faith around.

Astrid's breath hitched. "It still feels wrong."

He nodded, but it was the kind of nod that acknowledged emotion, not evidence. "It often does."

His eyes flicked to mine—measuring, almost cautious.

Did he expect me to agree with him? Or did he remember the girl who'd shown up at the station every day for weeks demanding updates?

Either way, the distance in that look told me something important: He didn't want me questioning this too hard.

That's where the first real crack formed. Not because he seemed dismissive. But because he seemed... certain. Too certain. As if he'd already decided the shape of the story before hearing all its pieces.

That certainty was the exact opposite of the man I remembered from Gwen's case, who hadn't rested, who hadn't let up, who hadn't allowed convenience to stand in the way of possibility. A man who once told my aunt, *We'll chase every lead, no matter how small.*

Now he was implying that there wasn't a lead to chase.

Astrid made a strangled sound, and Carson's expression shifted into that controlled sympathy again.

"I understand you feel blindsided, but I'm simply relaying what my officers observed."

Astrid's fingers curled into fists at her sides. "And the ferry? You said you were checking that, too."

"We checked the manifests. There's a ticket purchased under Priya Shah's name on the first ferry out, the morning after you last saw her. Credit card on file matched the one she used to pay her rent."

Astrid looked like he'd slapped her. "That doesn't—"

"One of the deckhands we spoke to thinks he remembers seeing her in line," Carson continued smoothly, skating over Astrid's protest. "Young Indian woman traveling alone, carrying a backpack and rolling suitcase. It's not a perfect confirmation, given the number of visitors we see this time of year, but it's consistent with the rest of what we've found."

Consistent. Evidence lined up in a neat row. If I'd been reading it in a case file, it would have looked tidy. A little too tidy.

"Then why didn't she answer her phone?" I demanded. "Why send an email instead of calling Dr. Thompson directly? She had time to buy a ticket, pack a suitcase, board a ferry, and write a formal goodbye to her advisor, but she couldn't spare a five-second voicemail?"

Carson's mouth thinned. "Ms. Reilly, we can't extrapolate intent from the absence of a phone call. People handle stress in different ways. Sometimes they avoid tough conversations."

"Yes, sometimes they do," I agreed, heat rising in my chest. "But we also both know how often emails like this get used to create the illusion of choice in situations where there isn't any."

"Madden." Astrid's voice was a warning and a plea.

I ignored it. Once I got going, it was hard to stop; that had been both my greatest asset in court and my biggest liability in life. "You're telling us she conveniently packed up, bought a ticket, vanished on the earliest ferry, and fired off a canned email to cover her tracks—right after a night where she was supposedly just working quietly at a bar and then failed to show up for the job that determines her future?"

Carson's eyes cooled a few degrees. "I'm telling you that there is no evidence of a crime. No sign of a struggle at her apartment. No reports of distress on the ferry. No witnesses indicated she left the island with anyone against her will. Every data point we have suggests she made a sudden decision to leave. People do that, Ms. Reilly."

"Not responsible grad students in the middle of a field season," Astrid burst out. "Not Priya. She doesn't even like taking a day off. You're talking about her like she's some flaky tourist who decided on a whim to bail on a beach week."

Carson turned his attention back to her, adopting that

conciliatory expression I was rapidly growing to hate. "Dr. Thompson, I understand that you're upset—"

"Do you?" Her voice cracked, and she pushed on anyway. "Because from where I'm standing, it looks like you're taking the first convenient explanation that lets you close the file and walk away."

He sighed, the sound heavy with put-upon patience. "We have limited resources, Dr. Thompson. An adult leaving under her own power is not a crime. We can't treat every abrupt departure as a kidnapping because it makes people uncomfortable."

The words scraped something raw in me.

"'We can't treat every abrupt departure as a kidnapping.'" I repeated softly. "That's interesting language coming from the man who preached 'leave no stone unturned' when my fifteen-year-old cousin disappeared."

His gaze snapped back to me, sharp now. "That was a child. This is not. Gwen's case was entirely different."

"Different because she was under eighteen," I said. "Different because you could justify pulling out all the stops. Press conferences. Search parties. Volunteers combing the island. But the bare bones are the same, Chief. A girl vanished. People who knew her insist it's out of character. And your first instinct—then and now—is to assume she wandered off with someone voluntarily."

Something flashed across his face then. Not guilt, exactly. Irritation tangled with something that looked uncomfortably like weary defensiveness.

"We did everything we could for your cousin," he said, and for a moment, the smooth professional façade cracked. "I have lived with the fact that we didn't find her for over a decade. Don't stand here and imply that my officers or I treat this lightly."

"I'm not implying anything. I'm saying the pattern looks the same from here: You decide what's likely, and you shape the investigation—or lack thereof—to fit." I'd seen officers do that. Tailoring the evidence to their own preconceived notions rather than following where the evidence actually led. But I hadn't thought Carson would be one of them.

His jaw flexed.

Beside me, Astrid looked between us, eyes wide. "Can we not make this into a pissing contest over ancient history while my student is still missing?"

"She's not missing." Carson seized on the one thing he could redefine. "Not anymore. You have an email from her. We have evidence she left the island of her own accord. Unless something concrete arises to contradict that, there is no basis for continuing this as an active missing person investigation."

"Concrete like what?" I demanded. "A body? Is that what it takes now?"

He stared at me, and in that moment, I saw exactly how he'd held onto his job this long. There was steel under the salt-bleached exterior. The kind that got more rigid, not less, when pushed.

"What I see," he said slowly, "is someone who spent years in big-city courts learning to see monsters in every shadow. And someone who experienced a terrible loss as a teenager that understandably warped her idea of what's probable."

The words landed like a slap. My spine snapped rigid.

"This girl is not your cousin, Ms. Reilly," he went on, relentless now. "And Sutter's Ferry is not Los Angeles. We followed procedure. We acted on the information we had. We conducted welfare checks, followed financial trails, and spoke to witnesses. We found no evidence of foul play. None. You may not like that conclusion, but that doesn't make it any less valid."

Astrid choked out, "So that's it? You're just... done?"

He glanced at her, softening his tone half a notch. "We'll keep the file on record. If new information comes in, we'll reassess. Until then, there's nothing further for us to do."

"For you to do," I corrected under my breath.

Carson straightened, smoothing the front of his shirt with an economical swipe of his palm. "As far as this department is concerned, the matter is resolved. Miss Shah appears to have left voluntarily. The case"—he met my eyes again, making sure I heard every word—"is considered closed."

NINE

RIOS

The marine lab had always looked smaller from the road.

A low rectangle of weathered siding and tinted windows, it sat just beyond the dunes, tucked behind a line of scrub like it was trying to stay out of the way. When I'd been a kid, it had been "that place with the tanks" we rode past on our bikes—a landmark, not a destination. I'd never had reason to come inside until Priya Shah disappeared.

This time, I pulled into the crushed shell parking lot just in time to see Chief Carson step out the front door. From the driver's seat, I watched him walk toward his cruiser. His stride was steady, unhurried. Not the loose, exhausted drag of a man who'd stayed up all night beating the bushes for a missing girl. Nor the tight coil of someone holding bad news and dreading the delivery. He moved like a guy coming off a long but ordinary day. The job, not a crisis.

Had the girl turned up after all?

He slid into his car and sat for a second, staring straight ahead. I caught a faint profile of jaw clenched and set mouth.

Then he shook his head once, like he was physically clearing out whatever thought had snagged him, and put the car in reverse.

He didn't look around. Didn't notice my truck or, if he did, didn't care.

The cruiser rolled out of the lot and turned back toward town.

I stayed where I was for a beat after he disappeared, fingers drumming on the steering wheel. Something about his posture nagged at me. Not guilt. Not satisfaction, exactly. More like... resolution. A man who'd reached a conclusion and was prepared to defend it.

I'd seen that resolution before. When that conclusion had been me as the scapegoat. It didn't leave me with a lot of faith about what I'd hear when I spoke with Astrid.

I killed the engine and headed inside. I followed the hand-lettered arrow for ADMIN/RESEARCH OFFICES down a short hall to an office with an open door.

Astrid sat behind the desk, elbows braced on the surface, fingers rubbing at her temples. Her hair was pulled into a messy knot that had clearly given up hours ago. Wisps stuck out in half a dozen directions. She looked like she'd been awake far too long. I wondered if she'd been here since she left Home Port last night.

Madden stood to one side, arms folded tight across her chest, weight shifted to one hip in a posture that screamed contained fury. Her jaw worked like she was grinding down words that would cost more than they were worth to say out loud.

Both of them looked up when I tapped on the doorframe.

"Hey. I just passed Carson on his way out. What happened?"

Astrid lowered her hands slowly, as if they were heavy. Her eyes were bloodshot and devastated. "He closed the case."

It wasn't the words so much as how she said them. Flat. Stunned. Like she hadn't quite accepted that the syllables were real.

I stepped fully into the room.

"He said it's resolved," Astrid continued. "That there's no longer a basis for treating it as an active missing person investigation."

"On what grounds?" I asked. "He suddenly find her on a beach towel somewhere, sipping a daiquiri and ignoring her phone?"

It wasn't funny. Nobody laughed.

Madden shifted her weight, eyes flashing with battle light. "On the grounds that everything conveniently points to 'she left of her own free will, so not our problem.'"

I glanced between them. "Walk me through it."

Astrid looked at the monitor, then back at me. "We got an email from Priya. It came in this morning."

"The timing is what—" Madden started, then caught herself. She gestured to the screen. "You should read it."

I moved around the side of the desk, tucking myself into the narrow space between Madden and the file cabinet. Up close, I could smell the faint scent of some floral shampoo and feel the tension vibrating in that slim frame, though inches still separated us. I registered the faint shadow under her eyes, the way she'd re-braided her hair too tight, as if control in that one area might compensate for the lack of it everywhere else. A crescent-moon dent showed in the skin by her thumb where she'd clearly been pressing her own nail.

My fingers itched to stroke that braid, down that stiff back.

What the hell? She's not a fucking cat.

I jerked my attention away from Madden to find the email already on screen.

It was short. Polite. Devoid of personality.

I read it twice. My brain, trained on years of statements and reports, automatically dissected it while my eyes tracked the lines.

Family emergency. No specifics. No mention of who, or what, or where.

Leave the island immediately. Past tense implied. It read like something written after the fact, not in the middle of an ongoing situation.

Won't be back for the rest of the season. Pretty definitive for someone supposedly blindsided by a crisis.

"Feels like it came out of a template," I said finally. "Like she searched 'professional resignation email' and copy-pasted the first hit."

"That's exactly what I said," Madden muttered.

Astrid rubbed at her temples. "She doesn't write like this. Not to me. She calls me Astrid. She includes memes. She sends me turtle GIFs." Her voice wobbled. "If something had happened at home, she would've called. She knows I would've understood. I told him that."

"Carson?" I asked.

"Yes." Her gaze slid to me. "They did a welfare check at her place this morning. Said most of her personal stuff was gone. Clothes, toiletries, electronics. No sign of a struggle. Then Carson comes in here and tells us she was on the ferry manifest, and acts like the email ties up the bow on the whole thing."

I straightened slowly. "Ferry manifest?"

"He says she bought a ticket on the first ferry out yesterday morning," Madden said, voice clipped. "Credit card on file matches the one she used to pay her rent. And a deckhand thinks he remembers seeing her in line."

"'Thinks,'" I repeated.

The word was doing a lot of work.

Astrid pushed away from the desk, standing because sitting was clearly too passive for all the emotion zinging through her body. "Young dark-haired woman—he said Indian, but who knows for sure—traveling alone, backpack and rolling suitcase. That's what the deckhand told them." She threw her hands up, helpless. "Have you seen the tourist traffic on that dock? That describes half the people getting off the damn ferry in July."

An exaggeration. But still, I could picture it. The terminal jammed with families and couples and groups of college kids, everyone lugging gear and coolers and tote bags, faces blurred by sun and motion. One tired ferry worker trying to sort tickets and keep an eye out for safety issues, not memorize faces.

"And all of this together was enough for him to decide she left voluntarily and stop looking," Madden added.

I leaned my hip against the file cabinet, letting the metal bite into my thigh while I processed. Email. Card charge. Vague witness ID. Apartment that may or may not have been packed by the time cops got there.

On paper, all of it added up to a neat, plausible narrative.

I'd seen neat, plausible narratives lie before. And something in all this was niggling at me.

"Who let them in for the welfare check?"

Astrid hesitated. "He didn't say. The landlord, I assume."

"I spoke to her landlord yesterday. Maria. Remember what I told you last night? She said the bed was rumpled, and most of Priya's stuff was still there."

"Oh my God," Astrid murmured.

Madden's fingers dug into her own arms, pressing the fabric of her shirt tight against her skin. "So either she didn't look properly, or Carson's officers didn't, or somebody's decided to... reinterpret what they saw to fit what they want to believe."

"I'm not saying anyone's lying," I said carefully. I'd learned early on that accusing cops of dishonesty, even obliquely, shut down conversations faster than a closed fist. "But I am saying the story seems to have changed overnight."

"Do you think that's enough to get him to reopen the case?" Astrid asked. "The police didn't know what she told you yesterday, and I'm so tired I didn't think of it while he was here."

I thought about the way Carson had looked walking to his car. Settled. Perhaps even relieved. Not the face of a man who'd want his authority challenged without iron-clad evidence.

"He's not exactly my biggest fan. I doubt he'd take anything I have to say seriously. Maybe if we speak to Maria again and clarify what she saw."

Silence fell for a moment, thick enough that even the muffled pump noise from down the hall seemed to fade. Outside the small window, the sky was a flat, washed-out blue, too bright and too blank.

Madden's gaze slid to mine. "We're going to need more."

Against my better judgment, I asked, "What did you have in mind?"

"Emails can be spoofed." The words came out like she'd been holding them in for hours and finally let them go. "Accounts can be accessed. People can be coerced into typing what someone else tells them to say. This email proves only that a message came from her account. Not that she sat there and carefully crafted it. And even that's not a guarantee if you have the right people with the right skills."

Astrid swallowed hard. "You think—"

"I don't know what I think," Madden cut in. "I just know that every part of this triggers my bullshit detectors. The timing. The vagueness. The way it all fits so neatly with the narrative Carson already wanted."

Her voice was rising. Not to a shout, but to that contained courtroom intensity that makes a jury sit forward.

I'd seen that before. Not from her—never from her—but from other lawyers I'd worked cases with. And against. The ones whose blood pressure shot up when something didn't line up.

She paced once, the short length of the office forcing a tight turn near the door.

"I've spent years reading case files where a supposed 'voluntary departure' started with an email that sounded exactly like that." She jabbed a finger toward the screen. "A neat little exit note that made everyone feel better about not asking too many questions. And later, once we got the rest of the story, we found out that the victim had been threatened, or drugged, or was dead before the message was ever sent."

Astrid closed her eyes briefly, then opened them, hating that possibility but unable to reject it.

I couldn't argue with Madden. Not about that.

"And the credit card?" I added. "All that tells us is that someone used her account to buy a ticket. Could've been her. Could've been someone else who had access to her wallet, or her computer, or anything with autofill set up."

"Carson dismisses that," Madden said. "He says there's 'no evidence of a crime.' No signs of a struggle, no screaming witnesses, no bloody handprints leading to the dock, so statistically she just decided to leave, and we're all overreacting because we care about her. Or because—" her mouth twisted "—we're still traumatized from the last time a girl vanished on this island."

That landed between us like a stone.

Gwen.

My chest tightened, the way it always did when her name came up, even indirectly. It wasn't just Madden who still carried that weight. Every time I walked past one of those posters, every time I caught myself scanning crowds for a face I knew I'd never see again, that summer came back in high-def.

"I'm not letting this happen again." Madden's words came out like brittle steel.

She stopped pacing, planted her feet, and uncrossed her arms. Her hands curled instead, fists forming and releasing at her sides like she needed something to hit that wasn't a person. "I'm not going to stand here and watch them shrug and turn away because it's complicated and inconvenient. Because the victim is an adult whose choices they can hand-wave. I've spent years watching cases fall apart because somebody at the beginning decided it was easier to assume a woman made a bad decision than to consider the possibility she was in danger. I am not doing that again. Not here."

Her gaze swung to me, pinning me in place. "Will you help?"

It was a simple question. Three words. But they hit me like a live wire.

There was a part of me that wanted to say no. To remind her that she'd once parroted the worst things this island said about me. That for years she'd been one more person who believed I was the boy who hurt Gwen, or at least the boy who failed her. That working alongside her felt like inviting someone to rip open an old wound that had never quite healed.

But under that was something older and louder. The memory of long-ago search parties. Flashlights cutting through darkness. Carson's voice on a bullhorn, calling Gwen's name into the trees. The sick, hollow certainty that we were already too late, even while we told ourselves we weren't.

Priya's name would never be printed on posters in quite the same way Gwen's had been. She was older. An outsider. Easier to reframe as someone who'd walked away.

That made it worse.

If the system was already folding up its tents because the story looked tidy on paper, somebody needed to keep digging. I'd been forced out of the Navy because I refused to let a predator skate by on technicalities. That part of me hadn't changed just because I no longer wore a uniform.

Madden's eyes held mine steadily, but there was a flicker underneath the anger now. Something like fear. Or maybe it was just the rawness of a woman whose faith—in systems, in people, in her own instincts—had taken hit after hit.

She'd been the last person I expected to ask me for anything.

And yet here we were.

I blew out a breath as the weight of the choice settled across my shoulders. It felt a lot like every other time I'd stepped into something messy, knowing it could end badly for everyone involved if we were wrong, but knowing we'd never forgive ourselves if we didn't try.

"Yeah." My voice came out rougher than I intended. "I'll help."

TEN

MADDEN

Maria Blackwell's house sat back from the road, a two-story salt-washed colonial with peeling shutters and a wide oak shading the drive. Priya's apartment was a small efficiency unit above the detached garage that loomed at the end of a worn concrete path. Mid-July humidity draped over everything like a wet blanket, making my clothes stick to my back. I hadn't missed this part of summer on the Outer Banks during my years in California.

When we stepped onto the small stoop beside the garage, Maria answered almost at once, dishtowel still in hand, as if we'd interrupted her mid-chore.

"Can I help you?" Her eyes flicked between us, lingering on Rios with a faint crease of recognition before landing on me.

I summoned a polite smile. "Hi. I'm Madden Reilly, and I believe you met Rios yesterday."

Maria's expression tightened. "You're here about Priya?"

I let my smile warm. "We are. We're here on behalf of Dr.

Astrid Thompson, Priya's boss. We were hoping you could help us clarify a couple of things."

"The police were already here this morning." She said it like a question.

"Right, and your cooperation has been so helpful."

The woman stood a little straighter. "Did they find something? Is Priya okay?"

"We haven't made contact with her yet," Rios explained. "We're... trying to make sense of some conflicting information."

Maria's brows knit. "Conflicting how?"

"You told him yesterday that when you checked the apartment, Priya's things were still here. Messy bed, clothes in closet, and the like."

"That's right," she said.

I exchanged a quick glance with Rios. His jaw tightened a fraction.

"The police are saying most of her belongings were gone when they looked," I said. "Neatly packed. Closets empty."

Maria stared. "Gone? No. No, that's not what I saw."

"I believe you," I said. "That's why we're here."

"Did you go up with the police earlier this morning?" Rios asked.

"No. They asked me to wait outside, so I let them in and waited at the bottom of the stairs." She exhaled long and uneasy. "Look—this whole situation is making me nervous. I've never had trouble with tenants before."

"I understand," I said gently. "I know we're asking a lot. But would you consider letting us inside to see it? You can stay right with us. We won't disturb anything. We just want to see what it looks like now compared to what you saw yesterday."

Maria didn't answer immediately. Her fingers tightened around the dish towel she'd been holding. Something flickered across her face—not quite fear, but the uncertainty of a person who realized her memory could become evidence, and she was terrified of being wrong.

Finally, she nodded. "All right. Give me a second."

She stepped back inside, retrieved a key from the small tray by the door, locked up behind her, and led us toward the apartment.

The climb up the narrow wooden stairs made the boards creak in the quiet. A few spiderwebs fluttered under the eaves. The door at the top looked freshly repainted compared to the sun-bleached siding around it.

Maria unlocked it and pushed it open, gesturing us inside.

The place looked like the model unit of an apartment complex, not somewhere an actual person had lived for a month. The futon-style bed had been made with clinical neatness, navy comforter pulled tight enough to bounce a quarter. The kitchenette countertops gleamed under the overhead light, every surface wiped down to an antiseptic shine. Empty sink, bone dry. Empty drying rack positioned at a perfect right angle to the window. Empty trash can except for a single scrunched paper towel, sitting too centered, as if it had been placed, not tossed.

The whole space felt sterile, devoid of the casual messiness that comes with actually living somewhere. No coffee ring stains on the counter. No water spots on the faucet. No dust gathered in the corners where someone might have missed during their regular cleaning routine.

Maria stepped just inside the door and stopped, her shoulders going rigid. "This isn't it. This... someone cleaned." Her hand drifted to the back of the dining chair as if she needed something solid to anchor herself to reality. The uncertainty in her voice was palpable—the tone of someone whose memory had just been called into question, even though she knew what she'd seen.

Rios stayed a few feet back from her, maintaining careful distance while his eyes swept the room in a slow, methodical pattern. I could see him cataloging details with that sharp, analytical gaze that missed nothing. Because I found myself wanting to watch *him,* I moved toward the closet to conduct my own examination, leaving him space to work.

The bifold doors stood ajar, revealing a sliver of empty space within. I nudged them wider with one knuckle, careful not to disturb potential evidence.

Nothing but a dozen mismatched plastic hangers on the rod, the kind of cheap hangers you'd find at any discount store. They hung at different angles, as if someone had removed clothing in a hurry without bothering to straighten what remained.

Behind me, Maria's voice carried a note of frustrated certainty. "Yesterday, there were shirts hanging here. Shorts folded on that shelf. A gray sweatshirt draped over the top of the rod. I remember it because I thought it was too warm for someone to need a sweatshirt, even with the AC running."

Rios didn't look up from where he'd crouched beside the small three-drawer dresser, his movements deliberate and respectful of the space. "What about her shoes?"

"Right there." Maria pointed to the small woven mat positioned beside the door. "Blue sneakers. A pair of brown leather sandals. And some beat-up flip-flops that looked like she'd had them forever."

"All gone now," I murmured.

Rios pulled the top drawer open just an inch, peering inside before opening it wider. Empty. The second drawer was just as empty, not even lint in the corners. The third drawer contained only one rolled pair of white socks shoved in the back corner, and a single bobby pin lying near the front like an afterthought.

Maria frowned at the sight, her confusion giving way to something closer to alarm. "There was definitely more before. I didn't go digging through her things—that wouldn't have been appropriate—but when I glanced in to check for any obvious problems, the drawers weren't empty like this."

I left them to continue their examination and moved toward the compact bathroom, noting how my footsteps echoed in the hollow emptiness of the space.

The shower rod still had a clear plastic curtain clipped in place, swaying gently in the breath of air I'd carried with me. The small vanity mirror above the sink was spotless except for a single faint streak in the top right corner, like someone had wiped away fingerprints in a hurry but hadn't been thorough enough to catch everything.

No toothbrush in the ceramic holder beside the sink. No toiletries cluttering the narrow shelf above the toilet. No hair elastic wrapped around the faucet base where someone might have kept it while washing their face. No evidence that anyone had ever performed the daily rituals of getting ready in this space.

The medicine cabinet wasn't quite closed. I nudged it open with my elbow—completely empty, not even an over-the-counter pain reliever or travel-sized shampoo bottle.

It was the kind of obsessive tidiness that wasn't natural, the result of someone systematically removing every trace of human habitation. Not that graduate students couldn't be neat —some of the most organized people I'd known had been academics—but this wasn't consistent with the impression Rios had gathered from his conversations yesterday.

When I stepped back into the main room, he had moved to the kitchenette area. He wasn't touching anything—didn't need to. The emptiness of the space spoke volumes on its own.

Maria ran her hand along the edge of the counter, her

fingers trailing over the spotless laminate surface. "This doesn't make sense. None of this makes sense."

"It's significantly different from what you observed yesterday." I chose my words with the careful precision of someone who might need to testify about this conversation later.

"Yes. Completely different."

"That's all we needed you to confirm."

She looked both relieved and guilty, the expression of someone who'd been second-guessing her own memory. "I don't know if I was imagining things. If maybe I was mistaken about what I saw."

"You weren't mistaken," Rios said with quiet conviction.

He wasn't looking at Maria when he spoke; his attention was fixed on the refrigerator door, where a faint smudged outline showed where a magnet had once held something in place. Probably a schedule, or a shopping list, or one of those casual notes people leave for themselves. Whatever it had been, it was gone now, leaving only the ghost of its presence.

"We appreciate your help with this," I said, meaning it. "You've been incredibly helpful."

Maria nodded, still visibly unsettled by the transformation of the space, and stepped out onto the stairs to wait while Rios and I took one final look around.

As soon as she was out of earshot, I let out a slow, controlled breath. "So. What's your read?"

Rios straightened from his casual lean against the counter, his expression grim. "Carson reported most of her belongings were already gone when they arrived to check the place out."

"And they are gone."

"Which means that part of his story checks out."

"But not the timing," I finished, the pieces clicking into place.

His eyes met mine—sharp and filled with the same growing disquiet I felt. "No. Definitely not the timing."

"Someone cleared this place out after Maria saw it yesterday."

"Or someone cleared it out before yesterday, but Maria didn't see the full extent of what was missing during her quick check."

I shook my head. "You heard the level of detail she provided. Specific clothing items, the type and condition of shoes, the contents of drawers she'd only glanced into. That kind of specificity isn't something you misremember overnight, especially when you're already concerned about a tenant."

He agreed with a slight, almost imperceptible tilt of his chin.

"This doesn't read like someone packing for an emergency departure," I continued, gesturing around the sterile space. "If Priya had needed to leave Sutter's Ferry in a genuine hurry—family emergency, sudden opportunity, whatever—she would have grabbed the essentials: toiletries, a couple of changes of clothes, her laptop, phone charger. Maybe a book gets left behind. Maybe one shoe. But she wouldn't have stripped her drawers down to a single pair of socks and a bobby pin."

"And she wouldn't have taken the time to wipe down surfaces," he added.

That observation caught my attention. "You noticed that too?"

He gestured toward the kitchenette area with one big, broad hand. "There's a streak on the laminate countertop—perfectly straight line, like someone wiped it down, paused to check their work, then wiped it again. People who are rushing to catch the ferry aren't worried about leaving behind crumbs or water spots."

Those hands looked so damned capable.

I gave myself a mental shake. "Same thing in the bathroom. The mirror has one streak in the top corner. Quick, efficient pass with a cloth or paper towel, but not thorough enough to get everything. And there are no signs of the cleaning materials here."

He folded his arms across his chest, settling back against the counter with the weight of someone processing unwelcome information. "This isn't her packing her own belongings."

"No," I agreed grimly. "So either she had one of her friends or colleagues come back here later yesterday to pack up the rest of her belongings to ship to wherever she's relocated—which we should verify—or someone else is trying to make it appear that she packed everything herself, and they had no idea that you'd already asked Maria to check the scene yesterday morning."

The air in the small apartment seemed to thicken with dread as the full implications settled over both of us.

From outside on the landing, Maria's footsteps shifted slightly—a subtle signal that she was growing tired of waiting for us to finish our examination.

"This isn't enough evidence to get Carson to officially reopen the investigation," I murmured.

"No, definitely not enough. We need to check the ferry security footage next."

"Agreed. If she did board yesterday's ferry as reported, we should be able to see her on the cameras."

"I've got someone who can give us access to those recordings."

I raised an eyebrow, not entirely surprised. "Of course you do." He was friends with Sawyer Malone, who was married to Willa Hollingsworth now. Her family owned the ferry company.

"Small island." He gave me a faint, humorless smile that

didn't quite reach his eyes. I found myself wondering what a real smile would look like from him. Had I ever even seen one?

I couldn't remember.

Uncomfortable with the thought, I stepped back toward the door. "Let's not keep Maria standing out there."

As we joined her on the landing, she locked the apartment again, worry etched across her features.

"You'll keep me updated?" she asked.

"Yes," I said. "We'll let you know if we learn anything."

"Thank you." Her voice was small. "I just... I hope she's all right."

"So do we," Rios said.

We started down the stairs, and I felt it settle between us— our first true shared certainty in this mess.

Nothing about that apartment matched Carson's story.

And both of us knew it.

ELEVEN

RIOS

By the time we pulled into the ferry terminal lot, heat bounced off the asphalt in shimmering waves. Out front, a line of cars waited in the staging lanes. The ordinary churn of people leaving the island. On any other day, I wouldn't have given it a second thought.

Today, every car felt like a potential lead we'd already missed.

The terminal's air conditioning hit like a slap after the soupy heat outside. The waiting area buzzed with the sounds of travel: rolling luggage wheels, kids whining for snacks, the faint echo of an announcement over the PA.

I scanned the lobby, looking for Willa, and spotted Roy, her big black pit bull, first. Easy to do, given he was the size of a small mountain. He sat like a particularly well-behaved statue as she spoke to an employee behind the ticket desk. She glanced up, eyes meeting mine before they slid over to Madden. The sight of us together made something unreadable flicker across her face before she smoothed it out with a careful, polite smile.

She crossed over. "Rios. Madden."

Roy lumbered to his feet and trotted over, big tail whipping. I gave him a scratch behind the ears, feeling the rumble of his pleased huff under my fingers.

"Hey, Willa." Madden's voice shifted into an odd formality, the syllables clipped. Her shoulders squared in that polished, courtroom way I was starting to recognize as some kind of armor. "It's a bit late, but congrats on your marriage."

Willa angled her head in gracious acknowledgement, her own posture taking on a bit of the polished edge she usually didn't bother with anymore. "Thanks." Her focus came back to me. "How can I help?"

"We need to see the security tapes for the past two days."

"I thought that might be it. Sawyer told me last night about Astrid's student, and the police were here this morning. They took a copy of the footage for themselves, but we still have ours on our server. Do you expect to find something they didn't?"

"Already have. That's why we're following up."

Willa frowned. "That sounds ominous. Come on. Elliott's in the security office." Willa hooked a thumb toward the back hallway. "He's been with us since before my grandparents retired. Knows the system better than the company that installed it."

Roy padded ahead like he knew the way, nails clicking on the tile. We followed Willa down the corridor, past a break room and a tiny HR office. The security room was at the end, door propped open with a plastic wedge.

Inside, three monitors glowed above a desk cluttered with coffee cups and a bowl of individually wrapped mints. A man in his fifties with a sunburnt neck and thinning hair swiveled in his chair when we stepped in.

"Boss." He tipped his chin at Willa. "Twice in one day? To what do I owe the honor?"

"Same reason, I'm afraid. This is Rios Carrera and Madden Reilly. Y'all, this is our head of security, Elliott Carver. They're helping look into Priya Shah's disappearance."

Elliott frowned. "Thought the police handled that."

"We're just being extra thorough," I said, which was far more polite than anything else I could manage.

"You want the footage from yesterday morning?"

"From about four-thirty to six-thirty," I said. "Ticket line, lobby, boarding ramp. Anything that would show the passengers getting on that first ferry."

"I already pulled that for the chief." Elliott spun back toward the monitors and started clicking through folders with practiced efficiency. "You want to go through the same files, or you want a wider window?"

"Let's start with the same," Madden said. "See what they saw. Or say they saw."

Willa glanced at her, the corner of her mouth tightening. It wasn't disagreement, exactly. More like silent alignment.

Elliott loaded up a four-way split-screen video: top left the parking lot, top right the ticket counter, bottom left the waiting area, bottom right the covered pedestrian walkway leading down to the ferry ramp. Timestamps glowed in the corner of each feed.

He clicked play. The footage rolled forward at normal speed—too slow for what we needed. Lines of people, blurry faces, bags, kids. Life.

"Speed it up until we get closer to boarding," I said.

He obliged. The movement on screen shifted from casual to jittery, everyone just a little too brisk.

I stepped closer, folding my arms over my chest as the digital world scrolled by. Madden stood to my right, arms at her sides, knuckles pale where her hands curled into loose fists. Willa stayed back near the doorway, one shoulder against the frame, Roy sitting pressed to her leg like a black shadow.

Casually, I glanced between the women. Objectively, they came from the same strata of island society—old family names, big expectations. Willa had cut herself loose from hers years ago, after her parents put her through unfathomable trauma in the wake of Gwen's disappearance. She'd made her own quiet path here on the island.

Madden, as far as I knew, had done the opposite. Ivy League law school. DA's office in LA. Textbook high-achiever track. I hadn't considered what that had cost her before. Now, watching the stiffness in her shoulders, I wondered.

On-screen, the timestamp ticked past 4:50 a.m.

I forced my attention back where it belonged.

"Elliott, can you flag any passengers traveling alone?" Madden asked.

He snorted softly. "In real time? Not really. But we can watch the line and see who matches your description."

I pulled my phone from my back pocket and swiped to the photo Astrid had sent me—Priya standing on the beach, hair in a low ponytail, wind tugging strands loose around her face. Brown skin warmed by the setting sun, dark eyes behind glasses. Small, warm smile.

I held the screen out so Elliott could see. "This is who we're looking for. Name's Priya Shah. Twenty-three. Five-four, maybe. Glasses most of the time, according to her advisor."

He studied the image for a long moment, then nodded and leaned in toward the monitors. "Okay. Here comes the line for the five-thirty."

We watched people filter into frame at the ticket counter—families juggling luggage, construction workers in reflective vests, a couple with matching duffels. Sped up, it all passed in a blur, but I trained my gaze on hair color, height, body type.

A figure with dark hair and a backpack stepped into view. My pulse kicked.

"Slow it to normal," I said.

The playback resumed at regular speed. A young woman in a tank top and leggings waited her turn, shoulders hunched. Her hair was pulled up in a messy bun, strands frizzed from the humidity. Medium brown skin; not as deep as some of the other passengers, but definitely not pale. She stood at about the height I'd estimate from the photo. No glasses that I could see, though the image resolution wasn't great.

"Could be," I said quietly.

Madden leaned closer, frowning. "We need a better angle on her face."

On the waiting area feed, the same woman appeared a minute later, now with a paper ticket in her hand. She took a seat near the windows, backpack at her feet. Her profile was turned away from the camera. She pulled out her phone, tapped at the screen, then shoved it back into her pocket.

"Zoom doesn't do much," Elliott warned. "These are fixed-angle cameras, not cinema quality."

"Try anyway," Willa said.

He enlarged the waiting room feed to fill the main monitor, then digitally zoomed in as far as the grain would allow. The image pixelated, exactly as he'd warned. The angle still wasn't giving us enough of her face. Chin, cheekbone, part of her nose. No full frontal shot that would let us say, yes, that's Priya or no, that's someone else.

"Does she have a rolling suitcase?" Madden asked. "Backpack only, or anything else?"

"Backpack," I said. "And..." I squinted. "Looks like a small duffel under her feet now."

"That doesn't match what Carson said." Madden's voice edged sharp. "He described a backpack and a rolling suitcase."

"People carry more than one bag," Willa pointed out gently. "She might have set the rolling one somewhere else."

We watched as the woman adjusted in her seat, pulling the backpack into her lap. At one point, she rubbed at the bridge of her nose like you might if you'd just taken off glasses. That sent a little ping of recognition through me.

"It's not nothing," I murmured.

"But it's not confirmation," Madden countered. "We can't say that's her. We also can't say it isn't."

The boarding call must've gone out; on-screen, passengers began to rise. Our maybe-Priya stood and shouldered her pack. This angle did show us one more thing—a flash of her profile, lips compressed, chin tucked down. Too blurred to really read her expression, but something about her posture screamed braced.

The view shifted to the walkway camera as people filed toward the ramp. From behind, all we had to go on were silhouettes and gaits. The young woman's stride was purposeful, not dragging, not stumbling. She didn't appear to be escorted or flanked. She didn't look back.

"She's alone," Elliott said. "If that's her."

"If," Madden repeated.

We let the footage play until the last of the line vanished down the ramp, then for a few beats more. No one matching her description came back the other way in that window.

Elliott finally hit pause. "That's the whole load. After that, the next timestamp jumps to the seven o'clock crowd."

The room felt smaller suddenly, the humming of the server fans louder.

"Okay." I rubbed a hand over my jaw. "Let's sum this up. We have a woman who could be Priya. Right height, right general build, dark hair, traveling alone, gear is consistent with someone leaving the island for more than a day trip."

"But we can't see her face clearly enough to confirm," Madden said. "And the bag details don't exactly line up with what Carson relayed."

"And we don't see her buy the ticket—just that she has one." I nodded at the ticket counter feed. "The card trail says that ticket was purchased with a card in Priya's name. But as we both know..." I glanced at her. "Cards get stolen. Or used under duress."

She met my gaze, understanding flashing there. "Or cloned. Or handed over."

"Or someone else bought the ticket for her entirely," I added. "We don't know if this woman is the person who used the card." And we didn't have the time-stamp of the purchase or the card number to get Willa's people to pull it up.

Elliott shifted in his chair, discomfort clear. "You saying someone could've faked all this? Just to make it look like she left?"

"We're saying it's a possibility," Madden said, voice even. "We don't have enough information yet to rule anything out."

At the edge of my awareness, I felt Willa's attention sharpen. When I looked over, she was watching the screens with a kind of pinched focus I recognized from too many people who'd sat through case updates. The words might change; the helplessness didn't.

"The police didn't stay to watch this with you?" I asked Elliott.

"No, sir. Chief's guys came in, asked for the time window. I copied the files onto a drive and handed it over." He rubbed the back of his neck, brow furrowing. "Didn't seem real interested in sitting down with me to go through it."

Of course they didn't. Why put in more work than necessary when the story already made them comfortable?

I bit back the comment. No point making Elliott defensive when he was being helpful.

Madden had her phone out now, thumbs flying over the screen. "I'm texting Astrid. We need to know if any of the other students could've come to Priya's apartment to pack up her things. Or if Priya has any other close friends on the island who might've done that."

"That's good," I said. "If someone was doing her a favor, they'll say so. That's the clean explanation."

"And if nobody did," Madden replied, "then someone else went in there and scrubbed her presence from that apartment after Maria saw it. Someone who believes this—" she flicked her eyes toward the monitors, "—is sufficient cover."

Her phone chimed a minute later. She read the message, mouth flattening. "Astrid says none of the grad students have been to Priya's apartment since she disappeared. Nobody's shipped anything for her, nobody's been asked to collect her things. And as far as she knows, Priya's only friends on-island are the other students and a couple of staff at the research station."

"So no one she knows of had a reason to be in her apartment," I said.

"Which doesn't mean no one was," Madden acknowledged. "Just that it would be out of the ordinary for Priya to ask for that kind of favor from anyone else."

Out of the ordinary. Like everything else about this situation.

Roy nudged his nose against Willa's hand, and she absently scratched his head, eyes still on the frozen image of the blurred woman in the boarding line. "You think she's still here." It wasn't really a question.

Madden's answer was immediate. "I think the story we're being given is convenient. That doesn't make it true."

"And what do you think?" Willa asked me.

I looked at the screens, at the timestamp, at the grainy image of the woman with the backpack. At the ghost-clean apartment in my memory and the landlady's trembling insistence that it hadn't looked like that yesterday. At Carson's relieved certainty that the case was closed.

"Honestly?" I said. "That we can't trust any assumption we didn't verify ourselves."

It wasn't a yes or a no. But the truth was, I didn't know what to think. The possibilities all tasted bad.

Elliott cleared his throat. "You want me to burn you a copy of this segment?" he asked. "So you can review it again later if you need to."

"That would be great," Madden said before I could. "Thank you. And if you could actually give us the full twenty-four hours on either side, that would be helpful."

I had to appreciate her thoroughness, even if I didn't exactly relish the thought of scrubbing through 48-hours of footage. It wouldn't be the first time.

While he queued up the export, Willa stepped away from the door and came to stand beside Madden. Up close, the contrast between them was stark—Madden in her neat, pressed shorts and blouse, hair pulled back tight, posture straight; Willa in a faded T-shirt and jeans, sun-bleached freckles across her nose, easy slouch. Two very different routes out of the same kind of pressure cooker.

"You doing okay?" Willa asked quietly.

Madden's jaw flexed. "Define okay."

Willa huffed a small breath that was almost a laugh, but not quite. "Yeah. Fair."

They stood in silence for a moment, Roy leaning into Willa's leg, Madden's fingers finally going still on her bag strap.

"If you need anything," Willa added, "beyond this, you know where to find me."

Madden's head jerked toward her, surprise and an odd vulnerability flickering across her face before the mask came down again. She nodded once, the movement short and sharp. "Thank you."

What was that about?

I didn't think the two of them had been friends back when. But both of these women knew what it was to lose the same important someone, so maybe that was a bond in and of itself.

Elliott handed me a USB drive. "This has all four angles you asked for," he said. "If you need more time windows, just let me know. I'll do what I can."

"Appreciate it." I slipped the drive into my pocket. "And if you think of anything else—anything off, any staff who mentioned something weird—call me." I rattled off my number. He typed it into his phone with care.

We stepped back out into the corridor. The hum of the terminal seeped in around us again, the ordinary chaos of people running for departures or starting a vacation.

Willa walked us as far as the waiting area, Roy trotting obediently at her heel. "You really believe Carson's just... sweeping this under the rug?"

Madden's lips pressed together. "I think he's chosen a narrative that makes his job easier. Whether that's negligence, incompetence, or something more deliberate remains to be seen."

Willa's gaze flicked to me. "And you?"

I considered all the effort he'd put into pinning Gwen's disappearance on me. How many other leads had he ignored because he'd decided I was the best scapegoat?

"I'm not ruling anything out," I said.

We stepped through the doors and back into the heat. The noise of the parking lot washed over us—engines, a honking horn, a kid crying because somebody had taken their spot in an imaginary game.

Madden shaded her eyes again, scanning automatically. "So, where does that leave us?"

"With a maybe on the ferry," I said. "A definitely on the apartment being altered since Maria first saw it. And a Chief who seems awfully eager to accept the simplest explanation."

"In other words, nowhere good." She let her hand drop. "We still don't know where she is or what actually happened to her."

"No," I agreed. "But we've eliminated one clean story. That's something."

She shot me a sideways look. "Are you always this optimistic?"

"Trust me, this is me being optimistic."

That earned me the barest ghost of a smile. It was gone almost as quickly as it had appeared, but I still caught it. Somehow that felt like my biggest achievement of the day. Which really wasn't saying much about the state of our case so far.

She tipped her head toward the lot. "Astrid's going to be waiting to hear what we found. Or didn't."

"I'll touch base with her," I said. "In the meantime, I keep circling back to what Jimmy at Home Port said—about how Priya liked to work there late."

"You think someone there might've seen her with somebody?" Madden asked.

"Bartenders notice patterns. Who sits where, who they talk to, who they avoid." I started toward the truck. "If Priya had more of a life here than the research station sees, odds are good it shows up there."

"Then how do you feel about lunch?"

TWELVE

MADDEN

Daylight elevated Home Port from a dive to a joint. The difference? A joint attracted working people who just wanted a break and a drink—a place to blow off steam and get good, cheap food. A dive attracted the kind of people already looking for a fight when they walked in. A place where the floor stuck to your shoes and the wrong kind of attention stuck to your skin. A joint was worn. A dive was dangerous.

I'd learned the difference between the two during my years in California, and I felt that difference now as Rios and I stepped inside. More eighties rock played from the corner speakers, but there was no sense of menace lurking in the shadows. I didn't think that was just because I had six-foot-plus of man who could handle himself by my side. Because, yeah, it was impossible *not* to be aware of that in the way he stepped into a space and automatically sized everything and everyone up. That competence was sexy as hell.

Or would have been in someone else less complicated.

Last night, I'd been too focused on the mission, too pissed

off at the police, and too worried about Priya to clock the danger that Rios had seen in an instant.

The danger he'd saved me from.

I was still confident that I could've handled it, but likely not as fast or clean as he had.

I'd walked in as if I owned the place because, in most circumstances, confidence got me results. I wasn't the weak damsel type, and I'd learned fast that I had to stand up for myself if I didn't want to get railroaded in a male-dominated field. But Rios hadn't been wrong that I'd been acting like a prosecutor instead of someone they'd have wanted to help. The truth was, I was out of my depth in a place like this.

I'd never come here growing up. My parents had always been very clear about which parts of the island were "for us" and which were "for them," and I hadn't been a rule breaker back then. I couldn't call myself one now, but I'd at least developed a healthy skepticism for everything I'd been raised to believe. So, as Rios and I stepped inside the bar, I stayed quiet and followed his lead.

He paused just past the threshold, eyes doing a quick sweep of the room. Doors, bar, exits, who was sitting where and with whom. It was fast and automatic—a scan I'd seen a hundred variations of from law enforcement, but never quite as... thorough.

My pulse gave a flutter I preferred to think of as heartburn.

He angled toward a table in the far corner, back to the wall, clear sightline to the front entrance and the hallway that led to the bathrooms and kitchen.

Most defensible position. Of course.

I slid into the seat opposite him, my back to the room. It made the hair on my neck prickle, a purely instinctive protest. I made myself ignore it. If something went sideways in broad daylight in a bar where a sunburned family of five argued over a basket of hushpuppies with—seriously, was that cheese dip?—we had bigger problems than table selection.

A waitress in cutoff shorts and a faded Home Port T-shirt came over with a loose smile and a pair of laminated menus. "Hey, y'all. What can I get started for you?"

"Sweet tea, please." Apparently coming home had resurrected my bred-in-the-bone preference for beverages that could double as syrup.

Rios tipped his chin in agreement as he accepted one of the laminated menus. "Same."

"Kitchen's got the lunch specials up on the board. Burger's always good. I'll give you a minute."

As she walked away, I took my own survey of the place. Despite the bigger crowd, it was somehow quieter than last night. No one was at the pool table in the back. A couple of older guys played cards at a corner table, the slap of their hands against the wood underscored by low mutters and the occasional cackle of laughter. Two men in work boots sat at the long, scarred bar, bright safety vests slung over the backs of their chairs. Behind the bar, a guy with a shaved head and forearms roped with muscle polished glasses with an intensity that suggested he'd been at it awhile. Not the same bartender who'd been on duty last night.

I grabbed the other menu, mostly to give my hands something to do. "We should talk to the bartender. And our waitress. Anyone who's likely to have seen Priya here regularly."

"That's the plan." Rios tucked his own menu between the condiments and the napkin dispenser. "We'll order, then ask while we wait for the food. People are more likely to talk if they think you're going to be around for a bit."

I eyed him over the top of my menu. "Is that a law enforcement trick?"

He shrugged one shoulder. "Just human nature."

Our teas arrived, beads of condensation already sliding down the sides of the plastic tumblers. The server—her name tag read KELSEY—set them down and pulled out her order pad. "Know what you want?"

"Fried fish sandwich," Rios said. "Fries."

I hadn't even read the menu. Given that no food had actually been appealing since my life blew up, I took her original suggestion. "Burger. With onion rings."

"You got it." She scribbled, then glanced between us. "Y'all been in here before? Don't remember seeing you at lunch."

"I was here last night, asking around about a missing girl." I didn't remember seeing Kelsey on duty, but it couldn't hurt to get it out there.

Something flickered across her face. "Yeah, right. The college kid? The turtle scientist?"

"Grad student," I corrected automatically. "Named Priya Shah. Have you ever seen her in here?" I pulled up her photo and tipped my phone toward Kelsey.

She chewed on the end of her pen as she considered. "We get a lot of new faces in the summer. Kinda hard to keep track unless they're regular-regulars, you know?"

"Priya liked to work late," Rios said. "Laptop, earbuds, coffee. Sat by herself. She was here night before last. That ring a bell?"

The waitress's brow crinkled. "Oh. That might be the girl Jimmy said always ordered coffee instead of beer? I don't work the late shift much. I'm usually done by nine." She tipped her head toward the bar. "You might wanna ask Tito. He does both sometimes. He'll probably remember more than me."

"Thanks," I said.

She gave us a quick nod and drifted away to drop the order ticket.

I looked to Rios. "Divide and conquer? You wanna take Tito? I can start with the card players in the corner."

"Works for me."

When he only continued to study me, I asked, "What?"

"I just kinda expected you to be like... a grilled chicken salad kind of woman."

Under most circumstances, I was. But something about that description rankled, so I simply arched a brow. "Does this look like the kind of place that would serve a good salad?"

The corner of his mouth gave the faintest twitch. "Fair point."

Without another word, he slid back his chair, leaving me wondering yet again what a full-blown smile from him would look like.

I took one last sip of my tea to wet my suddenly dry throat before heading toward the card game. Both men glanced up as I approached, and I stood straight in the face of their assessing gaze. It didn't feel skeezy. More like absent appreciation for a decent-looking woman.

The one on the left tipped his well-worn captain's hat back an inch so he could see me better. "There something we can do for ya, missy?"

I tried a polite smile and let a little more of the southern drawl that I'd worked to stamp out bleed back into my voice. "I sure hope so. I'm looking for somebody. A girl. Wanted to know if you'd seen her." I showed them Priya's photo.

Both men set their cards down and pulled out reading glasses to study the photo more closely.

"I reckon I'd remember seein' a pretty little thing like that," hat guy said.

"She in some kinda trouble?" the other one asked.

"We're not sure. Nobody's seen her in a couple of days. She

was here two nights ago, so we're checking with the staff and patrons."

Hat guy stroked his beard. "We're not usually here that late."

I shoved down the sense of disappointment. "Thanks for looking all the same. Keep your eyes peeled?"

"Sure." Hat guy nodded at his companion. "If there's anything to hear down on the docks, Earl will have heard it."

Earl frowned, his bushy gray brows drawing together. "Not sure if it has anything to do with this, but I caught wind somebody saw somebody almost get mugged right outside not too long ago."

I straightened. "Outside here?"

Earl nodded.

"When was this?"

"More than a week ago, I'd say."

"Any idea who the witness was? Or the victim?" I pressed.

Earl shook his head. "'Fraid not. Wish I could be more help."

There was no way to know if this was related to Priya's disappearance or not, particularly without speaking to the source. "I appreciate y'all's time."

I made the rounds to the other occupied tables, showing Priya's photo and getting a lot of concerned glances but no actual information. No one else mentioned the mugging. Then again, daytime patrons were probably a whole different set of people from the night crowd.

Spotting Kelsey swinging out of the kitchen with a couple of baskets in hand, I returned to our table.

I thanked her for the food just as Rios slid back into his chair.

Once she'd walked away again, I asked, "Any luck?"

"Bartender's seen her before with the other students, but

not recently. He's gonna ask the staff in the back. Didn't get anything out of anyone else. You?"

"Our card players mentioned a rumor about someone getting mugged outside sometime last week, but they didn't know who got attacked or who the witness was. Hard to judge if it has anything to do with this since Priya was seen after that."

Rios hummed a noncommittal note and picked up his sandwich.

Sensing he was thinking, I let the silence settle and dug into my onion rings.

Eventually, I realized he was watching me again. As my mouth was full of fried deliciousness—God, when was the last time I'd had onion rings?—I simply arched a brow.

"Why did you ask for my help with this?"

It was a fair question considering what he believed I thought of him. I washed down the food with more tea.

"Astrid mentioned you used to be military police."

The way his face instantly shut down told me more than denial would have. A shutter dropped behind his eyes, cutting off access to something I hadn't realized I'd even seen. He clearly hadn't expected me to be aware of that.

"So that's it? I happened to have police training?"

I didn't blow off the question. Because that wasn't the answer. When I'd blurted out my request, his police training hadn't even crossed my mind.

"Because when I look at you, I see someone with the same drive to find the truth that I feel. Someone who isn't going to give up because it gets hard or complicated." I studied him back, noting the tension in his shoulders, around his mouth. "I see somebody who also understands how 'used to be' feels when it wasn't fully your choice."

His gaze snapped back to mine, sharper now. "How do you know it wasn't my choice?"

I could have backed off. Accepted the rebuke and changed the subject. That would've been the polite thing, the safe thing.

But if we were going to do this—really work together—there wasn't much point in polite lies. And maybe this would mean more than my fumbled apology at his boat.

"Because you were a man accused of something heinous, and you chose to go into a field where you protect people from that exact kind of harm. Because when Astrid mentioned a missing woman, your first instinct was to start looking before anyone asked you to. Because you walked into an ugly situation the other night and shut it down without hesitation or expectation of thanks. Sure, there's a healthy dose of 'good guy' in there. You're constantly proving you're not the monster people believed you were. But there's also an element of unfinished business. Transference, if we're going to be clinical about it. I know something about that."

His fingers tightened around his glass. For a heartbeat, I thought he might get up and walk away.

Instead, he leaned back, studying me like I was a puzzle he hadn't realized he'd sat down to solve. "You get all that from one line on a résumé?"

"I get all that from watching you. And from spending half my career reading people who were lying to me."

"I'm not lying."

"No," I agreed. "You're just... editing."

His mouth flattened. He stared over my shoulder for a long beat, as if he were watching some internal film. "You're not wrong about some of it," he said eventually.

I stayed quiet, letting him pick what he wanted to put on the table.

Eventually, his mouth twisted into a parody of a smile. "Transference, huh?"

"My old therapist would be thrilled I acknowledged it," I muttered.

"Ex-therapist?" he asked.

I gave him a look. "I didn't pack her in my carry-on."

Something like amusement flickered across his face. It faded quickly, but it was there. "So, what are you transferring? Gwen?"

Weren't we both?

But I'd give him this honesty.

"I became a prosecutor because I wanted to put monsters away. I watched what Gwen's disappearance did to my family, to this island, to you. How the lack of answers hollowed people out. I thought if I could be the person who got answers—who put bad guys in prison—it would help balance the scales."

"Did it?" The question held no judgment.

"Sometimes." My throat felt raw. "I did good work. I know I did. But the system isn't as black and white as I wanted it to be. It took me longer than it should have to accept that. Longer still to see the ways I'd helped preserve a system that failed people like Gwen. People like Priya. Even people like you."

I met his gaze squarely. "I don't want Priya to become another name on a list of victims the system failed. I don't want her to suffer the same fate as my cousin. Not if there's anything I can do to stop it."

He held my eyes for a long moment. "That why you left LA?" he asked softly. "Because you stopped believing in the system?"

"Partly." I took a sip of tea to buy myself a second. "Also, because I screwed up. Professionally. Publicly."

He didn't flinch. "Heard something about that."

I grimaced. "I'm sure you did. The Sutter's Ferry gossip

mill is still primed and pumping. But I'm not ready to unpack all of that yet."

"Fair," he said again. "For the record, you're not the only one who stopped believing in systems."

"I figured," I said. "You're living on a boat, Carrera. That doesn't exactly scream faith in institutions."

That pulled the ghost of a real smile out of him, and I could tell the full wattage version would be lethal. "Yeah, well. At least the ocean doesn't lie to your face."

We ate in silence for a few minutes. It wasn't comfortable, exactly, but it wasn't hostile either. Just... thick with unsaid things and the clink of cutlery against plates.

My mind drifted back to Gwen. To the posters, the press conferences, the search parties. To Carson standing in my aunt's living room, voice grave, saying they were following every lead.

I set my fork down a little harder than necessary. "I can't stop wondering," I said.

"About?" Rios asked.

"How many leads went cold because he was so fucking focused on you," I said bluntly. "If Carson hadn't latched onto you as his prime suspect, if he'd been a better cop, if he'd been more open-minded, more aware of the evidence instead of his own prejudices—would we have found her?"

The question hung between us like a live wire. I didn't take it back. Couldn't. It had been eating at me since yesterday, gnawing at the roots of everything I'd believed about that investigation.

Rios set his sandwich down carefully, fingers flattening against the edge of his plate. His eyes were very dark, very calm. "You want the polite answer or the honest one?"

"Honest," I said, even though I wasn't sure I did.

"The honest answer is we'll never know," he said. "There

probably were leads he ignored because he'd decided I was his guy. Or there was nothing to find. Even if he'd been perfect, we might still be sitting here with nothing but questions. That's the thing about missing persons. You don't always get to know how badly you fucked it up."

Guilt flickered across his face, quick and sharp.

"But I'll tell you this much," he added. "If Carson had been a better cop, he wouldn't have written you the story you needed to hear."

My stomach lurched. "What story?"

"That the system works," he said. "That the grown-ups had it handled. That somebody was going to pay. That you could believe in all that and build your life around it. That's what you did, isn't it? You built a career on the idea that he'd done his job right."

The words hit with surgical precision. It was infuriating how accurate he could be when he chose.

"You're not wrong," I said quietly.

"Trust me," he said, voice low. "Realizing the person you hung your faith on didn't deserve it? That'll screw you up just as much as being the one they tried to hang for it."

A shadow fell across the table, interrupting whatever response I might've made. "Excuse me. You're the ones asking about the missing girl, right?"

I looked up. A woman stood there in a polo shirt with the marina logo, her blond hair pulled back in a low knot. She held a half-finished basket of fries in one hand, the other worrying at a napkin.

"Yes." Hearing my prosecutor voice snapping into place, I worked to soften it. "We are."

She flicked her gaze to Rios, then back to me, as if measuring which of us was safer. "I'm Lacey. I work at the marina office. I couldn't help overhearing."

Rios's posture shifted almost imperceptibly—alert, open, not threatening. "What'd you hear?"

"Some of the guys at the docks were talking last week," she said. "Said one of the deckhands—Willie Sanders, works night shifts mostly—claimed he saw some girl get jumped behind this place. Back alley by the dumpsters. Said she fought the guy off and took off. I didn't think much about it at the time—drunk stories, you know? But then someone said the police were looking into a missing student, and..." She shrugged, uncomfortable. "I figured maybe it mattered."

My heart gave a little kick. "Do you know Willie personally?" I asked. "Could you point him out to us?"

"Sure." She nodded quickly. "He runs with the crew down at Slip B, works on the *Sea Breeze* when she's in. Tall guy, sunburned, dark hair. Usually high as a kite, if we're being honest." Her mouth twisted. "But I don't think he was lying about seeing something. He looked... rattled."

I exchanged a look with Rios. There it was. A new thread.

"Thank you," I said to Lacey. "You did the right thing coming over."

"If it were me, or my sister..." She trailed off, then shook her head. "Anyway. Good luck."

She moved away, back to her table, shoulders tight.

Rios leaned in, eyes on mine, sandwich forgotten. "Looks like we've got a dock to visit," he said.

I felt the familiar burn of purpose flare in my chest, sharp enough to cut through the doubt and fear for a moment. "Let's go see what Willie Sanders really saw."

THIRTEEN

RIOS

The *Sea Breeze* was an old boat who showed her age in the rust spots along her mostly white hull. The green trim might've been bright once, back when I was young enough to be something other than a cynic. Now it was a pale imitation that hit somewhere between mint and seasick. A few guys were working onboard, hosing decks, checking lines, doing the million small chores that kept things afloat. Nobody paid me much attention. Another guy on the dock didn't mean much.

But they noticed Madden.

Of course they did. Pretty woman, all neat and tidy and smelling, inexplicably, of fresh flowers. She'd look like temptation personified to guys who'd been out on the water for days or weeks at a time. Hell, she'd been occupying way the hell too much of *my* brain today, when it should've been fully on the case. It wasn't her looks—though she was unquestionably attractive, even winnowed down by stress and poor sleep. It was the whole package. I loved a puzzle, and the more time I spent with her, the more it became clear that Madden Reilly was a big one.

Which didn't matter one good damn because we were only allies in the name of running an investigation the cops were ignoring. Once this was over, we'd go our separate ways. So I shoved my reluctant fascination down deep into the mental what-the-fuck locker and shut the door.

If she was aware of the attention, she didn't show it. She simply strode down the dock as if she owned it, head held high, shoulders back. Somehow, it wasn't the kind of entitled strut I associated with her parents. This felt like confidence rather than privilege. As if it never occurred to her that there was anywhere she didn't belong.

I couldn't decide if that was bone stupid or envy inducing.

Either way, I edged just a little closer. It was unlikely anyone would bother her with me around, but I wasn't taking the chance.

At the gangplank, she hesitated, and I noted the unconscious flex and clench of her fingers. Maybe she wasn't quite as confident as she appeared.

"How do we handle this?" she murmured.

"We ask." I curved one hand at my mouth and hollered, "Ahoy!"

Two guys on deck glanced my way.

"Willie Sanders around?"

The closer of the two men jerked his head toward the end of the pier and continued coiling line. I followed the direction of his nod and spotted a man slumped on an overturned five-gallon bucket, elbows on knees, phone in his hands. I moved in his direction, noting the messy, overgrown brown hair and peeling sunburn on the back of his neck.

"Willie," I called.

His head whipped up. For a second, he froze, and even

from a distance I spotted the too bright eyes and semi-glazed expression. Then he saw Madden, clocked both of us together, and bolted.

He came off the bucket fast, phone nearly flying out of his hand, heading for the narrow slot of dock between boats like he was going to sprint up the ramp and pretend he'd never seen us.

I moved without thinking, stepping sideways into his path.

He tried to dodge around me. I caught him by the upper arm. Not hard enough to hurt. Enough that he knew he wasn't getting loose unless I wanted him to.

"Easy," I said. "We're not the cops."

"Man, let me go," he blurted, breath already a little ragged. "I didn't do anything. I'm not holding, I swear—"

"I don't care what you've got in your pockets," I said. "We're here because of what you told people you saw behind Home Port. That's it."

That bought me half a second. He stopped pulling, eyes flicking to Madden.

Her expression was steady, controlled. Not the hard-edged prosecutor from the other night. Just... focused.

"We're trying to find out what happened to a girl who's gone missing. Lacey at the marina office mentioned you'd seen something. It might help. That's all we're after."

Willie swallowed. His pupils were blown, swallowing almost all the color of his irises. Whatever he'd taken wasn't subtle.

"You promise you're not with Carson?" he asked.

"If we were, you'd already be in cuffs," Madden said. "We're not looking to get you in trouble. We just need the truth."

He looked between us again, weighing his options. There weren't many. Jumping in the water wasn't going to help him, and he knew it.

"Fine," he muttered. "We can talk. Just... not right here."

He jerked his head toward the *Sea Breeze.*

I let go of his arm, keeping myself between him and the ramp out of habit, not distrust. He stepped onto the boat with the easy balance of somebody used to moving on wet decks. I followed, then turned to offer Madden a hand out of reflex. She ignored it and hopped down on her own, landing light. Of course.

Willie dropped back onto a bench built into the stern, heel bouncing against the boards. Up close, the jitter in him was even more obvious. His fingers tapped an unsteady rhythm against his leg. "So, you wanna know about the girl."

"Start with when," I said. "The night you saw something behind Home Port."

He scratched the back of his neck, eyes unfocusing a little as he chased the memory. "Uh. Few nights ago."

"Few, as in two? Three? A week?" Madden's phone was already in her hand, screen dark but ready.

He squinted. "Had that big haul of flounder. We got in late. That was... four nights ago. Yeah. Before the storm came through."

Four nights put it two days before Priya vanished. Close, but not perfect.

"Okay," I said. "Walk us through what happened."

Willie blew out a shaky breath. "I was heading home. Cut through by the back of Home Port. Faster than going up by the office."

"What time?" Madden asked.

He gave a helpless little shrug. "After midnight. Closer to one? I don't know. We didn't dock 'til late."

"Had you been drinking?" I asked.

"Couple beers," he admitted. "Nothin' crazy."

"Using anything else?" I kept the cop and the judgment out of my voice.

He raked a hand through his hair. "Couple hits. Took the edge off. I wasn't... gone. But I wasn't church clean either."

Fine. I'd worked with worse.

"Go on," I said.

"I hear something." His foot sped up on the bounce against the deck. "Sounded like... scuffling? At first, I thought it was just something in the trash or some drunk guy. Then I heard this noise. Like somebody got hit hard. Or shoved. Made my stomach drop."

"What did you do?" Madden asked.

"I went to check it out," he said.

Which made him brave or stupid, or a little of both.

"Didn't walk right into the light—I'm not an idiot. I eased up by the corner, tried to keep to the shadows."

He swallowed, throat working. His gaze shifted somewhere over my shoulder, out past the pilings. "Some guy had a girl pinned against the wall. One arm across her chest, the other on her shoulder. She was pushing at him, trying to twist away. He had her jammed in close. I... I thought he was gonna—" He cut himself off, jaw clenching.

"Did you get a good look at him?" I asked.

"Not his face," Willie said. "He had a cap pulled down and a hood up. White guy, I think. Not real tall. Maybe couple inches shorter than me. Dark clothes. He was... solid. Not huge, but not little. I mostly saw shape."

"And the girl?" Madden's voice softened.

"Smaller," he said. "Maybe a little over five feet? She had dark hair, swinging around. Her skin wasn't pale. Darker. Tan, maybe. Hard to tell with the light and all."

"What was she wearing?" I asked.

"Tank top. Jeans," he said after a second. "I think. It all happened fast, okay?"

"You're doing fine," Madden soothed.

He nodded like he was trying to believe her.

"What happened next?" I asked.

"I thought about yelling," Willie said. "Or going in hot. But the dude had fifty pounds on her and probably twenty on me, and I was alone and not totally sober." Shame flashed across his face. "I hesitated. Couple seconds. Then she kneed him. Hard, from the sound of his choke. She shoved him off, cracked him with her elbow, and he crashed sideways into the wall."

He lifted his hand to his own face like he remembered the impact himself.

"She took off toward the front. Fast. I mean, she was gone. Didn't even see me. He kinda lunged after her, but he was doubled over. Ended up half-stumbling the other way."

"Away from the front of the bar?" I confirmed.

"Yeah," Willie said. "Street side to the back."

"You didn't follow her," Madden said. Not accusing. Just naming.

"No." The word came out small and a little ashamed. "By the time I got my feet moving, she was gone. So was he. I walked around front. Music was going, people laughing, nothing looked wrong. I told myself she made it inside. I... I should've gone in and checked. Or called it in. I know that. I do." He gripped the edge of the bench hard enough his knuckles whitened.

"Did you see her face at all?" I asked.

"Just a flash when she ran under the light," he said. "Side view. Hair in her face. I couldn't pick her out of a lineup on that."

I pulled out my phone and brought up Priya's photo again. "Could it have been her?"

He stared at the picture for a long time. Too long.

"Maybe," he said finally. "She's the right size. Dark hair. Skin kinda like that. But... it was dark. And I was high. And I only saw her from the side for, like, half a second. I don't wanna say yes and screw you over if I'm wrong."

"If you had to put a number to it?" Madden asked. "How sure or not sure are you?"

"Forty percent," he said, almost immediately. "Like... not nothing. Not enough to swear on."

Honesty. I'd take that over a convenient certainty any day.

"Okay," I said. "Forty percent we're talking about the same girl. Sixty that we're not. Either way, someone was attacked out there."

"Yeah," he said. "That part, I'm one hundred on."

"Did you tell anyone?" Madden asked. "Besides the guys on the dock."

He shook his head. "Who's gonna listen? 'Hey, Chief, your favorite stoner deckhand saw some shit in a dark alley while he was high.' They'd laugh me out of the station. Or write me up for something else."

He wasn't wrong about how that would go. Not with Carson.

"How did Lacey find out?" I asked.

"Told some of the crew next day," he said. "I guess it made the rounds. She asked what was wrong. I told her. She's... you know. Decent. Didn't act like I was making it up."

Madden slid her phone back into her pocket. "Can you take us there?" she asked. "Show us exactly where you were, where they were."

He winced. "Now?"

"Now," I said. "While you're talking about it."

He shifted on the bench, heel tapping faster. "Look, I

wanna help. I do. But I'm not... clear right now. You want details to stick, I should... maybe not be like this."

It was a fair point. Sloppy recall now would give Carson ammunition later if this ever came up in any formal context.

"When's your next run?" I asked.

"Tonight," he said. "*Sea Breeze* goes out at eight. I gotta be here by seven."

"And you're back?"

"Depends on what we pull," he said. "Midnight, one."

"Tomorrow morning," Madden said. "After you dock, eat something and sleep an hour or two. Then call us. We'll meet you behind Home Port, and you can walk us through it in daylight."

He hesitated. "You really think that'll make a difference?"

"If this girl is the one who's missing," Madden said, "every detail matters. If she's not, someone else was attacked, and that matters too. Either way, you're the only one who saw what happened. We need you clear."

Something about *you're the only one* landed. His shoulders slumped.

"Yeah," he said. "Okay. Tomorrow. I'll find you."

I rattled off my number; he punched it into his phone with clumsy fingers.

"Don't disappear on us, Willie," I said. "We're trusting you."

He nodded hard. "I won't. I swear. I should've done more that night. I'm not screwing this up again."

I believed him. I also knew how easily good intentions were lost between now and sunrise.

FOURTEEN

MADDEN

We didn't speak at first as we walked up the ramp from the *Sea Breeze* to the main dock. The old boards creaked under our feet, the sun hitting that bleak hour of midday misery that made you question your life choices. From here, Home Port sat, a simple slab of weathered gray between the pilings—not menacing, just... ordinary. Which somehow made it worse.

I kept my voice low. "So, on a scale of one to ten, how useful was that?"

Rios huffed a breath that resembled a laugh. "Five. We've got confirmation of an assault, a general time frame, and a rough description of both the victim and the attacker."

"And a reminder that Carson has no idea any of this exists because nobody trusted him enough to make a report."

"That, too."

We reached the top of the dock. I stopped, turning to look back toward the *Sea Breeze*. Willie had returned to the overturned bucket, elbows braced on his knees, his head bowed like he was trying to physically hold himself together. Not exactly an ideal witness under the best of circumstances.

I continued turning the information over in my head. "How likely is it that Priya was attacked and didn't say anything to her friends or adviser?"

Rios considered the question. "Without knowing her? Hard to say. Some women keep quiet. Or they need time. Or they don't want to relive it. If she was the victim... yeah. Kidnapping would be a hell of an escalation."

"Is it an escalation? Or did he simply manage to finish what he started?"

"Fair point. If it wasn't Priya, then we've got at least two women of similar build and physical profile being targeted in the same area in under a week." A muscle in his jaw ticked. "Either way, somebody's hunting in that alley."

I blew out a long breath. "Terrifying how easily that sentence comes out of your mouth."

"Wish it wasn't," he said quietly. "But yeah."

We started toward the parking lot. He matched my pace without comment.

"Do you think he'll call tomorrow?" I asked.

"I think he wants to do one thing right," Rios said. "We'll see if that's enough to get him there."

I nodded. "Tomorrow, then."

"Tomorrow."

We walked in silence a few more steps before I said, "You want to go back inside Home Port?"

"Do you?" he countered.

I considered. The staff had been cooperative earlier. No one had hesitated; no one had seemed evasive. And after the chaos of last night's shift, if anyone had witnessed an assault behind the building—even secondhand—they'd have mentioned it when we showed them Priya's photo.

"I doubt we'll get anything new," I admitted. "If they'd heard about the mugging, they would've said so. And from the sound of it, Willie's story never made it past the dockhands."

"Agreed," he said. "But we can take five minutes and look at the alley in daylight."

Which made sense. Doing nothing didn't sit well with either of us.

We cut between the buildings into the narrow stretch behind Home Port. The space smelled like sun-warmed asphalt and old beer—not exactly comforting, but not sinister either. A couple of dented dumpsters hunched against the fence, one with a lid propped open. Ordinary. Forgettable.

Except it wasn't.

I'd looked at thousands of crime scene photos in my career —freeze-framed violence rendered into evidence. They were horrible, but they were... buffered. A degree removed. A thing you studied rather than inhabited. I'd gotten good at being objective about it in order to do my job.

But standing in the place where a woman had actually been attacked?

That felt different. And I couldn't stop the image that flickered up, unbidden and sharp: Gwen backed against a wall just like this. Gwen fighting. Gwen losing. Not that this was what had happened to her, but it was all too easy to fall into imagining the worst with her face.

My throat tightened. I forced myself to look at the siding, at the dumpsters, at the narrow mouth of the alley. Focus on reality. On the victim still missing, not the one who'd been gone for more than a decade.

Rios dropped into that quiet, observant mode he had—the one that made him seem larger, steadier. "Somewhere here. Willie wasn't precise, but... this general area."

"Close quarters," I murmured. "He wanted her trapped."

Rios moved toward the wall, glancing back at me. An invitation, not a command. I stepped beside him. The boards were rough under my palm. I imagined a woman's shoulder slamming against them, the scrape of old wood tearing skin. My stomach clenched.

"He had her pinned," Rios said. "Arm across the chest."

He lifted his forearm and braced it against the wall near my shoulder—near, not touching, not blocking. But close enough that his warmth bled into the air between us. My breath hitched.

God. Not now.

"And probably the other hand here." He hovered it near my opposite shoulder.

The space around me contracted, the wall hard at my back, him solid in front of me.

A simulation. Nothing more.

But my body didn't care about the logic. A pulse of traitorous awareness curled low in my belly. I hated that.

"She reacted fast," Rios went on. "Probably instinct rather than training. Nothing about it would've been clean."

He shifted to demonstrate, adjusting his stance, and in the process, his thigh brushed mine for the briefest second. It wasn't intentional. It wasn't sexual. It wasn't anything.

Except my body lit up like I'd been plugged straight into a wall socket.

Absolutely humiliating that she'd decided *now,* with *this man,* was the perfect moment to wake back up again.

Thankfully oblivious to my plight, he continued, "She would've driven her knee up. Hard. Anywhere she could land it. Then shoved him off, probably wild and unbalanced."

"Messy." My voice came out a little too thin. "Desperate."

"Exactly."

He stepped back immediately, giving me space. Respectful. Controlled. It should've helped.

It didn't.

Because the second he moved, the ghost of my own imagination filled that space again: a woman pinned, gasping, fighting. Gwen's face flickering over a stranger's. A decade of what-ifs pressing in like the heat.

I swallowed. "Being here is a lot different than looking at photos."

Rios's eyes softened, just barely. "I expect so."

I wrapped my arms around myself for a beat, grounding. Trying not to think about Gwen. Trying not to remember the way my body had responded to him like an idiot hormonal teenager. Trying not to obsess about how much I wished any of this made sense.

We walked through the rest of the positions Willie described, but nothing else hit as hard as that first moment—me against the wall, him close enough to steal my breath.

And the worst part?

I couldn't tell whether the grief or the attraction was more dangerous.

Probably both.

Reaching for logic as if it were the last life raft on the *Titanic*, I scanned the alley again. "There's no reason for a woman to be back here alone. This isn't a shortcut. It doesn't lead anywhere except the dumpsters. So why was she here?"

Rios followed my line of sight. "Came out the back door to get away from someone inside, maybe."

"Or something more benign. She stepped out to take a breath, a call, anything—and he followed her."

"Exits are chokepoints," Rios murmured. "Anyone watching would've waited for her to be alone at one."

A chill crawled across my arms, despite the heat. "If she

was ducking someone inside, you'd think a staff member would've remembered that."

"Not necessarily," he argued. "Packed bar, loud, drunk tourists. One guy bothering a girl isn't memorable unless it escalates."

"Or unless someone reports it," I said. "Which she might not have done. Especially if she handled it herself."

We both looked back toward where he'd bracketed me against the wall moments earlier. Hardwood siding, rough and splintered. A place to pin someone and swallow the struggle if no one happened to be walking past the mouth of the alley at exactly the right moment.

I swallowed hard. "And if she did escape someone inside, that means there's a good chance of a prior first encounter. Either that night or some other time. He followed her out. Which means this wasn't impulsive. He was already targeting her."

Rios's expression darkened in a way that made my pulse jump—not fear, but recognition. He'd seen predators. He knew how they behaved.

"Whoever it was," he said, "he didn't pick that alley by accident. And he didn't pick her by accident either."

The logic landed like a stone in my stomach.

If the woman Willie saw was Priya, then she'd been scared enough, pressured enough, threatened enough to flee out a bar's back exit.

Which meant she'd already been unsafe inside before the attack even happened.

And if it wasn't Priya... then someone else on this island had been hunted, and nobody had noticed.

The thought nauseated me.

Rios turned back toward the main street. "Come on. There's nothing else to see here."

He was right. The alley had shown us all it was going to.

Unfortunately, some of what it showed, I didn't want to see.

It was too easy—far too easy—to picture Gwen in a place like this. To imagine a moment where she'd stepped away from the bonfire, just for a breath, never imagining someone had followed.

My eyes burned.

We stepped back into the sunlight and walked toward the parking lot. The quiet between us this time was a shared weight instead of a strain.

I tugged open the passenger door of his truck and slid inside. "Okay, the next logical step is verifying whether that email really came from Priya."

"Yeah," he said. "We need metadata. IP logs. The works."

"Which requires a warrant," I reminded him. "A warrant neither of us can get. I don't have standing. You're not law enforcement anymore."

A beat of silence.

Then, softly: "There are... other ways."

I looked at him sharply. "Do I want to know?"

He shook his head once. "Probably not. But I can take care of it."

A twinge of discomfort flickered up my spine. "Carrera—"

"You want to do this by the book," he said. "I get that. I respect it. But we don't have access to the book anymore. If we want to find her before something worse happens, we do what we can with what we have."

He wasn't wrong.

And the ends did justify the means. This time.

"Fine," I said. "Just... be careful."

One corner of his mouth lifted. "Always am."

"Good. Because while you're doing whatever it is you're not telling me about, I have another angle to work."

He frowned. "Which is?"

"What if Priya isn't the first?" I asked. "I don't mean Gwen. I mean other disappearances. People who went missing and got written off as tourists who wandered off, or left the island, or whatever benign explanation Carson preferred."

"You think there are others." He didn't pose it as a question.

I didn't have quite that much confidence in my theory. "I don't know. Maybe. Can't hurt to check. I'm submitting a FOIA request for every missing persons report filed on this island for the last fifteen years."

"That's a lot of paperwork."

"And if even one case fits a pattern..." My stomach tightened. "I'm not letting her become another unsolved file."

He studied me for a long moment. "Carson won't hand those over."

"The FOIA exists for a reason," I said. "If he stalls, that tells me something too."

He nodded slowly. "All right. You pull on that thread. I'll follow the digital one."

"We update each other," I said.

"Yeah," he agreed. "No surprises."

I wasn't sure I believed that—about him or about this case. Not when every hour I spent with him was decimating everything I'd ever thought about him. Not when he was starting to feel like the one stable thing in the chaos of this island. But it was what we had.

"Tomorrow," I said.

"Tomorrow," he echoed.

And for the first time since we started this, it felt like we were actually moving forward.

FIFTEEN

RIOS

After I dropped Madden back at the research center so she could pick up her car, I pointed my truck north and let the road unwind. The two-lane strip that ran the length of Hatterwick on the west side of the island wasn't long enough to get lost on, but it gave me ten decent minutes of quiet where I wasn't focused on the case.

Instead, I thought about Madden.

The woman who'd sat across from me at Home Port, onion ring grease on her fingers, talking about transference and monsters and losing her faith in the system wasn't the privileged island princess I remembered. She'd walked into this thing clearly expecting me to tell her to go to hell and asked for my help anyway. Apologized without being pushed. Looked me in the eye and called bullshit on the idea that becoming "used to be" with your life's work was always a choice.

There'd been no way she could know how close to home that hit. Maybe that's what bothered me most: she saw more than I'd expected. Certainly more than I wanted her to.

I wasn't sure what to do with that.

I'd once lambasted her for making assumptions about me, and hadn't I done the same to her? The idea didn't sit well with me.

Madden was... fierce in a way I hadn't expected. In the middle of day trippers and vacationers and islanders going about their ordinary summer routines, a grad student had vanished—and Carson had decided it was easier to pretend she'd just gone home.

Instead of trusting the system with the blind faith she'd had at seventeen, Madden had refused to accept his edict. She'd thrown herself into an investigation she really had no personal stake in, and she'd asked me, of all people, for help. And it didn't seem to be because I was the only available option. She seemed to legitimately trust my capabilities as a cop. Or, at the very least, my motivations for being willing to keep pushing.

I'd seen the sharp-edged prosecutor as we watched that maybe-Priya on the ferry footage. When we'd walked the alley where someone had been pinned and nearly brutalized, I'd seen the way she paled, the way her throat worked. Saw her blink hard, like she was holding back something that would knock her off her feet if she let it out. Real-life investigations didn't have the distance she'd been accustomed to from police reports and crime scene photos. But it was more than that.

The memory of Gwen was still right there under her skin.

As it lived beneath mine.

Madden had taken her trauma and turned it into a career, putting bad people in cages. I'd taken mine and gone into the part of the process where you found enough truth for someone like her to lock those doors. Different paths, same target.

I hadn't expected to have anything in common with her. Least of all, the same fundamental driving force.

Life didn't offer up many chances to revise old judgments,

and I had no idea what to do with the fact that she'd handed me one. Or with the simmer of entirely inappropriate awareness I'd felt as we'd blocked out the attack in the alley.

Sutter House came into view at the crest of the dunes, saving me from going further down that mental rabbit hole. The big bastard of a house that had been in Willa's family since the island had been settled some century and a half before. She'd inherited it upon the death of her grandparents, along with the ferry company and pretty much everything else, save for some provisions for her elder brother, Jace. A great big middle finger to her parents. Sawyer had done some polishing and upkeep since he'd moved in, and everything about the place screamed history with comfort.

I spotted his truck and Willa's Jeep in the free-standing garage. Awesome. I'd get tag teamed.

That was a price I'd willingly pay for what I needed to do. I'd told Madden there were other ways to get to the email data we needed. Now came the part where I made good on that promise.

I parked in front of the house and slid out of the truck. Roy's booming bark pulled my attention to the deck around the side. His whole body vibrated with the force of his wags, but he didn't leave his post. I circled around to find Willa and Sawyer lounging in a pair of Adirondack chairs with drinks and a tray loaded with meats, cheeses, and crackers.

I gave Roy's head a scruff and moved up to join them.

"Wondered if we'd end up seeing you today." Sawyer lifted the bottle in his hand. "Beer?"

"Sure."

He shoved out of his chair and went inside, leaving me with his bride, who eyed me with a mix of interest, speculation, and worry as she tapped one finger against the bowl of her wineglass.

I dropped into another chair. "What?" I knew what was coming, but I wouldn't make it any easier on Willa than I would on one of my sisters.

"Sawyer had already told me you were looking into things with the missing grad student even before you showed up at the ferry company this morning, but how exactly did you end up working with Madden Reilly of all people?"

Lifting one shoulder in a shrug, I reached for a cracker and some cheese. "She asked for my help."

Sawyer came out the door with a long-neck bottle, top already popped. "What interest has she got in all this?"

Reasonable question. One I'd prepared for.

"Apart from being friends with Astrid, this whole thing is triggering her about Gwen. She wants to make sure the case gets the attention it actually merits, rather than Carson's bullshit acceptance of the too-convenient answer."

"What answer is that?" Willa asked.

I explained Carson's declaration this morning that the case was closed.

"Huh. Thought Madden was one of his biggest fans," Sawyer observed.

I took a pull of the beer. "Apparently, the scales have fallen from her eyes. Now she's starting to question everything about how he handled Gwen's case."

"Including you?" Willa raised a meaningful brow. "Sawyer mentioned she'd apologized."

I inclined my head in acknowledgement. "To be fair, she did that before all this happened. It was awkward as hell, but after spending today with her... I think she really means it. Not saying we're gonna end up besties or some shit, but we can both admit we're different people now and put aside any differences in the name of finding Priya Shah."

Sawyer narrowed his eyes. "And I'm guessing that brings us to why you're actually here."

Thank God. I wasn't gonna get roasted over the coals further about this weird partnership with Madden. We could get down to business.

Over a half dozen more crackers and cheese, I explained everything we'd uncovered so far in our investigation.

"We're at a dead end until we manage to talk to Sanders sober, and even then, I'm not sure how much help he'll be. The next logical step is to verify whether the email actually came from Priya's account. Neither Madden nor I have the channels we'd usually use for that."

"Ah," Sawyer nodded in understanding. "You need to get up with Dax."

Dax Gregory was a friend of Sawyer's. Former naval intelligence, before he retired, he'd run in a lot of the same circles Jace did now. These days, he was making bank doing God knew what in the private sector. Dax had been the one to uncover the link to who was after Willa after her grandparents died. He trafficked in information and wasn't usually precious about how he got it, so long as it was being put to good use in helping people. I couldn't think of anyone better for this.

"If we can. I know he's sometimes taking jobs that pull him as off the map as Jace is these days, but if he's around and can work whatever magic he usually pulls off, it could save a lot of time. And we're all aware time is of the essence with a missing person's case."

"Then let's see if we can get ahold of him." Sawyer immediately fished out his phone and began tapping at the screen. "I'll text him. If he's available, he'll call. I gave him your number."

By the time we'd decimated the rest of the charcuterie board, and I'd polished off my beer, my phone vibrated. Unknown caller flashed on the screen.

"Hello?"

"Carrera. Didn't expect to be hearing from you. You looking for more dirt on the brass you tried to take down?"

For a moment, I only sat there with my mouth hanging open. Who was I kidding? This was Dax. Of course he was well informed about shit that even half the upper brass didn't know about.

"Uh, no, actually. I'm on Hatterwick. Involved in a missing person's case of a young woman the chief of police believes has just gone off on her own."

I all but heard his interest sharpen. "You don't think so?"

"Evidence doesn't line up."

"Lay it on me."

Dax listened as I took him through it. When I'd finished, he whistled. "One of these days, Carson's gonna piss off the wrong person with his lackadaisical approach to law enforcement."

"May I be around to see it when it happens."

"You need me to see what I can dig up in terms of an electronic trail for this girl? Figure out if the email could've been spoofed or whatever?"

"Yeah. It won't be admissible, but we're not trying to get a conviction. We're trying to find a missing girl before something awful happens to her."

"I'm in. Give me everything you've got on her."

I reeled off Priya's name, her previous address, phone number, email address, and everything else Astrid had given me.

"All right," Dax said. "Give me a second."

There was a pause. Keys clicked faintly on the line. I stayed quiet, waiting, phone pressed to my ear, eyes tracking the waves down on the beach where they rolled in with steady inevitability.

"Okay," he said at last. "Phone's not active. Battery's either dead or it's been powered off."

I hadn't really expected anything else, but the confirmation hit harder than I expected. "Last location?"

More clicking. A longer pause this time.

"Last ping hit a tower servicing the ferry terminal."

"When?"

"Little after six in the morning yesterday."

I closed my eyes. Busy. Public. And the last place Priya had allegedly been seen. What did it mean that it was the last place her phone had pinged?

"And the email?" I asked.

"Yeah, I'm checking that now." Another beat. "It wasn't spoofed. Header matches the device. Whoever sent it had her phone in their hand."

I dragged a hand over my face. "So either she sent it herself—"

"—or someone had possession of the phone," Dax finished. "Yeah."

The implication sat between us, heavy and ugly.

"That's the quick triage. Anything deeper than this—texts, email content, whether someone was leaning on her—that's going to take real time. I've got something sensitive I need to wrap tonight, but I'll dig in properly tomorrow."

That was far more than I'd been hoping for. "Any light you can shed will help. I appreciate this, man."

"No problem. Anything I can do to take down the fuckers of the world. Best to Sawyer and Willa. I'll be in touch ASAP."

He'd clicked off before I could say another word.

"He says hi to both of you. And we'll see what he comes up with on the rest."

"Does that mean dead end until you hear back?" Sawyer asked.

"Maybe. Maybe not. Her phone last pinged near the ferry terminal."

Willa straightened. "Do you want to organize a search of the building? The surrounding area?"

I considered. "There's no way to know if the phone was powered down or destroyed. For all we know, it got hurled overboard, in which case it would be a waste of manpower. Let's hold off on that for a bit, until or unless Dax comes back with more. In the meantime, I want to circle back to her coworkers and friends. See if any of them recall any point this summer where she was acting strange or upset or nervy. There's no specific indication that the woman Sanders saw attacked behind Home Port was Priya, but if it was, seems like they'd have noticed her behavior changing in the days after. They probably would've mentioned it before if there were, but you never know. And Madden's chasing down another angle." My focus shifted to Willa. "Maybe one you can help with."

"How's that?"

"You've been back for more than ten years now. Do you remember hearing about any other missing women in that time?"

"Certainly nobody local. The island gossip tree would've been lit up with that. I can't say that I'd have remembered anyone else. I spent so much time keeping to myself. Bree or Caroline are probably a lot more likely to have come across rumors like that, since they both work more with the public directly."

"Fair point. I'll touch base with them."

Willa reached for Sawyer's hand. "Do you think there's some connection between Gwen and Priya?"

"Directly, no. No reason to believe there would be. I think Madden's looking at establishing Carson's pattern for handling that type of case since Gwen. Not sure exactly what she hopes to get out of it, but it's another line to pull."

Having gotten what I came for, I pushed to my feet. "Thanks for your help. And the snacks. I'm gonna head on. See if I can talk to the other grad students again before they head out for their evening observations. Maybe swing by the Brewhouse if I can catch Bree."

Sawyer pulled me in for a back-thumping hug. "Don't be a stranger, brother. And let us know if we can help in any way."

"Will do."

Feeling lighter than I had on my arrival, I loaded back into my truck and headed back toward the village. There were more questions to ask before the day was through.

SIXTEEN

MADDEN

Subject: Public Records Request – Missing Persons Files

Chief Carson,

Under the North Carolina Public Records Act, I am formally requesting digital copies of all missing persons reports submitted to the Sutter's Ferry Police Department from January 1, 2011 to present, including:
- initial report
- follow-up notes
- investigative supplements
- closure or status determinations

This request is for public records, not confidential case

materials. If any portion must be redacted, please cite the specific statutory exemption for each redaction.

Please acknowledge receipt of this email today. For transparency, I have copied the Town Clerk.

Electronic delivery to this address is preferred.

Regards,

Madden Reilly

CC: Barbara Channing, Town Clerk

By the time I made it through my third draft of the FOIA request, my eyes burned. I read it one more time to double check for typos—as if that would make anyone more inclined to cooperate—and hit send. The email vanished off the screen, leaving me staring at the empty inbox like something might magically appear to justify the effort.

"Congratulations," I muttered. "You've sent one bureaucratic request. Gold star."

I pushed back from the tiny dinette table on the *Second Wind* and scrubbed my hands over my face. A half-empty mug of coffee cooled next to my laptop, the surface sheen gone dull. I took a sip anyway. Bitter. Lukewarm. Fitting for the past fifteen hours of research.

The other tab I'd left open showed the *Seaside Sentinel's* online archive. I'd fallen down that rabbit hole at eleven last night, chasing headlines: petty thefts, noise complaints, seasonal ordinances, the occasional human-interest piece about somebody's impressive tomato harvest. Nothing about vanished women. Nothing about tourists who didn't make their checkout times. Nothing about patterns.

Just Gwen.

Always Gwen.

I'd reread those articles, too. That had been a mistake. It was one thing to know the words by heart. It was another to see them again—the grainy yearbook photo, the hollow-eyed photos of my aunt begging for any information about her daughter, the confident assurances from Chief Carson that gave way to the exhaustion of "We have not forgotten."

My sleep after that hadn't been sleep so much as a slow drowning in old images. Gwen's laugh. Gwen's empty bedroom. The bonfire. The way I'd sat in the back of Carson's office at seventeen, listening as adults talked about my cousin like she was a puzzle instead of a person. She'd ceased to be Gwen and had instead become her disappearance.

I stared at the laptop until the letters blurred.

None of this told me whether Priya was the first since Gwen. Or just the first one who had people who refused to let her be written off.

A voice cracked across the water, sharp enough to jolt me out of my spiral. "Reilly!"

I blinked, shoved my chair back, and stepped out of the cabin into the bright slap of morning.

Rios stood on the deck of his boat in the next slip over.

Shirtless.

For a second, that was the only detail my brain registered. Broad chest, shoulders cut with muscle and scattered with old scars, a line of dark hair arrowing down as he wiped sweat off his neck with a towel. The sun glanced off the damp planes of his skin like the universe had decided subtlety was overrated. I spotted dark lines of ink on the curve of one biceps, but I couldn't make out the design from here. Not that my brain was doing a whole lot of processing just now.

Holy hell, the Navy had done incredible things for that body.

My mouth went dry.

He hooked the towel around his neck and lifted his chin. "You alive over there?"

Barely.

"What?" I managed.

He jerked his thumb toward the dock, all business. "We heard from Sanders. Get dressed. We're going."

Right. Willie Sanders. The dockhand. Our only known witness.

I dragged my eyes up to Rios's face. Only marginally safer territory, because scruff darkened his jaw in a way that made him look deliciously dangerous. Like every good girl's bad boy fantasy come to life.

Words. They were a thing I normally knew how to use. How did they work again?

"Yeah. Okay. Give me five." I retreated into the cabin before I could humiliate myself further by openly ogling him like a thirsty barfly.

"Get it together," I muttered at my reflection in the tiny bathroom mirror.

My cheeks were still flushed from sleep—what little I'd managed—and far too much screen time. I splashed cold water on my face until my skin prickled, then did the world's fastest triage: ponytail, a swipe of eyeliner and mascara, clean t-shirt, jeans that could handle whatever grime today had on deck. Boots. Willie Sanders was not a judge I had to impress. As I dressed, I tried not to think about the fact that my first truly coherent thought of the day had been *Rios is hot* instead of *Find the missing girl.*

One was a problem. The other was a priority.

By the time I stepped back onto the dock, he was already there, leaning against his truck with his arms folded. Mercifully, a gray t-shirt now covered his torso. Less distracting. Also, somehow worse, because it clung to all those muscles that would now be living rent free in my brain in all their tan, sweaty glory.

"Ready?" he asked.

"Yeah." My voice came out steadier this time. Progress.

I climbed into the passenger seat and tugged the door shut. He backed out of the marina lot and turned us toward the narrow spine of road that ran north.

For a minute, the only sound was the hum of the engine and the low rush of the wind through the open windows. I tipped my face into it, appreciating the hint of salt in the air instead of the smog I'd have gotten in Los Angeles. A part of me really was happy to be home, which hadn't been a certainty when I'd impulsively driven cross-country to be here.

My skin prickled with awareness, and I glanced over to find Rios watching me, expression inscrutable.

Not at all sure what he'd see, I defaulted to business. "I sent the FOIA request. Every missing persons report on Hatterwick in the last fifteen years. We'll see how much Carson tries to stonewall."

Rios turned his gaze back to the road. "Carson always stonewalls."

"True. But he can't magically make the existence of public records disappear. If there's nothing else... that's something. If there is, I want to know."

"Yeah." He tapped the steering wheel with his thumb, a small, restless rhythm. "I spoke to my contact last night. He confirmed the last ping of Priya's phone was in the vicinity of the ferry terminal at six in the morning day before yesterday. Since then, it's been switched off or destroyed."

I glanced toward him. "Do I want to know who this contact is?"

"Probably not. But we're not building a case for you to prosecute. He also confirmed that the email did come from her device."

"From her device, but no way of knowing if she was the one who sent it," I murmured.

"Exactly. He's doing some more digging to see if he can find any electronic trail of harassment."

I definitely didn't want to know about that. Anybody who could get access to that information without a warrant was breaking a multitude of laws.

"I went at it from a different angle and hit up the grad students again last night. Asked if they'd noticed anything off with Priya the past week—anyone bothering her, weird phone calls, that kind of thing. Nothing. No change in behavior they can point to."

"None of the usual signs of her being harassed," I translated. "So that theoretically cuts one possible connection between the alley attack and her disappearance."

His glance showed approval for my having intuited his line of thinking.

"Unless she didn't feel safe saying anything," I added.

"Could be," he allowed. "But if she'd been jumped behind Home Port and still showed up to work like nothing happened... that tells us something about how she handles shit, too."

"Self-contained," I said. "Private."

"Yeah."

We fell quiet as the village thinned behind us. Businesses

gave way to clusters of small houses, then to stretches of marsh and scrub broken up by the occasional weather-beaten mailbox. The sky was a washed-out blue, already hinting that we were in for a scorcher.

"So, you heard from Sanders?" I prompted.

"Yeah. Texted a little after three this morning. Said he was back in and gonna crash for a few hours but was happy to talk to us this morning if we met him at his place."

"Sounds like he's still willing to help, at least." Guilt had been written all over Willie's face yesterday, even through the high. "Assuming he didn't lose his nerve."

"Or that he didn't get high again and ruin our shot," Rios muttered. "Gotta temper our expectations of what we're gonna get out of this interview."

I didn't answer. The possibility of another failed lead sat between us, heavy and unwelcome.

We turned off onto a side road that dead-ended into a cluster of low apartment buildings crouched near the salt marsh. The siding was faded, the parking lot cracked, but a few potted plants on stoops and a kid's bicycle chained to a stair rail made the place feel lived in rather than abandoned.

As Rios scanned the building, I noted a tightness in his jaw. I wondered what he saw here. Something that reminded him of old cases? Or something that reminded him of growing up on this side of the island? I dimly remembered that his neighborhood had been a few streets over. I'd picked his sister Gabi up a few times to drive her, Gwen, and Willa to a few things. I knew their home life hadn't been a good one, so I didn't push. If Rios was thinking of his past, walking into a place like this as an adult carried a weight. One that was none of my business.

He pulled into a spot in front of a ground-floor unit with a crooked screen hanging half off the window track and killed the engine. "You ready?"

"No," I said honestly. "But that's never stopped me before."

We climbed out. The air smelled like low tide and old oil from someone's perpetually leaking truck. A dog barked list-lessly in the distance. Willie's door had a faded four stenciled on the frame. Rios knocked—a trio of crisp raps that spoke the universal language of official enough to be taken seriously.

We waited.

Nothing.

He knocked again, harder this time. "Sanders! It's Carrera!"

A television murmured from somewhere in the building. An air conditioner unit churned away. No movement sounded from inside. No voice.

"Maybe he's still asleep. You said he texted around three, right?"

"Yeah." Rios frowned at the door like he could see through it. "Could be."

He knocked a third time, an impatient pulse of knuckles against wood. "Willie. You told me to come by this morning. We're not the cops. Open up."

Silence.

The unease that had been tapping at the base of my skull slid up a notch.

"I'll check the back," I said. "See if there's another entrance."

He looked like he wanted to argue, but what was he going to say? Don't investigate? On a missing-person case?

"Stay aware," he said instead.

"Always," I shot back.

The space between buildings was narrow, choked with overgrown shrubs and trash that had blown free of someone's can and never been reclaimed. Sand and grit slid under my boots, and a spiderweb I didn't see until the last second streaked across my arm like a ghostly thread. Behind the building, each ground-floor unit had a small concrete patio that overlooked a strip of dying grass and the marsh beyond, the kind that came standard with cheap plastic furniture and unrealized aspirations.

Willie's patio had one chair, a cracked ashtray, and a sliding door with the blinds half-drawn.

And the door itself... wasn't quite closed.

The latch hovered a hair's breadth from engaged, the glass parted just enough to show a thin line of darkness inside.

Every hair on my arms stood up.

People forgot to lock doors. People were careless.

But people who'd texted investigators at three in the morning, promising to help find a missing woman, probably wouldn't leave their door like that when they'd invited company over a few hours later.

"Rios!" I called his name sharper than I intended.

His footsteps pounded down the side path a moment later; he emerged around the corner, every muscle of his body shouting ready for action. "What is it?"

I pointed. "The door's not secure."

His whole body stilled in that particular way it did when he was slotting into some bone-deep training. "Okay. Stay out here."

He tugged a bandana out of his pocket and wrapped it around his hand so he could ease the door further along its track with his covered palm. It slid open with a soft scrape.

"Sanders?" His voice carried into the dimness. "Willie, it's Carrera."

No answer.

The smell hit first—stale beer, old takeout, and something underneath that made my stomach twitch. Not quite rot, but headed in that direction.

Against my better judgment—and his explicit instruction—I stepped in after him, keeping my hands tucked against my sides to avoid touching anything.

The main room looked like every cliché of an overworked, underpaid blue collar bachelor's apartment: pizza boxes, fast food wrappers, an overflowing trash can in the corner, a sagging couch with a suspicious stain in the middle. An ashtray on the coffee table overflowed with butts. A glass pipe lay beside it, dulled by use.

"Willie?" I moved carefully past the couch. "It's Madden Reilly, remember? We talked yesterday."

No sound. No movement. The apartment had a feeling of emptiness, though I couldn't put my finger on why.

Rios peeled off toward the kitchenette, scanning counters and sink, his gaze snagging briefly on an empty prescription bottle lying on its side. Even from here, I could see the label had been peeled halfway off.

I headed for the hallway.

There were only two doors—one slightly ajar on the right, one wide open at the end. The open door showed a stacked washer and dryer. The near door probably led to the bedroom.

"Willie?" I tried again, loud enough that if he'd simply passed out, he should have heard me. "We're here to talk about what you saw. You wanted to help."

Still nothing.

My pulse ticked faster.

I nudged the bedroom door with my knuckles, and it swung wider with a complaint of un-oiled hinges.

The room was a disaster—clothes everywhere, sheets in a tangle, an oscillating fan pointed at the bed. The blinds were mostly closed, slats tilted just enough to let in a dull stripe of light.

The bed was empty.

Then my gaze tracked to the floor at the far side, toward the bathroom doorway.

A bare foot stuck out. Toes splayed, skin waxy.

For a second, the world narrowed to that one image—foot, tile, dirty baseboards.

I rounded the bed in three quick strides and dropped to my knees on the bathroom threshold.

"Willie?" I said, even though I already knew.

He lay face-down on the tile, one arm pinned awkwardly under his chest, the other stretched out as if he'd been reaching for something or trying to crawl. His cheek was smashed against the floor, jaw slack. A dark bruise marred the inside of his elbow, but that could've been from any number of things— IV, blood draw, hard living. I didn't see a pool of blood, no obvious trauma.

"Come on," I muttered, because saying it made doing the next thing easier. "Don't do this."

I carefully stepped into the bathroom and pressed two fingers to the side of his neck, hunting for the flutter of life where a carotid pulse should be.

I'd touched a lot of people's throats in court photos. In evidence. In autopsy reports.

This was very, very different.

No barrier of glossy paper. No buffer of time and professionals between me and the moment.

Just skin. Too cool. Too still.

I pressed harder.

Nothing.

The absence was louder than any beating heart.

"Rios!" I barely held back the tremor.

His boots thudded down the hall, then stopped in the doorway behind me.

"What've you got?"

I lifted my face to him, fingers still stupidly on the place where life should have been.

"He's dead."

SEVENTEEN

RIOS

"...and unless you're planning to charge either of us with something, Chief, this is where you let us go." Madden's voice was cool and precise, every word edged in steel.

Carson bristled at that, color rising in his cheeks as he shoved his hands on his hips. "You're not an ADA anymore, Counselor. And he—" a jerk of his chin at me "—isn't law enforcement. Whatever you two think you're doing, I suggest you remember where your authority stops."

"Since we have none, our authority stops right here on this sidewalk. Where you have no legal cause to detain us further."

It took everything in me not to smirk. Or applaud. Or both.

The marsh hummed in the mid-afternoon heat beyond the parking lot, indifferent to a dead man on a bathroom floor. Behind Madden, crime scene tape already blocked off Willie Sanders's apartment. CSU was inside, and an officer was posted by the door. He looked vaguely familiar and kept glancing our way. At first, I'd thought it was at me, but it was her he was watching, his mouth drawn into lines of concern.

Carson scowled at the pair of us. "Get out of here, and stay out of my way."

"Trust me," Madden murmured under her breath. "I'd love to."

He stalked off toward his cruiser, shoulders tight, barking something at one of the uniforms. I watched him go, a familiar cocktail of resentment and weary contempt twisting under my ribs.

Half of me had been braced for cuffs. For the old dance of "just come down to the station so we can clear a few things up," which somehow never applied to anyone but me.

Having Madden there—calm, controlled, clearly stating the timeline and making it crystal fucking clear we'd had neither means nor opportunity—had been a shield I hadn't known I'd get to have. She'd been clinical with her answers, precise with her terminology, and absolutely ruthless about procedure.

Her willingness to use her expertise in my—our—defense said more about her inclination to trust me than perhaps anything else.

Beside me, she'd gone very, very still. Shoulders drawn in a fraction. Mouth a line. I knew that look. Now that the immediate threat was past, her adrenaline was wearing off, leaving the crash behind.

"Come on. Let's get you home."

"I'm fine." Automatic. Brittle.

"Sure," I agreed. "You can be fine on your boat."

Madden cut me a sidelong glance but didn't argue when I began steering her toward the truck.

"Madden."

We both turned at the voice. It was the cop who'd been posted at the door. He shot me an inscrutable look before focusing back on her.

"You okay?"

"I'm fine, Grant."

Grant. My brain filtered back through years and names, even as I glanced down and saw WILLOUGHBY on his name tag.

"Are you? What the hell were you even doing here?" He glanced at me again, at the hand I still held at the small of her back, and the *with him* was implied.

Madden's shoulders squared. "The job your boss refused to do."

Grant opened his mouth to speak, but she cut him off. "We have to go."

I resumed steering her back to the truck.

The moment we were shut inside, she tugged on her seatbelt. Or tried. Her hand trembled, and she struggled to slot the tab into the latch. Carefully, I closed my fingers around hers to stabilize it and pushed until the belt engaged.

Madden didn't meet my gaze as she muttered. "He was my high school ex."

I hadn't asked, but I didn't point that out. Instead, I said, "Ah," and released her hand to crank the truck.

The drive back to the marina was quiet. She said nothing as she stared out the passenger window, one hand clamped white-knuckled around the strap of her purse. The muscles in her jaw worked, like she was chewing on words she didn't trust herself to say.

I let the silence sit and pushed down my own urge to replay every second between stepping through Willie's sliding door and finding him on the bathroom floor. The smell. The angle of his arm. The cold under my fingertips when I'd checked for a pulse myself, just to be sure. Too late for CPR. Too late for anything but the call.

He'd wanted to do one thing right.

Now he was a body at a crime scene, and whatever he'd

seen behind Home Port had died with him. Unless he'd left something behind we hadn't found yet. Not that we'd get the chance to search his place under the circumstances.

I turned into the marina lot and pulled into my usual spot. "Come on. I'm clearing your boat."

She blinked around like she'd forgotten where we were. "I don't need—"

"Humor me. The guy we were supposed to talk to turned up dead. I'm not leaving you alone in a place that could be compromised without making damn sure it's safe."

She opened her mouth like she was going to argue, then stopped. Some of the fight bled out of her shoulders. "Fine."

I walked the dock ahead of her, habit making me sweep the surrounding boats with my eyes for anything out of place. Nothing but the usual evidence of life—lines creaking, flags flapping, someone hammering on a distant deck. No watchers. No shadows diving out of sight. Only a bright island afternoon, with no one any the wiser that a few miles away, a man had died.

She unlocked the cabin door of the *Second Wind* and stepped back to let me go in first.

I moved through the space methodically, checking the tiny head, the closet, the storage compartments where someone could've tucked themselves if they were really determined and really bendy. No signs of intrusion, no shifted shadows, or new smells. Nothing.

Satisfied, I stepped back out. "All clear."

"Good." She ducked around me to get inside, setting her bag down with more force than necessary. The neat ponytail had loosened, until curls escaped on either side of her face. My fingers itched to tuck them behind her ears.

Opening one of the galley cabinets, she retrieved a bottle of something amber and two short glasses. No ice. She poured, handed me one, and dropped onto the bench opposite the table like her strings had been cut.

I slid into the seat across from her. For a moment, we simply stayed there, the small space filled with the soft creak of the hull as she wrapped both hands around her glass. She stared into it like she could find answers in the reflection.

"You okay?" I asked.

Her laugh was short and humorless. "Define okay."

"Not in shock. Not about to pass out. Not planning to go find Carson and eviscerate him with pure rage alone. For starters."

She swallowed a mouthful of whiskey with only a slight tightening around her eyes. "I'm not in shock. And I'm not going to faint, because I've never fainted in my life, and I'm not planning to start now."

"And Carson?"

She tipped her head back against the wall and stared at the ceiling. "Can I reserve the right to eviscerate him later?"

The dry delivery had one corner of my mouth kicking up. "Always."

Silence settled again, heavier this time. The kind that buzzed with unsaid things.

"You did good out there, with Carson. You protected the scene; you were clear on the timeline. You kept him from rail-roading us into an interrogation room because his favorite suspect happened to be on the premises when a body turned up."

Her gaze cut to mine, sharp and incredulous. "I... did my job. My old job. Muscle memory."

"Sure," I said. "But it mattered. Having you there mattered." More than I'd realized it would.

She looked away, throat working. "You mean having

someone else there mattered. Someone whose name isn't synonymous with 'unsolved murder' in these parts."

She wasn't wrong, but that wasn't all of it.

"Yeah," I said quietly. "That too."

She swallowed more whiskey before setting the glass down with exaggerated care. "We found a dead man. A man who was supposed to help us find a missing woman. And the chief of police would rather we disappear than admit he should have been paying attention to either."

"That about sums it up."

Her lips trembled, barely. She pressed her lips together until it stopped.

The crash was coming in fast now. Color draining, shoulders sagging. I could see the fight between *hold it together* and *I can't do this anymore* happening right behind her eyes.

"Madden." I leaned forward, bracing my elbows on the table rather than reaching for her hands as I wanted. "Talk to me."

She shook her head once. "You don't want to hear what I have to say."

"I'm pretty sure I do."

Her laugh scraped out again, rougher this time. "What if it makes you hate me again?"

That hit me in the sternum. Because at some point I had stopped hating her. "I'm not really in the habit of hating people who help me find the truth. Even when they've been wrong about me before."

She flinched as if I'd struck her. "That's just it. I'm starting to realize exactly how often I've been wrong. And how many people paid the price for it."

Ah, here we were.

I sat back, gave her space, but kept my voice steady. "California."

Her fingers tightened around her glass. The amber liquid rippled. "Yeah. California."

"You wanna talk about it?"

"Honestly, no."

"Then why are we having this conversation?"

She stared at me across the table, eyes dark and tired and raw. "Because you keep showing up. You keep doing what I always told myself I did—chasing the truth, no matter how ugly it is. And because I saw yet another person die around the margins of a case where the system should've protected them. And if I don't say this out loud, it's going to eat me alive."

I nodded once, because that was a sentiment I understood. "Okay."

"In California," she started, fingers tracing the condensation ring on the table, "I had a case. Big one. High profile. The kind of thing careers are built on—or wrecked by."

She rolled her shoulders like she could shrug off the memory. It clearly didn't work. "I was a wet-behind-the-ears newbie and definitely not lead on the case. I was the grunt. But a week before trial, the senior lead had a stroke. Rather than risk requesting a continuance so additional counsel could be brought up to speed, the DA let me take it on. I bulldogged it. Got the conviction. A monster got put away, and we'd made the world safer."

She took another sip of the whiskey. "Fast forward to a few months ago. A civil rights attorney decided to examine old convictions handled by the lead detective on that case. She found... inconsistencies. Patterns. Witnesses who recanted under oath, saying they'd been pressured to identify a suspect they weren't sure of. Alternate leads that were never followed. Reports that never made it into the file."

The muscle in my jaw ticked as I worked out the implications. "He buried exculpatory evidence."

"Yeah." Her mouth twisted. "He buried a lot of things. Including a tip, in my case, suggesting someone else had been seen near the victim's building that night. Someone whose M.O. matched another unsolved assault three neighborhoods over. A tip he never told me about. One that never made it into my file."

My stomach went cold. I'd seen this movie. Too many times. Bad cops with tunnel vision. Or worse.

"The conviction was overturned?" I asked, even though I knew the answer.

"Overturned and vacated," she said. "The man I'd prosecuted walked out of prison. He'd lost five years of his life. His marriage. His job. His health. Because I believed the wrong person. Because I believed the system was infallible if I just worked hard enough inside it."

She swallowed hard, eyes shining. "I stood in court and listened to that judgment read. I watched him look at me. He didn't yell. He didn't curse. He didn't even ask for an apology. He just... looked. Like I was one more cop who'd ruined his life and was going to go home afterward and sleep like a damned baby."

"You didn't," I said quietly.

"No." Her laugh was wrecked. "I didn't."

She scrubbed a hand over her face, careful not to smear her eyeliner. "The media had a field day," she said. "Poster child for prosecutorial overreach. How many other cases did she screw up? How many innocent men are behind bars because of her? It didn't matter that I'd prosecuted in good faith. That I didn't know about the withheld tip. In their eyes, I was part of the problem."

"And in your eyes?"

She stared at me, and this time there was no shield at all. Merely naked, exhausted honesty. "In my eyes, I was the problem. Because I didn't ask enough questions. I didn't push hard enough on the gaps in the detective's story. I wanted the narrative to be clean and righteous, so I didn't dig into the gray. I bulldogged that case because I trusted the badge and the system behind it. Because I needed justice to be something I could hold up and say, 'See, Gwen? This is what should have happened for you.'"

That was the bone-deep root.

She sucked in a breath. "So when you ask why I believed Carson back then, that's why. Because my whole world was built around authority being right. Because this island needed a villain, and he handed them one. You." She flinched at the word. "And I needed to believe the adults in charge weren't going to fail us. Because if they did, if justice could be that wrong, then Gwen was gone and nobody paid for it. And I couldn't—" Her voice broke. "I couldn't live with that."

The confession hung between us, raw and bleeding.

I sat with it. With her. She hadn't been obligated to confess any of this. Not to me. Maybe especially not to me. But here we were, with her sitting broken open, with her mistakes on the table between us.

"You know what the shitty part is?" I said after a minute. "I get it."

She blinked. "You... do?"

"I was never going to like being on the receiving end of that kind of tunnel vision," I said. "But I understand the part where you needed the story to make sense. Where you needed there to be a monster whose face you could put on the bad thing, so it didn't all feel... pointless."

She laughed weakly. "That doesn't excuse it."

"No," I agreed. "It doesn't. But it explains it. There's a difference."

She picked up her glass again and set it back down without drinking. Her hand shook.

"It's happening again," she whispered. "That same blind spot. That same willingness to take the easy out instead of living with uncertainty. Carson decides Priya 'just went home,' and everyone breathes a sigh of relief. No more missing posters. No more press conferences. No more having to look at the fact that a girl is gone and nobody knows where. And I can't help wondering if he did the same thing thirteen years ago. With you. If he had other leads and he simply... didn't bother."

I thought of Willie, cold on the bathroom floor. I thought of Carson's face at the apartment, wary and irritated in equal measure. Not grieving. Not shaken.

"Would you be surprised?" I asked.

"No. And that might be the worst part." Her shoulders hunched, as if she were bracing against a blow I didn't intend to deliver. "I'm sorry," she blurted suddenly. "Not just in that vague 'sorry I believed the wrong thing' way. I'm sorry I never questioned the story. I'm sorry I didn't look at you and think, 'Wait. This is a kid I know. A boy my cousin trusted. Maybe I should examine this a little more critically instead of accepting the narrative that makes my fear easier to carry.'"

Her breath shuddered out. "I'm sorry I failed you. And Gwen. And all the people I put away without seeing the ways the system could crush them."

The words hit harder than I expected. Something in my chest that had been calcified for years gave a reluctant crack.

So many people would've taken this and buried it in the name of retaining their sense of self identity. But not Madden. No, she dug all the way down to the ugly truth of it because it was important to her that she do better.

I respected the hell out of her for that.

The system would've been a lot better off if more people were brave enough to do that self-examination.

I exhaled slowly. "You can't change what you did at seventeen or twenty-eight. Or any of it. You can only change what you do now."

She looked up at me, eyes wet. "And what am I doing now, Rios? Besides chasing ghosts and harassing a police chief who'd rather I vanish in a puff of smoke than keep asking questions?"

"You're doing the thing the system failed to do," I said. "You're looking at the gray. You're refusing to take the easy answer when it doesn't fit the evidence. You're putting your faith somewhere better than a badge or a title."

"Where?" she asked, almost desperate.

"In the work," I said simply. "In the questions. In the people who've proven they'll bleed for the truth."

Her gaze searched mine. "You mean you."

Yeah, and that meant more to me than I was ready to analyze, so I pressed on. "And you."

The silence that followed was dense and charged.

She broke eye contact first, scrubbing at one cheek with the heel of her hand in a gesture that was more frustrated than vain. "I don't know how to not be angry. At them. At myself. At...everything."

"Yeah," I said. "I'm familiar with that particular flavor of rage."

She huffed out something that might have been a laugh if you tilted your head and squinted. "How do you live with it?"

I studied the proud line of her spine and the tension around her mouth. The familiar exhaustion in her eyes.

"Badly sometimes," I said. "Better when I'm not doing it alone."

She looked back down at her empty glass. "I don't really know how to not do things alone."

"I noticed," I said dryly.

Her lips twitched.

I hesitated for half a second before deciding to hell with it. "Can I ask you a weird question?"

"Compared to what we've already covered?" she asked. "Shoot."

"When's the last time somebody gave you a hug?"

Her head jerked up. "What?"

"Hug," I repeated. "You know. Arms. Squeezing. Human contact that isn't hostile cross-examination."

She blinked. "I—why does that matter?"

"Because you found a dead man today, went toe-to-toe with a hostile cop, and confessed one of your biggest professional failures to the guy your hometown wanted to lynch, and you're sitting here holding yourself together with sheer spite. That's impressive. It's also exhausting. And sometimes the thing you need isn't another drink or another argument. It's somebody else holding some of the weight for a minute."

Her throat worked. "I'm fine."

"Bullshit."

Her eyes flashed. "I don't need—"

"I didn't say you needed it," I cut in. "I asked when the last time you had it was."

She opened her mouth. Closed it. Looked away. "I don't remember." Her answer was so quiet I almost didn't hear it.

Something in my chest twisted. "Can I give you one?"

Her head snapped back toward me. "Why?"

"Because you look like you're about to shatter. And because I'm very good at this particular form of first aid."

She let out a strangled sound that might've been half laugh, half sob. "You're serious."

"Deadly. If you say no, I'll respect that. But the offer stands."

She stared at me for a long beat, every line of her body broadcasting resistance. Independence. The fierce, lonely pride of somebody who'd learned early that needing anything from anyone was dangerous.

Slowly, she stood.

My pulse kicked up. I rose too, giving her plenty of space. Letting her close the distance if she chose.

For a second, she only stood there, fists clenched at her sides, breathing like she was about to go into a courtroom instead of a hug. "This is stupid."

"Probably," I agreed. "A lot of the best things are."

Her mouth quirked despite herself. With visible effort, she took one step forward. Then another. Until she was close enough that I could feel the heat of her. She hesitated again. I kept my arms loose at my sides, open invitation instead of demand.

"Just... don't say anything," she said.

"Scout's honor."

She made a soft, annoyed noise before she stepped into my space and pressed herself against my chest, arms coming up in a quick, almost defensive wrap around my ribs.

I closed my arms around her. Not too tight. Just enough.

She was stiff as a board for a full five seconds. Then ten. At last, with a quiet, shaky exhale, something in her gave way. Her shoulders dropped. Her forehead tucked under my jaw. Her fingers uncurling from fists to flat palms against my back.

That subtle surrender hit harder than any punch I'd ever taken.

I felt it like a tectonic shift—that moment when someone who doesn't trust easily puts themselves, literally, in your arms. A weight settling against me that wasn't physical so much as... soul-deep.

I couldn't quite stop myself from tucking my cheek against her hair. "Got you."

She didn't answer. But her grip tightened.

We stood like that for a long moment. The boat creaked. The world continued outside—waves and wind and distant engines—but inside the *Second Wind,* it was only the two of us and the sound of our breathing.

Eventually, her arms loosened. She stepped back, blinking fast, jaw clenched like she could force every emotion back into its box by sheer will.

"Thank you," she said, voice rough.

"Any time," I said.

She huffed. "Don't say that if you don't mean it. I might take you up on it."

"Good," I said. "I'd rather you take me up on a hug than on, say, beating the shit out of Carson in a grocery store aisle."

Her laugh came out more genuine that time. "Tempting."

"Extremely. But I like you out of jail."

Her eyes searched my face again, softer now. "I'm still mad at myself," she said. "And at the system. And at Carson."

"Good," I said. "Stay mad. Just don't let it blind you again."

She nodded, slow. "I'm trying."

"I can tell."

I stepped back, giving her space again. Letting the air cool between us, even though every cell in my body was suddenly, acutely aware of her. The way she smelled—soap and salt and something warm and feminine. The way she'd felt, solid and small at the same time, pressed against me.

Dangerous, that awareness.

I cleared my throat. "All right," I said. "You need a nap and a snack, and we need reinforcements."

Her mouth quirked in amusement. "Do I?"

"You do. Find that snack and have a lie down. I'll get

everyone together and figure out when and where we're meeting."

"You're very bossy for a man with no authority," she muttered.

"Comes from being right a lot," I said.

She rolled her eyes, but there was no real heat in it. "Fine. I'll try to sleep. Call me when you've got details."

"I will."

I headed for the door, pausing there with my hand on the frame.

"Madden?"

"Yeah?"

"You didn't fail me today," I said. "Whatever else you think you've done in the past—you didn't fail me today."

Something flickered over her face. "Don't you dare start making it easy to like you, Carrera," she said softly. "I don't have the bandwidth for that."

I flashed a quick grin. "Too late." And stepped out onto the dock before I could see her reaction.

EIGHTEEN

MADDEN

The drive to Sutter House took less than fifteen minutes, but my nerves managed to age a decade with every mile. Rios didn't say much, and strangely, that helped. The silence between us wasn't hostile anymore. It was... bearable. Companionable, even—if I didn't look at it too hard.

But that didn't help the swooping sensation in my stomach when he pulled up in front of Sutter House. I'd been here before, years ago, for one function or another, back when Willa's grandparents had effectively run the island. But I'd never been here as part of the group. Rios, Sawyer, Ford, and Jace had all been older. Willa and Gabi were younger. I'd gone to school with all of them, grown up on the fringes of their orbit. Always Gwen's cousin. Always the one who preferred rules and routines to bonfires. Never quite inside the circle. Never hated exactly, but not beloved either. I hadn't fit. Not with them. Honestly, not really with anyone.

Now I was walking into what amounted to their inner sanctum beside the man they all knew I'd once maligned.

Fantastic.

Rios cut the engine and looked at me. "Ready?"

"No, but I'm good at faking it." I blurted it out before I could think better of it.

He huffed something like a laugh, and the warmth of it skated over my skin like a touch, dragging my brain back to what it had been like to be wrapped up in him. A hug. A completely platonic friend sort of thing to do. A gesture that had shaken me more than I knew how to admit, not just because of the inconvenient attraction I was struggling to deny, but because I simply wasn't accustomed to physical affection and support.

Which was probably a terribly sad commentary on my life overall.

Realizing he was now standing in front of the truck, one brow arched in expectation, I slid out and followed, adjusting the strap of my bag. Why had I even brought it? As if I was going to show up with a PowerPoint? I tried to match his unbothered stride as he headed for the side entrance.

Just before we reached the porch steps, his hand slid to the small of my back. Barely a touch. Just a warm anchor guiding me forward.

My breath stuttered. He didn't seem to notice he'd done it.

I absolutely did.

The kitchen door swung open before either of us reached it, Bree's voice barreling out ahead of her. "Finally! We were two seconds from—oh." She stopped when her gaze landed on me. Not hostile. Not warm. Just... taking my measure. "Hey, Madden."

"Hi," I managed.

A blur of fur streaked past her legs. Roy, tail whacking everything in reach. A second dog followed, gold to his black.

The pair of them bounded around us, wriggling with joy at seeing literally anyone. Roy barked once, then immediately shoved his entire head under Rios's hand for pets. The shepherd mix came for me.

I crouched to greet her. "Hi, sweetheart."

"That's Keeley," Bree said. "She loves everyone."

The dogs apparently had fewer reservations about me than the humans. Fair enough.

"She's adorable."

"And the love of Roy's life," Willa added from just inside.

Sawyer appeared behind her, looping his arms around her waist. "Pretty sure that's still you, Wren."

"Come on in, y'all," she invited.

With nowhere else to retreat, I trailed them all to the kitchen.

It buzzed with activity—pots simmering, cutting boards covered in vegetables, multiple conversations happening at once. Ford stood at the stove, stirring something fragrant and spicy, while a guy I didn't recognize chopped cilantro with knife skills that suggested he'd had a lot of practice. Gabi perched on a counter stool, sorting tortillas into neat stacks. The moment she spotted me, she moved to the fridge and began filling a glass with water.

She thrust it in my direction. "Drink. And sit. You look wrung out."

"I—" My brain stalled, trying to reconcile this no-nonsense doctor with the dreamy romantic who'd been one of Gwen's besties. "Thank you."

I took the glass more because refusing Gabi Carrera seemed like an act of hubris. As I settled at the long butcher-block island, she added a plate of sliced mango and some tortilla chips.

I blinked at the spread before glancing at Rios. "Is this a family trait?"

"What?"

"Ordering people to sit and eat."

"Damn right. It's a time-honored Carrera tradition to solve everything with food." Rios brushed past me to grab a beer from the open fridge. His arm grazed my shoulder—barely there, the most incidental contact imaginable—and yet a spark zipped straight down my spine.

I stared determinedly at the mango.

Bree dropped onto the stool opposite mine. "Okay. Tell us what the hell happened. The island gossip train is going wild, saying y'all walked in on a dead guy."

The guy I didn't know snickered. "Slow your roll, Bree, and give the woman a chance to actually do some of that eatin' before jumpin' to the punchline." His rolling drawl was all bayou as he turned his attention to me. "I'm Daniel LaRue, by the way. Gabi's other half."

"Um, hi. Madden Reilly." Though I guessed he already knew that. I wondered what Gabi might have said to him about me before they'd shown up for this confab. "And I don't mind getting into it, if that's how y'all want to do things."

I wasn't exactly clear on what we were here to do, but Rios obviously wanted to loop these people in. His people.

At least it would give me something to *do* other than sit here on my ass while the rest of them moved around the kitchen with the well-honed chaos of a family. My own family hadn't been anything like this, and I felt extra out of place not knowing my role here beyond that of outsider.

Rios's hand brushed my forearm as he plucked a slice of mango from the plate, and something fluttered again behind my ribs. "I got the timeline. You got the details?"

"Sure."

As the rest of them continued prepping food, we ran through it—from Willie's wee-hours text to finding him in the bathroom, unresponsive and showing lividity that told us he'd been gone too long for intervention. By the time we'd finished, the rest of the ingredients had gone into a pot on the stove, which smelled like spicy heaven.

Gabi winced. "Damn."

Ford muttered a curse under his breath. Sawyer shook his head.

"Overdose." My voice came out just a little ragged. "That's going to be the line."

Rios slouched against the counter, snatching another slice of mango. "It fits. At least on paper."

I slanted a look at him. "You don't believe it."

"I believe he used," he qualified. "We saw the paraphernalia. We saw him high yesterday. But he texted me in the middle of the night to set that meeting. People planning to help don't usually plan to die before breakfast."

My mouth twisted. "People planning not to die do it all the time."

"Overdose is the preliminary ruling," Daniel said. "I heard chatter from local LEOs over the radio driving in. As you said, they found paraphernalia, and with his record..." He trailed off, expression tightening.

Mild surprise flickered through me. "You're on the radio how, exactly?"

"I'm Coast Guard. Task force covering drug traffic up and down this stretch of coast. We work pretty close with local agencies. Even when they don't like it."

"Ah." What more was there to say than that?

"If they want to slap a bow on it, OD is easy," Ford said. "People will believe it."

The truth of that reality had me rising to Willie's defense.

"But he asked us to meet. Why would he reach out if he planned to get high enough to kill himself before we even got there? He was nervous, yes, but he wasn't self-destructive. He was scared. There's a difference."

"Could've meant to do a little to take the edge off and misjudged the purity," Daniel offered, though his tone suggested he didn't quite buy it.

Gabi crossed her arms, doctor mode activated. "Did you see needle marks?"

"One on the inside of his elbow," I admitted. "But with him? Could've been anything. I don't think it was an opioid OD. No pinpoint pupils. No foam. His coloring wasn't quite right for respiratory depression. And the timing doesn't line up with what he told Rios."

Daniel lifted his brows. "Damn. You've seen some things."

A humorless smile tugged at my mouth. "My job put me in contact with a lot of witnesses who used. A lot of defendants, too. And that doesn't touch the crime scene photos and police reports from other ODs. You learn patterns."

"And this didn't fit." Rios's voice was steady, but something colder lurked underneath. A steel thread I hadn't noticed in him before.

"No," I agreed. "It didn't. He wasn't weaving when we saw him last. He wasn't sweating or shaking. His attention was scattered but coherent. He looked... overwhelmed. Not intoxicated. Not fully. He was in enough of his right mind to be aware he wasn't in his right mind and needed to sober up before we talked further."

"Withdrawal?" Ford asked.

"Maybe," Gabi said. "But sudden death from withdrawal is rare. And his body position—face down, arm outstretched— doesn't scream collapse. It screams... interruption."

The room went quiet, weight settling over the conversation like humidity before a storm.

Sawyer broke it first. "Let's say it wasn't an accident. Why him? Why now?"

"Because he saw something," Bree said bluntly. "That's what you said, right? He saw someone getting assaulted behind Home Port. And now he's conveniently dead? Come on. That's not coincidence."

Daniel scrubbed a hand over his jaw. "Small islands breed a lot of rumors. But one thing I've learned working narcotics here —if someone needs to disappear, drugs make a great cover story. No one asks questions they don't want the answers to."

An icy shiver slipped beneath my skin. "He was trying to do something good. God, he was scared, and he still stepped up. And he ends up on a bathroom floor."

I felt more than saw movement beside me. Rios's hand slid briefly to my knee—steady pressure, warm, protective—before he pulled it back. He didn't look at me. Didn't acknowledge it.

I, on the other hand, forgot how breathing worked for a moment.

Willa spoke softly from her stool. "Could this be connected to Priya? If someone hurt her, maybe Willie saw something they didn't want repeated."

Ford set down his spoon with a quiet clank. "Hell of a coincidence if not."

"Or deliberate timing," Sawyer said. "Priya goes missing. Willie starts talking. Suddenly he's dead."

"But no signs of forced entry," Gabi said. "No struggle."

"Because whoever did it didn't need force," I murmured. "If you know someone's habits—their vulnerabilities—you just need opportunity."

Everyone looked at me.

I flushed under the attention but kept going. "If he was using, anyone with access to his supply could tamper with it. Or swap it. A hot shot—something laced with fentanyl—would do the job and leave just enough plausible deniability for a quick ruling."

Daniel nodded slowly. "We've seen that up and down the coast. Cheaper product, higher purity, inconsistent cuts. Most ODs are a combination of bad batches and lack of tolerance. Easy for an ME to shrug and say, 'he overdid it.' Especially if whoever's running the local show is nudging them to keep things simple."

"Especially if the chief is already leaning on them to call it quickly," Bree said. "Which Carson would absolutely do."

Another beat of heavy silence.

"So, now what?" Willa asked.

"They're going to call it accidental," Rios said. "Carson's already decided. Which means whatever Willie might have told us theoretically scared someone enough to shut him up."

"Objection. Speculation." The words were out of my mouth before I could think better of them.

Everyone stared at me.

Heat crawled up my throat. "Sorry. Habit."

Rios's dark eyes sparked with humor rather than insult. "No, keep going, Counselor. Follow the thread."

"We can't *be certain* that someone killed Willie specifically because of what he was planning to tell us. We'd like to think that the assault he witnessed was connected to Priya somehow. But it might not be. There's no evidence to that effect. No trail. If we assume that it *is* connected, we're no better than Carson, trying to make the situation fit the narrative we want to be true." And after what had happened in California, I was more wary than ever of getting it wrong.

Rios angled his head. "Fair point. The guy used illegal

drugs. No matter what he was going to tell us, that lifestyle puts him in contact with a lot of potentially bad people. He could've had an outstanding debt to his dealer or been killed for any number of other reasons. If he was killed at all rather than over-dosing himself by accident. But I don't think that changes the bottom line for how we approach this. If he was murdered, our looking around further in any way is liable to provoke a reaction from somewhere."

The dogs whined near the pantry door, picking up the tension rippling through the room.

I swallowed hard. "If that's true... if someone's willing to kill to keep a secret, you're right, we're going to have more push-back. Maybe worse." I caught myself and corrected. "Rios and I are. You all... shouldn't be on the front lines of this."

Surely that hadn't been Rios's intention in bringing them in on this?

"Madden's right," he confirmed. "We're the ones actually poking the hornet's nest. No reason to expand the threat to y'all."

Sawyer nodded. "We can't stop you two from digging. Wouldn't if we could. But we can insist you don't do it alone. You check in before you go anywhere shady. You don't meet scared dockhands or pissed-off bar staff without somebody knowing where you are and when you're supposed to be back."

"And if something smells like Carson might interfere," Ford added, "you bring it here before you bring it anywhere near him. We'll figure out the best way to handle it."

"Agreed," Daniel said. "I've got my own chain of command to deal with. Officially, I can't be involved in your missing-persons crusade. Unofficially..." He shrugged. "If I hear things that sound like they touch your case, I'll pass them along. Quietly. And if you run into issues with Carson, I might be able to help with an end run by going to my own superiors."

I wasn't sure what the Coast Guard could do with a local investigation, but maybe they had contacts at the federal level. Right now, that was getting way ahead of things.

Rios leaned forward, planting his forearms on the island. "We keep going. We keep looking. But we're not reckless about it."

His eyes flicked toward me, and something unspoken passed between us—agreement, responsibility, something heavier I wasn't ready to name.

I nodded once. "I'm not backing off."

"Didn't figure you would," Daniel said quietly. "Just...be smart about where you put yourself while you're chasing this."

I sat back a little, drawing slow breaths into my lungs. The kitchen was warm, loud, alive. It shouldn't have been threatening—but being surrounded by this many people watching me, expecting things from me, needing me to know things... it felt like sitting in front of half a dozen judges.

Then Rios shifted beside me. His hand drifted to the middle of my back—absent, instinctive, reassuring. A touch he might've given Gabi or Ford or Willa without thinking.

But I wasn't them.

My whole body went still.

He didn't seem to notice what he'd done, moving his hand away as he reached for a beer someone passed down the counter. Everyone else kept talking.

That touch burned me like a brand. And worse—I missed the warmth the second it was gone.

Get a grip, Reilly. Focus.

Heat pressed against the windows. Roy and Keeley flopped to the tile at our feet. The pozole simmered. The light slanted gold across the counters.

And even in this bright kitchen, surrounded by people who had every reason to distrust me, gooseflesh rose across my arms.

Because we all knew the truth now.

Willie had probably been silenced.

Which meant someone else was already watching—already moving.

And if Rios and I kept pushing, we might be next in their sights.

NINETEEN

RIOS

I didn't decide to go to her boat.

I woke with the haze of yesterday clinging to my brain—unprocessed adrenaline, a montage of Willie Sanders flipping like a slide show through my brain, the feel of Madden cautiously sagging into me, as if she'd never thought to have someone taking the weight, let alone trusted someone to actually do it.

By the time my brain kicked in, I was already showered, dressed, and had vaulted onto the deck of the *Second Wind*. The cabin was still dark, though sun peeked through the collection of masts around us. I considered turning around. A run would be more productive in burning off this edge. She wasn't my business. I wasn't her boyfriend, her brother, or her anything.

Except in this weird, convoluted way, we were temporary partners. And I couldn't shake how she'd said, "I don't remember," when I'd asked when she'd last been hugged.

I knocked.

There was a long enough delay in response that by the time the door cracked open, my brain had already conjured a few dozen horrific scenarios where someone had sneaked aboard in the night and taken her as Priya had been taken.

Instead, Madden squinted out at me, hair flattened on one side, an oversized T-shirt with Minnie Mouse offering a flirty wave hanging off one shoulder, and the barest edge of sleep shorts peeking from beneath the hem. Her feet were bare, revealing toes painted a shockingly vibrant hot pink, and her eyes were puffy in a way that suggested she'd actually slept.

"Rios? What are you doing here?"

I refused to acknowledge the way that sleep-roughened voice felt like fingers stroking over my skin or all the ways that absurd and surprising Minnie Mouse t-shirt was improbably sexy.

"Making sure you eat. Get dressed. We're going for breakfast."

Her brows drew together. "Good morning to you too."

"Morning." I leaned a shoulder against the frame and tried not to look like I was gaging how many steps it was from this door to the berth she'd stumbled out of in the back. "Come on. Before the bakery line wraps around the block." *And before I do something that confirms my current insanity.*

She just stared at me for a beat, like she was trying to decide if this was a hallucination or a kidnapping. "You don't have to—"

"Eat first," I cut in. "Argue with me later."

Something in her expression flickered. Not quite a smile. Not quite surrender. "Is this a Carrera thing?"

"Yes." Right now it was sure as hell a me thing.

"Bossing people into meals?"

"Also, yes."

She huffed a half laugh that did annoying things to my chest. "Five minutes."

The door shut in my face.

I took that as a win.

As I waited, my phone vibrated in my pocket. I fished it out and spotted a text from Overwatch. I hadn't put anyone in my contacts under that name and assumed Dax had added it himself. If the name hadn't given me a clue, the content certainly did.

OVERWATCH:

Dug through texts and emails. No evidence of harassment, threats, or pressure. If someone was leaning on her, they were careful—or it wasn't happening digitally.

So we were no closer to an answer than we had been before. My gut told me Priya wasn't being harassed. If she had been, there'd have been a sign *somewhere*. Instead, we'd found nothing. So either the girl had nerves of steel, or we were barking up the wrong tree. Which would imply her disappearance was about something else.

But what?

Madden came back faster than I would've guessed, hair pulled up into a twist that managed to appear both efficient and entirely casual, jeans hugging long legs, a soft gray tank under a light cardigan that wouldn't last ten minutes in the July humidity. Sunglasses perched on top of her head, purse over her shoulder.

"All right, Captain Bossy," she said. "Let's go."

"Captain was Gabi's rank fantasy for me, not mine," I muttered as we stepped onto the dock.

A corner of her mouth kicked up. "You let her call you that?"

"You try telling my sister no when she's got a head of steam."

"I'll pass."

I kept my mouth shut about what Dax had sent as we walked in step down the dock, toward the path that led to the boardwalk. Boats bobbed around us, halyards pinging against masts, and gulls wheeled overhead, already on the lookout for careless tourists with morsels to snatch. The news could wait until I'd plied her with coffee.

I had every intention of heading toward Panadería de la Isla. Best conchas this side of anywhere, and their coffee could revive the dead. But as we hit the main boardwalk, something else snagged my attention.

A shadow that didn't quite belong.

I clocked it in the reflection of a shop window first—a slim figure in a ball cap and sunglasses half a block back, moving when we moved. Could be nothing. Plenty of people walked the boardwalk in the morning. Nothing overtly off, but my hackles rose nonetheless.

We stepped past another storefront, and I caught the reflection again, this time in the side mirror of a scooter parked at the curb. Same guy. Same distance.

Again, could be nothing. He could be headed to the bakery same as us, and that still wouldn't be weird. But something in his body language pinged my radar.

Without thinking about it, I slid my hand to the small of Madden's back, steering her gently but firmly away from the bakery turn and down the side street instead.

She stiffened at the touch. "I thought we were—"

"Change of plans." I lowered my head like I was aiming for her ear—which, technically, I was—and let my mouth brush close enough to feel the faint shiver of her breath. "We've got a tail. Eyes forward."

She stilled under my hand.

"Are you serious?" she murmured.

"Yeah. Skinny guy, cap, sunglasses. Been behind us since just past the marina. Haven't seen his face yet."

"And you decided the appropriate response was to get all cozy?" Damn if that dry sarcasm didn't make me want to grin.

"If he thinks we're paying more attention to each other than our surroundings, he's less likely to spook." I let my arm slide more fully around her waist, pulling her into my side like this was a morning stroll with my girlfriend instead of evasive maneuvers. "Plus, it makes it easier for me to glance over your shoulder."

She hooked her own finger in my belt loop. "You're enjoying this."

"Professionally," I lied.

Because the truth was, for all the tension, for all the bad possibilities, I was dangerously aware of the way she fit against me. The heat of her body through that thin tank, the clean scent of her skin—soap and something citrus, like she'd somehow bottled a shower in the five minutes she'd been inside.

Focus, Carrera.

We walked another half block. I kept my head bent, ostensibly listening to something she'd said, actually using the angle to scan the reflections in car windows, shop glass, any shiny surface that would give me another look at the guy behind us.

He was still there. Same distance. Same lazy-not-lazy stride. He adjusted his hat with a quick, nervous motion.

"Okay," I murmured. "We're gonna make a right, then a left into the alley behind the surf shop. Narrow space. When we hit the corner, you keep going like normal. I'm going to peel off. When he passes, I'll handle the rest."

"Define 'handle.'"

"Not with bullets," I promised. "Probably."

"That's so reassuring."

We turned right. The bakery fell away behind us, the smells of sugar and yeast replaced by hot asphalt and cut grass. Another right would've taken us toward the residential streets. Instead, I cut left, tugging her gently into the narrower space between two buildings where the shade dropped the temperature by ten degrees, which unfortunately did nothing to minimize the rank damp of dumpsters.

"Ugh," she muttered. "You really know how to show a girl a good time."

"Stick with me, Counselor. Full service."

The alley jogged once, creating a blind corner. Perfect.

At the turn, I gave her a little push forward. "Keep going. Don't look back."

She shot me a glare but did as I said, continuing down the alley, shoulders squared like she belonged there.

I flattened myself against the wall, just out of immediate sightline, counting in my head.

One. Two. Three—

Footsteps scuffed on the concrete. Light. Hesitant.

As soon as the guy cleared the corner, I stepped out, grabbed a fistful of the front of his T-shirt, and slammed him—not hard, but not gently, either—against the brick.

He let out a yelp that cracked upward in pitch. Up close, he was even skinnier than he'd looked in the reflections, possibly mid-twenties, dark hair curling out from under the cap, stubble patchy along his jaw. His sunglasses hung half off his face.

"Hey, hey!" he protested, hands flying up.

"Morning," I said calmly. "Enjoying your stroll?"

"Man, what the—"

"Who are you, and why have you been on our ass since the marina?"

His gaze flicked past my shoulder, where Madden had

stopped and turned despite my instructions, because of course she had. When she saw that I wasn't about to put the guy through the wall, she stepped closer, but not close enough to crowd.

"I—I'm Miguel," he stammered. "Please, I'm not—I'm not trying to— It's not like that."

"Like what?" I tightened my grip just enough to make the brick scrape the back of his head in a way most people found motivational.

He swallowed hard. "Kelsey said you were asking questions. About the girl. About... what happened behind Home Port."

I felt Madden's attention sharpen beside me.

"What about it?" she asked.

Miguel looked back and forth between us, sweating now. Up close, I recognized him from behind the bar's swinging kitchen door—dishwasher, runner, whatever the hell needed doing. Always moving, never saying much.

"I know who it was," he blurted. "The woman. The one the drunk guy attacked. She... she wants to talk to you. But only you. No police."

"Why didn't she say anything when we were there?" Madden demanded. "We talked to everybody. Twice."

"She wasn't there." Miguel's throat bobbed. "She's been home since it happened. She's scared. She doesn't trust the police."

Well, I could hardly blame her there.

The pressure of my hand eased on his shirt, just a fraction. "Do you trust us?"

Miguel licked his lips. "You... you talked like you cared about the girl missing. About what happened. Kelsey said you were not with Carson. That you were looking because someone had to." His gaze darted to mine. "You were a cop before, yeah?"

"Something like that," I said.

"And you?" He looked at Madden. "She said you were a lawyer."

"I was a prosecutor in L.A.," she said evenly. "I'm not anymore. I'm not here in any official capacity. Neither is he."

Miguel hesitated. Then nodded, like he'd made a decision he wasn't entirely happy with but couldn't see another option.

"She told me if I could find you, to bring you," he said. "Today. While Carson is busy with... with the other thing." The way he said it told me word of Willie's death had already spread.

"Where?" I asked.

"I... I'll take you," he stammered.

I weighed the possibility that this could be some kind of setup. This kid I could take apart in my sleep. But he could have bigger buddies. Still, this didn't have the stink of a trap.

My grip finally dropped. "All right. You walk ahead. We'll follow."

His eyes widened. "You don't trust me?"

"Not yet," I said. "I make it a habit not to give my back to strangers until we've at least had breakfast."

Madden snorted softly. "Such high standards."

Miguel raised both hands in a halfhearted "have it your way" gesture and moved past us toward the street.

I fell into step on one side of him. Madden took the other. It felt... weirdly like a protective formation.

We didn't head back toward the boardwalk. Miguel cut across, taking a few side streets I knew well, leading away from the polished up, tourist-focused part of town and into the kind of neighborhood I'd grown up in—small, tired houses with peeling paint and kids' bikes left on side lawns, cars in various states of operability parked half on, half off the street. Heat clung to the asphalt, rising in waves. A lawn sprinkler ticked uselessly at a patch of crabgrass. Someone's radio played faint bachata from an open window.

Eventually, he stopped in front of a small, one-story duplex with a sagging porch and flowerpots riotous with color. The house was worn, but the flowers were thriving. Somebody here cared.

Miguel gestured toward the house. "Let me go first."

We hung back while he climbed the two steps and knocked a quick pattern on the frame. The door opened just a crack, chain still on. A woman's voice snapped something sharp in Spanish.

"*Es Miguel,*" he said quickly. "*Traje a los que preguntan. No a la policía, te lo juro.*"

The chain slid. The door opened wider.

The woman was small. Late twenties, maybe younger, black hair pulled back in a low knot, dark eyes wary as hell. Fading bruises shadowed the side of her jaw and at the edge of her collarbone where her T-shirt dipped. She wore cutoffs and a soft, faded tee. Her gaze flicked over us, cataloging every threat.

"This is them?" she asked Miguel.

"*Sí.* The lawyer and the... ex-cop," he said. "They say they just want to know what happened."

Her eyes narrowed. "You stay outside," she told him in Spanish. Then, to us, with an accent but careful diction: "You come in. But I do not talk to police. Ever. You understand?"

"We're not the police," Madden affirmed—in perfect Spanish—before I could answer. Her voice had gone into that low, even register I was starting to recognize—prosecutor mode without the sharp edges, all calm reassurance and control. "We don't work for them here. We're just trying to figure out what happened behind Home Port the other night and whether it has anything to do with the girl who's missing."

The woman studied Madden for a long second. Then stepped back. "Come."

The inside was small but neat—living room barely big enough for a couch and a coffee table, kitchen table shoved against a wall, a tiny shrine in one corner with a candle burned low in front of a saint's picture. The air smelled like cleaning products and the tail end of last night's beans.

"Sit." She pointed at the table. "I do not have much, but I can make coffee."

"You don't have to—" I started.

"I am not talking to strangers without coffee," she said flatly. Then, with a quick flick of her gaze to me: "Sit. You look like a man who drinks too much bad coffee. This is better."

Well. She wasn't wrong.

I sat. Madden did, too, perching on the edge of the chair like she was ready to bolt if this went sideways. Her eyes kept drifting to the bruises on Rosa's throat, the fingerprints ghosting along her upper arm. No question someone had attacked her.

"I'm Rios. This is Madden." I waited to see if she'd fill in the gaps.

"Rosa," she muttered, moving with efficiency, filling a small pot, measuring grounds. When the coffee was on the stove, she came to the table, sat opposite us, and folded her hands. "Okay. You ask."

Madden's gaze softened, even as her posture straightened almost imperceptibly. "Miguel said you were attacked outside Home Port?"

Rosa's hand fluttered toward the bruising before falling again. She nodded.

"Can you tell us what happened the night you were

attacked?" she asked. "In your own words. Whatever you remember."

Rosa blew out a breath, eyes sliding to the window for a second before coming back.

"I work late," she began. "You know. We close; we clean. That night, Nicole sends the bartender home early. It was not so busy. Mostly tourists too drunk to notice."

I flipped through my mental roster of Home Port employees we'd spoken to. Nicole was one of the night servers.

"What night was this?" I asked. "Three nights ago? Four?"

"Three nights before the girl disappeared," she said. "I remember because Nicole was talking about her. The scientists from the station. She likes them. Good tippers." A faint smile ghosted across her mouth. "I do not see this girl, but I hear about her."

"Okay," I said. "Go on."

"I take the trash out." Rosa's hands tightened briefly, knuckles whitening. "Kitchen is hot. Smells like... fried everything. I like to get air for a minute. I go out the back, to the alley. There is light, but only a little. I put the first bag in the big bin." She swallowed. "Then someone grabs me from behind."

Madden's fingers curled around the edge of the table. "How?" she asked softly. "Arm around your throat? Your waist?"

"Here." Rosa touched her own chest, right under the collarbone. "One arm across, like a bar. The other—" She clamped a hand over her mouth, demonstrating. "He pull me back, fast. I drop the other bag. I cannot scream. I smell beer and something... stronger. Like cheap cologne and sweat."

"Could you see anything?" I asked. "Clothes, height, build..."

"He is taller than me." Her mouth twisted. "But that is not

hard. Maybe your height," she added, flicking her gaze toward me. "Strong. Not like... big, big, but tight. He wears a hoodie with the hood up. Dark. Cap under it, I think. I see the brim when he move his head." She shuddered. "He tries to pull me between the dumpsters. Away from the door. Toward the back street."

"Did he say anything?" Madden asked. "Anything at all?"

Rosa's eyes turned distant. "He say..." She swallowed. "'Quiet now.' Or 'easy now.' Something like that. His voice is low. Not shouting. Like..." Her face pinched. "Like he has done this before."

My jaw clenched.

"What did you do?" Madden's voice stayed even, but I could hear the tremor under it. She knew the answer. She just needed Rosa to say it.

"What I learned to do when men think they can put hands on me." Some steel slid into her tone. "I stomp on his foot. Hard. I have boots. He makes a sound. His grip loosens. I twist, bite his arm." She mimed the motion, fast and practiced. "He swears. I cannot hear all the words. Accent is... not heavy, but not like yours. Somewhere between. He tries to grab again, but I am small. I drop. Knee him in the cojones."

"Do you know where you bit him? Which arm?" I was building a picture of prospective defensive wounds she'd inflicted on her attacker.

Rosa frowned and laid a hand on her forearm. "Here. Opposite me, so... right arm."

"What happened after you kneed him in the balls?"

With a shrug that was probably meant to be casual, she continued. "I get free. I run."

"Before you ran, did you notice any other places you might have hurt him? Y'all were fighting in tight corners. Near the back wall of the building?"

"He crash into wall when he let me go. I didn't stay to see how."

Fair enough. Either way, this more or less matched what Willie had reported. "Where did you run when you got free?"

"Away. I get away, and I call back saying I was sick."

"You didn't feel comfortable reporting to the police?" Madden asked.

"They make trouble. A report mean questions. Maybe they look in the kitchen at the workers. Ask about papers." Her gaze cooled. "I do not have the papers they like."

Undocumented. Which added a whole other layer to this mess.

"So you came home," I confirmed.

"Yes." Rosa's mouth flattened. "I had bruises. I do not go back for a few days. I tell them I am hurt. Which is also true. Miguel, he come to check on me. Saw the bruises and got angry. He wanted to go fight someone. But who? A shadow? A voice?"

"And you decided to talk to us," I said. "Why?"

"Because the girl is missing," she said simply. "And Miguel says you care. The police do not. They say she go home. I do not think that is true. I know what it is when someone wants to disappear on purpose. I have seen women run." Her fingers worried at the hem of her shirt. "She did not run. She was taken. Like someone tried to take me."

Silence fell for a beat, heavy and thick.

Madden pulled up a photo on her phone—the one Astrid had given us of Priya, laughing near a marsh platform. She pushed it gently across the table.

"Have you seen her?" she asked. "Anywhere? At Home Port? On the street?"

Rosa studied the picture. "Not in Home Port. I keep to the kitchen. But..." Her eyes narrowed. "Maybe near here. Once or twice. Walking this way. I do not know her, but she looks... familiar. Where does she live?"

"A couple blocks over," I said. "On Marshview."

"Then yes. I have seen her," Rosa said. "From behind. Ponytail. Backpack. We do not... talk. I see her and think she is just another student. There are many."

Madden's gaze met mine over the table.

Ponytail. Backpack. Long, dark hair. Brown skin. About the same height. About the same build.

The image of the ferry security footage flashed in my mind —grainy, distant, a girl with dark hair and a backpack boarding. The authorities had taken it as gospel that it was Priya.

But from behind...

Madden sat back, fingers going still against the photo. I could see it hitting her, too. The new angle. The new, awful possibility.

"What if he had the wrong woman?"

TWENTY

MADDEN

"What if he had the wrong woman?"

The question landed in the cramped kitchen like a door slamming. For a beat, even the coffee pot seemed to hush, the soft burble of it suddenly too loud and too intimate, the sound of normal life intruding on a conversation about dark things that shouldn't exist in a place with fresh flowers outside the window.

Rosa's face stilled. Guarded.

Rios didn't move at all, but tension came off him in a wave —a sort of heat that lived in the jaw and the hands.

I hated myself for speaking the question aloud. Not because it wasn't possible, but because saying it made the world tilt. Including every assumption we'd made in following Priya's trail.

Rosa glanced toward the window, as if checking whether the street had changed while we'd been inside. When her gaze came back to me, it had sharpened into something hard and bright. "You think she was taken because of me."

"No." The word came out too fast. Too emphatic. Like I could shove the idea away by force. I forced myself to breathe. "No. I think she may have been taken because of... the conditions. From behind, in the dark, with a hoodie and a hat and someone who doesn't care enough to learn a name—"

Rosa's hands curled on the edge of the table. "It is still because of me."

Rios's chair scraped back half an inch. "No," he insisted, voice low. "It's because of him."

Rosa's eyes flicked to him, something like relief flashing there before it got crushed back down under survival instincts.

I swallowed. My throat tightened, as if my body was trying to reject the air.

"Rosa," I said carefully, "the reason this matters isn't blame. It's scope."

She frowned slightly.

"If Priya was a mistake," I continued, "then she was taken by someone who had a target in mind. A plan." Which meant we needed to determine whether the target was Rosa specifically or simply someone like her. The answer would change the entire trajectory of this investigation.

I forced my voice to steady. "We need to ask you some direct questions. And you can tell us to go to hell at any point."

The weight of Rios's gaze was almost palpable, but he didn't interrupt, which I took as tacit permission to continue with my line of questioning.

Rosa didn't smile. "Ask."

"Has anyone ever threatened you?" I asked. "Outside of work—on the street, near your home, on your way somewhere—anyone ever told you to watch yourself, to keep quiet, to stop walking a certain route?"

Rosa shook her head. "No."

"Have you ever had someone try to get you alone before?" I

asked. "Not like what happened behind the bar—maybe someone offering you a ride, someone waiting near your door, someone you noticed more than once?"

Her mouth tightened. "Men look. Men speak. I ignore."

"And have you ignored anyone recently who didn't like being ignored?" I pressed.

Rosa's eyes flashed, irritation crossing her face. "I ignore all men. It saves time."

Rios made a sound that might've been a laugh in a different universe. It wasn't here.

I nodded once. "Fair. But I need to know if there's anyone who might have fixated on you."

Rosa's gaze slid away for a second. Back to the window. Back to me.

"There is a man," she said slowly, like each word had to pass through a filter of risk. "I see him sometimes."

"Where?" Rios asked immediately.

"On the street. Near the marina. Sometimes near the market." She hesitated. "Once, maybe twice, near my building."

My pulse kicked.

"Not at Home Port?" I asked.

Rosa shook her head. "No. I do not work out front. Customers do not see me. I do not see him come inside."

That mattered. A lot.

"Describe him," Rios said.

Rosa stared at the table. "Older. Not old. Maybe... late thirties? Forty. Hair short. Always clean. He wears nice shoes. Like he is not from here."

Not from here.

That phrase always mattered on islands.

"Facial hair or clean shaven?" Rios asked.

Rosa gestured to the center of her face. "Skinny beard here."

"A goatee?" he asked.

She nodded.

"Does he speak to you?" I asked.

"No, he smiles." Rosa's lip curled. "Like he knows something I don't."

Rios leaned forward, forearms on the table, posture controlled but coiled. "Did you see him the night you were attacked?"

Rosa shut her eyes briefly. "I do not know. It was dark. He came from behind."

"Okay." I kept my tone even. "That's something, but it doesn't mean it's him."

"It could be anyone." Rosa's voice was tight. "That is the point. Anyone can watch you. Anyone can follow you. And no one notices."

The truth of that ached like a bruise.

"What about your life here?" I asked softly. "Do you have family on the island? A roommate?"

Rosa's mouth flattened. "No family. I live alone."

"Friends who check on you?" I asked.

Her gaze lifted, direct and unflinching. "Friends are dangerous."

I nodded like I understood, because I did.

Friends asked questions. Friends noticed absences. Friends created ties that could be pulled. And for certain groups, that posed a potential threat. Or at least leverage.

"All right," I said. "Let me ask the question another way. If you didn't show up to work for a week... would anyone report you missing?"

A beat.

Rosa looked down at her hands again. Her fingers tightened. "No," she said simply. "They would say I left."

My chest went tight.

Rios's hand flexed where it lay on the edge of the table.

"Okay," I whispered, more to myself than anyone.

This likely wasn't about Rosa personally but about the place she occupied in society. Disenfranchised. On the fringes. A woman of color. Alone. Someone who likely wouldn't be missed. My gut screamed all of this spoke to scope.

Someone had potentially nabbed Priya, believing her to be Rosa. A mistake. But there'd been no body found. So maybe they believed she'd "do" for their purposes.

What was the likelihood that she'd been the only one?

Slim, to my mind.

I forced myself to keep going because I didn't have the luxury of spiraling. "Rosa, you mentioned you've heard things."

Her gaze snapped up. "I did not say that."

"You didn't," I amended. "But you didn't say you hadn't." It was a guess. A good one, based on how Rosa's expression sharpened with suspicion.

I watched her compute the quick mental math of whether talking to us was worse than staying silent.

Rios didn't push. He didn't interrupt the flow of the questioning I'd picked up. He sat solid and still and let the silence do what it did.

I had always been good at silence in court. Let the witness fill it. Let the jury feel it.

Rosa's throat worked. "There are rumors. Not... official. Just... women say things."

"What things?" I asked.

Rosa shook her head once, frustrated. "Be careful. Don't walk alone. Don't take the back streets. Don't go home late."

All standard warnings most women received at some point or another. But this seemed like more.

"Because of this?" Rios asked, voice quieter now.

Rosa hesitated before nodding once. "Because sometimes women go and do not come back."

My pulse stuttered. "How often?"

Rosa's eyes narrowed like the question itself was naïve. "How would I know? We do not put it on Facebook."

I swallowed. "Does anyone talk about where they go? If there's a place? A person? A car?"

Rosa shook her head. "Just... gone."

My stomach rolled.

This was exactly how predators thrived. Not through invisibility. Through disinterest. Through the world deciding a certain kind of missing person wasn't a problem worth solving.

Rios's voice cut in, controlled but edged. "Has anyone said it happened to someone they knew?"

Rosa nodded slowly. "One girl. Seasonal. She worked at the hotel. Not long. She stopped answering her phone. Her roommate said she left in the night."

"And no one checked?" I couldn't keep the anger out of my tone.

Rosa's gaze sharpened. "Checked with who? Police? They ask for papers. They ask for names. They ask if she used drugs. They ask if she had a boyfriend. They say maybe she went with him."

I pressed my lips together so hard they hurt.

"And another," Rosa said quietly. "A girl who cleaned houses. People said she return to her country."

"But she didn't," Rios said.

Rosa's shoulders lifted in a tiny shrug. "I do not know."

But her face said she did. Or at least, she believed she did.

I took a slow breath and forced myself back into control. Rage didn't help. Rage made promises.

"And these rumors," I asked, "do they stay within your community? Undocumented workers, seasonal people—"

Rosa's mouth tightened. "Not only."

My heartbeat ticked faster.

"Not only," I repeated.

Rosa's gaze flicked to the door, as if she expected someone to walk in because she'd said too much.

"Girls who come for summer. The students, or sometimes the tourists. People say they leave. But..." Her voice roughened. "Some girls do not leave."

My scalp prickled.

Priya.

Not the first. Just the one who didn't fit the easy story because someone got careless and made a mistake.

I held Rosa's gaze. "Is there anything else you've heard? Anything that comes up more than once?"

Rosa hesitated. "They say it happens to women who are alone."

Rios's jaw clenched.

"Alone." I echoed, the word tasting like rot.

Rosa looked down again, fingers twisting in her shirt hem the way someone did when they were trying not to cry.

"Rosa," I said gently, "you did the right thing telling us any of this."

Her laugh was sharp and bitter. "The right thing is expensive."

I felt that settle into my bones, because she was right.

"I know," I said softly.

Rios pushed back from the table, not abruptly but decisively, like he had to move or he'd break something. He paced two steps in the tiny kitchen, then stopped, hands on his hips, staring at nothing.

His restraint was almost worse than anger.

Rosa watched him with wary eyes. "What?"

Rios turned back to her, expression controlled. "What I'm

hearing is that even if we find the right questions, we have nowhere to take the answers without the risk of getting you hurt."

Rosa didn't answer. Because the silence was the answer.

I stood slowly, forcing my body to obey me. "We can't promise you anything, but we can promise we'll keep looking. We won't forget this."

Rosa's eyes met mine, and for the first time there was something like emotion there—something that wanted to believe. "People forget." The words weren't unkind. Merely a statement of fact.

"Not this time." I meant it enough to scare myself.

Rios stepped closer to the table, lowering his voice. "If you hear anything else—anything—don't tell Miguel to follow us again."

Miguel's name made Rosa glance toward the door.

"Tell him to leave word with Kelsey," Rios continued. "Or have her call—" He caught himself. He didn't want her to have our numbers. A number could be found. Traced. Used. "No. Just... tell Kelsey to find me. At the marina. Quiet."

Rosa nodded once.

I hesitated, then added, "And if you feel unsafe—if you see that man again, the one with the nice shoes—tell Kelsey. Tell Miguel. Tell someone."

Rosa's mouth twisted. "And do what? Stay inside forever?"

I didn't have an answer that wasn't insulting, so I didn't give one. "Just... don't be alone if you can help it."

Rosa's eyes hardened. "Women are always alone."

The words followed us out the door like a curse.

Outside, the sun hit me full in the face, bright and uncaring. The neighborhood looked exactly as it had when we arrived—quiet, lived-in, with small signs of pride tucked into worn structures. Hanging baskets, a painted mailbox, a child's chalk drawing on the sidewalk.

Normal.

That normality felt obscene.

We walked for a block without speaking.

"We're still getting breakfast," Rios announced.

It took me a beat to understand what he meant.

"What?" I asked stupidly.

He glanced at me, expression unreadable. "I promised you breakfast."

The words were simple. The intent wasn't. He was giving us an action because otherwise we'd stand in the street and let the fear eat us alive.

"I'm not hungry." How could I possibly think of food with all the implications swirling in my head?

"Yeah, you are."

I huffed a breath that might've been a laugh if my throat wasn't tight. "You're insufferable."

"Carrera trait." As if to settle the matter, he cupped my elbow and angled us back toward the boardwalk, toward the tourist part of town that pretended nothing bad could happen under all that bright sunlight. As we walked, my mind kept snapping back to Rosa's answer.

No one would report her missing. They'd say she left. And if she left, no one had to look.

Something cold and hard settled behind my ribs. This wasn't only about Priya anymore.

It probably never had been.

TWENTY-ONE

RIOS

Madden unlocked the cabin of the *Second Wind* and stepped inside without a word, setting the paper bags on the counter like the motion itself was automatic. No commentary. No deflection. No attempt to make it lighter.

That worried me more than if she'd snapped.

I'd only been inside her boat twice before. Once, briefly. Once longer—after Willie—when everything had gone sideways and we'd ended up here because there was nowhere else quiet enough to sit with the aftermath. I hadn't paid much attention then. My focus had been on her breathing, the way she'd gone still when the adrenaline wore off, the careful distance she kept between herself and anything that might tip her into feeling too much.

This time, I absorbed the rest as I did a quick scan. Not because anything had changed. Because I had.

The boat was small and functional in the way borrowed things always were. Nothing extravagant. Nothing precious.

But there were choices layered into it—quiet ones, easy to miss if you weren't looking for them.

A plant near the window, angled deliberately toward the light. Not decorative. Alive. Maintained.

Books stacked beside the berth, not tossed there but arranged so the spines lined up clean. Not legal texts. Not work. I spied a thriller by Cope Shepherd, and some romance names my sisters loved. Things she'd read for herself.

A soft blanket was folded at the foot of the bed. The kind of blanket more about comforting textures than warmth. For some reason, that made me think she'd had little real softness in her life.

She hadn't been here long enough to redecorate. She hadn't had time to reinvent the space. And given she was borrowing the boat, she probably didn't intend to. But still she'd attempted to cozy the place up. To create a buffer. A space where the world couldn't reach her all at once.

It stood in stark contrast to my own situation—crashing on a boat that wasn't mine, living out of a duffel like I was still deployed, everything provisional, nothing rooted. I told myself it didn't matter. That it was temporary. That I didn't need more than that.

She'd told herself the same thing.

The boat didn't agree.

I closed the door behind us and stayed where I was for a beat, watching her the way I'd learned to do when someone was holding themselves together by will alone.

Instead of sitting, she leaned back against the counter, arms folded loosely, eyes unfocused—already somewhere else.

I recognized that look. The slow, dangerous inward turn of someone connecting dots they didn't want to see.

"Madden."

Nothing.

I unpacked the food without asking. Set the pastries out. Poured coffee into the mugs neatly stored behind a little railed shelf. I nudged a plate toward her. "Sit."

She gave me a look that might've been reflexive irritation if it hadn't been dulled around the edges. "I'm not—"

"Sit," I repeated, firmer this time.

She hesitated. Then complied, sliding onto the bench seat and drawing her knees up slightly, like she was trying to make herself smaller without meaning to.

That did something ugly to my chest.

I sat across from her and waited. Let her pick at the pastry. Let her take a sip of coffee. Her shoulders stayed tight, like she was holding herself together by will alone.

"Okay," I said finally. "Talk to me."

Her fingers stilled. "I am talking to you."

"No, you're spiraling quietly and hoping I don't notice." I leaned back just enough to keep from crowding her, even though every instinct I had wanted to close the distance. "Which isn't going to work."

She huffed a breath. "You don't have to babysit me."

"I know. I want to." Color me surprised.

That got her attention.

Her gaze lifted, sharp despite the exhaustion. "That's not—"

"Don't," I cut in. "Don't lawyer me. I'm not making an argument. I'm stating a fact."

Silence stretched between us, thick but not hostile.

She broke it. "I can't stop circling around what Rosa said."

"I figured."

"She's not the target," Madden said quietly. "Not specifically."

I nodded once. "No."

"She's a category."

That time, I didn't answer right away.

Instead, I cataloged what I'd missed before—how her stillness wasn't stiffness, how her reserve wasn't snobbery, how the control she carried wasn't distance but containment. She cared. Deeply. Enough that she had to keep a tight lid on it or it would drown her.

Madden winced. "I hate that you already know that, because it means you're ahead of me."

"I'm not. I'm just coming at it from a different angle."

She shook her head. "Priya doesn't fit the pattern."

"No."

"She was noticed," Madden said. "She had people looking for her immediately. She had resources. Family. A paper trail."

"And that makes her noisy," I said.

Her jaw clenched. "Which means if she was taken intentionally, she'd be a terrible choice."

"But if she was taken by mistake," I finished, "that changes the math."

She met my eyes. "It changes everything."

I leaned forward, forearms braced on the table. Controlled fury buzzed under my skin, waiting. "You believe there are others." She'd already implied as much when she'd put in the FOIA request.

She didn't hesitate. "I think there have to be."

That settled in my bones.

Madden shredded another pastry. "Rosa wouldn't have been reported missing. Neither would the hotel worker. Or the house cleaner. Or any of the women she mentioned. They disappear, and the story fills itself in. They went home. They left town. They made choices."

"And nobody looks past that," I said.

"Because looking costs something," she replied. "And the people who would have to pay don't think it's worth it."

She took a shaky breath. "If Priya was the oops... then she's only visible because someone fucked up."

I nodded slowly. "Which means whoever did this isn't operating on impulse."

"No, they're operating on risk assessment."

I studied her face—the way her eyes had gone distant, analytical, sharp-edged with fear she wasn't acknowledging out loud.

"You're thinking trafficking," I said.

Her gaze snapped back to mine. "Yeah. I am."

The word hung between us, ugly and heavy.

She began ticking points off on her fingers. "No body. No evidence of escalation. No ransom. No public spectacle. If they'd needed to get rid of her, she would've turned up. Somewhere."

"That's what's bothering you," I said.

"Yes."

I leaned back, rubbing a hand over my jaw. "I'm not going to tell you you're wrong."

She winced. "That's not comforting."

"It's honest. And honesty's all I've got right now."

She stared down at her coffee. "I haven't heard back about those FOIA requests. It didn't occur to me to ask about unidentified remains. I should follow up with that."

"You can," I said. "But you're probably not going to like what you get."

She looked up. "Why?"

"Because if you're right—if the targets are the women least likely to be missed—it's possible no one ever filed a report. No paper trail. No official disappearance. Just... absence."

The words landed hard.

Her hands curled around the mug, knuckles whitening.

"That means the system didn't fail. It worked exactly the way it was designed to."

I didn't argue. Because she was right.

"And it means that even if I get files back, they'll be incomplete. Or sanitized. Or empty."

I reached across the table and covered her hand with mine.

She stilled, but she didn't pull away.

"You're not wrong," I said quietly. "But that doesn't mean there's nothing to find."

She swallowed. "It means the people who know things are afraid."

"Yes."

"Because they're undocumented. Or using. Or tied to something they don't want dragged into the light."

"Yes."

"And because talking to police has historically made things worse, not better."

I held her gaze. "You're not wrong about that either."

Her shoulders sagged a fraction, like naming it cost her something. "Willie knew something, and he didn't feel safe sharing it at the docks. I don't think his putting off talking to us was entirely about being high. And Rosa—even telling us was a calculated risk on her part."

I squeezed her hand gently. "You did good back there."

She scoffed softly. "I asked questions. That's literally my job."

"You asked them carefully. That's not nothing."

Her eyes flicked up, searching my face.

"I thought you were reckless," I added. "When we first started this."

Her brows drew together. "You did?"

"Yeah," I said. "I thought you were smart and angry and used to bulldozing your way through things."

She snorted. "That's... not entirely inaccurate."

"But I was wrong about the dangerous part," I said. "You're not reckless. You're deliberate."

She stilled.

"You're measuring consequences," I continued. "You're choosing them. That's not someone chasing danger. That's someone deciding what they're willing to pay."

Her voice was barely above a whisper. "I don't know how else to do it."

"I know." And I did. Because I'd lived that way too.

Silence settled again, this one heavier but steadier.

Finally, she exhaled. "I don't know what the next step is."

"That's okay," I said. "We don't have to know yet."

She looked at me skeptically.

"We do need to know one thing," I added.

"What?"

"That you're not doing this alone."

Her mouth curved faintly, sad but real. "I wasn't planning to."

"Good," I said. "Because whether you like it or not—"

She raised a brow.

"—you're one of my people now."

The words were out before I'd fully examined them.

She blinked.

"That's not a legal term," she observed.

"Lucky for you," I replied. "It's not a negotiable one either."

She shook her head, but there was something like relief in her eyes.

I stood and moved around the table, tugging the blanket off the berth and draping it over her shoulders before she could object.

"Eat," I said. "Then we'll follow up on the FOIA stuff. And

we'll figure out how to hear from people who don't feel safe being heard."

"And if I'm right?" she asked quietly.

"Then we get smarter," I said. "And quieter."

She nodded.

And for the first time since we'd left Rosa's house, it seemed like the ground under our feet had stopped shifting.

We didn't have answers.

But we had the shape of the problem.

And that was enough to keep going.

TWENTY-TWO

MADDEN

The email arrived before my second cup of coffee.

From: **Barbara** **Channing**
<clerk@hatterwick...>

Subject: Response to Public Records Request

My stomach dropped.

Barbara Channing had been the town clerk since I was in middle school. She'd been at every council meeting, every town hall, every "we care" press conference after Gwen disappeared. Always composed, always efficient, always the gatekeeper of paper and permission.

The email was politely cold.

Thank you for your request.

Pursuant to applicable public records statutes...

Certain materials have been withheld or redacted...

Four attachments. Only four.

I clicked the first PDF, heart thudding like I could will it into being useful.

Black bars. So many of them it looked like someone had taken a Sharpie to my hope.

Names removed. Addresses removed. Dates blurred into vague ranges. "Ongoing investigation." "Pending review." "Referred to appropriate agency."

I scrolled faster, desperate for any scrap that wasn't sanitized.

There were references to "an incident," "a complainant," "a witness statement." Whole paragraphs where the only readable words were "the" and "and."

The second PDF was worse. A single-page memo explaining why additional records were exempt.

The third looked promising until I realized it wasn't even for the case I'd requested—an unrelated call log that technically fell under the same umbrella of "public safety documentation." A compliance trick. Give me something so they could say they'd responded.

The fourth was an itemized list of withheld documents, like a menu of everything I wasn't allowed to see.

Interview notes. Supplemental reports. Evidence logs.

All marked WITHHELD.

I sat very still.

The boat shifted gently under me, as if nothing in the world had changed. As if the air didn't suddenly feel thinner. As if a person could read "WITHHELD" a dozen times and not want to tear something apart with her teeth.

Rios had warned me yesterday. He'd said it with that maddening calm, like he'd seen this movie before and already knew the ending.

Don't get your hopes up.

I'd nodded like I was reasonable and experienced and not still—*still*—hoping with some part of me that the system would accidentally tell the truth if I asked the right way.

I stared at the screen until my eyes burned. Then I slammed the laptop shut hard enough that the whole boat seemed to flinch.

"Fuck you," I whispered to no one.

Not Barbara. Not even Carson.

The machine. The whole gleaming apparatus of procedure and policy and *we can't comment at this time* that existed to protect itself first, always.

Because this wasn't a delay. This wasn't bureaucracy.

This was a deliberate chokehold.

I could practically see the fingerprints on it.

Carson had been furious at the scene of Willie's death. Furious I'd challenged him. Furious Rios had challenged him. Furious we'd stood there like we had the right to ask questions.

And now he'd reminded me what power looked like on a small island.

It looked like four PDFs and a condescending smile.

My phone buzzed again—an incoming text—and for one absurd second, I thought it might be Rios. Checking in. Making sure I was eating. Making sure I wasn't spiraling quietly like he'd accused me of.

But it was just a bank notification.

The man himself was off to his sister's for family breakfast this morning, which he'd notified me of, even though he had no reason to. I wasn't his keeper. I didn't know exactly what I was.

My brain turned over what he'd said yesterday. *You're one of my people.*

What the hell did that make us? Friends? Partners? I sure as hell didn't know, and I didn't have any means of clarifying that mystery right now.

I set my phone down and pressed my palms to my eyes.

Okay. Fine. If the official channel was blocked, I needed an unofficial one.

A quiet one.

A human one.

I opened the laptop again—more carefully this time, like it might bite—and forwarded the email to a folder labeled FOIA / Hatterwick. Then I copied Barbara Channing's exact wording into a note, because I was not going to trust my memory when I inevitably decided to fight this later.

And I would fight it.

Just... not by charging headfirst into the island's one police department and handing Carson a target he could use against people like Rosa.

My fingers hovered over my contacts list.

Devon Washington.

If anyone understood what it looked like when people vanished without paperwork—when "missing" was a privilege granted by whether anyone considered you worth searching for —it was Devon.

He'd built his podcast, *Unaccounted*, around that exact premise. Shining a light on the cases of the marginalized. Proving they were not forgotten.

He was also three time zones away. Which meant it was early as hell in California.

Devon was an early riser, though. Had been since we met in college. The kind of person who did morning runs and made real breakfasts and somehow still answered crisis calls with his whole heart intact.

I hit call before I could chicken out.

He picked up on the second ring.

"Madden," he said, voice warm and alert. No grogginess. No irritation. "Okay, baby. You don't call me at ass o'clock unless something's wrong."

I exhaled, a tight laugh scraping out of my throat. "Hi."

"Nope," he said gently. "Not 'hi.' Talk."

I closed my eyes and leaned my forehead against the cool edge of the table. The boat rocked faintly beneath me, a reminder that the world kept moving whether systems worked or not.

"I hit a wall," I said. "A hard one."

Devon's modulated voice was steady. "Start at the beginning. What kind of wall?"

"FOIA. Local request around a missing person's case. Small jurisdiction. Everything that matters is redacted or withheld."

There was a beat of silence I knew for what it was—recognition.

"All right. And you're calling me because this isn't just one missing person, is it." He didn't pose it as a question.

"No," I admitted. "It's not."

"Okay," Devon repeated. "Slow down. Give me the outline. Not the names yet. The shape."

I drew a breath, organizing it the way I would've before a jury. Clean. Linear. No emotion unless it served the point.

"Small island," I began. "One town. One police department. A lot of people who pass through seasonally. Workers, tourists, students. One woman recently disappeared—she doesn't fit the profile of someone who just... leaves. And in the course of looking for her, I've stumbled onto something else."

"Something that doesn't live on paper," Devon concluded.

"Yes. And I'm worried that if I handle this wrong, someone's going to get hurt."

Because he knew me, Devon's tone shifted—still gentle, but sharper at the edges. Protective. "We are not getting the people who already have the least protection hurt because the system refuses to do its job."

"I know." Relief and frustration collided inside me. "That's why I'm calling you."

"All right," Devon said. "Tell me."

So I did, breaking it down with precision from beginning to end. "I think whoever took Priya meant to take someone else," I continued. "Someone like Rosa. Someone who wouldn't be reported missing, because the story would fill itself in. She left. She went home. She didn't want to be found."

"And you think that's the point," Devon said.

"Yes."

"And now you're asking yourself how many times that story has been used," he finished.

A chill ran through me. "Yes."

Devon exhaled slowly. "Okay. Then FOIA was never going to hand you the answer."

"I know," I said. "But it should have given me *something*. Now I need options that don't rely on Carson. Or local resources. Because there aren't any."

"Right," Devon said. "Tiny island. One town. Everybody knows everybody."

"Exactly."

"All right." He shifted into *Unaccounted* mode—the voice he used when he was telling a story that deserved respect.

"Then you build your own map. Not from what the system recorded. From what the system ignored."

I gripped the edge of the bench. "How?"

"First," Devon said, "you widen your sources. Missing persons databases."

"NamUs," I said automatically.

"NamUs, yes," he confirmed. "But also state-level databases. Some states have separate missing persons bulletins. And don't just search by name. Search by region, date ranges, age ranges. Look for 'last seen' near ferry terminals, marinas, tourist areas."

I scribbled notes fast, my pen scratching over paper.

"And don't assume people were ever entered," Devon added. "But you'll find some—the ones whose families had enough stability to report. Those become your anchor points."

"Okay," I said.

"Second," he continued, "archived news. Not big outlets. Local papers. Community newsletters. That kind of 'so-and-so hasn't been seen' blurb."

I frowned. "On an island like this, that's..."

"Exactly," Devon said. "It'll be small. But that's good. Because small data sets show patterns if you're patient. And you, my darling, are fabulous with patterns."

I swallowed. "What else?"

"Third," Devon said, "community networks. The underground ones. You already found one—Rosa."

My chest tightened. "I can't put those people at risk."

"You don't have to," Devon said. "You don't ask them for names on a recorded line. You ask for structure. Where do they share warnings? Who do they trust? What places do they avoid? What prompts them to change their routines?"

I stared at the plant by the window, leaves pointed like little spears. "Structure."

"Yes," Devon said. "Because structure tells you the predator's hunting ground without anyone having to expose themselves."

I wrote it down.

"And fourth," Devon added, "transportation and lodging."

My brow furrowed. "Lodging?"

"Hotels. Vacation rentals. Seasonal housing," Devon said. "People who come and go. Employees who rotate. Places where someone can disappear and the story becomes 'she went home.'"

I felt my pulse pick up. "And transportation."

"Yes," Devon said. "Your instinct is the ferry."

"I have a friend who can access ferry records quietly," I said. Willa would help if Rios asked. She'd probably help even if I did.

"Good," Devon said. "Now they don't conveniently keep some tab of women traveling alone. What they do keep is transaction logs. Ticket sales. Vehicle manifests if vehicles are involved. Time stamps. Payment methods. Sometimes plate numbers—depending on their security and whether they track for billing or capacity. And if they don't track plates, they still track cars as units. And units leaving should roughly match units arriving."

I sat up straighter. "So you look for anomalies."

"Exactly," Devon said. "One-way patterns. Cars arriving and never leaving. Return tickets purchased and never used. Clusters of one-way foot passengers on certain days. Cash purchases at weird hours. And—this matters—repeat vehicles. The same unit showing up in patterns that don't make sense for a local."

The moisture in my mouth evaporated. "That's..."

"That's how you build a map without asking people to bleed," Devon said quietly.

I swallowed hard. "And if I can get those logs..."

"Pull once," Devon warned. "Don't poke it repeatedly. One quiet request. One clean pull. Then you analyze offline. Somewhere no one's watching."

My hand shook slightly as I underlined it.

"Okay," I whispered.

"Fifth," Devon said, "digital footprints. Not fancy. Not hacking. The stuff people leave behind without realizing it."

"Like what?"

"Social media. Public posts. Tagged locations. 'Girls trip to Hatterwick!' Photos at the boardwalk. Then silence. And message boards—travel forums, seasonal worker groups, migrant community networks. Places where people warn each other."

My stomach twisted. "So... I post?"

"Carefully, as a person looking for information about missing loved ones," Devon said. "Or you post through a third party. Or you use *Unaccounted* as a signal boost later once you have enough to protect your sources."

Later.

When this was safer.

If it ever got safer.

I closed my eyes. "This is going to get ugly."

Devon's voice softened. "It already is, sweetheart. You're just looking at it directly now."

I swallowed past the pressure in my throat. "Rios says the same thing, just with more... growling."

Devon chuckled, warm and real. "I like him."

"You would," I muttered.

"I would," Devon agreed. "Because he's protective and angry and he's trying to do right by people a system chewed up. That's my favorite genre of man."

Despite myself, I laughed, and it cut through the fog.

Devon turned serious again. "Madden. You said the town clerk responded."

"Yes."

"Okay," Devon said. "Then you assume the police are watching your moves now. Which means you don't go knocking on doors. You don't message the clerk again. You don't create noise."

"I know."

"You do the quiet pulls," Devon said. "Ferry logs through your friend. NamUs and state databases from your laptop. Use a VPN. Archived local news. Public social posts. Then you connect dots."

"And I need to update Astrid." The words tasted bitter because it meant telling her we still didn't have her student.

"Yes," Devon said gently. "But you don't go to her with panic. You go with structure. With the shape. With what you can promise: that you're looking for the people no one looked for."

I wasn't sure I could wait that long to give her something. But still, I said, "Thank you," and meant it.

Devon's voice softened again, the friend behind the podcaster. "Anytime. And Maddie?"

He was the only one who'd ever used the diminutive.

"Yeah?"

"You're not crazy," he said. "You're not overreacting. This is what it looks like when people disappear in the gaps. The fact that you're seeing the gaps means your eyes are working."

I pressed my knuckles to my mouth, grounding myself in the pressure. "Okay."

"And," Devon added, a little lighter, "if you want, when this is over and you're not actively living inside a nightmare, I'm going to drag you on *Unaccounted* and let you talk about why systems fail. Because the world needs to hear it from someone who's been inside them."

I made a sound that was half laugh, half something sharper. "I'll think about it."

"That's my girl," Devon said.

We hung up, and the boat was quiet again—except now my silence had edges.

Tools.

Paths.

A way to move forward that didn't rely on Carson's permission.

I opened my laptop and started building my own map.

TWENTY-THREE

RIOS

By the time I pulled up to the rental Ford shared with Bree, it was evening but nowhere near dark. July on Hatterwick meant the day hung on like it had something to prove. The sun was still up, bright and stubborn, throwing hard light across the pavement and making heat shimmer over the road.

Evening should've meant I could stand down.

My brain didn't get the memo. Case mode was a bitch. Once it latched on, it didn't want to let go.

Ford swung the front door open before I even got halfway up the walk. "About time. We're starving."

Sawyer was already sprawled in the living room, boots off, like he'd decided the couch was his and the rest of the world could file a complaint. "We weren't sure if you'd make it."

I was torn between relief that I'd been able to and frustration that I *was* able to because the case had stalled out. "I wasn't gonna miss seeing you assholes."

I automatically scanned the room, clocking the absence of female energy. "Where are all your girls?"

Ford rocked back on his heels. "My bride to be is at the Brewhouse tonight, ostensibly to confer with Monty about a new beer but really to keep an eye on Ed and the Graybeards to make sure they don't get into too much trouble."

"It's the trouble that keeps them young," Sawyer insisted.

"Try telling her that. Anyway, Peyton took Keeley and is off with Mimi plotting world domination. Otherwise known as our wedding."

I snorted. "Are you sure they should be left unsupervised?"

Ford grinned. "Together they are a force of nature. Honestly? Bree's happy someone else is doing the planning because that's not her jam. She just wants to be married at the end."

"Let me just say elopement was pretty great," Sawyer opined.

Ford pointed at him. "For all that my moms helped you two elope, they have at least minimal expectations of us. There will be a proper wedding, even if it's small. I'm more focused on finding a house big enough for the three of us plus Keeley. This place is fine, but it's... tight."

"Tight like 'cozy' or tight like 'teenager will murder you in your sleep if she trips over the dog again'?" I asked.

Ford's grin turned into a grimace. "The second one. Although she doesn't have a leg to stand on considering she keeps sneaking Keeley into her bed. Hopefully, after tourist season is over. Nothing moves here until the island decides it's done making money off people who don't live here."

"Smart," Sawyer said. "Wait it out."

Ford pushed off the wall. "Beer?"

"Yes." Because just now it sounded like a lifeline and not a beverage.

He returned a minute later and started passing out bottles.

I arched a brow at the lack of label. "What are we drinking?"

"One of Monty's latest creations. They're testing some for the new bottled line."

Sawyer squinted at the bottle. "How's he supposed to know which ones we like?"

"Apparently the bottles are color coded. I can't remember shit, so you get what you get," Ford declared.

I took a long pull. Cold. Clean. Bitter at the end in a way that reminded me I was alive. "Bless Monty for being damned good at his job."

"I'll drink to that," Sawyer announced, holding up his bottle.

We tapped with a satisfying clink.

Ford dropped onto the armchair and looked between us. "Food?"

"Thai," Sawyer said immediately.

I blinked. "You just—"

"I know," he said, smug. "You both want Thai. Don't argue with me."

Ford laughed. "He's right. Thai it is."

We did the whole dance—what we wanted, who was ordering, the small negotiations that meant nobody had to make a decision alone. Ford grabbed his phone, put in the order, and then we settled in like this was what we'd always done.

Like life hadn't sunk its teeth into all of us at one point or another.

I tried to settle into the couch and let my shoulders drop. Tried to feel the cushion under me, the bottle in my hand, the familiar weight of my friends in the room.

Because I knew they'd note my distraction and ask sooner or later, I took the offensive, looking to Sawyer. "What's going on in your world?"

His mouth quirked. "Well," he said slowly, like he was about to announce he'd joined a cult or taken up interpretive dance, "looks like I get to get used to the pitter patter of little feet."

Ford and I both stared at him.

The words landed in my head like a grenade.

"Holy shit," Ford said at the same time I said, "Is Willa pregnant?"

Sawyer barked a laugh and shook his head. "She is not."

My lungs started working again.

"She's taking on a new foster dog," Sawyer went on, like he hadn't just casually spiked all our blood pressure. "I don't think either of us is quite ready for the human variety of pitter patter. And if we are, we can always borrow Peyton."

Ford made a noise that was half laugh, half wounded dad. "She's *fourteen*," he bemoaned. "My kid is a full-blown teenager."

"And a truly awesome kid," Sawyer said, no hesitation.

Ford's expression softened in a way that made my chest ache. "She really is."

I took another swallow of beer and let myself smile. "Hopefully, she'll get in a little less trouble than we did at that age."

Sawyer's brows lifted. "That's a low bar."

Ford pointed at me like I'd personally offended him. "She absolutely maxed out my capacity for handling trouble when she conducted a murder investigation last spring. She's toeing the line."

I huffed a laugh before I could stop it. "Still can't believe you let her out of the house after all that."

"I considered putting her in an ankle monitor. Bree insisted that was overkill," Ford grumped.

Sawyer's gaze slid to me, not pushing, just... there. "Speaking of investigations, dare we ask how the case is going?"

There it was.

I'd known it was coming. These were my people. They weren't going to pretend my life hadn't been eaten by something ugly.

"Slow." Anything but blunt honesty would be a lie. "We're pretty sure it's bigger than Priya."

Ford's posture shifted, a fraction more alert. Sawyer's expression sharpened, but his voice stayed calm. "What makes you think that?"

I gave them the bones of it—how it had come into focus, how the pieces had started to suggest something wider. Not the kind of details that would turn this into a briefing—because I needed the escape of just hanging with them. Just enough that they understood why my nerves were still humming under my skin.

Ford's jaw worked. "Fuck."

"Got it in one." I took another pull on my beer. "We had to go update Astrid today."

"How is she holding up?" Sawyer asked.

I swallowed. The beer didn't help with that particular burn. "Devastated. She finally got in touch with Priya's parents in India. They're flying back to the US as soon as they can."

Ford's eyes narrowed. "That'll light a fire under Carson's ass."

I almost laughed. It wouldn't have been humor. It would've been bitterness wearing a smile. "I'd like to think so, but I'm not holding my breath."

Sawyer's gaze held mine. "So now what?"

I tipped my head back against the couch for a second and stared at the ceiling like it could hold me up. "Now we try to find evidence of the pattern and hope it'll give us some new leads to follow. Madden's working on that."

Ford's eyes flicked, quick and not subtle. He didn't say it, but I could hear it anyway: Madden. Her name still carried history for me like salt carried in the air.

During the update with Astrid, she'd gone still as stone, absorbing her friend's grief, and I'd watched her do what she always did when she couldn't fix something—go quiet, go sharp, go inward. So I'd stopped by the *Second Wind* before I came over here tonight, both because I'd wanted to let her know I'd be out for a bit and to check on her. She'd already been elbow deep in online research and had waved me away. Once I'd have taken that as depersonalization. Now I knew better. It was a coping mechanism.

Control what you can. Don't drown.

And it was certainly safer than her going out there questioning anyone face to face.

Not that we'd had any leads on *who* to question in the past couple of days.

Finally, Ford observed, "You two seem to work pretty well together."

I looked at him. He wasn't accusing. He wasn't teasing. He was just... noticing. Like Ford did.

"Kinda didn't expect that," Sawyer admitted. His gaze stayed on me, steady. "Not after... well." He let the rest hang there without forcing me to pick it up.

I exhaled through my nose. "You mean after I hated her," I said flatly.

Ford winced, but I kept going because it was true and because I was tired of pretending the past was less sharp than it had been.

"You seem to have put it behind you," Sawyer said carefully.

I considered my words. "For all that this island tries to calcify people at their worst moments, we aren't the mistakes we made in the past."

Ford's expression softened, like he was relieved to hear me say it out loud.

"When she made that apology," I continued, "she wasn't just blowing smoke. She's done the work. Continues to do the work. That's more than most people do." I took another sip, letting the cold anchor me. "She really gives a damn. That goes a long way with me."

Sawyer nodded once. That was a sentiment he understood.

"And," I added, because truth was truth, "she's hella smart. Beyond all the bookish valedictorian shit we remember from high school. I've certainly worked with worse partners over the years."

I heard how that sounded the second it left my mouth—like I was placing her in a category I hadn't expected to exist. Like I was saying partner and meaning more than colleague.

That was... something I wasn't ready to unpack.

Ford and Sawyer both looked like they wanted to say something. Ford's mouth even opened.

The doorbell saved me.

Ford headed for the door, and I shifted on the couch, relief and irritation tangling together. I hated how much I needed rescuing from my own mouth lately.

Ford came back carrying bags that smelled like heat and spice and edible comfort. He set them on the coffee table like an offering.

We did the routine—pulling food out, passing containers, the casual choreography of people who'd done this a hundred times. I took a bite of something that made my eyes water in the best way, and for a minute my brain actually quieted, focusing on spice instead of bloodless patterns, and I shifted the conversation yet again, aiming for more normal.

"So, we taking bets on how long it is before Jace surfaces again?"

Sawyer let out a low whistle. "Oh, I'll take that action."

I pointed at him. "Of course you will. You live for chaos."

"I live for entertainment," Sawyer corrected. "Chaos is just a bonus."

Ford grinned.

And just like that, the conversation devolved into banter—ridiculous, familiar, easy—and it reminded me that no matter how ugly things got, no matter how hard the island tried to freeze people into the worst moments of their lives, I still had this.

These were my brothers.

And in a world that kept handing me reasons to feel alone, I was so fucking grateful for that.

TWENTY-FOUR

MADDEN

I had three tabs open for missing persons databases, two more for regional boards where people posted everything from "lost dog" to "my neighbor's cousin saw a UFO," and one spreadsheet that was rapidly becoming the only thing in my life that seemed like it obeyed any form of logic.

The spreadsheet was winning.

I copied the wording from my last post, tweaked two lines to fit the rules of this forum—no last names unless public record, no personal contact info, no "call me," only "message me here"—and hit submit.

The page refreshed. My post dropped into the thread like a stone into a lake. No splash. Just a quiet, stubborn presence.

I stared at it for a second longer than necessary, waiting for that tiny dopamine ping my brain insisted should come with doing the right thing. It didn't. It hadn't in days. It was like my system had burned through whatever "reward" chemical it used to keep me functioning and decided we were on our own.

My stomach reminded me it existed with a hollow, reproachful twist.

Right. Food. Humans required food. Ideally, before they turned into brittle, irritable monsters.

I dragged myself up from the little table in the cabin and stepped into the narrow galley. The boat shifted under me with that subtle rock that was just enough movement to remind me I wasn't on land. I opened the small fridge, stared at the contents, and made a decision that was both deeply practical and, if my father had his way, a prosecutable offense.

Bread. Cheese. Butter.

Grilled cheese.

I pulled out what I needed, set a pan on the stove, and turned the knob. The click-click-click of ignition sounded too loud in the quiet cabin. The pan warmed. The butter hissed. I laid the sandwich down and watched it sizzle, the scent of browning fat and bread doing more for my mood than it had any business doing.

While it cooked, I reached into the cabinet above the sink and pulled out the box of MoonPies I'd bought at the island market earlier that week. Chocolate. Because if I was going to do this, I was going to commit.

I set it on the counter like a bribe to my future self.

The grilled cheese browned on one side. I flipped it and watched the edge of cheese start to melt into a glossy line when my phone lit up on the counter beside me.

Dad.

For a second I stared at the screen. There were a lot of ways to interpret a call from him. None of them were "checking in because he missed me."

I turned the stove down out of reflex, wiped my fingers on a dish towel, and picked up the phone.

"Hello?" Because that was what you said, even when you knew who was on the other end.

"Madden." My name, as always from him, sounded like a title. As if he were addressing someone he expected to perform.

I braced without moving. "Hi, Dad."

"I have a few minutes," he said. "I wanted to speak with you."

Not *how are you?* Not *are you okay?* Not even *do you have time?*

I stared at the grilled cheese, at the edge of bread darkening too quickly now that my attention had shifted. I turned the heat off this time and slid the pan off the burner. "Okay."

His pause was less like silence and more like the moment a man took before he began a speech he'd rehearsed. "I saw your name come up."

My spine tightened. "Where?"

"In a piece. Online." He said it like the internet was a distasteful neighborhood he only visited when he had to. "A mention, not an article. But your name was there."

I kept my voice even. "There are a lot of mentions."

"You know what I mean."

The scandal. The resignation. The narrative that had grown around it because the public loved nothing more than a clean story where someone fell from a height.

"I'm not doing interviews."

"I'm aware. That's part of the problem."

I turned from the stove and leaned my hip against the counter, gripping the edge with my free hand hard enough to anchor my body while my mind did the mental acrobatics a conversation with my father required.

"I'm not interested in being managed," I said.

"You're not in a position to be interested or not. You're in a position to be strategic."

There it was. The word that covered everything for him. Strategy. Optics. Positioning. Performance.

I swallowed and kept my voice neutral. "I am being strategic."

"You're being stubborn," he insisted. "There's a difference."

I listened to myself breathe. In. Out. I felt the pull—the old urge to smooth, to soothe, to make my tone softer so he wouldn't think I was being "difficult." The old calculus that said if I adjusted correctly, maybe I'd get the smallest flicker of approval.

I didn't adjust this time. "I'm not going back into that environment."

"You don't get to decide what environments you go back into."

I didn't miss the flash of real irritation.

"You earned your degree. You clerked. You worked. You built a résumé that people would kill for. Harvard Law, for God's sake. And now you're letting a moment define you."

A moment.

That's what he called it. Not months. Not years. Not a set of choices. Not a moral injury. Not the kind of pressure that bent a person until the only way to stop breaking was to step away.

I stared at the MoonPie on the counter. Chocolate. Cheap. Comforting. A thing he'd never buy because it didn't signify the right kind of taste.

"I'm not letting a moment define me. I'm choosing what I'm willing to do."

"What you're willing to do appears to be... nothing."

The edge of my control prickled. Heat bloomed behind my eyes—anger, frustration, the old shame trying to slip in.

"I'm working." I said.

"At what? Madden, you can't simply vanish and expect this

to resolve itself. The world does not work that way. Reputations do not recover on their own."

I closed my eyes for a fraction of a second, because I couldn't afford to roll them and still claim adulthood. "I'm not trying to recover a reputation. I'm trying to live with myself."

Silence. The kind of quiet that meant I'd stepped outside the script.

When he spoke again, his tone had cooled. "Living with yourself is easier when you're employed."

A humorless laugh threatened. I swallowed it down. "I'm fine."

"You're not. You are wasting time. You should be applying. You should be putting your name in front of the right people. You should be speaking to firms who understand that these situations are survivable if you handle them properly. You are—" He paused, and I heard him choosing a word he believed would land as motivation, not cruelty. "—You are capable of better than this."

Better than this.

As if "better" was always upward. Always visible. Always impressive.

I let my gaze drift to the window, to Rios's boat in the slip next door. He'd gone to see Ford and Sawyer for a couple of hours of normal. Of human.

Something twisted in my chest—a brief, irrational wish that he'd step out onto the dock right then, like he could hear the tone of my father's voice from across the water and decide to intervene.

He wouldn't. He couldn't.

But the thought of him—of his blunt, unsentimental steadiness—did something to me anyway. It reminded me there were other definitions of "better."

"I'm not applying to those jobs," I announced.

"And why not?" My father's voice sharpened. "Because you want to prove a point? Because you want to punish yourself? Because you've decided to be... principled?" He said principled like it was a youthful phase people outgrew.

"Because I don't want that life. And I'm not going to chase it just to look like I'm doing what I'm supposed to."

"You were raised to have options," he snapped. "You were raised to use them."

There was the crux. Not love. Not understanding.

Investment. He had invested in me. Time, money, expectation. I was supposed to yield returns.

I could perform right now. I could soften my voice, give him a palatable version. I could promise I was "exploring options." I could say I had meetings. I could feed him the kind of language he recognized as progress.

And perhaps if I did it correctly, I'd get that thin slice of approval. Not love. Never love. Approval. That was what had always mattered in our household.

I didn't feed him. "I am using them." I stayed calm because calm was armor. "Just not the way you want. Now, I have to go."

His breath hissed, quiet but audible. "Madden—"

"I have something on the stove," I lied, because it was easier than saying, *If I stay on this call, I'm going to say something we can't unsay.*

A tight pause. "We'll speak again," he said. Like it was a decision he got to make alone.

"Okay." I ended the call.

For a few seconds, the boat was too quiet. My skin, my throat, both seemed too tight. Not in a panic way—more like my body remembered what it was like to live under constant evaluation, and it was bracing for the next critique.

Carefully, I set the phone down on the table and turned back to the stove.

The grilled cheese was darker than I'd intended. Not ruined, just... overdone on the edges. Story of my life.

I slid it onto a plate anyway and carried it to the table. I sat down and took a bite.

The crunch was satisfying. The cheese was molten. The salt hit my tongue, and for a second my brain went blank in the way it only did with simple pleasures. I let the flavor ground me until my shoulders dropped from around my ears.

A ding from my computer indicated something new hitting my inbox. Compulsively, I toggled over, and my pulse jumped as I spotted a reply. Not from email, but from the forum messaging system tied to one of the posts I'd made earlier. The subject line was generic: *RE: Your post.*

I opened it.

The message was short. Casual, almost careless. And it made my scalp prickle.

I might have info. Not posting it here. If you're serious, we can talk. In person.

I read it again, slower.

I might have info.

Not I saw her. Not I know her. Not I'm sure.

But still—information. Something. A thread that wasn't frayed to dust.

My body reacted before my mind could discipline it. I sat up straighter. For a second I was already moving through next steps: where, when, how fast, what questions.

The impulse was immediate and absolute: now.

And then, just as fast, another voice cut in. Rios. Flat and certain.

Don't run at the first thing that looks like a door. Make sure it's not a trap.

I exhaled through my nose.

I didn't want to admit he was right, but—he was right.

I flexed my fingers and put them on the keyboard.

I'm serious. I'm not discussing details here. Name a public place and a time. I won't come alone.

I read it once to make sure it said what it needed to say and nothing it didn't.

Then I hit send.

The message whooshed away into the void.

My hands were steady. My heart was not.

I reached for my phone and tapped out a text to Rios.

MADDEN:

Swing by on your way back from hanging with Ford and Sawyer. I've got something to show you. Not an emergency.

Once the message sent, I finished the grilled cheese and grabbed one of the MoonPies. The first bite was sweet, soft, and utterly ridiculous. Perfect. I ate it too fast and went back for another in a small show of defiance. I'd eaten little enough lately that it wasn't as if the extra sugar was going to do any harm.

I carried my second dessert back to the berth along with my laptop. I closed down my email, my browser, and everything else work related. I was too tired, angry, and raw to chase more leads tonight. That was how mistakes got made.

And I was done making mistakes for the sake of momentum.

I kicked my shoes off, curled into the berth and queued up

the *Great British Bake Off,* because watching strangers care intensely about pastry was the safest possible way to let my brain uncoil without falling into a pit. As the familiar theme music washed over me, some of the tension unraveled, leaving my eyes heavy. They slid closed before a single word could be said about soggy bottoms.

TWENTY-FIVE

RIOS

I tipped my phone like I was checking the time, but I was really looking to see if I'd gotten another text from Madden.

Nothing.

Just the one she'd sent a couple of hours ago, still sitting there like it hadn't decided what it was yet.

MADDEN:

Swing by on your way back from hanging with Ford and Sawyer. I've got something to show you. Not an emergency.

I'd almost left right then.

But she'd said it wasn't an emergency, and I was supposed to be here—supposed to be doing something normal, letting my brain stand down for a while. So I'd stayed. Had another beer. Let Sawyer run his mouth. Let Ford argue about wedding logistics like that was the most important problem in the world.

The niggle hadn't gone away. It rode in the back of my skull, persistent as a bad tooth. I told myself the compulsive checking of my phone was habit. I'd hardly had the kind of downtime as a civilian for my nervous system to figure out how the fuck to do quiet yet.

Still.

When headlights swept across the living room wall and a car pulled up outside, I looked up automatically.

Peyton came in a minute later with Keeley at her heels, tail wagging like a metronome of joy, as if she hadn't just spent the last several hours with her favorite human. Mimi's car was already pulling away.

"Hey," Peyton dropped her bag and bending to hug the dog. "Did I miss anything?"

"Just Sawyer being wrong about everything," Ford said.

Sawyer scoffed. "Objectively false."

I stood before I could get pulled into another round of banter. "I'm gonna head out. Early start."

Ford frowned. "You sure?"

"Yeah." I moved toward the door. "Peyton, good to see you again."

Sawyer stood as well and stretched. "I should get home to my wife before she decides to bring home more than one more dog."

Peyton brightened. "Y'all are getting a new dog?"

"A foster," Sawyer corrected.

Because I knew he'd get sucked in by her enthusiasm, I kept moving. Ford caught me at the door. "Text if you need backup."

I nodded. "Will do. Thanks, brother."

Outside, the air was finally cooler, the day's heat loosening its grip now that night had settled in for real. July nights on Hatterwick were like that—heavy but quieter, the island exhaling after squeezing everything it could out of daylight.

Most of town had gone dark. A few pockets of light still glowed toward the boardwalk and downtown, but the marina was usually subdued at this hour. Boats rocked gently in their slips, lines creaking, the water slapping soft and lazy against hulls.

I drove with my phone sitting in the console where I'd notice any new incoming messages.

Nothing.

I was halfway down the road toward the marina when my brain registered something wrong before I consciously saw it.

Light.

Not the steady, contained glow of dock lights or cabin lamps. This was brighter. Erratic. Flickering in a way that didn't belong.

I slowed, eyes narrowing, scanning past the silhouettes of masts and rigging. I still couldn't see the source—too many boats between me and the inner slips—but my pulse kicked up anyway as I whipped into the nearest parking spot and opened the door.

As soon as I did, I smelled it. The stench of smoke rode the air like a warning.

I bolted down the dock, looking for someone, anyone, to help. The closer I got, the thicker the air became. Acrid, biting, laced with something that made the back of my throat sting.

Gasoline.

A part of me knew before I rounded the corner. The kind of knowing that didn't come from logic or deduction, but instinct.

The *Second Wind* was on fire.

Flames licked up the side of the hull, hungry and bright, reflecting off the dark water in violent, distorted shapes. Smoke poured upward, thick and black, smearing the night sky.

"Madden!" The shout tore out of my chest. "Madden!"

No answer.

My heart slammed hard enough to make my vision tunnel.

I scanned frantically—dock, water, neighboring boats—looking for her, for any sign she'd made it out.

Nothing.

A couple of people stumbled out of nearby boats, half-dressed, confused, drawn by the noise and the light.

"Call nine-one-one!" I yelled without slowing. "Now!"

Someone fumbled for a phone. Someone else swore.

I was already on the dock, sprinting, the heat rolling toward me in waves. I launched myself onto the *Second Wind*, and my boots hit the deck hard.

Brutal heat punched up through the soles, the planks hot enough that instinct screamed move before my brain finished catching up. Flames wrapped the exterior of the cabin, crawling fast and loud, chewing through anything they could take. The sound was enormous—roaring, crackling, a constant violent rush that swallowed everything else.

I went straight for the cabin door.

The handle didn't move.

Not resistance. Not warped wood or swollen metal. Nothing at all.

I looked down and saw a bike chain looped through the handle and padlocked to the rail, the metal already blackened, the lock glowing dull and angry in the heat.

Someone had deliberately locked her inside.

Rage snapped through me, sharp and cold.

I reached automatically for the fire extinguisher bracket beside the door.

Empty.

Of course it was.

"Extinguisher!" I barked, turning my head and shoulders just enough to see the dock.

Something heavy came flying through the smoke a beat later. I braced and caught it against my chest. The impact knocked the air out of me as metal rang against bone. I ripped the pin free and squeezed the handle as I turned back.

White powder blasted out in a hard, forceful stream, knocking the flames down from the door and rail, buying me precious, narrow seconds. The heat eased just enough that my lungs stopped seizing.

I dropped the extinguisher and grabbed the metal boat hook from its bracket. I shoved the hook through the chain, planted my foot against the rail, and hauled sideways with everything I had. The lock shrieked, metal protesting, then failed with a sharp crack as the hasp snapped.

The chain fell away.

I yanked the door open.

The air inside punched out like a physical blow.

Heat and smoke blasted into my face, so dense it felt solid, the kind that stripped oxygen and turned every breath into a fight. The cabin wasn't burning yet—it was baking, sealed tight, cooking from the outside in.

I dropped low and crawled inside.

Visibility was almost nothing. Smoke rolled thick and gray, the heat pressing in from every surface. My lungs burned. My head swam.

"Madden!" I shouted, though I couldn't hear myself over the fire.

No answer.

I swept my arm out blindly, and my hand hit something soft.

Her.

She was on the floor near the kitchenette, collapsed on her side. Unmoving. Her skin was hot to the touch, her breathing shallow and uneven—smoke and heat had taken her down before the fire could finish the job.

"Fuck," I rasped.

I didn't waste time checking responsiveness. I hooked one arm under her shoulders, the other under her knees, and lifted.

She was limp.

Dead weight.

Her head lolled against my chest as I turned back toward the door. The fire outside roared louder, the structure of the boat protesting as flames climbed higher, heat slamming into my back like a shove.

I ran.

Across the deck, fire snapping at my legs, the planks melting the soles of my boots. I hit the edge and jumped, landing hard on the dock with a jolt that rattled my teeth.

Hands reached for her immediately.

"I've got her," someone shouted.

"Clear!" I barked. "Get her clear—now!"

They moved fast, dragging her farther down the dock as I dropped to one knee, chest heaving, lungs screaming, skin burning where the heat had kissed it too long.

Behind me, the *Second Wind* finally gave up.

The fire breached the cabin in earnest, flames tearing through as the interior ignited, heat blasting outward and driving everyone back. The sound was violent, final.

I didn't look.

Instead, I crawled to Madden's side, shaking hands finding her pulse, counting shallow breaths, my entire world narrowing to one hard, undeniable truth—

Someone had tried to kill her.

And I'd gotten there in time.

TWENTY-SIX

MADDEN

"—I'm fine. I don't need a bed."

The voice cut through the dark before anything else did.

Firm. Controlled. Strained around the edges.

Rios.

"I said I'm not going anywhere." He was closer now. "You can treat me right here."

Someone else answered him, sharper. "You don't get to make that call."

Another voice—calmer, professional. "Sir, you've got burns that—"

"I said I'm staying."

The words landed with a stubborn finality that my fogged brain latched onto like a lifeline.

Cool, dry air filled my lungs before I was ready for it. The faintly metallic taste made me wince, my first instinct to fight it —until I realized there was nothing to fight.

I was breathing on my own.

In.

Out.

In.

Out.

Light followed sound, sliding in under my eyelids until I blinked them open.

The ceiling above me was white and too close, the light flattened and unforgiving. My eyes burned as if I'd been crying for hours, though I couldn't remember doing that. My throat was scraped down to something tender and swollen, and when I swallowed, it hurt.

My sluggish brain struggled to process. Hospital?

No. No hospital on Hatterwick.

The clinic.

Something tugged lightly at my face when I shifted again. I lifted a hand, disoriented, and stopped when warm fingers closed over mine.

"Madden. Hey. Easy. You're okay."

Rios's voice was right there. Close enough that I felt it vibrate through his chest where he leaned over me. I turned my head carefully this time, slower, and found him standing at the side of the bed, one hand gripping the rail like he'd anchored himself there and refused to budge.

Only now I saw why someone had tried to move him.

He looked... wrecked. Soot streaked the side of his jaw and his neck, smudged into the collar of his shirt, which was burned through in places. One sleeve had been cut clean off, revealing skin that was red and shiny, already swelling. His wrist was wrapped in fresh gauze, the white stark against the grime.

A nurse stood a step behind him, clearly mid-task, clearly not winning whatever argument had just been happening.

"You're okay," he said again, like he needed me to hear it. "You're at the clinic."

I tried to speak. What came out was barely sound.

He leaned closer. "Don't push it."

I let my head sink back into the pillow, the effort of holding it up suddenly too much. My chest clamped tight, like there wasn't quite enough room inside it, even with the oxygen flowing. The mask fogged faintly with each breath.

"What... happened?" I asked, the words rough.

His jaw tightened a tiny fraction, but I saw it beneath the scruff shading his jaw. "There was a fire."

The word landed with a strange lack of impact. Fire was abstract. Fire was something that happened to other people.

Memory stirred anyway—oppressive heat. The air itself turning against me. The latch that wouldn't move no matter how hard I pulled.

"And you—" I tried again. "You—"

"I got you out," he said simply.

Something inside my chest lurched. I looked at him more closely and saw the tremor he was fighting in his hands, the way he was bracing himself like the ground might still give way beneath us.

"You scared the hell out of us," Gabi said from across the room.

I hadn't noticed her there. She gathered some kind of materials from a tray and advanced on her brother with a scowl that said she wouldn't be put off.

"Us?" I echoed faintly.

She shot me a look as she reached for the burn on his arm. "Yes, us. And before you start arguing, you're staying on oxygen. You had smoke inhalation, and you lost consciousness. You don't get points for toughness." Her gaze shot to Rios. "Neither do you."

"I'm fine," I said automatically.

She didn't even look up from the task. "You're stable. That is not the same thing."

Rios shifted, his thumb brushing once over my knuckles. "Just listen to her."

There was no edge to it. No command. Only concern, bare and unguarded. It hit me harder than the reprimand would have.

For a few minutes, we stayed silent as Gabi efficiently cleaned the burns, dabbed them with some kind of ointment, and covered them with gauze.

The nurse came and checked my vitals, the cuff squeezing my arm until my fingers tingled. She murmured something to Gabi, something I couldn't quite track, then adjusted the oxygen flow and smiled at me in a way that probably meant to be reassuring.

"You're doing well. Keep breathing slow like that." She glanced at Rios, then back to Gabi. "Fire department called ahead. Police are on their way."

The word police cut through the fog in my head.

"The police?" I asked.

Rios's eyes flicked to mine. There it was again—that subtle shift, the way his posture changed as if he'd taken on more weight.

He looked at Gabi. "Can we have a minute?"

Gabi's mouth flattened. "One," she said. "After that, they're coming in whether you're ready or not."

She herded the nurse out with a look and pulled the door closed behind them. Background sounds dampened to a soft hum.

Rios didn't sit. He stayed standing, close enough that I felt the heat that wasn't heat radiating off him, the restless energy of someone whose body hadn't yet accepted that the danger had passed.

"What's going on?" I asked.

He took a breath. Let it out slowly, like he was bracing himself. "Madden, the fire wasn't an accident."

The words slid into the space between us and stayed there.

I stared at him, my brain snagging on the wrong part of the sentence. *Wasn't an accident* still left room for malfunction. Faulty wiring. A bad fuel line. Anything that didn't involve intent.

"What do you mean?" I asked.

"The cabin door was locked. From the outside."

My stomach dropped. "Locked how?" The question came out thin, like I already knew the answer and didn't want to hear it anyway.

He shifted, and that careful pause told me he was choosing his words. "There was a bike chain looped through the handle. Padlocked to the rail."

For a second, my mind refused to cooperate. Locked. From the outside. My thoughts skidded, trying to reroute.

"That doesn't—" I stopped myself. Swallowed. Tried again. "The latch wouldn't move."

"I know."

The memory surged up, vivid and immediate. Me yanking at the handle. The spike of irritation that had turned to fear as the heat pressed in. I'd told myself it was the boat. Old hardware. Something warped.

Not this.

"Someone..." My voice wobbled. I cleared my throat. "Someone locked me in."

"Yes."

The oxygen hissed steadily as my breathing sped up. I brought it back under control, one breath at a time.

The room was suddenly too small. The ceiling too close. My skin prickled as the rest of it sank in, fast and brutal. I squeezed my eyes shut and saw the flames consuming the boat. My temporary home. My last link to Gwen.

Asleep. I'd been asleep.

I'd queued up something mindless and let myself drift off without a second thought.

I could have died.

Something broke loose—not panic exactly, but a surge of emotion that had nowhere to go. My chest tightened, a sharp ache blooming beneath my ribs as the implications stacked up faster than I could process them.

Rios moved without hesitation. He stepped closer and wrapped an arm around my shoulders, pulling me in carefully, mindful of the oxygen line. I leaned into him, my forehead pressing against his chest, breathing him in—smoke and salt and something solid underneath it all.

His hand came up between my shoulder blades, firm and steady.

"I've got you," he said quietly.

For a moment, I let myself believe that meant everything.

A knock sounded at the door.

Rios straightened but didn't pull away entirely. "Yeah?"

The door opened, and Grant Willoughby stepped inside, still in his cop's uniform. I hadn't seen him since Willie Sanders's apartment. Had barely even given him a thought.

His gaze flicked to me, to the oxygen, the IV, and the way Rios hadn't moved more than a step away. Something crossed his face—surprise, concern, maybe a flash of something he didn't quite manage to shove down.

"Madden," he said, carefully. "I'm sorry. I didn't realize you were this—"

"Hi, Grant," I said.

He nodded once, visibly pulling himself back into professional mode. "I need to take a statement."

Rios's arm tightened slightly.

Grant noticed. His eyes lingered there for a fraction of a second before he looked down at his notebook. "You're the one who called it in," he said to Rios.

"Technically, someone on the dock called it in while I was retrieving Madden."

Grant blinked. "Right." His tone softened as he turned to me, but there was tension under it, like he was bracing for what came next.

"Madden," he said, "what do you remember?"

I took a breath and tried to filter through the haze still covering my brain. "I was working earlier. Research. Then I shut everything down for the night. I was watching TV in bed." I paused. "I must have fallen asleep."

The memory sharpened, dragging sensation with it.

"I woke up because it was hot," I continued. "And because I smelled smoke. I tried to get out, but the door wouldn't open. I thought the latch was malfunctioning."

My chest tightened as the panic resurfaced. Rios's fingers brushed my arm, grounding without interrupting.

"It just kept getting hotter," I said. "And I couldn't get out."

"You didn't hear anything before that?" Grant asked. "Footsteps? Voices?"

I shook my head. "No. I was asleep. I didn't know... I didn't know I was locked in."

Grant stopped writing, his gaze snapping to me. "Locked in?"

"So I was told." I looked to Rios to pick up the thread of the narrative.

"Carrera, take me through it in order, will you?"

Rios gave his account without embellishment. One cop speaking to another. Fire already established, smell of gasoline, blocked door, chain and padlock, getting me out. Through it all,

I felt the tension vibrating in Rios's frame and watched Grant's pen move faster as the details stacked up, his jaw tightening as the picture sharpened.

When Rios mentioned the chain, Grant looked up sharply. "Chained?"

"Yes."

The word echoed in my head again, heavy and awful.

Grant exhaled slowly and resumed note-taking. "What happened next."

Rios's tone remained flat and businesslike as he walked through the rescue, but I could too easily imagine the roar of the flames, the heat he'd fought through to get to me. What he'd risked staying long enough to battle the chain, to get me out.

He'd risked his life to save mine.

The bloom of that realization left me breathless even before Grant quietly asked, "Is there anyone you can think of who might want to kill you?"

TWENTY-SEVEN

RIOS

The question hung there like a live wire.

Who might want to kill you?

I'd known it was coming. I'd known it since the second I saw the chain on the door, since the stench of gasoline hit the back of my throat and my body chilled with certainty. But up to now I'd been focused on doing the thing right in front of me. Getting the lock off, door open. Getting Madden out. Getting her to treatment.

But there was no next right thing in this moment. No action to distract from the brutal reality she faced.

Madden didn't answer right away.

She looked at me instead.

Not for reassurance or permission. For calibration. As if she needed a gauge of how much truth she should reveal for the sake of the case. And that said everything about where her faith in the system stood.

And where her faith in me stood.

That faith absolutely cut me off at the knees. Because it

said she believed I was the good guy. That I was worthy of trust above and beyond this man who'd once meant something to her as part of a system she used to trust. She'd decided I was a touchstone. A protector.

Something tight and sharp shifted unmistakably in my chest. This was the part I couldn't protect her from. Not with my body. Not with speed or force or adrenaline. This was the part where survival turned into consequence.

"I'm sure you're already aware that we believe Chief Carson prematurely closed the Shah case." Though her voice rasped, it remained steady in a way that cost her. "As I implied when we spoke at Willie Sanders's apartment, we've continued looking into her disappearance."

Something flickered over the other man's face. Discomfort. With the way his department was being run? Hard to tell. I didn't get the sense that he was Carson's lackey, but I wasn't sure where he stood.

"Were you not warned off doing exactly that?" Grant asked.

Madden's chin lifted in a faintly mutinous tilt. "Technically, we were warned off the investigation into Willie Sanders' murder, which was never our focus to begin with."

A muscle jumped in Grant's jaw, but he didn't correct her or call her out on the technicality. "What exactly have you been doing?"

Madden only blinked at him. "Other than speaking to everyone the department spoke to about Priya's disappearance? Whatever research we can. Since Carson conveniently made sure that my FOIA request was stonewalled, I haven't spoken to anyone directly."

Of course she wouldn't betray Rosa.

Grant pinned her with his gaze, but Madden only stared back at him.

Finally, he sighed. "Do you have any reason to think that your involvement has... upset someone?"

It was my turn to stare at him. The restraint it took not to snap back surprised me. Maybe because I was past rage now. Past shock. What was left was colder. Heavier.

"You mean aside from the fact that someone chained her inside her boat and set it on fire?" I said.

The silence that followed was loaded.

Grant angled his head in acknowledgment. "That's fair."

He asked a few more questions after that, but they were procedural. Loose ends. Time stamps. Who knew what. None of it went anywhere useful. Whatever line had been crossed tonight hadn't left a paper trail behind, and given the remains of the boat had sunk, there was unlikely to be much in the way of physical evidence to process.

Finally, Grant closed his notebook. "If you think of anything else—anything at all—please call."

She nodded.

Grant hesitated, eyes flicking between us again—taking in the oxygen, the IV, the way I hadn't moved more than a foot from her side since he walked in.

"Take care of yourself," he added, quieter.

The door closed behind him with a quiet, deliberate click that sounded far too final for a room this small.

For a second, I expected the world to rush back in. To hear voices in the hall, the scrape of shoes, the hum of movement that meant things were still happening. Instead, there was only the low hum of the oxygen and the faint buzz of the overhead lights.

Too quiet.

I stayed where I was, standing close enough to Madden's bed that I could reach her without leaning, far enough away that it still looked like restraint instead of instinct. My hands ached with the need to do something—anything—and there was nothing left to do.

No fire to fight.

No door to break through.

No one to pull out of harm's way.

Just the knowledge that someone had tried to kill her, and the sick certainty that if the timing had been even slightly off, I'd be standing in this room alone. Or not standing at all.

Madden lay back against the pillows, oxygen still in place, her skin pale beneath the harsh clinic lights. The color had come back to her cheeks since the dock, but she looked wrung out in a way that went deeper than smoke or shock. As if her body had finally been allowed to stop and hadn't yet decided whether it was safe to start again.

At last, I dragged a chair closer and sat, elbows braced on my knees, hands hanging uselessly between them. The burns on my arm throbbed now that the adrenaline had fully burned off, a deep, pulsing ache that felt almost welcome. Pain I understood. Pain I could catalog and endure.

This—whatever this was—I had no system for.

"You okay?" I asked.

It was a useless question. We both knew it. But it was the only one that didn't feel like pushing.

She nodded anyway. "I think so."

I didn't call her on it. Didn't tell her that "I think so" was what people said when they were still sorting through the wreckage. When their brain was stacking the facts in neat little piles because if they didn't, the emotional reality would hit all at once and knock the air out of them.

I'd been there.

Her eyes flicked to the gauze on my arm. "You should've let them take you to a bed."

I snorted under my breath. "Not happening."

She studied me for a long moment, like she was filing the answer away for later. "Why?"

Because if I'd let them move me, I'd have had to step away from you.

Because the image of you trapped behind that door won't stop replaying, and I need to know you're still breathing.

None of that came out.

"Because I'm fine."

Her mouth twitched. "Liar."

That almost cracked something in my chest. Almost.

The silence that followed was heavier than the last one, pressing in on all sides. I stared at the floor, at the scuffed linoleum and the faint smear of soot my partly melted boot had left behind, and tried not to let my mind go back to the marina.

Tried and failed.

I still felt the heat of flames on my skin, still smelled the gasoline underneath the burning fiberglass. "Madden."

She shifted slightly, the blanket rustling. "Yeah?"

I looked up at her, really looked, and the breath caught in my chest in a way I didn't have language for yet. She wasn't crying. Wasn't shaking. She was watching me with that sharp, assessing focus she used when she was thinking something through.

"I need you to understand something," I said.

Her brow furrowed. "Okay."

"This wasn't random." I kept my voice level, even as something dark and furious curled tighter in my gut. "Whoever did this didn't just get lucky. They came prepared. They knew the boat, the layout, and how long it would take for heat to build."

She absorbed that without flinching.

"They chained the door because they wanted time. They wanted smoke. Confusion. They wanted you trapped long enough for..."

Her fingers curled into the sheet as I trailed off. "For me not to get out."

"Yes."

The truth settled between us, heavy and unmovable.

She closed her eyes for a moment, breathing in the oxygen. I watched her throat move as she swallowed, watched the way her jaw set like she was bracing against something internal.

"Madden, they could try again."

I needed her to hear that. To understand it.

Her eyes opened, and she shoved the canula off, as if she wanted to be extra damned sure I heard her reply. "I can't stop."

There it was.

Not bravado. Not defiance.

Resolve.

"You should. At least for a while." I didn't want her hurt. Didn't want her in harm's way.

Those sharp eyes stayed steady on mine. "That's easy for you to say."

I frowned. "Why?"

"Because you're trained for this," she said quietly. "You know how bad it can get. You chose that life. I didn't."

The words weren't an accusation. Just a statement of fact.

"And yet," she continued, "someone still decided I was a problem."

My jaw clenched.

"You could have died." The words scraped out rough with an emotion I didn't have a name for.

"I know."

The calm way she said it was what undid me.

"That's not a shrug-it-off statement." Heat crept into my voice. "That's a line you don't cross without it changing everything."

Her gaze held mine, unwavering. "It already has."

I stood, the chair scraping softly against the floor as I moved closer, drawn by something I'd been pretending not to feel for days.

"Can *you* walk away?" she demanded.

The question hit me square in the chest.

I knew she was asking if I could walk away from the case. But I saw her as she'd been on the dock—soot-streaked, pale, and so very still. I saw the version of her that might have been zipped into a black bag if the night had gone a little differently.

I saw the part of myself that had already crossed a line the moment I decided her fight was mine too, and the question I answered was whether I could walk away from *her*.

"No."

The truth of it settled over us, into me.

Madden Reilly wasn't who I'd have picked in a million years. But I hadn't known her before. She was complicated. Sometimes difficult. And fucking fascinating. This unwavering commitment to doing the right thing, even when it might cost her everything... Brave, stubborn, brilliant, beautiful woman.

I couldn't stop myself from reaching for her, from gently cupping her jaw. Something flickered across her face—surprise, relief, something softer threading through it.

"You're an eternal surprise, Counselor," I murmured.

That surprise brightened to something that might've been pleasure as I closed the distance between us and brushed my lips to hers.

For one, two, three heart-stopping beats, she froze, and I worried I'd crossed a line. But just as I would have pulled back, apologized, she reached for me, hands curling into my T-shirt and tugging me closer. I fought not to sink too deep because she'd been through hell. Then her mouth opened beneath mine, and it was like we'd both finally found oxygen. Or perhaps we both just needed the reminder that we'd survived tonight. As the taste of her flooded into me, my pulse stuttered, and my fingers tightened in her hair.

One of her hands slid along my jaw, scraping against the stubble in a way that made me growl like some big damned cat. I leaned into her touch, wanting a hell of a lot more than this...

"Contrary to popular opinion, this particular variety of swapping oxygen is not actually more effective than the classic medical intervention."

At the sound of my baby sister's voice, I stood bolt upright. Every cell of my body protested, *We weren't done yet.*

Madden blinked up at me, dazed, her lips pretty pink and kiss swollen.

Gabi's gaze flicked between us, unimpressed and unsurprised all at once. "I've got discharge instructions. And before either of you argue, you're staying at Caroline's tonight. Both of you. No exceptions."

Her look told me there wasn't a chance in hell she was keeping this juicy detail from our older sister. Right. I'd cross that bridge when we got to it.

Madden glanced at me, something bright and unsettled still in her eyes.

I exhaled slowly, tightening my fingers on hers. "Let's get out of here."

TWENTY-EIGHT

MADDEN

Hoyt came to get us himself.

I registered that fact the way I registered everything else after the clinic: distantly, as if it belonged to someone else's night. Someone else's emergency. He didn't say much beyond that everything had been contained, which seemed like a strange word to apply to something that had erased an entire floating square of my life from existence.

Contained.

As if fire respected boundaries.

I opened my mouth to protest out of reflex. I didn't need this. I didn't want to be an imposition. I could manage. I always managed.

But the protest stalled halfway to my throat, because the truth crept in sideways.

Neither Rios nor I had our vehicles.

And somewhere between the clinic room and Hoyt's truck, it finally sank in that the only things I actually still owned were whatever was in my car. Everything else—clothes, books, notes, mementos, the stupid coffee mug I'd had since law school, the last physical trace of Gwen's life I'd still been able to reach—had been on the *Second Wind.*

Past tense.

There was no question the boat had been destroyed. No question whatever hadn't burned had sunk. I didn't need anyone to say it out loud for me to be certain. The absence echoed already, like a phantom limb I hadn't yet learned not to reach for.

My throat hurt. My head hurt. My body felt like it had been wrung out and left to dry somewhere it didn't quite belong.

So I didn't fight.

I climbed into the truck and let the door shut behind me.

Rios stayed close. Not hovering, exactly—he wasn't that kind of man—but near enough that I sensed him without looking. His presence registered on a level below thought, like pressure or gravity. I couldn't tell if he was waiting for something else to happen—for someone to jump us, for me to finally crack—or if he needed me close for his own reasons. Like perhaps he needed the reassurance that I was still breathing.

The idea of that last one slid in unexpectedly, and something warm unfurled in my chest.

Which unfortunately made me think of the kiss.

Which immediately took that warmth and set it on fire.

I stared out the window and told myself not to analyze it. Analysis was dangerous territory tonight. Analysis led to spirals, and spirals led to questions I didn't have the bandwidth to answer.

The truck slowed. Turned. Stopped.

Caroline and Hoyt's house sat quiet and dark, the kind of late-night stillness that meant the children had been put to bed hours ago and the adults had made the fragile transition from managing to waiting. The porch light was on.

Caroline was already in the doorway.

One moment I was standing just outside the door, still orienting myself to the house, still vaguely aware of the night pressing in around me, and the next she'd wrapped her arms around me. No questions. No pause to assess whether I wanted it.

Just contact.

"Oh, honey," she murmured, brief and low, pulling me in against her shoulder somehow, even though I was taller than her by about four inches. She smelled like clean cotton and something faintly herbal, and the absolute *momness* of it hit me sideways. Because I'd never had anything like this from my own mother.

She pulled back just enough to look at my face, hands still on my arms, thumbs pressing lightly as if checking I was solid. Her gaze flicked over me in quick, practiced passes before turning sharply toward Rios.

The Spanish came fast and familiar, a tumble of syllables I was too tired to follow but didn't need translated. The tone told me enough: relief threaded through with scolding, affection sharpened by fear that had already burned off.

Rios answered in kind, quieter, defensive but conceding ground. The exchange had the cadence of siblings who'd done this dance their whole lives.

Caroline exhaled through her nose and released me, already pivoting away. "Okay," she said, brisk now. "Come on."

She disappeared down the hall and returned almost immediately with her arms full. She set the stack on the chair beside the door and added a toiletry bag on top.

"These should work," she said. "They're clean. Bathroom's up the stairs and down the hall. Towels are in the cabinet."

I stared at the pile longer than made sense. Pajamas. A toothbrush. Ordinary things that suddenly seemed enormous because it came bundled with the reminder that I had nothing. Nothing of my own to change into. Nothing familiar to anchor me.

I shut that thought down immediately.

There would be time for grief later. Time to inventory loss and decide how to survive it. Right now, all I could manage was the present moment, and the present moment required oxygen and vertical posture.

"Thank you." The word barely made it past my abused throat.

She waved it off like it was nothing, already moving again. "Take your time."

Then she paused, glanced back at me, and something in her expression gentled with assurance. "You're safe here."

Rios opened his mouth.

Caroline cut him off without missing a beat.

"If you think either of you is going back to that boat, think again. Madden, you're in the guest room. Rios, you're—"

"With her." The words landed fast and solid, with no hesitation in them at all.

I opened my mouth. Closed it again.

Part of me wanted to protest. Another part—a quieter, more honest part—was already clinging to the idea like a life raft.

"I'll take the floor. Nobody's getting to you again."

That did it. Whatever argument I might have mounted dissolved. The image of him between me and the rest of the world was so deeply comforting it almost hurt.

Caroline's expression shifted into something thoughtful. Whatever opinions she had about this development, she kept them to herself. There was more bustling. Extra bedding pulled from a closet. Efficient, purposeful motion that communicated *you are safe here now* without requiring additional reassurance.

And then suddenly, impossibly, we were alone.

The guest room was dim and quiet, the air cool against my skin. Rios handed me fresh towels and the borrowed pajamas, along with the small collection of toiletries Caroline had assembled like a professional emergency responder.

"You go ahead and shower." He nudged me gently toward the bathroom, as if momentum alone might keep me upright.

The water helped. For a little while, I lost myself in the mechanics of it—the simple act of standing still and letting warmth wash over skin that had been too close to fire. I focused on getting clean, on rinsing the smoke from my hair, on breathing through the lingering rasp in my chest.

I kept my brain turned off by force.

I knew it wouldn't last. I knew the thoughts were waiting to devour me on the other side. But I clung to the reprieve with everything I had.

When I came out, Rios was already changed.

Pajama bottoms. Bare chest. Wet hair, proof he'd used another bathroom.

I deliberately did not stare.

Which, unfortunately, did nothing to stop my eyes from registering the sculpted lines of muscle, the strength of him rendered unguarded by the domesticity of the moment. The bandages on his arms helped. Visual punctuation marks reminding me why this wasn't the time for anything but survival.

"You holding up?"

"I didn't know what to do with..." I held up my clothes.

They were worse than I remembered. Soot-stained, singed, ruined beyond denial. My hands started to shake before I managed to stop them, the reality of loss crystallizing in that small, tangible pile.

Rios took them from me gently. "I'll take care of it."

He set them aside and pulled me into his arms before the tremor turned into something bigger.

The solid pressure of him anchored me, kept my feet on the floor when everything inside me wanted to float off into panic or numbness or both.

"Someone tried to kill me." The words came out flat, like a statement of fact I hadn't yet processed.

"Yeah. But they didn't succeed."

His hands moved slowly up and down my spine in a steady, grounding rhythm.

"Only because you were there. You were *there,* Rios. Risking your life for me."

"It's what partners do." He said it simply. As if this arrangement we'd fallen into had always been. As if I had any idea what it was like to count on someone like that.

I clung tighter to him. "Jesus, if you hadn't come—" I stopped myself before the image finished forming. Before my mind could supply the version of the night where I didn't make it out.

"But I did come. I wish to God I'd come sooner. Maybe I could've caught the bastard. But your text said it wasn't an emergency."

"Text?" The memory flickered back into place, absurd in the context of everything else. "Oh, my God. With everything else, I forgot. I—someone wants to meet with me."

He went still. "Who?"

"I don't know. Someone on one of the forums I posted on. We hadn't set any details yet. I wanted to get your take before I agreed to anything. But whoever it was said they might have some information."

"About Priya? About someone else missing?"

"I don't know. It was pretty vague. I messaged them back to get more details."

He paused, gears visibly turning. "Was this a public forum?"

"I mean, behind a login, but public in the sense anyone can sign up, yes." Even as I said it, the pieces started to align in a way I didn't like. "You don't think that had something to do with the fire?"

"If it does, that says someone's watching what you're doing a hell of a lot closer than we suspected. Somehow, somewhere, you've managed to step on someone's toes enough that they thought they'd scare you off."

I didn't miss how he was trying to downplay it now. For himself? For me? I didn't need that.

"Let's call a spade a spade. It was a murder attempt."

Rios shuddered.

My hands flexed against his chest. "I haven't come this far to be scared away now."

When his eyes met mine, I braced myself for an argument.

Instead, he cupped my cheek. "I know. And that's what scares me."

The idea of this man being scared of anything, least of all on my behalf left me feeling unmoored, clinging by my fingertips to some kind of emotional roller coaster that had no safety bar.

After a long humming beat, he nudged me toward the bed. "You need rest."

I crawled beneath the covers, the mattress welcoming and unfamiliar. The moment I lay down, I missed his arms.

"You don't have to sleep on the floor." I forced myself to say it out loud.

"I've slept on worse."

"I..." I drew in a breath, steadying myself. "I think I'd feel better if you were over here with me."

The pause stretched. My heart thudded loud in my ears. "Okay."

He climbed into the bed beside me, careful and deliberate, then reached out to turn off the light. Darkness settled.

For a long moment, we lay there, both of us staring at the ceiling we couldn't see, the silence filled with things neither of us was ready to say.

"About earlier," he said.

I needed absolute clarity about *which* part of earlier he meant. I knew which one I was thinking about. "The kiss?"

"Yeah."

I braced myself for the gentle letdown, the insistence that it was just a heat of the moment thing, a mistake.

"Look, I'm not trying to push you into anything. That would be a dick move. But I'm into you. I'm going to protect you through this, no matter what, even if you don't feel the same."

The inner teenage girl I pretended not to have squealed outright. *He likes me! He really likes me!*

"I... I'm into you, too." Admitting it was more terrifying than the fire. Because this wasn't about survival—this was about choice.

He shifted, and suddenly I was tucked against him, his body curved protectively around mine. "Good. That makes things easier."

I relaxed into him by degrees, inch by inch. "You call this easy?"

"Oh, sweetheart, nothing about you is easy. Easy is boring. But not having to fight myself simplifies my life."

"Oh." Because what else could I say to that?

I felt his smile when he kissed my temple, soft and sweet. "Go to sleep, Counselor."

And somehow—impossibly—I did.

TWENTY-NINE

RIOS

I woke up with the taste of smoke in the back of my throat.

My eyes opened on a ceiling I didn't recognize. Pale, smooth, with a faint hairline crack running toward the corner. Guest room. Caroline and Hoyt's. I lay still long enough to take inventory—burns pulling on my arm under the fresh gauze, grit in my hair I hadn't managed to rinse out completely, a dull ache behind my ribs from too much adrenaline and too little sleep.

And Madden.

She curled into my side with the kind of trust that hit me harder than the fire had. One arm tucked between us, her hand rested on my stomach, fingers slightly curled, as if only in sleep could she let herself even think of holding on. Her hair was loose, spilled across my chest and the pillow, and without the armor she wore when she was awake, she looked... younger. Softer around the mouth. Her lashes were dark against her cheeks, her brow smooth for the first time since she'd stepped back onto this island and started digging.

I watched her breathe.

Slow. Even. No rasp. No panic.

My chest loosened a fraction, like some part of me had been holding a fist tight all night and was only now learning how to unclench.

Her pajamas had slipped off one shoulder, showing the curve of skin there, pale in the early light. I didn't touch it. Didn't move. I didn't trust myself to move without wanting more than I had any right to want.

I'd kissed her.

That fact sat in my head like a live round. I'd said what I meant, and I meant what I'd said, and still my body kept replaying the moment like it was trying to learn it by repetition. The shape of her mouth under mine. The way she'd grabbed my shirt and pulled me in like she'd been starving.

I'd spent years getting good at control. Good at putting a lid on whatever wanted to spill out. That kiss had cracked something. Now it was like the damn thing was looking for the seam again.

Madden shifted, making a tiny sound in the back of her throat. Her hand tightened once on my stomach, then relaxed.

My instinct was to pull her closer. Keep her there. Keep her safe. The other instinct was to get up and make sure every door in this house was locked.

I chose the second one because I could do it quietly.

I slid out from under her arm with careful patience, moving an inch at a time like I was disarming a bomb. The bed gave a soft creak. Madden didn't wake. She rolled onto her side, tucking her hand under her cheek, and for a second she looked like she'd never had to be strong a day in her life.

Something sharp twisted low in my gut as I stood there, shirtless in borrowed pajama bottoms.

Someone had tried to burn her alive.

Fury burned through me so hot, it was almost calm. Maybe

I couldn't fight all of Madden's demons, but I was going to find the son of a bitch who'd done this and make sure he never got the chance to terrify her again.

I pulled on one of Hoyt's borrowed T-shirts and stepped out into the hall. The house was quiet in that way a house only got when kids were asleep or gone. Given the angle of the light, I was banking on the latter because Logan usually hit the ground running by six AM and let everyone know it.

Caroline sat at the kitchen table, hair pulled into a messy knot, a steaming mug beside her as she scribbled something on a notepad. A grocery list or schedule or some other sign of normal domesticity.

She looked up the second my foot hit the tile, eyes sweeping over me in a single pass in that assessing gaze she'd learned years ago, when I'd started taking on our father to keep him from going after her or Gabi. Those eyes asked, *How bad is it?*

What she actually said was, "There's coffee."

With a grunt, I crossed to the pot and filled one of the waiting earthenware mugs Ford's Mimi had made. Then, I joined my sister at the table.

"Where are the little monsters?"

"Ibby took them so I'd be free to help with whatever."

"Nice of her."

"She'll want a family dinner soon, if you're going to be around long enough."

Caroline's mother-in-law had essentially adopted all three of us when Caroline married Hoyt. Not that Gabi and I had been around much for her to mother. But I heard the implied question beneath my sister's statement. The statute of limitations on keeping my own counsel about my departure from the Navy had run out.

"I'll be around. I'm not sure what's next, but I'm no longer in the Navy."

I waited for the third degree. For the gasp and outrage.

But Caroline only nodded. "Good. Maybe choose something safer as a next profession." Then she winced. "Although given you just hurled yourself onto a burning boat last night, perhaps I should save my breath."

"I don't plan to make a habit of it."

She sipped her coffee. "What about Madden? Do you plan to make a habit of her?"

"We're still figuring that out."

I braced for the judgment. For the reminder of how Madden had once behaved toward me.

But again, Caroline surprised me by only nodding. "She's got scars. I think a lot more of the kind that don't show."

It was a more astute observation than I'd expected her to have made this quickly.

When I said nothing, she sipped more coffee. "Gabi said y'all had your tongues down each other's throats at the clinic last night."

Heat crawled up my neck. "Gabi has a big mouth."

My sister's lips twitched into a grin. "Of course she does. When was the last time we met a woman you were involved with? Never. Not since high school."

I didn't point out that was because, after high school, everyone on this island had believed I was some kind of predator.

"I'm allowed a private life."

"Of course you are. But as that private life is sleeping in my guest room—with you—you'll allow me a little curiosity."

"Someone tried to kill her, Caro."

The faint amusement faded. "Yeah. I know what that's like."

Fuck. Of course she did. Our father had tried to kill her. Twice. Before Hoyt put an end to it.

"Answer me one thing: is this thing between you because of the circumstances or because of her?"

How could I even answer that? "I wouldn't have gotten to know the real her without the circumstances, so both, I guess."

The stairs creaked, and my head snapped up.

Caroline's mouth twitched. "Relax. That's her, not a hitman."

I swallowed a mouthful of coffee that burned on the way down. "Funny."

Madden appeared in the doorway a minute later, face pale, eyes heavy. She still wore the borrowed pajamas, and her posture curled in a little, as if she hadn't yet decided whether to be embarrassed or grateful. Parading around the home of a semi-stranger in sleep clothes probably left her feeling a little exposed.

When her gaze landed on me, her shoulders dropped a fraction, and her face softened with relief, like I was an anchor point when her world had tipped entirely off its axis.

That trust had something in my chest squeezing.

She strode on into the kitchen with a stiffness to her posture that hadn't been there in the bed, like she'd put her armor back on out of habit and didn't know how to take it off again in front of an audience.

I rose from my chair and snagged her hand, pulling her into me. Her body stilled for a second. Then she exhaled like she'd been holding her breath since the fire and let herself sink into my arms. Her forehead pressed against my shoulder. She swallowed once, and I felt the little tremor she tried to hide.

I flattened both hands against her spine and brushed a kiss to her temple. "There's coffee."

"Thank God." The rasp in her voice was as much sleep as smoke, and the heartfelt words had me smiling, just a little.

"Sit. I'll get you a cup."

Carefully releasing her, I nudged her toward an empty seat.

Madden's gaze darted toward Caroline, color in her cheeks. "Good morning."

"Morning." Caroline's tone was bright and brisk, as if she hadn't just watched her brother hold a woman like his life depended on it. "Rios has the caffeine handled. Are you up to food? I've also got a neighbor who dropped off a bag of clothes before sunrise like we're running a disaster relief station."

Madden blinked. "A neighbor did what?"

Caroline waved a hand. "People heard. People talk. They bring things when they don't know what else to do."

Madden's expression tightened. Pride, maybe. The reflex to refuse help. I recognized it because it lived in me, too.

Caroline stepped closer, her voice gentling. "It's not charity. It's community. Believe me. I've been where you are. Take the help."

Madden's throat bobbed before she tipped her chin in a small nod.

I set a mug in front of her and lightly rested a hand on her shoulder in a touch that said *I'm here* without making her look at it.

She lifted her own hand and laid her fingers over mine with a little squeeze of gratitude. With the other, she picked up the mug and brought it to her lips. Her eyes widened. "You actually know how I take my coffee?"

"I pay attention. Besides, it's hard to forget when you use half as much sugar as coffee."

"I'm not that bad."

"You like coffee syrup," I accused, liking that the teasing put a little spark back in her eyes.

"And you apparently drink motor oil."

Caroline lifted a finger. "I do not make motor oil. However, you have him on battery acid status. Who wants breakfast?"

"I think I could eat something soft. Maybe eggs or oatmeal or something?"

"Coming right up." Caroline rose from the table and picked up a bag from the end of the counter. "Here, take these and see if anything will work for you. I know you don't want to sit around in PJs just now."

Madden frowned at the bag but took it and the coffee back upstairs. I watched her go, a heat in my chest that had nothing to do with desire and everything to do with the fact that she'd been so close to dying and was walking away from me now on her own two feet.

Caroline had just hauled a carton of eggs out of the fridge when the doorbell rang.

I froze, my body going cold and ready in the same breath. "Stay here."

"Rios, I'm sure it's just—"

"Here," I insisted.

I moved to the front door without making noise. Checked the side window first. A man stood on the porch.

Grant Willoughby. He looked like he hadn't slept. He wore civilian clothes and a faint shadow under his eyes. He held some kind of expanding folder, and his stance was tense. That couldn't bode well.

I opened the door a crack. "Willoughby."

"Carrera. Is Madden still here?"

"Is there something new about the fire?" I demanded.

"No. Not yet."

"Then why are you here?"

"To help."

Footsteps sounded on the stairs behind me. "Grant?"

Grant's eyes shifted past me, and his professionalism slipped. His face softened with something that looked a lot like concern. "Madden." The way he said her name carried history.

I didn't like it, but I opened the door fully.

Grant stepped inside like he knew he shouldn't be here and had decided to do it anyway. His eyes roamed over her. Thank God she'd gotten dressed in some of the donated clothes—capri pants and a T-shirt. I watched him fight the mask back in place as she came to stand beside me.

"What are you doing here?"

Grant's hand tightened on the folder. "I shouldn't be."

She only angled her head in question.

"Carson's been blocking you," Grant continued, voice tight now. "And if it was just you being you, I wouldn't—" He cut himself off, jaw working. "I watched what happened last night. When Carrera gave his statement, I watched the way you looked when you understood that someone had locked you in."

Madden's throat bobbed. Her eyes flicked to me and back.

Grant swallowed. "So I pulled what you requested. The stuff he's been sitting on."

Madden stilled.

My pulse ticked up.

Grant held the folder out like it weighed fifty pounds. "Non-redacted. Copies."

Madden stared at it like it was a bomb. "You're serious."

His voice softened. "Yeah."

Madden's hand lifted halfway, then stopped. "Are you sure about this? You're breaking all kinds of rules giving this to me."

"Yeah. If anyone finds out I did this, I'm done. But I don't like what he's doing. And I don't like what happened to you. If this will help you get what you need without putting you in more crosshairs, it's worth the risk."

Madden's hand finally moved. She took the file with careful fingers, as if too much force would tear it.

Grant's eyes flicked down to her hands. To the soot that still lived under her nails despite the shower. To the faint tremor she controlled.

Then his gaze slid to me. The look wasn't jealousy or suspicion. It was a simple, brutal question between men.

You'll protect her?

"Yeah." *With my life.*

Grant nodded once, like he'd expected that answer and needed it anyway. He shifted his weight, glancing toward the door. "I should go."

Madden's voice caught. "Thank you."

He hesitated. His expression softened again. "Don't make me regret it."

"I won't," she promised.

He gave one last glance toward me, then turned and left. The door closed behind him with a quiet click that felt too loud.

The house went still again.

Madden stared down at the envelope in her hands like she was holding a key and a knife at the same time. Her breathing had changed—shallower, faster. Her mind was already racing down corridors of paper and dates and names.

I stepped in close and wrapped an arm around her shoulders.

She didn't stiffen this time. She leaned into me like it was instinct now.

Her voice was quiet. "He risked his job."

"Yeah," I said.

Madden's fingers tightened on the envelope. "He's scared."

"He should be."

She swallowed. Her eyes lifted to mine. "So are we."

The words were plain. Honest. No bravado.

The weight of them settled over my shoulders, and I didn't shrug it off. "Yeah," I said again. "We are."

Madden looked down at the envelope once more. Her thumb traced the edge like she couldn't stop touching the proof that the system could bend.

Her shoulders squared. The familiar steel slid back into her spine.

I tightened my arm around her. Not to restrain her. To anchor her.

"We're gonna need some room to work," I said. "But first, breakfast."

THIRTY

MADDEN

By the time the light outside the dining room windows shifted from afternoon to early evening, the table was gone.

Not literally—Willa's solid oak monstrosity still occupied the center of the room—but whatever sense of it as a place meant for meals and massive holiday celebrations had vanished under layers of paper, file folders, legal pads, the laptop I'd borrowed from Willa, Rios's notebook, and three mismatched coffee mugs that all belonged to other people. We'd moved over here to stay to avoid endangering Caroline's family, and because there'd be more space and privacy for digging into this next layer of investigation.

Sutter House had turned into a war room.

I hadn't planned it that way. I'd told myself I was just going to skim. Get a feel for what Grant had risked his career to hand me. One pass through the files so I knew what I was dealing with before I decided where to dig deeper. But we'd done little more than dump our things—mostly Rios's things and my donated wardrobe—into the guest room before doing a deep dive.

I couldn't stop myself from stacking. Sorting. Lining things up in ways that were instinctive rather than conscious—dates to the left, names to the right, open cases separate from closed, anything involving disappearances flagged with bright yellow tabs I'd found in the junk drawer. I'd dragged chairs out of the way and started taping photocopies to the wall with blue painter's tape like I'd been doing this my whole life instead of improvising in someone else's dining room.

Across the room, Willa's foster dog—currently on temporary loan for our sanity—snored like he'd personally paid rent. He'd claimed the spot by the bay window after a single lap of the dining room, plopped down with a grunt, and made it clear the only thing he was willing to investigate today was whether the sunbeam moved.

The dog was massive and ridiculous in a way that made him necessary. Some kind of mastiff mix with the heart of a marshmallow and the soulful eyes of a poet. I'd fallen for him on sight. Not that I was in any position to have any sort of pet, let alone one that weighed almost as much as I did. But I appreciated the company. Every time I moved too fast or muttered under my breath, his head lifted, dark eyes tracking me with calm, steady interest.

"You're judging me," I told him without looking.

His tail thumped once against the wall.

Rios snorted from the other end of the table. He'd been there the whole time, having claimed one corner of the table early, pulled his notebook close, and started reading alongside me like it was the most natural thing in the world for us to be doing this together.

Which, disconcertingly, it was.

We'd fallen into a rhythm without ever naming it. I read a

file, flagged it, and slid it across to him. He skimmed, annotated, sometimes asked a question or made a quiet sound that told me something didn't sit right. When he finished, he passed it back, and I logged the relevant details into my spreadsheet—name, age, last known location, date reported missing, status.

As far as I could tell, none of the missing had been found.

That alone was enough to make my stomach knot.

"What database are you cross-referencing?" Rios asked after a while.

"Three: missing persons, NCIC summaries, and a scraped dataset Devon built a couple years ago from news archives and nonprofit reports. It's not perfect, but it catches a lot of cases that never made it into official systems."

"Devon?"

"He's a close friend from law school. He started the *Unaccounted* podcast after his cousin disappeared."

"I've heard an episode or two. Specializes in disappearances of the marginalized, right?"

"Yeah."

"He's good at what he does."

"Yes. He is."

He nodded, absorbing that without comment. He didn't ask how I had access to something a podcaster had built or why I trusted it. He trusted me. That was becoming a theme.

The dog padded forward and dropped onto the rug at my feet with a huff.

I stepped back from the wall, marker uncapped, and stared at what I'd built so far.

It wasn't random.

That was the problem.

At first glance, the cases looked scattered—different years, different circumstances, different reasons for initial dismissal.

Runaway. Voluntary disappearance. Left town. No evidence of foul play. But once I stripped away the labels and started lining up what mattered, patterns emerged like bruises under skin.

Age range clustered tighter than it should have.

Almost all women.

Most were reported missing by roommates, coworkers, or casual acquaintances. Very few by immediate family.

And every single one had last been seen in a liminal space —bars, marinas, parking lots near transit hubs. Places where people came and went. Places where it was easy to vanish without causing a ripple.

I circled a date on one page and then another on a different file.

"Rios."

"Yeah."

"Look at these."

He circled around the table and leaned over my shoulder, close enough that the heat of him soaked into me without it being distracting. Much. I pointed, tapping the marker against the paper. "Different cases. Different years. Same two-week window."

He frowned. "Seasonal."

"Exactly."

"High tourist season," he said. "Temporary workers. Boats coming and going."

My jaw tightened. "People who won't be missed right away." The marker squeaked as I underlined another name harder than necessary.

Rios said nothing as he returned to his own pile.

We kept working.

Time blurred the way it always did when I was deep in something that mattered. The dog shifted positions. The light outside changed angles, slipping toward that golden hour preceding full night. At some point, a sandwich materialized at my elbow. I could only assume Rios was doing the Carrera thing and feeding me because I couldn't be bothered to stop long enough to do it myself, but I was too deep in the work to ask.

I was halfway through another file when I realized my shoulders were creeping up toward my ears.

I forced them down and took a breath.

The file in front of me was older. Ten years back. Closed. I scanned the summary, eyes moving faster now, the way they did when my brain was already jumping ahead.

Missing. Female. Early twenties. Last seen leaving work. Dismissed as voluntary.

I slid it to the side and reached for the next one in the folder.

This one was thinner. Fewer pages. Fewer notes. A closed case with the kind of administrative finality that suggested no one had ever expected it to go anywhere.

I skimmed the left side first—name, age, physical description. Nothing leapt out at me until I caught myself pausing on the "last seen" line.

Bar. Again.

Different name. Different year. Same category of space.

I didn't comment. I just marked it and passed it to Rios.

He read in silence, brow furrowing deeper the longer he continued. When he handed it back, he didn't need to say anything.

Another file. Another bar. Another marina-adjacent parking lot. Another woman in her early twenties with no immediate family in the area and a report filed by someone who hadn't seen her for a few days and finally thought, maybe this isn't normal.

The shape of it was starting to seem unmistakable.

I capped the marker and leaned back in my chair, folding my arms. "Okay."

Rios looked up from the file he was holding. "Okay, what?"

"This isn't random disappearance. It's not even serial in the way people usually think of serial. It's selective."

"Explain that to me like I'm not already halfway there."

I pushed up to pace, and the dog lumbered to his feet to follow like a faithful shadow. "If this were opportunistic, we'd see wider variation. Different ages. Different circumstances. At least a few cases where someone reappears or there's credible evidence of a voluntary exit. But this—" I gestured at the wall where I'd amassed a collage of awful. "This is curated."

His jaw tightened. "You're saying someone's choosing."

"Yes." I didn't soften it. "And they're choosing people who can disappear quietly."

He exhaled through his nose, slow. "That tracks with what I'm seeing. No struggle noted. No witnesses who can give more than vibes and impressions. No follow-up pressure from families. Adults, not teenagers who'd have parents who'd make noise."

"And no bodies," I added. "Which matters."

Rios set his file down and leaned back in his chair. "You've been circling around this idea since before the fire."

I met his eyes. "Human trafficking."

He didn't flinch as I continued.

"I didn't want to say it out loud until I could support it. Because people hear that word and immediately jump to sensationalism. But this is logistics. It's infrastructure. Boats. Seasonal labor. Transient populations. It's not dramatic—it's efficient."

He nodded slowly. "And Sutter's Ferry sits right where it shouldn't."

"Exactly." I pointed to the dates again. "These clusters? They line up with peak traffic. When no one's paying attention to who's new and who's leaving."

Silence stretched between us, heavy with the weight of things being named.

Rios reached for another file. "If this is trafficking, where does Priya fit?"

"That's the problem," I said. "She doesn't."

He looked up.

"She doesn't match the profile," I continued. "She's educated. Connected. Her disappearance caused noise. That's not what you want if you're moving people like cargo."

"So she's either an outlier," he said carefully, "or a mistake, as you concluded when we met Rosa."

My stomach tightened. "Or she crossed paths with someone who wasn't following the same rules."

Rios didn't respond right away. He flipped the file over, then frowned.

"What?"

He turned it slightly so I could see the tab. "This one's still open."

I followed his gaze.

Gwen Busby.

For a second, everything in the room seemed to still.

I'd known her file would be in here. I'd requested all missing persons cases. There was no reason hers wouldn't be included. And yet, seeing her name on the tab hit differently than I'd expected—like finding something familiar in a place it didn't belong. "I didn't realize they'd kept it active."

"They haven't," Rios replied. "Not really."

That made my attention sharpen. "What do you mean?"

He slid the folder across the table toward me but didn't open it. "You should look."

I hesitated.

It wasn't fear, exactly. It was... weight. Fourteen years of knowing how this case had been treated. The searches. The flyers. The slow tapering off of effort until it had all become past tense, even though no one had ever said the words.

I pulled the folder closer and opened it.

The left side was exactly what I expected. Gwen's photo. Her details. Her last known movements. Notes I could've recited from memory. I skimmed them quickly, like touching something hot just to confirm it still burned.

Then I shifted to the right side. Procedural documentation near to an inch thick. Logs. Reports. Years of nothing. A final entry noting lack of actionable leads. But the top page was newer than the rest. The date alone was enough to make my pulse spike. Recent. Last year.

I read it once. Then again.

Evidence submitted. Digital media. Related to ongoing investigation.

My fingers tightened on the edge of the paper, and I all but stopped breathing.

Rios stilled beside me. "You didn't know." It wasn't a question.

I looked up at him. "Know what?"

He didn't answer. He just held my gaze, something raw and uneasy flickering there.

And in that moment, I understood the truth he hadn't meant to reveal. He had context I didn't. Did everyone?

The war room walls closed in just a fraction.

I looked back down at the page, at the proof that something had happened long after the rest of us had been told there was nothing left to find.

My voice came out steadier than I felt. "What is this, Rios?"

He didn't look away. "It's something you need to see."

And suddenly I knew—whatever was on the other side of that explanation, nothing about Gwen was going to stay contained anymore.

THIRTY-ONE

RIOS

By the time Ford showed up, the dining room looked like it had been occupied by a small, determined militia.

Paper covered every surface. Painter's tape marched up the walls in straight, stubborn lines. Madden's borrowed laptop sat open beside a legal pad full of tight handwriting, and my notebook had turned into a mess of arrows and circles and dates. Somewhere in the middle of it all was a bowl of pretzels Willa had set down, but nobody had touched them.

The dog—Willa's foster fail-in-waiting—lifted his heavy head when the door clicked, gave Ford a single assessing look, and dropped his chin back onto his paws like Ford hadn't passed inspection.

Ford came in quietly, shoulders tense, a thumb drive held between two fingers like it might burn him. Bree followed close behind, face pale, eyes fixed on the floor until she looked up and found Madden.

Madden wasn't in the dining room anymore. Not exactly. She was there physically, perched at the edge of a chair with her knees drawn in and a mug of coffee braced between her hands. But she'd pulled that mask I hadn't realized she'd shed back on, and the woman who sat before me was quieter. Too controlled. That kind of control wasn't calm. It was bracing.

Gabi slid in behind Ford and Bree, eyes scanning the walls in a single sweep. She let out a low whistle, then caught herself when she saw Madden's expression. Daniel came in last, hair damp, in civilian clothes instead of his Coast Guard uniform, but his face was that of a man never fully off duty.

Sawyer came down the hall from the kitchen, Willa right behind him with a bottle of water and a second pot of coffee like she'd anticipated we were about to do something that would drain the room of oxygen.

No one said hello. No one made small talk. Everyone's eyes shifted to Madden.

She looked at Ford. "You have it?"

Ford nodded once. He held up the thumb drive.

Bree's hand slid into his without ceremony. Ford squeezed back like he needed to anchor both of them in the same moment.

"How exactly is it that you have this?"

"My daughter found the flash drive. Miles came after it, held us at gunpoint trying to finally get his hands on the information that had been used to blackmail him for years."

Madden's face paled. "Oh, my God."

One corner of Ford's mouth twitched in reluctant pride. "Peyton hit him with a stun gun long enough for me to take him down. After that, I made copies of the files before turning the original over to the police because, frankly, I don't trust Carson further than I could throw him, and I figured someone should have backups."

"Sensible. I suspect evidence has a habit of disappearing on this island if it makes the wrong people nervous." Madden's eyes shifted to the drive. She stared at it like it was the last card in a game and she was afraid to see what was on the other side.

Willa cleared her throat. "We can go into the living room. Bigger TV."

Madden's eyes flicked to her, then to me, then away again. "Sure."

We moved like the room was full of tripwires.

The living room at Sutter House was comfortable in a way that made no sense with the tension packed into it. The couches were soft, the rugs comfortably worn, the throw blankets folded with Willa's precise attention. The windows looked out over a strip of dunes and the darkened water beyond. Moonlight threw everything into silver and shadow like it wanted to soften the edges of what we were doing.

It didn't help.

Willa hooked another laptop to the TV without speaking before gesturing for Ford to take over. He didn't look at Madden while he plugged the drive into the side. Bree hovered close, her fingers still wrapped around his hand. Daniel took the armchair nearest the door. Sawyer and Willa sat together on one couch, shoulders squared. Gabi sank onto the other couch, her knees bouncing once before she forced them still. I ended up standing for a second because sitting felt too much like settling in, then I took the chair closest to Madden.

Madden sat on the edge of the couch like she might need to launch herself across the room at any moment. Her coffee mug was gone now. Empty now, her fingers kept flexing and closing as if she was holding something invisible and sharp.

Ford's cursor hovered over two files. "Are you sure you're ready for this?"

"She lived it," Madden bit out. "I can survive watching it."

Grainy cellphone footage filled the TV. Miles Busby, younger, face sharper, shoulders narrower, stood in front of the faded logo of his family's marina. The camera shook like whoever was filming didn't care about quality. Whoever was filming cared about the threat.

Madden's body froze as an off-screen voice spoke conversationally about an offer. Miles outright refused to launder dirty money through the family business. When the fist shot into frame and hit Miles in the gut, Madden flinched hard enough her hand jerked against the couch cushion. She caught herself immediately, like she was offended by her own reaction.

The attacker kept his tone easy. He made it sound like a business deal. Either Miles took the deal or someone he cared about paid the price.

Miles spat on the ground and snarled, "Fuck you."

Madden's breath came shallow. Her eyes didn't blink. She looked like she was watching evidence she'd already known existed, but the reality of it was landing differently now that it was playing in front of her like this.

The video ended.

For a second, no one moved. The only sounds in the room were the ocean outside and the hum of the laptop fan.

Madden's voice came out low. "That's—"

"Yeah." I didn't know what else to offer her in that moment. Yes, that's your cousin. Yes, that's your family's blood. Yes, someone decided they could put hands on him and call it leverage.

She swallowed once. "That was the one used in court for Miles's trial."

Ford nodded without looking at her. "Yeah."

Her eyes shifted to the second file on the screen.

There was a weight to that movement that made my stomach tighten. I knew what was coming. I'd known since Ford showed me last year. Since Bree had gone white and silent and then angry. Since we'd all sat in a room and let the reality settle, and none of us had been able to move for a long minute afterward.

Madden didn't have that. She had only the name Gwen Busby that lived in every part of this island's history and in every part of her own.

Ford's hand hovered over the trackpad. He looked directly at Madden for the first time since we'd sat down. "You sure?"

Madden didn't hesitate. "Play it."

Ford clicked.

The second video was worse. Not in quality. It was actually less grainy than the first. Though the light was dimmer, it was still plenty bright to show metal walls behind a trembling body.

Gwen. Just fifteen years old. Duct tape across her mouth. Wrists bound behind her back. Dark hair tangled around her face, eyes huge and wet, darting like an animal trapped in a place it couldn't understand.

Madden made a sound that wasn't a word. It didn't come from her throat so much as from somewhere deep in her chest, the kind of sound you made when your body reacted before your mind could shape it into language.

The camera panned across Gwen's form with slow deliberation, like the person filming wanted the viewer to see every detail.

Then the off-screen voice spoke.

"You were warned, Busby. We own you now."

Madden's hand flew to her mouth. Her eyes didn't leave the screen. Her whole body locked. She didn't blink. She didn't breathe. She sat like she'd been nailed to the couch.

The video cut to black. The TV screen went dark, reflecting all of us back in a distorted, dim mirror. Ford's laptop cursor hovered. No one moved.

Madden lowered her hand. Her voice was quiet, which was worse than if she'd shouted. "You knew?"

No one answered fast enough.

She turned her head slowly, looking at each of us as if she couldn't make sense of why the room was full of people who'd sat with this without her. "All this time you knew?" Her gaze landed on me and held. "You knew?"

My chest tightened. I opened my mouth. Nothing came out on the first try because there wasn't a clean sentence that would fix it. "We didn't know," I said, because the words mattered and because the truth mattered even if it was messy. "We suspected."

Her eyes narrowed. "You saw this."

"Yes." I didn't look away. I didn't let myself soften it with qualifiers. "We saw it."

"And you didn't tell me."

My jaw clenched. "We thought you already had the context."

"Why would you think that?" Her voice didn't rise. That was the part that made my blood run colder. She wasn't spiraling. She was cutting.

Because you're family, I wanted to say. *Because this island devoured your cousin and then fed you a story that everyone could live with, and I assumed the people who loved you would have told you everything they'd learned, even if it tore them apart.*

Instead, I said the part that mattered. "We didn't deliberately keep this from you."

Madden stared at me like she didn't believe I could use the word deliberately and mean it.

Gabi shifted, hands twisting in her lap. "Madden—"

Madden's head snapped toward her. "You too?"

Gabi's chin lifted, eyes shining. "Yes."

"And no one thought I might want to know?"

Willa leaned forward, voice steady. "We weren't aware you

didn't."

Madden's attention swung to her, the accusation sharp enough to draw blood. "How could you not know?"

Willa didn't flinch. "Because you left. Because you built a whole life away from here. We thought you'd already made your choices about what you could handle. And we didn't have any idea what the authorities might have told your family."

Madden's throat worked. She swallowed hard, eyes flicking back to the dark TV screen as if she was checking whether Gwen was still there.

Bree's voice came small. "I'm sorry."

Madden looked at her, and something in her expression shifted—not softened, exactly, but redirected. Bree hadn't owed her anything. Bree hadn't been part of Gwen's life as a kid. Bree had come into all of this later and still had been the one to watch a fifteen-year-old girl on a grainy screen and carry that horror forward.

Ford's arm tightened around Bree's shoulders. "We should've asked. We should've checked."

Madden's gaze returned to me.

There it was again. That direct line between us that felt like a wire pulled taut. She didn't just want an apology. She wanted the truth of what it meant.

"What am I supposed to do with that?" Her voice finally cracked around the words. "What am I supposed to do with that, Rios?"

I could've answered as a man. I could've answered as someone who wanted to pull her into my arms and tell her we'd fix it, we'd burn the world down if we had to.

But she didn't need romance in that moment. She needed competence. So I answered as the thing I was trained to be. "We figure out what it changes. And what it doesn't."

Her eyes narrowed again. "It changes everything."

"It changes what we can say out loud," I agreed. "It changes the shape of Gwen's disappearance. It changes what was done to her and why. But it doesn't give us a location. It doesn't give us a name. And it doesn't give us anything we can take to a courtroom without blowing up the person who handed you those files."

Daniel shifted, voice low. "And it doesn't tell us where Priya is."

Madden's shoulders went rigid. For a second, I thought she might lash out again. Then her face tightened like she'd bitten down on something sharp. "Carson has had this video for a year. Both of them. One spoke to motive and was made a part of public record during my cousin's trial. The other would have been a procedural nightmare and added nothing from a prosecutorial standpoint, so it seems they buried it. *He* buried it. Maybe not at first, but at the end of the day, it was just like all the others."

Willa and Gabi both straightened. "Others?"

Ignoring them, I kept my focus on Madden. "Seems like it. Yeah."

Madden scrubbed both hands down her face. "Fifteen. She was fucking fifteen years old, and she was part of this."

Her skin had gone gray with grief and horror, and when they opened, those hazel eyes were shattered.

The dog crossed over and leaned his big bulk against her with a little whine. She folded over his back, wrapping around those beefy shoulders and pressing her face into his neck.

No one said a word. What could we say after what she'd just seen? We'd all had our own emotional responses to seeing the footage. It didn't improve with repetition. The only real answer we had was that something truly horrible had befallen someone we'd all cared about.

Eventually Madden straightened, shoulders squaring, chin

lifting. I recognized the shift. This wasn't the Madden who'd asked what she was supposed to do with it. This was the Madden who built cases and made arguments and refused to let emotion be the only thing driving the room. "What do we do now?"

It was the only thing that fundamentally mattered, and I didn't have a good answer.

"We thought—we'd hoped—Carson would be looking into all this," Willa said.

"Should have known better," Gabi muttered darkly.

Ford's voice was a little ragged. "If he's not gonna act, we take the copy to someone else."

"Who?" Madden demanded. "The State Bureau of Investigation? The feds?" Her eyes cut to me. "Do you have any sense of what would actually happen if we took this off the island?"

I did. I had too much sense of it. "If you hand over copies of evidence that was part of a case file without going through the department, you risk compromising the chain of custody. You risk whoever currently has the authority using that as an excuse to discredit it. And you risk Grant's job if anyone traces how you got what you got."

Madden's mouth tightened. "So we sit on it."

"We don't sit on it." That word hit too close to what Carson had done for two decades. "We decide what we can do without getting someone else burned."

Sawyer exhaled, frustrated. "We're back to the same place."

Willa's voice stayed steady. "Not exactly. Now Madden knows. That matters."

Madden's gaze dropped. For a second, the steel slipped and something raw showed through. "It matters that I didn't know."

It was an accusation and a confession all at once.

I shifted closer. "I'm sorry."

Her eyes lifted to mine. She didn't soften. She didn't accept it. Not yet. But she heard it.

Gabi swallowed. "We didn't do it to hurt you."

Madden looked at my sister again, and this time the edge in her expression eased a fraction. "I get that." The words sounded like effort. "I'm not—" She cut herself off, jaw tight. "I don't know what I am right now."

Fair.

Gabi leaned back, wiping at her eyes with the heel of her hand like she was angry her body was betraying her. "What it means is Gwen didn't vanish into the ocean. Someone took her."

"And they filmed it," Madden said, voice flat.

"And they sent it," Daniel added. "At some point."

Ford's shoulders tightened. "It was on that flash drive with the other file. The guy who was blackmailing Miles kept it."

Madden's eyes turned distant for a beat, brain already moving. "So it survived thirteen years in someone's possession."

"Yeah," I said.

Her gaze sharpened again. "Which means people protected it."

Or used it. Or traded it. Or kept it as leverage the way they'd kept Miles as leverage. The implications branched out fast enough my head hurt.

Madden looked down at her hands like she couldn't make sense of them. "And none of this helps Priya."

It wasn't a question. It was a verdict.

Willa leaned forward again. "We don't know that."

Madden's laugh was short and humorless. "We don't even know where Priya's phone was beyond a last ping at the ferry terminal. We don't have a location. We don't have a suspect. We don't have anything we can legally force."

Sawyer's jaw tightened. "We have eyes. We have instincts."

"Instincts don't get her back," Madden said.

I watched her face as she said it. It wasn't just frustration. It was fear. Fear with teeth.

Because now she'd seen Gwen on that screen, and she could finally name the thing she'd been circling around since the beginning. This island didn't just lose women. This island fed them into something that moved through the water and out of reach.

Madden's chest rose and fell fast. She pressed a hand flat to her sternum like she was trying to steady her own breathing.

Though every cell in me wanted to hold her, to offer comfort, I didn't reach for her. Not in front of everyone. Not with the room already watching her bleed.

A phone began to ring. Madden jolted, pulling hers from her pocket. We'd picked up a replacement at the general store earlier in the day, but I didn't think she'd done anything to set it up other than having her number ported over. One glance at the screen and her already gray face chilled. She rose to her feet, stroking one hand along the dog's back. "I... have to take this."

She was already stepping into the hall when I heard her stiff, "Hello?"

Everything broke up quickly after that. Dark had already fallen, and everyone had work tomorrow. There was nothing more to be done tonight except figuring out a way to get Madden to let me back in.

THIRTY-TWO

MADDEN

"Madden." My father's voice came over the line, clipped, precise. Annoyed.

"Yes." I didn't say his name. Didn't call him Dad. I never did. There was no version of this conversation that benefitted from pretending we were the kind of people who used casual greetings.

"Why am I hearing about a fire involving my former brother-in-law's boat from someone other than you?"

My step hitched. Of course he'd heard. And of course he couldn't be bothered to ask after my wellbeing. He was just irritated that information had reached him without passing through the proper channel.

I leaned my shoulder against the wall halfway up the stairs. "I wasn't aware I owed you a briefing."

"You owe me common courtesy." A pause. "And judgment. Which you've never had enough of when it comes to that island."

My jaw tightened. Damn it. He knew I was here. That hadn't been part of the plan.

Of course, the police would've contacted my uncle. He owned the boat. It would've been standard practice. For all I knew, Carson was trying to make a case that I was an arsonist. I should've thought of that and headed Uncle James off at the pass before he'd had a chance to contact my father.

"Did you think I wouldn't find out?"

It didn't really matter whether he meant my being on the island or the fire.

Unwilling to have this conversation near the others, I continued up the stairs and stepped into the guest room we'd been given. "I didn't think about you at all."

Silence snapped tight on the line. I'd broken protocol. I always did eventually. But I didn't have it in me to be more than brutally honest, just now. Not with the image of Gwen's terror etched into my brain.

"So you went back," he said.

When we'd moved, he and my mother had effectively cut ties with Hatterwick. They'd assumed I had, too.

"I'm handling some things," I hedged. "Temporarily."

A sharp exhale. "Handling what, exactly?"

The weight of the last few hours pressed against my ribs—the images, the implications, the way Gwen's face had burned itself into the backs of my eyes. None of that was information he was entitled to. None of it would be met with care.

"I'm working. That's all."

"That is not an answer." His voice rose a notch—not shouting, but projecting. Commanding. "You disappeared from that place years ago, and now you resurface in the middle of a police incident tied to family property? Do you understand how that looks?"

I disappeared? As if they'd spirited me away in the night? But there was no sense in correcting him. Not when all he cared about was optics.

"Yes. It looks inconvenient."

"It looks irresponsible." Another pause, heavier this time. "You were supposed to be past this. Past them. Past that place."

He'd never understood why I'd never be past Gwen. He never would.

I swallowed. "I am." It wasn't a lie. It just wasn't the whole truth.

"You've wasted enough time chasing problems that aren't yours," he continued. "I did not support your education so you could go back and insert yourself into island drama."

Drama.

Something in my chest hollowed out, and I closed my eyes. "I didn't ask for your support." Because why would I ask for a thing that would never be freely given?

"No," he snapped. "You demanded it. And I provided it with the expectation that you would apply yourself to something worthwhile."

I demanded it. As if my Ivy League education had been entirely *my* idea and not a form of pacification I'd hoped might earn me a glimmer of acceptance. Ignoring the bruise he'd struck so effortlessly, I forced my voice to remain even. "This conversation isn't productive." It was a phrase I'd learned early. The one that let me disengage without provoking escalation. "If you have concerns, you can put them in writing."

"You will not dismiss me," he said sharply.

The phone disappeared from my hand.

I gasped and turned, heart slamming into my ribs.

Rios stood there, jaw set, my phone already at his ear as he shut the door. "That's enough." The calm of his voice was almost frightening.

Dad barked something I couldn't hear.

Rios didn't flinch. "You don't get to speak to her like that."

Another bark. Louder this time. Dimly, I registered the sound of engines outside. Everyone else was leaving.

Rios's gaze flicked to me for half a second—checking, not asking—then turned distant again, like he'd locked onto something far more important than the man on the other end of the line.

"She's been through a traumatic event. Someone attempted to murder her. And since you didn't bother to ask—no, she's not injured. She's alive. She's safe. And she doesn't owe you an explanation on your timetable."

I was frozen. Rooted to the floor.

Dad's voice rose, sharp enough that I caught fragments. *Who the hell are you? This is family— You have no right—*

Rios didn't raise his voice. He didn't need to. "If you can't speak to your daughter with basic respect, you won't speak to her at all."

He ended the call. Just like that.

I stared at him, my heart still racing, my hands numb at my sides. My phone seemed heavier when he pressed it back into my palm, like it had absorbed the impact of something it had never been meant to carry.

Rios didn't say anything right away. He just watched me— really watched me—with an expression I couldn't read and didn't have the strength to try.

I thumbed the phone entirely off, wanting to shut down my father's last avenue of reaching me. "You didn't have to do that."

"Yes, I did."

I swallowed. "He's my father."

"I know." Something in his voice shifted. Not anger. Understanding. The kind that came too easily.

I folded my arms across my chest, as if they might keep me upright. "I usually handle him."

"I heard how you handle him." The words landed harder than anything my father had said.

I laughed once, short and broken. "Congratulations. You've just witnessed my childhood."

His jaw tightened.

I waited for the familiar follow-up. The *but he means well.* The *he wants what's best for you.* The rationalizations I'd started out repeating, then perfected myself over decades.

Rios didn't offer them.

Instead, he stepped closer. "You don't deserve that."

The room tilted.

In reflex, I shook my head. "It's fine."

"No," he insisted, firmer now. "It's not."

The truth of that hit me like exhaustion. Bone-deep. I slid down onto the edge of the bed because my legs stopped pretending to hold me.

Rios crouched in front of me, bringing himself level with where I sat perched on the edge of the bed. He didn't touch me yet, waiting instead with his hands pressed to the mattress on either side of my thighs, creating a cage of care I didn't know what to do with. The heat of him radiated toward me, but he held himself back, giving me space even as he invaded it. "I'm sorry for not seeing it sooner."

I frowned, confusion warring with the exhaustion that weighed down my limbs. "Seeing what?"

"All of it. Why you don't rest. Why you don't ask for help. Why you think you have to be perfect to earn space." His voice was low, steady, each word deliberate. "Why you've spent your whole life trying to prove you deserve to exist."

My throat closed, the air suddenly too thick to draw into my lungs.

He exhaled slowly, the sound carrying a weight of regret. "I should've figured it out earlier. I didn't. I'm sorry."

That apology—quiet, unqualified, asking nothing in return—hit somewhere deep and tender, a place I'd armored over so thoroughly I'd forgotten it existed.

I pressed my lips together, fighting the urge to deflect. To joke. To minimize what he was offering me. "I didn't ask you to—"

"I know. You shouldn't have to."

Something gave way then. Not dramatically. Not with tears or broken confessions. Just enough that my shoulders sagged and my eyes burned with the pressure of emotion I'd been holding back for what felt like years. Was this truly what it meant to be one of his people? To have someone see the wounds you'd hidden and tend them without being asked?

Rios rose from his crouch and settled beside me on the bed, his weight causing the mattress to dip. He pulled me into his chest with a gentleness that undid something else inside me. I didn't stiffen this time, didn't brace against the contact. I went willingly, forehead pressing into the solid warmth of his shoulder as his arms came around me like they'd always known exactly where to go, how to hold me together when I was threatening to come apart.

No one had ever stood between me and my father before. No one had ever believed I was worth the conflict, worth the risk of his displeasure. But Rios had done it without hesitation, had put himself in the line of fire as if it were the most natural thing in the world.

I breathed him in—salt and soap and something indefinably solid, something that spoke of safety—and let myself stay there, let myself lean into the strength he offered so freely. I could rest, just for a moment. Just long enough to remember what it felt like.

Then he murmured, "I've got you," his voice rumbling through his chest and into my bones, and the last shred of my resistance faded like morning mist under the sun.

How was I supposed to stand against this man who'd had every reason in the world to hate me and instead seemed to be the only one who truly understood me? Who saw past all my carefully constructed defenses to the scared, exhausted woman underneath?

Lifting my head, I cupped his cheek, feeling the scrape of stubble against my palm, as I searched those deep, dark eyes that saw far too much. That had always seen too much, even back when we were younger and I'd been so determined to look anywhere but at him.

I was the one who closed the distance, brushing my mouth to his in a kiss that started soft, tentative. I'd intended it as a way to express my gratitude, because words were failing me just now, tangling on my tongue before I could shape them into anything coherent. Instead, just as had happened at the clinic, we ignited at the touch, the spark catching and blazing into something neither of us seemed capable of controlling. His arms tightened around me, and I pulled him closer, threading my fingers into the thick silk of his hair. A faint shudder ran through his body as I licked the seam of his lips, as if he was using every shred of his formidable control to hold himself back, to keep from consuming me whole.

Sexy, noble man.

To clarify my position on that particular issue, I shifted, swinging one leg over his thighs and settling myself in his lap, where I got ready confirmation that he wasn't immune to this heat sparking and crackling between us. The hard length of him pressed against my core, and a bolt of pure need shot through me. Pausing, I pulled back just long enough to take his face between my hands. "Rios."

His gaze burned into mine, pupils blown wide with desire even as concern flickered at the edges. "We don't have to—"

"I know."

"You've been through a terrible shock." His voice was rough, strained with the effort of doing the right thing even when his body was clearly voting for a different course of action.

Impossibly, the corner of my mouth twitched upward. "I'm thinking perfectly clearly right now." To emphasize the point, I rocked my hips against him, grinding down in a slow, deliberate motion that had his eyes nearly rolling back in his head.

Those eyes dropped to half-mast, heavy-lidded and dark with want, and his hands grabbed my hips, seeming torn between pressing me closer and unseating me entirely. "Are you sure about this, Counselor?"

I gave him the only truth I could. "You're the only thing in my life that makes any sense at all right now."

Rios surged up with a speed and strength that stole my breath, and my arms and legs automatically tightened around him in response. Not that he was about to let me fall as he turned and settled us back on the bed, all that warm, hard, muscled weight stretching out over me in a way that made me feel deliciously trapped. His eyes burned into mine, serious despite the desire etched in every line of his face. "Tell me to stop at any point, and I will."

But I wouldn't stop him. I wanted this. Wanted him. Wanted to lose myself in sensation and forget, at least for a little while, everything that was crumbling around me.

In answer, I kissed him again, pouring everything I couldn't say into the press of our lips, whimpering as his tongue swept into my mouth in a claiming that sent heat pooling low in my belly. His hips ground against my center, and the friction was maddening. I needed so much more than this layered friction. I was desperate for skin on skin, to him inside me filling all the empty, aching places.

My fingers closed over the hem of his t-shirt, tugging it up so I could finally get to the hard planes of muscle I'd been fantasizing about since I'd seen him shirtless on the boat next door. He jerked his mouth away from mine only long enough to drag it over his head in one fluid motion, tossing it to the floor without looking. Then he did the same to me, stripping off my t-shirt and the plain white bra beneath. His curse was reverent as his gaze raked over my exposed skin before he lowered his mouth to take one budded nipple between his lips.

I muffled my cry, my back bowing off the mattress as I bucked for more pressure, more of that delicious friction. His tongue circled and flicked while his teeth grazed just hard enough to send sparks of pleasure-pain shooting straight to my core. It had been so very long since I'd let anyone close enough to touch me like this, and even then, it had never been this consuming, this overwhelming. Maybe because I struggled to trust people—men in particular.

But I trusted Rios.

He lavished so much delicious, focused attention on my breasts—alternating between them, sucking and licking and nipping until I was writhing beneath him—that I hardly noticed he'd worked his hands between us to unfasten my jeans until that big, broad palm slid beneath the fabric of my under-wear, his fingers cupping the growing heat. My head fell back on a moan that was probably too loud, too revealing, but I couldn't bring myself to care. It was too much sensation and not enough, all at once. I widened my legs as much as the denim would allow, arching into the touch, inviting more. Begging without words.

And, oh, he gave it, dragging one blunt finger through my folds, gathering the wetness he found there before circling my clit with it and then doing it all over again, over and over, building a rhythm that had my hips rocking to meet him, chasing the pleasure he was doling out in carefully measured increments.

I gasped his name, equal parts plea and demand, past the point of pride or pretense.

"Need more, pretty girl?" The endearment, combined with the rough edge to his voice, sent another wave of heat through me.

"Yes." At my hissed admission, he finally slipped a finger inside me, and the stretch and fullness made my inner walls clench greedily around him.

My body clenched, desperate for more as he began to thrust, in and out, his thumb finding my clit and circling in time with the movement. One finger became two, and the fullness was almost enough. Almost. But not quite.

"Let go for me, Madden. I've got you." The words were both permission and command, his breath hot against my ear.

On a cry that might have been his name or might have been something more incoherent, I broke apart, trusting that he'd keep his word and wouldn't let me fall as pleasure crashed over me in waves that seemed to go on and on.

He eased me down slowly, gentling his touch as the aftershocks rippled through me, then stretched out beside me like some giant, contented cat, that sensual mouth twisted into an unmistakable look of male satisfaction that should have annoyed me but somehow didn't.

"Better?" His voice carried a thread of smugness that definitely would have annoyed me under other circumstances.

I lolled my head toward him, my limbs heavy and loose in a way they hadn't been in longer than I could remember. "It's a start."

Those eyes gleamed with humor and renewed heat. "Only a start?"

Digging deep, I mustered sufficient muscle control to roll toward him, hooking a finger in the waistband of his jeans where they rode low on his hips. "This was not a one-sided proposition."

"It can be. I'm not expecting—" He started to protest, ever the gentleman, but I wasn't having it.

I pressed my lips to his in a deliberate bid to shut him up, to end this ridiculous notion that I was some fragile thing that needed to be handled with kid gloves. When I pulled back, I held his gaze. "I appreciate this noble streak of yours. That you want to be absolutely sure that I'm sure, that I'm not making a decision I'll regret tomorrow. I am sure." I brushed my mouth over his once more, softer this time. "I want you in my bed, Rios. I want you in me."

He stared at me, searching my face with an intensity that felt like being read at the cellular level, looking for long enough that my heart began to sink and brace for rejection, for him to decide I was too broken, too complicated, too much trouble. But apparently he finally saw whatever he'd needed to see, some confirmation that this was real and wanted, because he pulled me closer again, his kiss deeper this time.

Neither of us spoke after that as we slipped into the wordless, timeless dance of stripping away the last barriers between us—jeans and underwear discarded in a tangle of fabric and fumbling fingers. We explored each newly exposed inch of skin with hands and mouths, learning the geography of each other's bodies, the places that made breath hitch and muscles tense. He left me only long enough to dig a condom from his wallet—a moment of practicality that somehow made this more real, more intentional—and sheathe himself with hands that weren't entirely steady.

And as the moon rose high above the ocean beyond the window, painting the room in silver light, he positioned himself between my thighs and slipped into me in one long, smooth stroke that had us both gasping. We followed the pull of our own tide, building and cresting and building again, chasing it with increasing urgency until we finally broke together, pleasure crashing over us like waves against the shore.

THIRTY-THREE

RIOS

Hunger drove us out of our room somewhere close to midnight. The upstairs bedroom door clicked softly behind us. The sound shouldn't have mattered. It did anyway. Everything felt like that lately—small noises turning into meaning, ordinary things carrying weight.

We froze in the hall, listening for Sawyer and Willa, for the dogs. Madden's pulse gave an erratic jump beneath my thumb as I brushed it over her wrist. We were grown-ass adults who had every right to leave anytime we chose, but it still felt a little like we were sneaking out, and I'd have bet my last dollar that wasn't something she'd ever done growing up. The idea of her doing it now made me grin in the dark.

On bare feet, we made our way downstairs to the kitchen. In the dim light over the stove, I took in Madden's tumble of dark brown curls and the way she wore my shirt like it belonged to her. The tight, braced tension she'd been holding onto since the video had eased, as if she'd finally found a place inside herself to set some of it down for a minute.

I told myself not to read into that.

I failed immediately.

"How hungry are you?" Hunger was a safe topic. It had rules and solutions.

Madden's mouth twitched. "Starving."

"We can raid the fridge. Guaranteed they've got something."

She made a face. "I know. It just feels weird. Like rummaging through someone else's drawers."

"That's because you've never let anyone give you anything without paying for it."

Her eyes flicked to mine, sharp even in the dim light. For a second, I thought she might argue. Instead, she let out a breath that sounded like surrender. "Probably true. But I still feel weird about it. Home Port?"

Rather than point out that your friends were absolutely the people whose drawers and cabinets you raided—I got the sense she hadn't ever had that sort of friends—I only nodded. "Yeah, we can do that."

She'd learn. But not tonight.

On the drive, I kept my attention split: half on the dark road ahead, half on the woman beside me. She said nothing, staring out the window at nothing in particular. I didn't get the sense that she wanted to put distance between us after what had happened. Neither did I think she was circling back around what she now knew—or at least suspected—about Gwen. Not yet, anyway. I wasn't sure how long that might hold once we hit the bar.

For once, I wished we had a Waffle House on the island. It was damned hard to hold on to the dark in the face of loaded hash browns, eggs, and coffee had in bright yellow booths at any hour of the day or night.

Home Port's parking lot looked like what it always looked

like after eleven: too many trucks, too few spaces, and the faint, constant hum of people who didn't want to go home yet. Music pushed out through the door every time it opened. A few guys leaned against a pickup tailgate, beers in hand, laughing too loud. Someone stumbled and caught themselves. Someone else shouted a goodbye that sounded like a threat.

Madden sat still for a beat before opening her door.

"You good?" I murmured.

She turned her head. In the dark, her eyes looked almost black. "I'm fine."

That was never the whole truth with her, but tonight I let it stand. I got out, walked around the front of the truck, and held my hand out.

After a moment's hesitation, her fingers slid into mine like she was testing what it was like to let someone lead without losing herself.

Inside, the noise hit us like a wall. The crowd wasn't a crush, but it was busy. Enough bodies that you had to angle your way through. Enough voices that any conversation could disappear into the hum.

That suited me. We'd stand out less in a crowd like this.

Madden's gaze flicked around the room in that way that told me she was assessing every person around us as a potential witness.

I kept us moving, two steps ahead of her, not in a controlling way. In a protective way. A difference she seemed to understand now.

We snagged a booth near the pool table, close enough to hear the smack of balls and the muttered insults between shots. The spot wasn't private exactly, but it wasn't in the center of the room either. We could see the door. We could see the bar. We could see the side hall to the bathrooms and the back exit that led to the alley.

Madden slid onto her bench and leaned back, stretching her legs beneath the table until her foot brushed my shin. Not an accident.

The electricity of the touch went all the way up my spine.

A server appeared, pen tucked behind her ear, eyes already tired. "Y'all know what you want, or you need a minute?"

"Burger," Madden said immediately. "Fries. And... onion rings."

The server's eyebrows rose. "Hungry."

"You have no idea," Madden muttered.

I ordered a basket of wings and fries because I could eat my weight in salt right now and still want more.

The server walked off, and for a second Madden stared at the scarred wood of the table like it had answers.

I didn't rush her. I watched the room.

A couple of regulars I recognized from my previous trips in here. One guy at the bar who kept checking his phone like he expected bad news. Two women in tank tops sharing a basket of something fried, laughing quietly, leaning into each other. A group of men near the pool table, louder than the rest, bodies loose with drink and arrogance.

Madden tapped her fingernail once against the table. A small sound. A tell.

"What?" I asked.

Her eyes lifted to mine, and something like reluctance passed across her face—like she didn't want to open the door she was standing in front of.

"I keep thinking about what you said," she murmured.

I kept my voice neutral. "Which part?"

She huffed a short laugh. "The part where you said it changes what we can say out loud, but it doesn't give us a name."

"Yeah."

Madden's gaze dropped again. "I don't like not having a name."

"No one does."

She leaned in a fraction. "You don't either."

It wasn't a question. It was an observation. The kind she'd always been good at and I'd always resented because she saw too much.

"You mentioned someone wanted a meet," I said, because that was actionable. Because that was a door we could push on.

Her eyes widened, and she cursed under her breath. "Oh my God."

My mouth twitched. "You forgot."

"I forgot." She pressed her palm to her forehead like she could physically push the thought back into place. "I have been —" She cut herself off. "Yes. I forgot."

"You've had a busy day or two," I pointed out.

Her glare was half offended, half grateful. "Shut up."

"You going to check it?" I asked.

She pulled her phone out and unlocked it, thumb moving fast. The screen glow lit her face, and for a second she looked younger in the blue light. Not softer—Madden didn't do soft easily—but less armored.

She frowned at the screen. "The poster pulled the thread."

It was my turn to frown. "What? Like it's gone entirely?"

"Yeah. No follow up, no DM. It's just gone."

I considered. "Did you have any sense of where they were?"

"No."

"If they were on Hatterwick and they heard about the fire..." I trailed off, letting the implication sink in.

Her cheeks paled. "They might have gotten spooked and decided it was too dangerous to talk."

I didn't like the math around that or the fear the idea of it put in her eyes. "Or it might be completely unrelated. You posted to a lot of boards, right? What would be the likelihood that the person who set the fire just *happened* to be on one and just *happened* to see the request for a meet and just *happened* to know it was you in time to set a fire on your boat two or three hours later? That's a lot of stretches."

Carefully, she turned off the phone and set it facedown on the table. "Well, I guess that's another potential lead cut off."

Reaching across the table, I laid a hand over hers. "We'll find another."

She turned her palm up and curled it around mine.

The server interrupted us, sliding plates onto the table with a practiced smile before vanishing again like she didn't want to interrupt whatever she sensed was happening at our table.

I nodded. "Eat."

She took a bite like she was proving she could still do normal things. I followed suit, salt and heat grounding me in a way I hadn't realized I needed.

We ate in silence for a few minutes, the noise of the room filling the spaces between us. We'd shared multiple meals over our time working together, and I marveled at how being quiet with her now was easy, even in the middle of chaos.

I didn't turn my head when I heard Priya's name. I didn't react at all. I let my attention drift the way it always did when a keyword hit.

"—told you she was gonna hustle you," one of the men near the pool table said, voice loud with alcohol and satisfaction.

"Bullshit," another voice barked back. "She didn't hustle me. She—she cheated."

Laughter erupted.

A third voice chimed in. "She did not cheat. She just played like she had eyes. Girl had aim."

"Yeah," someone else said. "And she took your money like it was her job."

More laughter.

Madden kept eating, unaware. She didn't glance around. I didn't think she clocked the conversation because her focus remained on her plate and the small patch of normal she was trying to keep. That was fine. Let her be lost in her thoughts for now.

I lifted a wing and bit in, shifting my gaze to the reflection in the framed black-and-white photo of the marina on the wall beside our table.

One man stood a little apart from the group. Still part of the circle—but off to the side. He held a cue loosely, not playing yet. He didn't laugh as hard. He didn't lean in. His shoulders stayed tight even while everyone else relaxed.

Someone nudged him. "You still sore about it, man? She cleaned you out twice."

His jaw flexed. "Drop it."

"Aw, come on," the first guy goaded. "You were sweet on her."

"Was not."

"Were."

The man's grip tightened on the cue. Not anger exactly. Something... stiffer. Like he was trying to hold a lid on something that wanted out.

He glanced toward the bar, then toward the door. Quick. A check.

Not unusual in a bar.

But the timing hit wrong.

"Maybe she'd still be around if you'd asked her out," another guy said, laughing. "Instead, you let her take your last twenty and said thank you, ma'am."

The man's mouth flattened. "She was smart," he muttered.

Not cute. Not hot. Not sexy. Smart.

That word snagged.

Smart meant he'd probably talked to her. Smart meant he'd seen her as a person. Smart meant the loss had landed differently than it might have for a total stranger.

Madden reached for another onion ring. I leaned in, voice low, casual enough not to trip her alarm. "Finish up."

She paused mid-bite and looked at me.

I didn't give her the explanation yet. I didn't need her head turning toward the pool table.

Her eyes narrowed slightly. "Why?"

"Just do it."

Madden's posture stiffened the way it always did when someone gave her an order. Then she exhaled, the edge easing. She trusted me. That was new. Still strange.

"Okay," she said, and took another bite.

I watched the group by the pool table without looking like I watched them, the way I'd been trained to watch: peripheral, relaxed, nothing that screamed cop. My body stayed loose. My attention did not.

The man with the tight shoulders took his turn at the table. He lined up a shot, hands steady, cue sliding forward with controlled precision. He made the ball. The guys around him cheered like that meant something.

He didn't smile.

He sank the next shot too. He missed the third by a hair and swore softly under his breath, not loud enough for the others.

His frustration looked real.

His tension looked more real.

Madden wiped her fingers with a napkin and slid her plate away. She glanced at mine. "You finished?"

"Yeah," I tossed down enough cash to cover the bill and a tip. I didn't want to wait on a check. I didn't want to linger.

We stood.

I didn't hurry her. I just placed my hand at the small of her back and guided her toward the door, letting it seem like we were leaving for the reasons people left bars late at night. Nothing urgent. Nothing alarming.

Outside, the ocean smell came in clean and sharp. I steered Madden to the side of the building, into a pocket of shadow near stacked crab pots and a leaning pallet. Enough cover that we wouldn't be obvious, but close enough to see the door.

Madden leaned back against the wall and let out a quiet laugh, breath visible in the chill. "This is hardly a place I'd expect you to get amorous."

I stepped in close and stole a brief kiss—quick, controlled, enough to look like the reason we'd ducked away. Her lips parted automatically, her hand sliding up to my chest like she'd forgotten what to do with herself and decided this was safer than thinking.

I pulled back before it could turn into something else. "Tempting," I murmured. "But no. We're here to wait."

Her eyes sharpened. "For what?"

Maybe for nothing. Maybe for everything. But there was no time to explain any of that to her because the door opened.

I pressed Madden back gently, one hand braced beside her shoulder, the other at her hip. I mimed shhh.

She went still instantly, body aligning with mine, breath quieting like she'd flipped a switch. Madden didn't do panic. She did control.

The pool player I'd been watching stepped out alone, keys jingling, head down. He looked over his shoulder once, quick and uneasy, before heading toward the docks.

I waited. Counted heartbeats. Let him get far enough

ahead that he wouldn't turn and catch us as part of the doorway light.

I leaned in, voice barely more than air. "Stay close."

Madden's eyes widened, but she nodded.

We moved off the wall and followed, keeping distance, using the shadows of pilings and parked boats the way I'd used alleyways overseas. The dock stretched out ahead, lights casting long, broken reflections on the water. Somewhere a buoy clanged softly, the sound dull and repetitive.

The man walked like someone with something heavy in his pockets that wasn't metal. His shoulders stayed tight. His head turned slightly now and then, not quite looking behind him, but checking.

He felt watched.

Good.

Madden's breath came steady at my side, her steps careful, quiet. She didn't ask questions. She didn't whisper. She trusted me to tell her when it mattered.

We reached the point where the dock split—one branch toward the charter boats, the other toward smaller working vessels tied up close. The fisherman hesitated before turning down the working side.

My pulse picked up.

I didn't like the way Madden's fingers brushed mine—only once—like she needed the reminder that I was there. For the first time all night, I wished she wasn't here. Wished I was on my own to follow this guy and satisfy the niggle in my gut. But she was here, and we couldn't risk losing him on the slim possibility my gut was right.

I gave her a brief squeeze back and angled us into deeper shadow as we followed the man from the bar.

THIRTY-FOUR

MADDEN

I crept beside Rios, nerves wound tight as we followed the man from the bar a couple miles from the marina. The shack squatted at the end of a rough lane that had never been properly paved and had been patched so many times after storms it looked like a scar map. Pines and scrub crowded the edges. The marsh pressed in, thick and alive, and the ground still held the day's heat in a damp, stubborn way that made sweat cling instead of evaporate.

The building itself looked like it had lost a fight with weather and kept showing up anyway. One side had been repaired with mismatched boards. One corner of the roofline dipped slightly, like it had shrugged off a hurricane and never fully recovered. Old storm debris still littered the periphery—broken pallets, a warped sheet of corrugated metal, a length of rope bleached nearly white. It was the sort of building that could've been used for a multitude of purposes over the decades. It was obvious no one came here for routine anything anymore. If anyone used it at all, they used it the way people used old outbuildings: overflow storage. A place you stuck things you didn't want to throw away but didn't need right now. A place no one visited unless they had a reason.

What reason would a man have to come here in the middle of the night?

No good one.

Rios and I crouched behind a tangle of stacked fish totes and crab pot frames half swallowed by weeds, our bodies angled toward the side door. He'd guided us here without a word, moving with quiet certainty across short distances that seemed longer in the dark because I couldn't see what I might trip over. The island didn't sprawl the way mainlanders thought places sprawled. Everything here sat within reach. That didn't make it safe. It just made it tighter. Harder to disappear without someone noticing—unless you knew exactly where people didn't look.

The air wrapped around us like a wet blanket. Mosquitoes whined near my ear. I resisted the urge to swat. Any sudden movement seemed loud, and though Rios hadn't said a word about what we were doing, I understood the need for silence.

The man from the bar crossed to the door without hesitation and unlocked it, slipping inside and pulling it closed behind him.

I exhaled a slow breath and leaned toward Rios, mouth close to his ear. "Okay, tell me what we're doing."

He kept his focus on the shack like an enemy combatant, but he leaned close enough that the warmth of his breath brushed my ear as he murmured, "At the bar, I heard his buddies running their mouths. About Priya. About pool. About her cleaning him out more than once."

I tried to keep my voice level. "That doesn't exactly scream motive for kidnapping."

"Not by itself."

"What am I missing?" Because we wouldn't be here if I hadn't missed something.

He shifted slightly, the smallest movement of his shoulders. "The way he reacted wasn't normal."

I glanced at the door again. The shack stayed silent.

"What does 'not normal' mean?" My brain didn't like vagueness. It wanted evidence. Names. Timelines.

Rios finally turned his head a fraction, enough that his mouth brushed the shell of my ear when he spoke. "He didn't laugh. He didn't play it off. He shut it down hard. Too hard. And when they teased him, he didn't get pissed the way guys do when they're being ribbed. Like he was afraid of saying the wrong thing. Maybe keeping a lid on something."

A chill threaded through me despite the heat.

I looked at the shack again, and my mind tried to shove the two images together—the broad, terrifying pattern I'd been building for hours, and this intimate, ugly, almost prosaic motive Rios was describing. A guy spurned. Or at the very least embarrassed by a woman.

I wanted to ask if that was enough. But I'd been a prosecutor. For some men, it was.

"You think he took her?"

Rios didn't answer quickly. That pause did more to spike my pulse than any dramatic declaration might have.

"I don't know. I don't think it's likely. But if I'm wrong and we walk away, I don't get to take that back."

There it was. The responsibility that was the bedrock of who he was. The reason he was the hero and not the villain he'd been painted as for years.

My mouth felt dry. "Okay. Then we wait."

Time stretched until my legs ached from crouching. Sweat dampened the back of my neck and the hollow between my shoulders. The mosquitoes grew bolder. The marsh made its own noises—frogs, insects, the occasional soft splash that might've been a fish or something bigger. There was no other habited structure in sight from here, but faint sounds reminded us both that people weren't all that far away. An engine started and died. A door slammed. A dog barked once and quieted.

Island sounds. Normal sounds.

Except nothing was normal.

While we sat there, my brain spun.

Priya leaving the bar. The ferry terminal. The last ping.

And then the other pieces I'd been staring at all day: women who vanished in liminal places. Boats coming and going. Seasonal clustering. The kind of infrastructure you didn't notice until you knew to look for it.

This—one fisherman and a beat-up old building—didn't erase that.

But it made room for an alternative: the messy human variables that threaded through bigger crimes and made them possible.

A man who knew her.

A man who'd watched her play pool and laugh and not care that he wanted her attention.

A man who couldn't stand the idea that she belonged to herself.

I hated that my mind went there. I hated that it made a kind of horrible sense.

The door scraped open, and my body locked.

Rios's hand lifted slightly, a silent command for stillness, though I'd already frozen. I couldn't have moved if I'd wanted to.

The man stepped out alone. He locked the door, glanced around, and headed back toward the marina and the bar without turning on any exterior lights. He moved like he expected no one to be here—which meant he either felt safe...

...or he felt entitled.

I waited for Rios to signal, to move, to do something.

He watched the retreating figure until it became nothing but a smear of darkness against the night. Then he waited—not just a few seconds, but several long, careful minutes—before finally rising from his crouch. His movements were deliberate, practiced, the kind of patience born from military training and years of knowing that rushing could get you killed.

I followed, my knees stiff and protesting after being folded beneath me for so long. My sneakers sank slightly into the damp sand with each step. The closer we got to the building, the stronger the odor became—and it wasn't the clean, sharp scent of fresh fish or the pleasant tang of salt brine that you smelled at the docks in the morning. This was something older, more layered. Ancient salt and rot that had soaked deep into wood and metal over years, maybe decades. The scent of a place that hadn't been properly scrubbed or maintained in a long time, not because it was forgotten, but because no one cared enough to bother anymore. Because it served its purpose as it was.

The door was secured with a thick padlock hanging from a heavy-duty hasp that had been bolted into the weathered boards. The lock itself looked relatively new, the metal still bright enough to catch what little moonlight filtered through the clouds. The rest of the building did not.

Rios crouched, examining the hardware for a moment before he pulled something from his pocket. One of those multi-tool things men carried with seventy-five uses. He flipped out one of the larger blades and went to work on the wood around the hasp—because old storm damage meant weak points, and weak points meant leverage. He worked carefully, controlled, until the board gave with a muffled crack that sounded horrifically loud in the quiet night.

Rios caught the door before it could swing wide and bang against the interior wall. He eased it open just enough for us to slip through sideways, one at a time, bodies pressed close to minimize the gap.

The smell hit like a fist.

I clamped my mouth shut hard enough that my jaw ached as I fought the gag reflex. Heat inside the building sat trapped and wet, thick with brine and something sourly organic that I couldn't quite identify and didn't want to. I had the distinct sense that fish had rotted here over the course of years, their decay seeping into every porous surface. Although one hot summer would be enough to bake the odor in forever.

Rios flicked on his phone flashlight. I did the same, beams slicing through the darkness to paint everything in harsh, jumping shadows.

The interior didn't offer any additional clues to what this place might have been in its former life. A couple of badly scarred work tables had been shoved carelessly to one side, their surfaces water-stained and warped. I spotted a busted commercial ice machine with a stained tarp draped over it like a shroud, stacks of plastic storage totes in various states of deterioration, coils of rope in different thicknesses, and fishing nets hanging limp and tangled from rusted wall hooks like tired ghosts of better days. A large chest freezer sat unplugged in the far corner, its lid cracked open just enough to make my skin crawl with awful possibilities—at least until I angled my light inside and saw that it was blessedly empty except for some dried brown stains I chose not to examine too closely.

The building turned out to be significantly bigger than it had looked from outside, with an odd, maze-like collection of rooms that bled one into another without clear purpose or organization. Each space held another chaotic hodgepodge of abandoned equipment and maritime detritus. This was exactly the kind of place someone could stash a person if they wanted to. Or hide a body. Because absolutely no one came here unless they had a very specific reason to.

I moved deeper into the labyrinth, my light sweeping methodically behind stacks of totes, around the hanging nets that brushed against my shoulder and made me flinch, past a precarious stack of broken plastic chairs that looked ready to topple. My own breath sounded unreasonably loud in my ears, almost drowning out the soft shuffle of Rios's footsteps behind me.

I found myself unconsciously counting potential hiding spaces the same way I'd learned to count and catalog evidence: corner, corner, behind, under, gap between—

A sound cut through the silence.

Not a voice. Not words. Just a small, choked whimper that was somehow more human and more desperate than any scream could have been.

I immediately turned my beam toward the back of the current room, my heart suddenly hammering against my ribs.

A narrow cot sat pushed against the far wall, half hidden behind what had been arranged to look like a casual wall of stacked crab traps and plastic totes. Someone had clearly tried to make it appear as though storage had simply been shoved back there and forgotten over time, allowed to accumulate naturally. The disguise was crude at best, amateurish even, but in the pitch dark, with no reason to do more than cast a casual glance around, it might actually work. It might be enough.

A figure lay curled on the cot in a defensive position. Bound with what looked like duct tape. Gagged with more of the same. Eyes wide and reflecting our flashlight beams with an almost animal terror.

My chest seized so hard it physically hurt, like someone had reached inside and squeezed. "Priya."

I bolted toward her without thinking, without caution, dropping hard to my knees beside the cot with enough force that pain shot up my thighs. "Oh my God. I'm here. We're here. You're safe now."

Her eyes flooded instantly with tears that spilled over and ran down her cheeks. She made a broken, muffled sound around the tape covering her mouth, her whole body jerking as if she didn't know whether to fight or collapse, whether we were real or some kind of cruel hallucination her desperate mind had conjured.

Realizing abruptly that she might not be able to see my face clearly with the flashlight shining in front of me, I quickly turned the phone around to illuminate my own features instead. "It's Madden Reilly. I'm a friend of Astrid's—we met over fish tacos. Remember?"

Rios was already there beside me, dropping into a crouch, his hands steady and sure as he pulled out another blade attachment on his multi-tool and began carefully cutting through the layers of tape.

The second the gag came free from her mouth, Priya sucked in a huge, shuddering gulp of air and immediately broke into wracking sobs. "Thank—thank God—I thought—I didn't think anyone—"

"It's okay." My voice came out rougher than I'd intended, scraped raw with emotion I was barely keeping contained. "You're okay now. We've got you. You're safe."

Her gaze darted frantically between us, back and forth, like she didn't quite believe we were actually real, like she was terrified we might disappear if she blinked.

"How long have you been here?" The question came out sharper than I'd meant it to, more like an interrogation than comfort, but my body was demanding answers, demanding a timeline, demanding something concrete I could grab onto and make sense of.

Priya shook her head hard, the movement jerky and uncoordinated. "I don't—I don't know for sure. Days, I think. Maybe? I lost track after..." She swallowed hard, her throat working visibly.

"Have you been in this building the whole time?" Rios asked, his tone carefully measured and calm even as he continued working on the tape around her wrists.

"Not the whole time. Not... not at first." She swallowed again and visibly winced, like the action hurt her throat. "Somewhere else before. I think. It's—everything's confused."

Rios's jaw flexed with barely suppressed anger, a muscle jumping beneath the skin. But he kept his voice deliberately calm and even. "This guy—the one who was just here a few minutes ago—is he the one who took you initially?"

Priya hesitated, and that pause—just a beat too long—made my stomach drop like a stone. "I don't... I don't know. Someone grabbed me from behind—" Her breath hitched audibly. "They grabbed me when I was leaving the marine center late. I thought—" She squeezed her eyes shut. "At first I thought it was just a mugging, you know? That they wanted my purse or my phone or something. But then it wasn't. It wasn't that at all."

I forced myself to stay perfectly still, to project steadiness and control, because she desperately needed someone to be steady right now. She needed an anchor.

"Did he hurt you?" Something dangerous threaded through Rios's carefully controlled tone—a simmering fury being held on a very tight leash.

"No." Priya's answer came almost too quickly. "No, he didn't—he brought food. Bottled water. I... I think he actually felt guilty about it?" She let out a single laugh, broken and ugly and completely humorless. "He kept saying he could fix this. That he was going to fix everything."

Fix what? I wondered, with a chill running down my spine. What the hell did he think he was fixing?

"We can talk about all the rest of it later." Rios sliced through the remaining bindings at her wrists and then moved down to work on her ankles. "Right now, we need to focus on getting you out of here. Can you walk? Are your legs okay?"

"I think so. I should be able to." She tried to swing her legs off the cot and immediately winced, her face contorting with discomfort as protesting muscles made their displeasure known after days of limited movement.

"That's completely normal after being restrained," I told her, keeping my voice as professional and reassuring as I could manage, even though white-hot fury was lighting me up from somewhere deep. "Your circulation was restricted. We'll take it slow, okay? There's no rush now."

Rios carefully slid one strong arm around her other side, supporting her weight. Together we got her upright, lifting her gently to her feet. She swayed once, badly enough that my heart leapt into my throat, but she caught herself with our help, breathing hard through her mouth.

He met my gaze over her head, and even in the glow of our flashlights, I saw the simmering rage in his eyes. "Hang tight, Priya. We're getting the hell out of here."

THIRTY-FIVE

Gabi got Priya down the hall of the clinic before the door swung fully shut behind us.

She didn't rush her—didn't crowd her, didn't treat her like she was fragile glass—but she stayed close enough to catch her if her knees buckled. One hand hovered near Priya's elbow; the other settled at the center of her back like a steadying point.

Gabi's voice stayed low and calm, the same tone she used when she walked a kid through stitches or talked an old man down from panicking about chest pain. "Okay, we're going to step into an exam room. You're going to sit down. We're going to get you some water, and we'll go from there."

Priya nodded. She didn't look at me or Madden. She kept her eyes on the floor like it might tilt under her feet if she lifted her head. She moved carefully, testing each step.

I followed at a distance I didn't like.

Gabi paused at an open doorway and guided Priya inside. Priya sat on the edge of the exam table with a wince, hands on either side like she was bracing for the world to shake again.

Gabi touched her shoulder once. "I'm going to close the door. Not to shut anyone out but to give you privacy. You tell me what you need, okay?"

Priya's throat moved. "Okay."

Gabi looked up at me over Priya's shoulder. "I've got her."

And this was why I'd called her to meet us here instead of taking Priya straight to the police station. Because I could hand Priya off to someone I trusted to take care of her.

Nodding, I stepped back and let the door shut. Only then did I finally take a full breath.

Not relief—not yet. I didn't have that kind of luxury. But something loosened anyway. We'd gotten Priya out. We'd gotten her to the one person on this island I trusted to assess her without missing anything, without letting anyone bulldoze her, without letting pride or politics set the pace.

Priya had said he didn't hurt her.

That mattered. It also didn't mean shit.

People said all kinds of things while they were still in survival mode. Sometimes they didn't know what counted as hurt until someone asked the right questions. Sometimes they didn't want to say the words out loud because then they'd have to live in a world where those words were true.

Gabi would get to the truth. Gabi would know if there were bruises under clothes, injuries she couldn't feel yet, signs that demanded a kit and documentation and a chain of custody that didn't leave room for anyone to shrug later and say, *No evidence.*

Madden's hand slipped into mine, and her head tipped to my shoulder. "We found her. *You* found her."

I'd followed my gut, and this time it had paid off.

That still hadn't quite sunk in. Maybe it wouldn't until the son of a bitch who'd held her actually got brought in and put in a cage. Maybe it would take longer than that. Some part of me still believed that missing women weren't problems you actually got to solve. They were a problem you lived with. One that became posters. Candlelight vigils. Shrugs. Rumors. Blame. Because that was what Gwen had been.

But we'd found Priya before it was too late.

"We need to call the cops," I muttered.

Madden's fingers tightened around mine. "It can wait a few minutes. I'm calling Astrid first. Priya needs one of her people."

I understood what she meant even though she didn't say it outright.

Astrid wasn't merely a friend. Astrid was safety. An adult Priya trusted. She would make the world feel less like a fluorescent hallway and more like something Priya could survive.

Madden released my hand and stepped a few feet away, phone already in her palm. She turned her body slightly like she was shielding the call from the rest of the world—not because she was hiding it, but because privacy was a habit she didn't shed easily.

I watched her mouth move as she spoke. I couldn't hear the words over the faint sounds from inside the exam room—drawers opening, paper crinkling, Gabi's measured questions—but I could read the shape of it. Short. Controlled. Urgent.

Madden ended the call and came back. "She's on her way."

"Good." I pulled my own phone out and dialed 911.

A voice answered, practiced and clipped. "Sutter's Ferry 911, what is your emergency?"

"This is Rios Carrera. We've recovered Priya Shah. She's at the clinic for medical evaluation. We have a suspect description and a location tied to where she was held."

The line went quiet for half a beat—not silence, exactly, but that subtle shift when someone's attention locks. "Repeat that?"

I repeated it. Slower. Clearer. I gave the clinic address, though there was only one on the island. I gave the basic facts I could without turning it into a story. I gave the location of the shack in the marsh, the condition of the door.

"I need an officer at the clinic," I said. "And I need someone moving on that location now, in case he goes back."

I waited for her to argue that I wasn't an officer and couldn't demand any such thing. But she only said, "Yes, sir. Units are en route."

I ended the call and looked down the hall toward the front.

The clinic wasn't open twenty-four hours. It didn't stay unlocked at midnight. Whoever came next would have to knock. They'd have to wait to be let in.

Which meant we had minutes. Not hours. Minutes.

Madden reached up to cup my cheek. "Hey. You okay being here again so soon?"

So soon? I blinked at her. Fuck. I'd just been here last night, with her after the fire. Christ, that was barely over twenty-four hours ago.

I reached for her, tugging her into my space bubble. "When all this is over, how do you feel about the notion of a vacation away from all of humanity?"

The corner of her mouth twitched. "Do you have a line on such a Shangri-La?"

"I can find a way to make it happen. I'm very motivated for some peace and quiet."

The other corner lifted. "Sounds like a plan."

She didn't say what we were both thinking—that this was a long way from over.

Someone pounded on the front door of the clinic. I instinctively dragged Madden behind me, even as Gabi stepped out of the exam room and made for the door.

Astrid burst inside, hair loose around her shoulders, eyes bright, cheeks already wet. She stopped short at the sight of

Madden, as if her body couldn't decide whether to run or collapse.

Madden crossed the distance in two strides, and Astrid met her halfway. They hugged hard. The kind of embrace that said I've been holding myself together by force of will, and now I don't have to for ten seconds.

"She's here?" Astrid whispered.

"She's here," Madden said into her hair. "She's alive."

Astrid made a sound that was half laugh, half sob. She pulled back and looked at Madden like she needed to confirm she was real. Her eyes snapped to me.

"Where is she?"

Gabi nodded toward the exam room. "She's stable. You can see her in a minute."

Astrid's hands lifted, hovered, and dropped to her sides, because she didn't know what to do with them. Fear did that. Relief did that.

Madden touched her elbow. "You're not alone."

Astrid nodded, swallowing hard. "Neither is she."

Gabi opened the exam room door. "Come on."

The room was small. Practical. Priya sat propped against the table now, a paper sheet crinkled under her thighs. An IV line ran to her arm, taped neatly. Her hands and ankles had been cleaned and wrapped in light bandages to protect raw skin and keep it from splitting again. The ugly redness around her wrists stood out anyway, a thin line where restraints had bit in.

Priya's eyes lifted the moment Astrid stepped in.

Something broke on her face. The expression tried to fold in on itself, overwhelmed.

"Astrid," she rasped.

Astrid crossed the space and took her carefully, mindful of the IV, arms wrapping around her shoulders, cheek pressed to her hair. Priya clung back like she was anchoring herself to the only thing she trusted to stay.

"I'm here," Astrid said, voice thick. "I'm right here."

Priya's breath hitched. "I thought—"

"I know," Astrid cut in. "I know. Don't—don't do that to yourself. You're here."

Gabi stepped slightly to the side, letting them have the moment without turning away from her work.

"She's dehydrated," Gabi said to all of us, brisk and matter-of-fact. "Underfed. No acute injuries so far. I'm finishing the assessment, and then we're going to get some calories into her. Nothing heavy. Something gentle."

Astrid pulled back, cupped Priya's face with one hand like she needed to confirm she was solid. "Did he—"

Gabi's tone stayed neutral. "I'm evaluating that."

"He didn't." Priya said it quick and fierce, like she needed Astrid to hear it. "He didn't hurt me."

Gabi didn't contradict or reassure. She only made a note.

Good. Let the facts be facts.

Another knock hit the front door.

Harder this time.

Gabi's jaw tightened. She walked out, and I followed, already knowing who it would be.

She opened the door, and Carson stepped in with Grant right behind him.

Carson took in the clinic in a single sweep, eyes moving fast —clocking Madden, clocking me. His face tightened with controlled frustration, the kind that didn't flare into anger until it found a target. He chose my sister.

"Why wasn't this brought directly to the station?" he demanded.

Gabi didn't flinch. "Because she's a patient."

"She's also a missing person—"

"And she came here first," Gabi said, voice flat. "Because her medical condition comes first. That's how this works."

Carson's attention snapped to me. "Carrera. What the hell are you doing here?"

Guess he didn't get the memo that I'd been the one to call it in.

Before I could answer, Priya's voice carried from the exam room doorway. "He found me."

Carson turned. Reset his expression into something more official. Less personal. "Miss Shah are you up to answering a few questions?"

Gabi stepped around him and planted herself as a physical barrier. "Brief."

Carson's mouth tightened, but he nodded. "Brief."

He and Grant stepped into the exam room. I stayed at the threshold with Madden, close enough to hear but not crowding Priya. Gabi moved to the side of the table, hand on the IV line, eyes sharp as a blade. Astrid stayed right by Priya's side, one hand holding hers.

Carson pulled a small notebook out. Grant stayed quiet, posture unreadable, eyes doing the same quick, thorough scan Gabi had done earlier.

Carson asked the expected questions first. "Do you know what day it is? Do you know where you are? Can you tell me your full name?"

Priya answered. Gabi watched her face while she did it, watching for drift, for confusion, for dissociation.

Then Carson moved into the meat. "The last anyone remembers seeing you was at Home Port a little over a week ago. Can you pick up from that night?"

Priya swallowed. "I was working on reports after the latest beach observation. Headed for home sometime around one-thirty, I think."

"On foot or by car?" Carson asked.

"On foot. I don't have a car on island. Sometimes I'll use my bike, but I don't like riding it at night." She stopped, eyes darting toward Astrid. "I know I shouldn't go by myself, but I'd done it before. And... well... I guess there's always the time it's not okay. Stupid."

Astrid squeezed her hand. "Don't think about that right now. What happened next?"

"Somebody jumped me."

"Did you get a look at your attacker?" Carson asked.

Priya shook her head. "Not clearly. It was dark. I didn't—" She closed her eyes, brow furrowing, trying to pull the memory back like it was something she could force. "I fought, but I didn't get a good look. Then he knocked me out."

"What do you remember happening next?" Grant prompted.

"I didn't know where I was. I—there was time where I wasn't... I don't know. I remember being moved. I remember water sounds. A motor at one point." She swallowed again, eyes shining. "I remember thinking maybe I was going to drown."

Which could have meant anything. This was an island. Very few places weren't near water. Had she been *on* a boat? Was that how Pool Guy had transported her? Had he been the one to transport her in the first place, or had there been someone else?

But neither Carson nor Grant asked any of those questions.

"Tell us about the man who held you captive," Carson ordered.

"I knew him from the bar. We played pool a few times. Friendly enough, I thought."

"You have a name?"

"Wes. I never got his last name."

I spoke up. "White male. Early thirties. Lean, 5'10', around

170. Sunburned skin. Longish dark hair. Tattoos on his right forearm—something in the American traditional style. Nautical themed. Olive green cargo pants. Gray henley. He came out alone. Locked up. Didn't look around like he was afraid."

"How did you even make the connection?" Carson asked.

I resisted the urge to say, *Because I did your job.* "Overheard him talking to his buddies about her at Home Port. Nothing overt, but his reactions struck me as odd, so we followed when he left and ended up out in the marshes."

Carson's jaw flexed once. "Where is this individual now?"

"Dunno. He headed back toward the marina. We didn't engage when he left, electing to search the premises for Priya. When we found her, we brought her straight here."

Carson didn't like that. I saw it in the tension around his eyes. He swallowed it anyway.

"Miss Shah," he said, voice tight, "did he harm you in any way?"

Priya shook her head quickly. "No. He brought water. Food. Not enough, but... he did." Her voice went raw. "He didn't let me go."

"Did he threaten you?" Carson pressed.

Priya's hands curled on the sheet. "He kept saying... I wasn't safe. He kept saying if I left, someone would find me."

"Someone," Carson repeated.

Priya's eyes squeezed shut. "I don't know who. I didn't see anyone else there. I just—" She looked at Gabi, pleading. "I just knew he believed it."

Gabi kept her expression neutral, but her eyes softened a fraction. "You're doing fine. Take your time."

Carson scribbled a few more notes before shutting the notebook with a sharp motion like he'd reached the end of what he could get without pushing her into a spiral. "We'll have more questions later. Right now, the priority is locating Wes and bringing him in. Where can we find you?"

Astrid stepped forward, voice steady. "She's staying with me."

Carson's gaze snapped to her. "We'll need—"

"She's staying with me," Astrid repeated, not louder, just firmer. "Her parents are arriving tomorrow. They're flying in. This is the news I'm giving them."

That landed. Even Carson couldn't argue with optics and humanity at the same time, not in front of witnesses.

He gave a curt nod. "We'll be in touch."

He turned to Grant. "Let's move."

Grant's eyes met mine as he stepped past. An acknowledgment—*I see what you're doing. I see what you found. I see that you didn't bring her to the station first, and I'm filing that away.*

Then he followed Carson out.

The door shut. The clinic quieted again.

Astrid exhaled shakily and turned to Gabi. "How soon can I take her home?"

Gabi checked the IV line and looked at Priya. "Give me a little more time for fluids and a snack. I want her steady on her feet first."

Priya's shoulders slumped with relief so sharp it almost looked like pain.

Madden's hand stayed in mine, grip still tight, like she needed proof this was real.

And I stood there in the doorway, watching my sister do what she did best—protect the person in front of her without asking permission—while the chief of police hunted the man who'd kept Priya locked up.

We found her.

Now the island would do what it always did—close ranks, demand neat answers, try to make this one clean.

And nothing about it would be clean.

THIRTY-SIX

MADDEN

Every muscle in my body protested as Rios and I crossed the threshold into the Brewhouse, as if my skin hadn't quite caught up to the reality that we were allowed to be somewhere ordinary again. The hum of the crowd, the scrape of chairs, the splash of laughter—they all sounded strangely muffled, like coming up from underwater too fast. Rios's hand stayed at my back until we reached the edge of the dining room. His thumb traced a silent check-in, anchoring me, even as he read the space for exits and threats. That sign of vigilance was such a comfort.

"I'll be right over there if you need me." He caught my eyes, waiting for my nod—my consent to let him go. I managed it, but barely.

He squeezed my hand—a flash of pressure, the kind you only give when words are too thin to hold everything you want to say—and slipped toward the bar where Ford and Sawyer waited. I watched him go, wishing I could go with him.

But that wasn't why we were here. I'd come to see Astrid

because we both needed a piece of normal, and that wouldn't come until the last of this was closed out.

I spotted her at a table by the windows, two drinks sweating onto napkins, a basket of fries untouched. She looked up as I approached, and for a moment, neither of us moved. The exhaustion on her face mirrored my own, etched deep and dark as bruises. When she stood, we slid into a brief, hard hug that said we were both still here. When we pulled apart, I saw how red her eyes were, and I didn't bother pretending mine weren't the same. There'd been tears of relief and exhaustion once we'd made it back to Sutter House and passed the news on to Willa and Sawyer.

We sat, shoulders slumping toward the sticky tabletop like we could rest our weight on it. Astrid shoved the fries at me. "Eat. You look like you haven't since—well. Since."

I took one, more for something to do with my hands than any real hunger. The salt stung the inside of my mouth. "I'm not sure I've eaten anything in the past several days that wasn't forced on me by one Carrera or another."

She gave a little huff, not quite a laugh. "We'll circle back to that."

The bar noise receded, and we sank into the kind of hush that only came after holding your breath for way too damned long. There was only the clink of ice in our glasses, and the steady, shaking exhale we both let out together. Some of the weight seemed to leave with it.

"How is Priya?"

We'd escorted the two of them back to Astrid's place from the clinic. Rios hadn't been willing to leave until he'd seen the security system himself and heard her lock the deadbolts and arm it. Even then, he hadn't wanted to go, but Chris Shelton, one of the local police officers, had shown up saying that he'd been put on guard duty.

Wes Mullowney hadn't been apprehended yet.

Astrid's smile was raw and real. "Safe. Her parents haven't let her out of their sight since they got in late this morning. She slept finally—really slept. Her mom cried so hard she made herself sick. Her dad keeps bringing her toast and tea like it's a cure for anything. But she's okay." She reached across the table and laid her hand over mine. "I don't know how to thank you for that."

"There's no need to thank me. I just did what needed doing." I winced. "And I kind of ignored you to do it. I'm sorry for that."

Astrid held up a finger. "First, I've known you for twenty years, and I know what you're like when you get into a project. Head down, no distractions. No reason for a case to be different. Second, you did what no one else was willing to do. You and Rios both." She stopped, closing her eyes for a moment. "I never thought it would go that far. I never thought you'd be in danger from poking around. Not really. When I heard about the fire yesterday, I—"

I squeezed her hand back. "Don't. I'm okay. Rios got me out. And it's not like you actively asked me to help. I inserted myself. I saw that Carson wasn't going to keep looking, and I made that call. I'm the one who brought Rios into the broader investigation. None of this is on you."

But it hadn't stopped me from dreaming of smoke and flames when I'd finally caught a few hours of sleep this morning. I'd probably be circling that for a while.

For a moment, Astrid looked like she was going to argue the point, but she only cleared her throat. "So, speaking of Rios." Her eyes flicked to the bar, where he stood with Ford, posture coiled like he couldn't help tracking the perimeter. Even as we looked, his gaze tracked to us—to me—and one corner of that sensual mouth lifted.

"I didn't see *that* coming."

I smiled back at the man who'd somehow become the anchor of my world. "Neither did I."

"I mean, if you'd asked me, I'd have said you didn't actually like him. But obviously you two had some serious, forced proximity chemistry going on with this case."

"It wasn't like that," I protested.

Astrid arched a brow.

"We learned how to respect each other's professional capabilities."

Her grin turned wicked. "I can imagine that he has all kinds of *professional* capabilities with that mouth and those hands..."

Heat burned my cheeks as my brain and body reminded me of exactly how true that statement was. "I'm not at liberty to discuss the confidential details of the case."

She hooted with laughter. "Good for you, girl! You deserve some good in your life. And from the looks of it, he's very good for you."

"I trust him. And I can't say that about many people."

"It's good to have someone you know will catch you if you stumble."

"I think, maybe, we caught each other."

She didn't say anything as the words hung between us, only blinked a little like she was watching her own personal Hallmark movie.

I watched him, absorbing the way he laughed—low and guarded—at something Ford said, the way he scanned the room every so often, always coming back to me. "He makes it easier to breathe."

I didn't realize I'd made the admission aloud until Astrid's hand found mine again. "Hold on to that. The world's not going to get simpler anytime soon."

That was the God's honest truth.

A comfortable hush slipped over us. I sipped my tea, feeling the cool spread through me, and with it the noise and texture of the rest of the Brewhouse. As if the volume on the world had been unmuted.

She let me sit in that silence. Perhaps she needed it too.

"I'm glad you're here," she said quietly. "Still here. Not—" Her voice broke, and she cleared her throat. "Not gone."

I squeezed her hand. "Me too."

"What's the plan now?"

"I hardly know." I hadn't come home to find a missing girl or fall in love with a man who'd once hated me.

The entire texture of my life felt different now, and there hadn't exactly been time to think about it. Plus, Rios and I hadn't actually talked about what came next. If there was a next. He was every bit as much in transition as I was, and the subject of us beyond our attraction hadn't made it on the docket of discussion.

But maybe, when all this was over...

Maybe.

That was as much as I was willing to count on at the moment.

A murmur swept through the bar. Something about the wave of it, building and flowing across the room, had the hair on my arms standing straight up. Astrid and I both looked around as Bree hollered, "Everybody quiet!"

All the patrons went silent as she pointed a remote at the big TV in the corner of the bar that usually played some variety of sports. I was out of my seat, trying to get close enough to read the headline scrolling across the bottom of the screen, even before the volume got loud enough to catch the newscaster's voice saying, "—ends in violence on the Outer Banks."

I couldn't make out the words until I'd reached Rios.

KIDNAPPING SUSPECT KILLED IN SHOOTOUT WITH POLICE

My brain began to buzz so loudly, I barely registered the rest of the report. Rios pulled me into him as the reporter continued to talk about how Wes Mullowney had fired on police after being cornered on his boat earlier in the afternoon.

Carson came on screen, looking appropriately sober. "The suspect was wanted for questioning in connection to the kidnapping of a local grad student recovered last night. The student is safe and recovering with family. The suspect's residence showed evidence of a planned abduction. There is no indication he was working with anyone else."

"It's over." The words swept through the crowd inside the Brewhouse, becoming another of those waves that rose to a crescendo of applause and jubilant cheers.

Rios and I only looked at each other. This was the nice, neat solution. An end that the public could cling to.

But he and I knew better. This was only one end to a much, much larger story.

THIRTY-SEVEN

RIOS

Sometimes, it was easier to let the rest of the island pretend it was finished. The papers called it closure. Carson played hero for the cameras—though Priya herself had made it clear in interviews that it was Madden and me who'd rescued her. But in the living room at Sutter House, none of us bought the neat and tidy resolution for a second. The air all but vibrated with everything we couldn't prove, and couldn't afford to ignore. While we'd celebrated Priya's safe return, we knew it wasn't finished. Not even close.

Madden sat beside me on the leather couch, one foot tucked under the other leg, fingers hovering over the laptop she'd seldom been without over the past week. Without Priya's case to work on, she'd dived back into the files Grant had given her, tightening up connections, highlighting patterns. To what end, I wasn't sure. Perhaps just to keep busy, to keep feeling as if she was doing *something* in the face of this insurmountable threat.

The rest of the crew were close, coffee table and every flat surface covered in mugs, notebooks, takeout boxes, the debris of a meal nobody remembered eating. Not a party, not a wake—a war council, every eye turned in, every back to the walls. A heaviness had settled, a tangle of hope and dread.

Nobody here was eager to move on, and nobody tried to force relief. I'd never been more grateful for these people and their refusal to look away. In their presence, I felt less alone—reminded that the urge to do something, even in the face of systems designed to grind us down, was its own kind of hope.

Daniel cleared his throat, the signal that whatever was coming wasn't gossip. "I did some diggin' in the wake of Mullowney's takedown. Somethin' about his name rang a bell. Turns out his name had come up in connection with a few boats we have our eyes on for drug running." He shrugged. "Nothing concrete, just chatter. Maybe nothing, maybe not. But his name's in the mix, and it's got the higher-ups glancing our way."

Sawyer leaned in, brow furrowed. "So he was mixed up in something?"

Daniel's mouth gave a wry twist. "Might be. Or might've just been there when they needed a hand. Nobody's sayin' he ran anything. Could be he just worked with the wrong crew."

Ford made a rough sound, his jaw tense. "Damn. Figures."

Something clicked in my head. Investigator's muscle memory. The wrong crew, the wrong time. Sometimes that was all it took, especially when the network was bigger than anybody wanted to admit. My frustration simmered, sharp as salt on a wound.

"So we've got a guy who might or might not be involved in drug running, who kidnapped Priya Shah for reasons unknown." I turned the pieces over in my head. "Ostensibly, he didn't physically hurt her, and she said herself he kept saying he'd done it to keep her safe."

"Where are you going with this?" Ford asked.

"Stay with me for a bit. If you've got channels to move product, it's not a leap to think you could move other cargo too. Drugs, guns, people. It's all the same to the folks at the top. And the ones who disappear are the ones nobody notices. We already had reason to believe Priya wasn't the intended target. If she was nabbed by mistake and was too hot to move, as it were, logic dictates they'd simply kill her and be done with it. But instead, we have Mullowney, who took her. Kept her. Because she was a face he knew. Someone he'd played pool with. Someone he had a human connection to. Harder to see someone you have a connection with—no matter how tenuous —as cargo."

Sawyer ran a hand through his hair, voice uneasy. "You think he was in over his head, realized it, and couldn't go through with it?"

"Maybe," I said. "It's a better explanation for why he took her but never assaulted her. If he was involved, I doubt it was anywhere higher on the food chain, or him removing her from the pipeline wouldn't have been such a problem for him. No real way to verify since he's dead."

Daniel nodded, face set. "If he was involved and bucked the orders from his higher ups, they'd have wanted to cut their losses. If the police hadn't killed him, someone else likely would have."

The silence took on an almost physical weight as the group collectively processed that new edge to the story. I glanced at Madden—her face was grave, her hand steady on the laptop, but her shoulders were tight, like she was bracing for an aftershock.

"What if—" Willa bit her lip, hesitant.

"What if what?" I prompted.

She pressed on, words stumbling out. "I mean, I hate to say this, but what if the police are involved somehow? What if the run-in that resulted in Mullowney's death was their way of taking him out? I mean, if someone wanted him gone..."

Nobody shot her down. We all understood the fear.

Madden's eyes met mine, and her voice was measured. "We can't know what's in Carson's head," she said evenly. "Maybe he's just willfully ignorant, because ignorance is safe. Might be it's more. Either way, the result is the same. He's failed everyone who didn't have the power to demand more. What we do have clear proof of is a pattern of gross negligence and failure to follow reasonable procedure that extends back fifteen years, at minimum."

Daniel shrugged. "From what I see, it's easier to let things slide than to risk making enemies. Everything I've seen in working with him shows he likes a neat file and a closed case."

Bree scowled. "So what? He'll keep sweeping this kind of case under the rug until someone makes it impossible?"

My own frustration rose—this endless inertia, this island-wide willingness to pretend because people needed at least the illusion of safety. I felt it in my bones, the way I used to sense the approach of a storm at sea. "Someone has to force the issue. That's the only way it ever changes."

Madden drew a slow breath, and with it the tenor of the room changed. "That's what I've been working on." She glanced around, making sure everyone was listening. "I put together a packet—fifteen years of missing persons, all the cases that never got a proper search, all the requests for information that were stonewalled. Every file that was closed for the sake of convenience instead of truth. I cross-referenced patterns—who disappeared, how long the cases stayed open, which files never made it to the press. The files I was slipped helped fill in a lot of gaps, but there's more from public record if you know where and what to look for."

Willa sat forward, eyes huge and earnest. "What do we do with it?"

Madden's eyes hardened. "He's spent all this time hiding behind procedure. So, I'm turning procedure against him. I'm sending everything I've found to the State Bureau of Investigation with an audit request. No name, no traceable connection. Every digital fingerprint's scrubbed. They'll have to open an inquiry. It takes the decision out of Carson's hands."

Ford loosed a low whistle. "That's ballsy."

Daniel looked at her with respect. "That's not something he'll expect."

Sawyer let out a sound that was half a laugh, half a groan. "He's gonna lose it. I hope someone has a camera on him when he finds out."

"He'll be getting a copy of the complaint himself," she added.

I frowned. "That's a bit like poking the bear. He might take it as a threat."

"It's not meant as a threat." Madden paused. "Well, not entirely. It's part of procedure that he be notified."

Bree leaned in, her tone sharpening. "Anonymous or not, he's going to want a scapegoat, you know. That's how men like him operate. He'll sniff around, try to intimidate, start rumors."

Madden's smile was thin. "That's why it's anonymous. I'm not stupid. But it's the only way to force him out from behind his desk. He's hidden behind policy and paperwork for too long."

Ford looked my way. "You'll watch her back?"

I nodded, meaning it with every part of me. "Always."

A low hum of agreement moved through the group. For the first time all night, something like hope flickered.

I caught Madden's gaze. "It's the right next step. And yeah, if he's actually dirty, it'll rattle his cage. So we stay sharp. We watch. We wait. And whatever comes, we face it."

THIRTY-EIGHT

MADDEN

Being out in public was weird, as I let routine fold over the part of me that kept waiting for the sky to fall. Two days had passed since I'd sent the packet. Two days marked by a hundred little anxieties pressed into every hour. I well knew that bureaucracy moved at a snail's pace. Had known it before I'd started down this path. But the fact that nothing had happened left me on edge. I kept half-expecting to look up from my phone and see a uniform, a summons, the beginning of a reckoning.

Instead, there was just the bakery: the soft click of the door behind me, the smell of yeast and cinnamon and coffee, and the low hum of local voices blending into the music piped from hidden speakers.

Rios and I reached the door together. He lingered at my side, his hand at my waist like he could absorb the leftover worry radiating off me. I sensed him cataloguing the space even as he leaned down for a kiss meant to reassure us both. "Don't let Astrid talk you into anything illegal while I'm gone," he murmured, lips at my temple.

I snorted, but the humor was thin. "If I do, I know who I want to come rescue me."

His smile flickered—faint, but real. "Be careful," he said, thumb tracing my hip. "I'm gonna go save Hoyt from an impending hernia. I shouldn't be long."

"You realize those are famous last words whenever the prospect of moving furniture is involved, right?"

"Hope springs eternal. Don't leave before I get back, okay?"

"Promise." I pressed my palm to his chest, letting myself take one long, deep breath. I didn't want him to leave; I didn't want to need him to stay. I wanted—God, I wasn't sure what I wanted anymore.

Abruptly aware that the low din of conversation had dipped, I glanced around to find most of the customers staring at us. But instead of the looks of judgment habitually shot in Rios's direction, I saw open curiosity and quite a few grins that held a distinct tone of *awww*.

An old woman parked at a table by the window flashed a toothy smile. "Good for you, sonny."

Her companion, who wore a lime green velour track suit, nodded and met my gaze. "Gotta appreciate a military man, sweetheart. They have *stamina*."

"Um?" I squeaked, feeling heat flame across my cheeks.

For his part, Rios merely looked amused. "Right. That's my sign to GTFO. I'll be back."

With a quick brush of a kiss that garnered more than one sigh, he stepped away, and I watched him disappear down the sidewalk, the sun striking off his glossy black hair, his frame receding into the ordinary bustle of the day. The bakery's bell chimed again as I moved inside, blinking against the shift from sunlight to shadow.

Astrid was already waiting with coffee and pastries, having staked out a small table near the window—a vantage point on the street and, I realized, a line of sight to the bakery's only exit. We settled in with only a few words, the comfort of familiarity making room for our mutual tension. The air inside was sweet and faintly sharp, warm from the ovens but not uncomfortable. There was a steady background of forks scraping plates, a barista calling out names, the front door swinging open and shut at intervals.

Astrid glanced at my face, her own mask slipping just enough for me to see the worry underneath. "Sleep?" she asked quietly.

"Some." The truth landed heavier than I meant. "Better than last week, but that's not saying much."

She sipped her coffee. "I guess it'll take a while to stop expecting danger around every corner."

She didn't know the half of it, but I wasn't about to be the one to disabuse her of the notion that the threat was over, so I shifted to talk of ordinary things, as if the right sequence of words might pull the world back into order.

Eventually, Astrid set her mug down and looked me over with that calm professorial gaze. "So. What about you? I mean, the whole reason you came here was to figure out what was next, and that kinda got derailed."

I hesitated. "I keep thinking the answer will just... appear. But it hasn't. I know what I don't want. I can't go back to prosecution. I'm not sure anyone would have me if I tried." I thought of my father and his demands. "I have negative zero desire to work in some high-powered firm, looking for some kind of prestige. That's not who I am, and it's not ever what I wanted, and I'm done doing anything just because my parents want me to."

"Good for you. So what *do* you want?"

The question bounced around inside me. I looked out the

window, watching a truck rattle past, a dog tug its owner toward the shade. "I want to do something that matters. I want —" I shook my head. "Hell, I don't know. I thought coming here would give me clarity. But everything that's happened has just... scrambled things more."

"You could get your law license in North Carolina," Astrid offered. "Stay. Open your own practice. Be your own boss for once."

I fiddled with my napkin. "That's a thought. But it feels huge. And risky. And I'm tired of fighting for everything. I'm tired, period."

She gave a small nod, understanding gleaming in her eyes. "Would you want to go somewhere else?"

I shook my head, more certain of that than anything. "I can't. Not now. I have unfinished business here." Now that I knew what was happening here, what Gwen may have been a part of, I couldn't just walk away.

Astrid grinned. "Is that unfinished business named Carrera?"

Heat crept into my cheeks. "Yeah, okay, he does factor in."

"Have you talked about what comes next?"

"No. There's been so much going on. We're just playing it by ear. And I don't want to press for any kind of answer or decision from him yet. I don't want him to feel like I'm issuing an ultimatum."

She waved that way. "Asking the guy you're involved with what his plans are is just reasonable information seeking, not an ultimatum. You're not saying, 'do this or else.'"

"Maybe not, but we're just so... new. Either way, I don't want to leave the island, and I can't stay camped out in a guest room at Sutter House forever. With my uncle's boat gone, I should really look at finding my own place."

"Well, with summer season shutting down, some of the

rentals should for sure be opening back up. No doubt you could find something on a month-to-month basis while you're deciding." She blinked innocently. "Maybe even a place with room for two in the closet."

I gaped at her. "You cannot seriously be suggesting we move in together this fast."

"Why the hell not? He'll need a place too, if he's sticking around, and why *not* have that sexy hunk of Latino goodness warming your bed?"

I didn't deny that I'd been doing exactly that in the time we'd been up at Sutter House. Or that I slept better with him beside me than I'd slept in longer than I cared to remember. "That seems like it's getting ahead of things."

"Okay, okay. I'll lay off. But I'm going on record as saying it's a good idea."

"Noted. Just keep your ears peeled for any availability, okay?"

"I can do that."

The conversation wandered from there—her research backlog, Priya's insistence on reclaiming a semblance of normal, the logistics of her parents' looming departure. She was a little softer than usual, a little less brisk; every so often, I caught her checking her phone, eyes flicking to the door. We were both waiting for things we couldn't name.

The bakery slowly emptied around us. A couple with a stroller lingered at the window. Someone came in for a box of pan dulce, left with a nod to Astrid. The staff started clearing tables, moving with the methodical energy of people counting down minutes to shift change.

Astrid sighed, checked her phone, and pushed her chair back. "I need to get going. We're so behind on things. But let's catch up again soon, okay?"

"Absolutely."

She squeezed my shoulder as we stood. "Soon. I mean it."

We hugged tight, and she left a warmth in her wake that I hadn't realized I'd needed. I watched her head out to the parking lot.

As Rios wasn't back yet—surprise, surprise—I ordered a fresh cup of coffee and settled in with my book to wait.

The quiet felt sharp now. My phone was a heavy weight in my pocket, but I resisted the urge to pull it out to check my email for the twentieth time or slip into doomscrolling. It wasn't as if I was expecting anything in particular. I hadn't provided real contact information, so even if the State Bureau of Investigation would contact me back to acknowledge receipt, they couldn't. And I didn't have any job applications out. Something I'd have to start thinking about soon.

I had savings enough to get me by for a while, but my father wasn't wrong that I couldn't exist without a plan forever.

When my phone buzzed, I flinched.

Slipping it out, I found a text from Astrid.

ASTRID:

FML. Got into a crash over on Seacrest.
Some idiot tourist missed the one-way sign.

A thin strand of fear wound through me. Astrid didn't over-react to minor things.

ME:

Are you okay??

ASTRID:

Ish? Police already called, but can you come?

I hesitated. I thought of Rios—his warning, the promise I'd made. I thought of Astrid, pale and shaking and only two blocks away. I weighed loyalty against caution and knew which would always win.

ME:

I'm on my way.

I fired off a quick text to Rios—

Astrid was in an accident on Seacrest. I'm heading over to check on her

—grabbed my bag and headed for the back door, short-cutting through the narrow alley behind the bakery that would get me there faster than the main street.

The sidewalk was nearly empty now, a few locals chatting by a delivery truck, the clatter of a dropped tray echoing from a nearby café. It was a sign of the true end of the summer season that the space wasn't choked with tourists. My shoes tapped against the pavement as I cut between buildings, heart pounding faster than the walk warranted.

I was already scanning the street ahead, looking for police lights, a cluster of people, Astrid's familiar car.

A hand clamped down on my arm from behind, so sudden and violent I barely got a breath. I dropped the coffee and twisted, trying to jerk away, but he was too strong. Another quick jerk and a second arm snaked around my throat, cutting off any sound but a desperate, animal whimper as he dragged me backward, feet scrambling for purchase on the uneven concrete.

"You just had to interfere," a voice hissed against my ear, low and rough, familiar in that awful way that meant I'd probably passed him on the street a hundred times. "Had to keep asking questions. You couldn't just die on that fucking boat."

I kicked, thrashed, clawed—every lesson in self-defense fighting to surface through panic. My elbow connected with something, but his grip only tightened. I got one hand up, tried to scratch, but he twisted my wrist until pain flared up my arm.

Something jabbed at my side, and my heart lurched.

Knife? No. Smaller. Needle.

The world began to tilt, the concrete blurring beneath me. I heard my phone clatter to the ground. My body wouldn't answer me—legs buckling, arms leaden, lungs burning for air I couldn't pull.

Everything swam and spiraled. I fought for another breath, enough to scream, but my muscles wouldn't obey.

"It's too damned bad your family's going to have another tragedy."

THIRTY-NINE

RIOS

I was already halfway back to the bakery, cursing my sister's predilection for falling in love with heavy furniture, when my phone lit up with a text.

I punched the screen so the truck would read it.

MADDEN:

Astrid was in an accident on Seacrest. I'm heading over to check on her.

I'd told her to stay put, but depending on how bad things were, of course she'd go check on her friend. I wasn't far, so I hooked a left and cut over three blocks to Sand Dollar Street, which ran parallel to Seacrest. At the first possible chance, I turned onto Seacrest proper and scanned for flashing lights and emergency vehicles.

But there was nothing, just a half dozen cars lazily driving down the mostly empty street.

Even with a basic fender bender, there wouldn't have been

time to get the vehicles clear and a police report made. So what the fuck was going on?

As I dialed Astrid, a bad feeling spun up in my gut.

"Hey, Rios."

"Where are you?"

A pause. "At the research station. Why?"

"You weren't just in an accident?"

"No? What's going on?"

"Nothing good. Gotta go."

I hung up on her and circled another block, driving too fast back toward the bakery, scanning streets and alleyways on both sides. Madden would've come this way on foot.

A flash of something caught my attention down an alley, and I threw the truck into park, leaving it running as I jogged down the alley. A cell phone with a spider-webbed screen lay on the cracked pavement. It didn't power on when I picked it up. I couldn't be absolutely sure it was hers. A little further on, a paper coffee cup lay on its side in a puddle of brown. I scooped that up and rotated it until I saw Madden's name scrawled on the side.

My blood ran cold.

Broken phone and dropped coffee equalled only one thing in my mind: She'd been taken.

Bolting back to the truck, I ran scenarios.

It had been two days since she'd sent the audit request. Two days since she'd poked the bear. What were the chances that the protections she'd put into place to ensure her anonymity had been sufficient? Not big enough.

My gut told me Carson had her. Who else had reason to come after her? I didn't have time to dwell on what the hell he planned to do with her. I needed to focus on where would he take her. He wasn't stupid. He couldn't keep her anywhere on the island—not for long. Which meant he'd want to get off island. He wouldn't be fool enough to take the ferry. That left a private boat. His own or one he had access to.

The marina.

I didn't know for sure, and if I was wrong, I'd lose precious time. But if I was right...

The moment I hit the driver's seat, I tore down the street and hit the group text with Ford, Sawyer, and Daniel.

ME:

Someone took Madden. I figure Carson. Need backup at the marina ASAP.

I'm coming, Counselor. Hang on.

The two miles seemed to stretch forever as I sped through stop signs and whipped around other vehicles. More than one pedestrian leapt back from the road. At least one flipped me off. I half expected one of the other island cops to end up on my tail, lights flashing. Fine. Let them help take down their boss.

But none of them showed by the time I screeched to a stop in the parking lot. Daniel was already there, and Ford was coming in hot behind me. I bolted for the docks, already scanning for that rangy, weather-beaten figure. He wouldn't be in the section with the sailboats. Not on a police chief's salary. And not the commercial fishing further down. Too many prospective witnesses. If he had a boat here, it would be somewhere in the warren of smaller slips.

I heard another truck door slam, and Sawyer shouted, "Go on. I'm right behind you!"

We garnered an assortment of confused looks from a handful of tourists as we fanned out to search. I ignored them, looking only for evidence that I was right.

It was the flash of bright blue tarp that caught my eye. Well out on the end of the oldest section of the marina, a figure struggled under the weight of some wrapped bundle draped over his shoulder. A bundle the approximate size of a woman.

I poured on the speed, dodging around a fisherman and his cooler, leaping over a pile of fishing tackle. He didn't hear me coming until I rounded the final corner and hit the long stretch of warped boards reaching out into the water. As he turned, the bundle shifted, and I caught a glimpse of a hand. Unconscious? Worse? I didn't dare think about it as I bellowed, "Stop!"

Carson hesitated, glancing back toward a boat nearly at the end.

"Don't you fucking dare, Carson!"

He whipped around fully as he realized the others were behind me. Lifting a gun, he aimed in our direction. "Don't come any closer!"

"Chief, put the gun down," Daniel called. "Let's not get hasty here."

"Hasty? I've devoted my fucking life to this island. To keeping it safe."

"But not for everybody equally," I growled.

Carson scowled. "Needs of the many, son. Sometimes you have to make sacrifices."

"That's not how the law works." Not how it was supposed to work, anyway.

He snorted. "This is so much bigger than the law. And when it all crashes down, know it'll be her fault."

What the hell did that mean?

"Put her down, Carson."

He glared at me with undisguised hatred. "You want her? Fine. Go get her."

Before I could make a sound, he heaved the tarp-wrapped bundle into the water.

Eyes on where it had gone under, I began to run, ignoring

Carson as he bolted further down the pier, presumably for one of the boats. I had to trust that my friends would go after him.

I leapt for where she'd disappeared. Water closed over my head, the waves shoving my body around before I managed to reorient and swim toward the bottom. This part of the marina wasn't as deep as the commercial section that had to make room for bigger boats, and I thanked God for it as I caught sight of blue. Kicking hard, I reached out, fingers closing over the plastic and hauling. It floated toward me with no resistance. She wasn't secured inside it.

I fought with the tarp, struggling to get past it to where she would've fallen to the bottom. There was no movement below, no evidence she was conscious. Was she still breathing when she went in?

Come on, baby. Hold on for me.

My war with the tarp had kicked up so much silt I was reaching blind along the bottom, desperation rising with every inch as my lungs screamed for oxygen. Then my hand closed over a foot. That foot was attached to a leg, and from there I managed to wrap my arms around the rest of her. Exhaling the last of my air, I sank fully to the bottom in a crouch, then shoved hard toward the surface.

I broke through with a gasp and a hacking cough. Sawyer was there, already reaching down to help drag her limp body onto the dock. Then he reached a hand down for me, hauling me out. I rolled to my back, gasping for only a couple of seconds before reaching for Madden.

She lay still and so very pale, eyes closed. Her hair was plastered across her face. I gently shoved it back and bent over her. "Madden. Baby, wake up. Come on, *cariño*, you've gotta wake up."

I pressed shaking fingers against her throat and almost

sobbed with relief when I felt the flutter of a pulse. She was alive.

Only then did I look back up the dock.

Carson stood on the deck of a boat, casting off with one hand while holding Daniel at gunpoint with the other. Daniel's own weapon remained steady, his training evident in the way he didn't so much as flinch. Neither did Ford's from where he stood flanking the other side, his body coiled and ready.

"Carson," Ford warned, his voice carrying across the water with lethal calm.

"Shoot his fucking engine!" I shouted, my voice raw from swallowing half the harbor. "Stop him!"

"I'm not going—" Carson's body suddenly jerked, his eyes going wide with shock. Red bloomed across his chest, and he collapsed to the deck just as a sound like thunder rolled across the water from the direction of the ocean.

He'd been shot, and not by one of us.

Sniper.

My mind raced through the implications even as my body remained frozen, half-crouched over Madden.

"Boat." Sawyer pointed out on the water where a lone watercraft bobbed in the distance, probably near to 750 meters out. "There."

Daniel was already on the radio to alert the Coast Guard, his Louisiana drawl clipped and professional as he rattled off coordinates and a situation report. But I suspected whoever the fuck had taken that shot would be long gone by the time they managed to mobilize. Ford didn't hesitate—he took a running leap and managed to land on Carson's boat with the same athletic grace that had landed him a track scholarship back in college.

I turned back to Madden, checking her pulse and breathing

again. Her eyelids began to flutter, and I squeezed her hand in mine. "That's it. That's my girl. Come on back to me now."

Out on the water, Carson's boat had already floated halfway to the sound by the time Ford straightened and shook his head.

Carson was dead.

I couldn't think about that just now because Madden's eyes finally opened, blinking blearily into mine.

"Rios?"

"Hey, *cariño*." I didn't have to force the smile of relief to my face.

She frowned. "You're all wet."

"I am. So are you."

From somewhere up the road, sirens began to wail.

"Gave us a scare, there," Sawyer told her.

Those long-lashed eyes only blinked as she tried to make sense of that. I gently pulled her into my chest. "It's okay. We just need to get you checked out at the clinic."

"Again?" she croaked. "Maybe that's where we ought to be paying rent."

On a rough laugh, I pressed a kiss to her forehead. "We'll talk about that."

Her eyes must've cleared enough to see beyond me because she tried to straighten. "Carson! He's the one who set the fire on the boat. He—"

"Is dead," I finished. "It's over."

At least for now.

On a long exhale, she slumped against me. "Good. Maybe we can take that vacation you talked about."

Holding her tight, I kissed her brow again. "I can make that happen."

FORTY

MADDEN

The ferry slid through the faint chop of Pamlico Sound, a subtle rise and fall of the deck beneath my feet as I stood at the rail, staring out at the sky painted with late-summer clouds. In the distance, a thin spine of land rose from the water, too far yet to see more than a hint of color, but I knew Hatterwick. It wasn't the same place I'd left, and I wasn't the same woman who'd made exactly this crossing two months ago. I felt so different coming back to it now, Rios at my side, his shoulder pressed to mine.

Everything had happened so fast. Carson's death had sent a shockwave across the island. There was no pretty story for what happened—no way to explain away a veteran police chief shot down on a dock, the crack of a sniper's rifle echoing off the sound. The Coast Guard had determined he'd been executed, most likely by someone connected to the drug running operation they were investigating. That piece wasn't common knowledge. What *was* common knowledge now was that Carson had been on the take, something SBI investigators had determined when they'd shown up by Labor Day with their badges and rental cars, all business and no interest in small-town mythmaking.

They'd found decades of payouts, small regular deposits, new appliances bought in cash, old debts erased. Everything tied back to the shoddy, dismissive work I'd uncovered in those missing persons files. Local officials weren't hiring a replacement chief until the audit was over. Half the councilmen were still fighting about whether the interim should come from "the outside." The only thing anyone agreed on was that there were more secrets still to come.

There'd been no further threats on my life. The summer's fever had broken, and the island itself seemed quieter for it. Unease lingered in the spaces between conversations—the way people looked away from the marina, the sudden hush in the coffee shop when the news came on. They knew now that none of it was over. Carson hadn't been a mastermind. He'd been a loose end. And I couldn't forget what Rios had told me he'd screamed: "This is so much bigger than the law. And when it all crashes down, know it'll be her fault." I didn't know what he meant, not fully. But I wondered what I'd started. What I'd set loose by refusing to let things stay buried.

But there was a limit to what Rios and I could do. That was why, after the investigation into Carson's shooting wound down, we'd left the island behind. We disappeared into the Blue Ridge Mountains—no phones, no internet, nobody but each other. We let the world shrink down to the basics: coffee, eggs, the hush of rain on a tin roof, and a king-sized bed in a cabin that scented with cedar and old quilts. We talked—long, wandering conversations about what we wanted and who we were now. We didn't come up with answers for everything. But we figured out the only things that mattered for sure: we wanted each other, and we wanted Hatterwick. For now, that was enough.

I felt changed. Less like someone running, more like someone—maybe, possibly—coming home.

As the ferry blasted the horn, announcing our impending arrival, Rios curled a hand around my waist. "Ready?"

I tipped my head to his shoulder. "Yeah. Let's do it."

As we wandered back to his truck, I spotted Peggy Garrett, who'd been assistant to Sutter's Ferry's mayors for the last thirty years. As she caught my eye, saw who I was with, I half expected her to duck her head and slip into her car. Instead, she squared her shoulders and walked over to us with purpose.

"Madden, Rios. I wasn't sure either of you were coming back to the island."

"Mrs. Garrett." I managed to work up a polite company smile. "We're not through with Hatterwick yet."

She offered a decisive nod. "Good. Thank you—" Her gaze slid to Rios. "Both of you—for doing right by the island. It means more to everyone than y'all can know."

Rios blinked, clearly taken aback by the thanks and what seemed sort of like an apology.

I tightened my hand on his arm. "Thank you. We appreciate that." The ferry horn sounded again, and I gave a little wave. "Time to load up. I'm sure we'll see you around."

We slipped into his truck, Rios behind the wheel. He stared straight ahead for a few long moments. "That was... different."

"Hopefully, it's a preview of things to come."

He angled his head in a way that clearly said he wasn't holding his breath, and I let the subject drop. He had a long and complicated history with this place, and he'd make his peace with that in his own time.

The moment our tires bumped off the ferry, he turned

north toward Sutter House. Willa and Sawyer were putting us up again until we made other arrangements, and they'd gathered everyone up for a party to celebrate our return.

The drive in front of Sutter House was already full of vehicles when we pulled up. The side door opened before we'd even made it out of the truck.

"There they are!" Willa's bright voice rang out. "About damn time."

Roy and the foster dog bulleted out behind her, racing over to us with madly wagging tails. Rios and I paid the necessary canine toll, handing out pets and ear scruffs and chest scratches until we could make it over to the house.

I barely had time to brace before Willa wrapped me up in a hug that held more fierce affection than I'd been prepared for. After a moment's hesitation, I hugged her back. She smelled like soap and something herbal, her hair pulled back in a messy knot like she'd been cooking.

"You look—" she pulled back, hands landing on my shoulders, eyes scanning my face. "You look good."

I had no idea how to answer that, so I just smiled and stroked my hand over the foster pup's ears, since he'd already attached himself to my hip.

Over Willa's shoulder, I spotted Sawyer yanking Rios into one of those back-slapping man hugs. "Welcome home, man. Come on in."

Everyone was gathered around the kitchen island, hunched over baskets of snacks and boards of charcuterie like cheerful gremlins. Bree was defending the salami and cheese from Ford. Daniel appeared to be calling dibs on the pepper jelly and cream cheese with crackers, and Gabi was at a blender making margaritas.

She stabbed the machine off and crossed to pull her brother into a fast, tight hug. Then she turned to me. I hesitated less than I had with Willa. It was hard to balk in the face of Carrera affection, I'd learned. They were a very *We will hug you, and you will like it* sort of family. I'd come to appreciate that.

"I'm really glad you're back."

"Me too." I meant it more than I'd expected.

Questions came cheerful and fast. How was the trip? Did the cabin live up to the hype? Had the weather cooperated? Did we actually unplug or just pretend?

"Both," Rios answered when Sawyer asked if we'd actually stayed off our phones. "We cheated once. Regretted it immediately."

"That tracks," Bree said, sliding a plate toward me. "Eat. The gouda is to die for."

Ford mock pouted. "You slapped my hand when I tried to get some."

"You haven't earned it today, slick."

He bent and whispered something into her ear that immediately had her cheeks going pink and her eyes sparkling. Bree handed him a cracker with cheese. "Sold."

Willa announced the chicken needed another half hour to marinate before going on the grill, so we all filled our plates with appetizers and headed out to the deck. September was still warm in the Outer Banks, but the brutal edge of summer had passed, and the ocean breeze made things comfortable. I sat on an outdoor loveseat, and the foster dog lay down across my feet. His heavy bulk against my legs was comforting, and I automatically reached down to stroke his silky ears.

Rios sat beside me and raised one knowing brow. "So, how's the island been treating everyone while we were gone?"

Bree popped an olive into her mouth. "Quiet. Too quiet, depending on who you ask."

"People are still talkin' about Carson. About everything. Expect that won't change for a while," Daniel said.

The name slid over me like a cold draft. I stiffened before I could stop myself. The dog shifted, pressing closer, his head now fully in my lap. I let out a breath I hadn't realized I was holding and kept petting him, grounding myself in the steady rhythm of it.

Rios felt it. I knew he did because his arm tightened just slightly around me. "There'll be time to talk about that later," he said calmly, not to shut it down, just to set it aside. "Tonight's about being back."

No one argued.

Willa cleared her throat, mercifully changing the subject. "We're just glad you're both okay. After... everything."

The conversation shifted again, meandering the way it did among people with so much shared history—small updates, shared jokes, the kind of easy overlap that came from long familiarity. And through it all, something loosened inside me. A tension I hadn't even known I was carrying.

At some point, Sawyer leaned back in his chair and eyed Rios with open curiosity. "So. What's next for you two?"

The room went quiet in that attentive, interested way—not invasive, just expectant.

Rios glanced at me, a question in his eyes. I nodded.

"We're moving in together."

There it was. Out in the open.

Bree's face split into a grin so wide it was almost comical. "Called it."

Ford dug out his wallet and passed a bill to his fiancée. "Hell. I figured it'd take another few months."

Sawyer gave a high five, and Willa just beamed.

"That's—" Gabi started, then stopped herself and smiled. "That's good."

My profound relief didn't put a waver in my voice. "So, we're looking for a place."

Rios nudged my shoulder with his. "With a yard."

I looked at Willa, my hand still resting on the dog's head. "Because I want to adopt him."

"I *knew it!*" Willa crowed, pumping her fist in the air. "I knew the minute he leaned on you."

The dog's tail thumped once, as if in agreement.

Bree laughed. "You're serious?"

"Completely," I said. "If Willa's okay with it."

Willa crossed the deck in three strides and dropped into the chair across from me, eyes shining. "I know a fellow sucker when I see one. And he obviously already adores you." She leaned closer, stage-whispering. "What's his name?"

I smiled down at him, at the soft brown eyes and the way he watched me like I was something solid he could trust. "Moonpie."

Daniel's laugh rolled out. "Moonpie? I'm bettin' there's a story there."

"Not a big one. I love chocolate MoonPies. He's exactly that color with a heart just as squishy."

Willa made a sound that was almost a squeal. "He does have a marshmallow center. Perfect."

Conversation surged again, energized now, the way it did when the future cracked open just enough to glimpse something good.

"So," Rios said, glancing around. "If anyone knows of a place..."

Bree and Ford exchanged another look.

"Well," Bree said slowly, like she was trying not to interrupt fate. "My cottage. We've been running it as an Airbnb, but it's open right now. Fully furnished. Two bedrooms. Fenced yard."

My heart started beating faster.

"You could stay as long as you want," Ford added. "Month-to-month. If you decide it's not the right fit, no harm done. We flip it back to short-term."

Bree smiled at me. "I'd rather have people I know there than strangers."

I looked at Rios. He was already looking at me, a question in his eyes.

"That sounds..." I trailed off, unable to finish.

Perfect. Safe. Ours.

Willa reached over and squeezed my hand. "Looks like you're home."

The word settled into me, warm and solid, no longer something I was circling or resisting.

Home.

I leaned back into Rios, the dog's weight anchoring me, surrounded by people who'd seen the worst of this place and still chosen to stand together.

For the first time in a long while, I didn't feel like I was waiting for the ground to give way beneath me.

I felt like I belonged.

EPILOGUE

RIOS

Mid-November on Hatterwick didn't resemble the brochures. No glittering sunburned crowds, no flip-flops slapping along the dock, no rental cars multiplying in the ferry line like rabbits. Only gray-blue water under a sky that couldn't decide if it wanted to rain, wind that carried a thin bite off the sound, and a ferry easing in like it had all the time in the world.

Ford stood with his hands shoved in his jacket pockets, shoulders slightly hunched, eyes on the ramp like he could will it down faster. Sawyer paced two steps, stopped, paced two steps back. He'd say it was because standing still made him itch, but I knew better. We were all keyed up. None of us said it out loud.

Jace was coming home.

"Any minute," Sawyer muttered for the third time in five minutes.

Ford shot him a look. "You got a stopwatch, or you gonna keep narrating the obvious?"

Sawyer smirked, but it didn't fully land. He scrubbed a

hand over his jaw and stared back at the ferry. "Just weird, is all."

Yeah. Weird.

It had been months since Willa's brother had been on island for more than a blink. Deep cover assignment, Naval Intelligence—half the time we didn't even know where he was, and the other half we pretended we didn't, because knowing was the kind of thing that could get people killed. We'd gotten a few texts when he could swing them. Mostly, we'd gotten silence.

Silence meant he was alive.

I shifted my weight and watched the ferry's ramp start to lower with a metallic groan. A couple of cars idled at the front —locals, mostly. People in work boots and sweatshirts. A woman with a cooler wedged between her knees. Nobody acted like this was anything more than a Tuesday.

My phone buzzed once in my pocket, and I ignored it on principle. Madden was probably checking in, but she knew where I was. She'd told me to tell Jace hi and not to let the guys haze him too hard on his first day back.

As if that was an option.

The ramp hit with a dull thud, and the first car rolled off. Then a second. Then the foot passengers started down, shoulders hunched against the wind, bags slung over their backs.

I saw him.

Jace looked like he always did at first glance—broad shoulders, easy stride, dark hair that needed a cut, bearded face set in that calm, watchful expression that made people underestimate him right up until it was too late. But the closer he got, the more I caught the edges: the way his gaze swept the dock, the parking lot, the ferry itself. The slight delay as he clocked exits. The tension in his posture that didn't belong to homecomings.

Deep cover didn't peel off like a jacket.

Sawyer spotted him and went still for half a beat, like his brain had to confirm it was real. Then he surged forward.

Jace's mouth split into a grin that was all white teeth and relief. "Well, hell."

Sawyer hit him first. It wasn't a delicate reunion. It was a full-body collision disguised as a hug, the kind of thing men did when they couldn't say *I missed you* without choking on it. Jace took the impact like he expected it.

Ford stepped in next, clapped Jace on the shoulder, and pulled him in close enough to thump him twice on the back. "Welcome home, asshole."

Jace laughed low. "Missed you too."

He turned to me. I stepped forward and gripped his forearm. He locked on, hand strong, familiar. We held for a beat longer than necessary. Not for show. For confirmation. Alive. Here. Safe.

I pulled him in for the obligatory back thump and squeeze. "Good to see you, brother."

"Yeah. Good to be seen." Jace stepped back, flicking between us, reading the room the way he read everything. "So what'd I miss?"

Sawyer didn't even hesitate. "Carson's dead."

Jace stopped walking so abruptly that his duffel bag swung forward and bumped his thigh. "He what?"

Ford's expression didn't change. "Sniper. The city asked Rios to step in as the new chief of police."

The words landed like a punch even though I'd heard them a dozen times in the last week from a dozen different mouths. The council. The interim administrator. The handful of locals who'd suddenly discovered they'd always respected me. The ones who still couldn't look me in the eye without remembering old rumors.

I rolled my eyes because if I didn't, I'd grind my teeth into dust. "Provisionally. I haven't given them an answer yet."

But it meant something that they were willing to trust me with the job. Willing to give me a chance to prove myself to this island I still somehow loved beyond reason. I was a little afraid of what that meant, hence my reluctance to commit. Madden had been the only one unsurprised. She'd simply shrugged and said that it was a sensible move on their part because they finally saw in me what she saw.

That meant something, too.

Jace's brows shot up, and he let out a low whistle that was half disbelief, half something like admiration. Then he shook his head, still trying to catch up. He fell into step again, moving with us toward the parking lot like he didn't trust himself to stand still.

"Well, holy shit. I've missed a damned lot. What are the chances I can get a comprehensive update over a beer?"

Ford jerked his chin toward his truck. "I'm marrying a brewery owner. We're always stocked. Let's go."

The drive to Ford's place took blessedly little time. As we piled into the house, we all immediately clocked it was empty, but for the wagging Keeley.

"Bree's at work. Peyton's at track practice. They'll see you later." Ford stuck his head into the fridge and pulled out bottles.

We ended up at the kitchen island, longnecks sweating slightly in our hands. Sawyer leaned on his elbows like he was ready to spill everything at once. Ford stayed steady, quiet, anchoring the room just by being there. Jace sat on a stool, posture relaxed but eyes alert, like he wasn't sure yet that he could let his guard down.

I watched him take his first sip. Watched the way his shoulders loosened a fraction. Beer couldn't fix what war did to a man, but it reminded you that you weren't alone in it.

"All right," Jace said after another swallow. "Start from the top. Last thing I knew, y'all were trying to keep the island from imploding."

Over our beers and a bag of nacho chips somebody dug out of a cabinet, we told him all of it. From Priya's disappearance to how Madden and I had ended up taking on the case, to the bigger rot we'd discovered because of it. All the way up to Carson's execution and the SBI's involvement.

"The audit's still ongoing. Probably will be for a few more months." I plucked another chip from the bag. "And that more or less brings us to where we are."

Jace took another sip before leaning back slightly, letting the information settle. When he spoke again, his voice was quieter. "I think they're right to ask you. It feels like acknowledgement, finally, that they see the man you really are, not who they believed you were back in the day. You were the one who helped expose Carson in the first place."

My throat tightened unexpectedly. Not because I wanted praise. I didn't. But because hearing that from Jace—who knew more about secrets than any of us, who'd seen the worst of people and still chose to come home—hit different.

"Not alone," I added.

Jace caught my gaze. "Which brings me to the other surprising piece of this. You and Madden Reilly. Never would have called that one. But if she makes you happy, man, that's all that matters."

"She does." The words came out simple. No qualifiers. No jokes. No armor.

Ford made a low sound of agreement. "They're cohabitating and everything."

Sawyer grinned like he'd been waiting for that opening. "We're taking bets on how long it takes him to propose."

I leveled them both with a flat stare. "We're taking things slow. She's got enough on her plate hanging out her own shingle here. Or will be. She's still waiting on the Bar to finish their investigation to get her license transferred. Not to mention, we both kinda feel like we're waiting for the other shoe to drop. Whatever is going on was bigger than Carson."

Silence stretched for a beat as we all sat with the truth of that.

Jace's gaze stayed on me, thoughtful. "All the more reason for you to take the job. Then you have the credentials and access to maybe do something about it."

I took a long drink, buying time. Because he wasn't wrong. He also wasn't living inside my skin.

"The thing is," I said finally, setting the bottle down with a soft click, "neither of us knows who we can trust outside our circle. So Madden's calling in some help."

Jace's brows lifted. "What kind of help?"

"You ever hear of that podcast, *Unaccounted*?"

His eyes narrowed slightly as he searched his memory. "True crime missing persons deal, right?"

"Yeah," I confirmed. "Guy who runs it is a good friend of hers from law school. He's been investigating this stuff for years outside the usual channels. She's tapping him for help. He's tied up with a case himself right now, but he's sending one of his people. She should be here sometime next week."

Jace made a quiet sound. "Hmm."

Sawyer narrowed his eyes. "You've got that *I know something but I can't say anything or I'd have to kill you* look."

Jace's mouth twitched. "Let's just say I have professional reasons for being in the area for longer than a 48-hour visit."

Ford stilled, the movement so slight I almost missed it.

Sawyer's grin faded into something sharper. Even I felt the shift—like the room had tilted a degree.

I caught Jace's eye. "Does that mean we can count on your help with this?"

He didn't hesitate. He stood, stepped around the island, and offered his hand. Not a handshake. A brother thing.

I met him halfway and clasped his forearm, grip tight, familiar, sealing a promise without needing paperwork or witnesses.

"Anything I can do, brother," he said.

OOOO, things are getting COMPLICATED, y'all! Before we jump into the final book in the Wayward Sons series—*Carry on Wayward Son* because obviously I had to continue to express my love of 80s music in Jace's book—don't miss out on Rios and Madden's bonus epilogue:

https://harperjacksonbooks.com/otos-be/

Meanwhile, ANSWERS ARE COMING about what happened all those years ago to Gwen Busby, and *you're not gonna believe everything that's about to come out.* Preorder your copy of *Carry on Wayward Son* today!

OTHER BOOKS BY HARPER JACKSON

Wayward Sons

- *Smoke on the Water: Hoyt and Caroline*
- *Won't Back Down: Sawyer and Willa*
- *Against the Wind: Daniel and Gabi*
- *All Along The Watchtower: Ford and Bree*
- *On the Other Side: Rios and Madden*
- *Carry On Wayward Son: Jace and Layla—Coming August 2026*

ABOUT THE AUTHOR

Harper Jackson has rescued her co-workers from a hostage situation, battled ninjas, and stopped international espionage—in her head anyway. Now that she's no longer busy devising ways to make staff meetings more entertaining, she's pouring that imagination into tales of breath-stealing, small-town romantic suspense. She believes that peach cobbler with ice cream is the best dessert ever and has a black belt in taekwondo to back it up. She lives in the Deep South with her husband and canine furbabies. Find out more about Harper and her books at https://harperjackson.com or explore the lighter side of her catalog as Kait Nolan at https://kaitnolan.com.

www.ingramcontent.com/pod-product-compliance
Lightning Source LLC
Chambersburg PA
CBHW071547030726
47593CB00001BA/61